THE
HIGHLANDER'S WILD FLAME

ALSO BY HEATHER MCCOLLUM

SONS OF SINCLAIR SERIES

Highland Conquest
Highland Warrior
Highland Justice
Highland Beast
Highland Surrender

THE BROTHERS OF WOLF ISLE SERIES

The Highlander's Unexpected Proposal
The Highlander's Pirate Lass
The Highlander's Tudor Lass
The Highlander's Secret Avenger

HIGHLAND ISLES SERIES

The Beast of Aros Castle
The Rogue of Islay Isle
The Wolf of Kisimul Castle
The Devil of Dunakin Castle

HIGHLAND HEARTS SERIES

Captured Heart
Tangled Hearts
Crimson Heart

THE
HIGHLANDER'S
WILD FLAME

HEATHER
USA TODAY BESTSELLING AUTHOR
McCOLLUM

Entangled Publishing, LLC
644 Shrewsbury Commons Ave., STE 181
Shrewsbury, PA 17361
Visit our website at www.entangledpublishing.com.

Amara is an imprint of Entangled Publishing, LLC.

Edited by Alethea Spiridon
Cover design by LJ Anderson, Mayhem Cover Creations
and Bree Archer
Photography by Shirley Green
Stock art by Fodor90/Gettyimages and
FedevPhoto/GettyImages
Interior design by Britt Marczak

Print ISBN 978-1-64937-649-7
ebook ISBN 978-1-64937-654-1

Manufactured in the United States of America

First Edition August 2024

AMARA

To Kathy, who is the bravest cancer-warrior I know. Despite the fire you've been forced to walk through, you are a beautiful heroine to your very core.

May you rise from the ashes like the phoenix.

Love you, friend.

The Highlander's Wild Flame is a forced proximity, enemies to lovers Scottish Historical romance, the first book in a new series by *USA Today* bestselling author Heather McCollum. However, the story includes elements that might not be suitable for all readers. Kidnapping, threat of burning alive, threat of rape, referral to past domestic abuse, and imprisonment scenes are mentioned in the novel. Readers who may be sensitive to these elements, please take note.

OLD ENGLISH AND SCOTS GAELIC WORDS USED IN
THE HIGHLANDER'S WILD FLAME

blaigeard – bastard

camelopard – early English name for giraffe

cù math – good dog

daingead – dammit

gu airm– to arms

Ifrin - Hell

mattucashlass – short dagger with both sides of the blade sharpened

Mon diah – My God

sgian dubh – short dagger with one side of the blade sharpened, often hidden on the body

siuthad – come on

tha no chan eil – yes or no

THE BATTLE OF SOLWAY MOSS

HISTORICAL NOTE

King Henry VIII wanted his nephew, James V of Scotland, to leave the Roman Catholic Church when England left, but King James ignored him. Henry, who hated to be ignored, sent English troops to set fire to some Scottish border towns. In retaliation, King James sent between 15,000 to 18,000 Scotsmen across the border into England to do the same.

Sir Thomas Warton, the English commander, managed to find approximately 3,500 Englishmen to stand against the Scots. They met on November 24, 1542 on a boggy heathland on the Esk River called Solway Moss. Due to confusion in the command of the Scots, the larger group of Scottish soldiers retreated, many getting caught in the bog and some drowning. The English were victorious and took 1,200 Scottish prisoners back to London. It was a devastating loss that demoralized James V.

For the most part, England's King Henry VIII treated the prisoners well, hoping to sway them to his cause. He even let some of the higher-ranking prisoners be exchanged for sons or other pledges, if they "assured" the English king that they would support his push to have his son, Edward, marry the Scottish heir, Mary, Queen of Scots. In some cases, the pledges also became "Assured Scots," swearing their allegiance to England, and they were released to return to Scotland. However, some prisoners were kept in England and "ill handled" like the two sons of the Earl of Glencairn.

Much to King Henry's irritation and likely fury, many of the "assured Scots" did not hold to their oaths to support England's plans for reformation and rule in Scotland. I could very well envision that some stubborn Scots pledges who refused to swear allegiance to England were kept prisoner and treated very poorly indeed.

PROLOGUE

"Out of suffering have emerged the strongest souls;
the most massive characters are seared with
scars."

Kahlil Gibran, 1883-1931, poet

Rory MacLeod let the growl sitting at the base of his
throat rumble out of him. Low and long, like a guttural tumbling of rocks, it sounded like a warning
rumble from a lion. After a year in Carlisle Castle's
dungeon, he looked the part with a mane of long,
dirty hair, scars, a full beard, and lips that pulled back
to show sharp teeth.

Perhaps this was part of God's required penance
for the devastating foolishness of his youth.

He growled again, and the sound had the desired
effect of making the English guards back up outside
the narrow, barred door. The barrels of their muskets
bobbed, showing that the English trembled.

"Move back," ordered one of the two guards who
carried an unconscious Asher MacNicol between
them. "Else we throw him in the moat."

Cyrus Mackinnon and Kenan Macdonald stepped
back. Rory would rather lunge, ripping into the
guards. A year of hell had brought out the beast in

him. He'd thought Kenan Macdonald and his clan were Rory's biggest enemy until he'd suffered the true foe, England.

He pressed against the damp stone wall, and the guards dropped Asher on the musty straw clumped on the floor of the cell that the four of them shared. Rory stared hard at the Englishmen until they looked away, swallowing in discomfort. His amber-colored eyes and disconcerting stare made most men look away even when he was washed and dressed properly as a Highland chief's son. Now he looked half beast, like his battle title implied. He would use every weapon he had against King Henry's men.

"God's teeth," a guard said, staring at Rory. He was new, and Rory had the sudden desire to open his maw and roar at him, to see if the man pissed himself.

"He's the Lion of Skye," another guard said. "Don't look in his eyes. It'll make you unable to move so he can rip your throat out."

Rory remained with the other two Highlanders while the guards backed quickly out, and one re-locked the barred door. "If any of you Scots bastards try to escape like him, you'll get the same treatment or worse." The portly man spat on the ground. "The only way out is giving your oaths to England and paying the ransom due to the king." The three Highlanders glared at him, and he ordered his men away.

The new guard cast a glance toward Rory, and Rory bared his teeth. The man's eyes grew round, and he skittered off. As soon as they were out of sight, the three men descended on Asher. Rory crouched next to the man whose back had been flayed open with a studded whip, leaving a bloody mess, raw and jagged.

He met the grim faces of the other two, all of them originally from the Isle of Skye, a western isle off bonny Scotland. "Bloody fok," he said and the other two nodded.

All four of them were hardened warriors and would fight England until their last drop of blood. They hadn't been captured at the embarrassing Scottish loss at Solway Moss but had been traded for more important family members after *they* were captured. Rory, Cyrus, Kenan, and Asher were left to pay the price of a weakened Scotland. Abandoned by their clans. Forgotten.

I'll send the ransom money within the month.

Alasdair MacLeod's words were a distant promise now. Rory had believed his father, until months went by without a word or a coin.

Kenan checked Asher's pulse. "He's alive. Let's get him to the pallet."

Cyrus punched his fist into his other hand. "We need to leave here now."

"Aye," Rory said. "But first we need to get Ash walking again."

"Damn fool," Kenan huffed. "Trying to leave on his own."

Cyrus snorted. "And telling Wharton to shove the other prisoners' bribes up his arse until he could taste the silver on his tongue didn't help him, either."

The fact was the four Highlanders from Skye hadn't been sent any coins with which to bribe Wharton to give them extra food and care. 'Twas as if their clans had decided they were already dead. Would Rory's older brother tell their cloistered sister,

Eleri, that he had died down in England even though he'd survived the battle at Solway Moss? Would she insist on a funeral even without a body?

"We need to work together," Rory said, his voice a low grumble. "Not break out on our own."

Cyrus, Kenan, and Rory lifted the MacNicol warrior and set him as gingerly as they could on the rumpled pallet. How easily they worked together now when at first they'd hated one another. The adage was true. *The enemy of an enemy is a friend.*

"I'll ask Mirella for clean water, some spirits, and rags," Cyrus said. Since he was the one who smiled the easiest, he'd been the one to charm the keeper's daughter when they were still treated as possible allies by King Henry. The English tyrant thought he could persuade Highlanders to his side against King James of Scotland. Rory didn't know who he hated more, the king or those Scotsmen who assured him they'd back English rule over Scotland and all Henry's religious dictates.

"Ointment, too," Kenan said. "Ash's back will fester."

"He might still die," Rory said, inspecting the weeping skin on the man's back. Ash had tried to escape with a small dagger but was overpowered by four guards with muskets and swords. Asher hadn't warned his cellmates he planned to attack when he was taken from their cell after volunteering to work on a new wall at the castle. They hadn't seen him for two days when Mirella snuck down to tell them he'd been caught and was being whipped.

"Wharton is practically starving us," Kenan said, his voice low. They did get two meals a day and ale, but for four warriors, the amount wasn't adequate to keep up their strength, especially while surviving the constant cold. "We need to get out."

Kenan went to the small, barred window cut through the stone wall and peered out at the damp grass that had grown green with spring. "If we were but birds to fly away," he said. Despair was making them all a bit mad. Kenan sucked in the fresh wind like it was a meal. "Da Vinci made plans for a flying machine," he murmured to himself.

"Where did Ash get the sgian dubh?" Rory asked, ignoring Kenan's ramblings.

Cyrus grabbed one of the woven blankets they'd each received from an anonymous benefactor for Beltane. Made from thick, warm wool, each one had come with a printed tag penned with their names. "I saw him picking away at the hem, plucking the strings," Cyrus said, pinching the edge and looking at it closely in the light from the window. But there'd been only one blade, and it was gone.

Rory grabbed his own blanket and slid his fingers along the bulky seam. A thin, hard object sat near a corner. "There's something here," he whispered and bit down on the threads binding the blanket. He plucked the threads away and worked a hard piece of iron from the hole he'd created. "'Tis...a key." He held it up. It had minimal teeth, so it could work in numerous locks. "A skeleton key." Glancing at the bars, he tucked it away quickly.

"Coins." Kenan worked them out of his own blanket. "Eight gold crowns."

Cyrus kept running his fingers around the edge of his blanket and shook his head. "I don't feel—" He stopped and held the edge to his ear. "But I hear something." He bit hard at a seam and pulled out a piece of paper. Without reading it aloud, he passed it to each of them.

The Renegade

Captain Bunch

Dock at Girvan Port

Cyrus looked up at Rory. "The Renegade? 'Tis a ship."

"One that will take us north to Skye?" Kenan asked.

Rory exhaled. "As long as it gets us out of England."

"If we work together, we have a chance of making it past the guards," Kenan said, stretching his arms overhead. He nodded at Asher. "All four of us."

The three looked at each other, the question of whether to leave the man who'd tried to escape on his own already answered. They were four enemies on the Isle of Skye, each of them belonging to a different feuding clan, raised to hate each other. But here in a dank cell in Northwestern England, they'd become brothers.

CHAPTER ONE

Claigan Beach – made of "minute pieces of calcified algae known as maerl. When maerl dies, the hardened skeleton is crushed by the action of waves, and then washed up on the shore where it is bleached to a brilliant white by the sun."

BritainExpress.com

WESTERN SHORE OF THE ISLE OF SKYE, SCOTLAND
25TH OF JUNE 1544

Rory MacLeod threw the short length of gray driftwood toward the lapping waves. Gus, his ancient wolfhound, loped after it. The whitecaps farther out in the bay off Claigan Beach churned up low waves. The water stretched onto the shore to grab and tumble the pebbles and shells, making them clatter against one another as they washed back into the sea.

Rory breathed in deeply of the sea air, letting the salt tang sting his nose. There was a hint of the smoke from the inland crop fields that were being burned to promote better growth, but the sea breeze pushed it back. Rory hoped the freedom in the wind would cleanse away the taint of imprisonment and betrayal that moldered in his chest like an illness. He preferred the outdoors now after being locked away in Carlisle dungeon for over a year.

Gus trotted to him, the driftwood stick caught in his

crooked teeth. "Cù math," Rory said, tugging it from the dog's bite. He threw it, and the wind caught the stick, hurling it into the salty froth. Gus turned, joy in his slow trot as he ran after it. Poor old beast. He'd likely been ignored while Rory was locked away.

He turned his face southward where his clan castle, Dunvegan, sat on a sheltered inlet from the sea, a hill blocking sight of the hulking fortress from the beach. How he'd longed for it and the surrounding hills, forests, and this very strand of unique white beach.

His brother, Jamie, said Rory had sold his soul to the devil to escape, because he'd worked with sons of their enemies on Skye. Rory rubbed a thumb across his palm where four knife scars sat in red lines, healed but not yet faded. "But I didn't sell my soul to England," he said, the words caught by the wind. If Jamie had traded places with their father instead of Rory, Jamie wouldn't have survived. It had taken the four Highland warriors, working together, to escape back to their homes on the Isle of Skye, each of them using their special skills and the anonymous gifts sent in blankets. The mystery of their benefactor had yet to be solved.

The wind blew the sweat dry in Rory's hair. He'd been training since dawn on his horse, Airgid, with the other MacLeod warriors on the moor outside the village of Dunvegan. The men had rotated, half training with sword and horse and the other half tending the fields of fire. Rory had taken his turn walking along the edge of the barley field that would grow all the better with the weeds burned away. So taking a dip in the cold saltwater would cleanse his body as well as his soul.

The caw of a bird made him look upward. He spotted the black crow and followed it, turning to scan the white crescent of beach where the blue-green water pushed froth up higher with the incoming tide. Smoke rose from over the hill in contrast to the cool view of tumbling waves.

His gaze lifted to Cnoc Mor a Ghrobain, a hill covered in green grasses and wildflowers, above the shoreline. A woman stood on the ridge, her full skirts tugged by the wind which caught her long, auburn hair, swirling it around. For a second, another lass from years ago flashed through Rory's memory, one who'd stood there being whipped by her own hair. But Madeline was no more, and yet his biggest shame haunted him still. He shook his head and refocused on the hill.

The field burned beyond the woman, and she moved forward out of the smoke. She raised her arms, and he could imagine her as a Celtic goddess leaving a swath of destruction behind her, her magic making her hair rise like rays of a sun out from her head. Unease pricked his shoulder blades even a decade after Madeline.

This woman was no phantom. She was likely a guest for his brother's wedding on the morrow. The bride traveled from Dunscaith Castle on the Sleat peninsula of Skye, which was a two-day slow ride to the south, so Macdonalds had been arriving over the last couple days.

The woman pointed down the shore from where he stood, yelling, but the wind snatched away her words. Rory turned to where she'd pointed, and his heart lurched.

"Shite!" He broke into a run across the shifting pieces of shell and crystallized seaweed toward Gus in the water. The dog was farther out than he should be, his wiry snout barely above the surface, his teeth clinging to the driftwood that Rory had thrown. "Daingead!" Rory cursed, yanking off one boot and then the other. The broken pieces of hardened seaweed jabbed into his feet, but non-lethal pain meant little, and he hardly noticed it as he ran toward the surf.

"Swim!" Underwater currents had been known to suck a man out to sea. Had Gus been caught in one? He was old, nearly eleven years now, and the large breed did not usually live past a decade.

Rory yanked off his tunic as he ran and unbuckled his belt, dropping his plaid wrap that would only weigh him down in the angry sea. Water sprayed up around him as he lifted his knees high, charging into the stinging iciness of the water. Gus's face went under a wave. With another leap, Rory dove, his hands pointed out before him. His fingers jabbed into the shaggy body of his best friend, and his arms wrapped around the struggling dog. They broke the surface together, water in Rory's eyes.

"I've got ye," he yelled, pulling the large, warm body against him as he pushed them upward, his feet shifting in the sand underneath, making him wobble. Saltwater stung his eyes as it dripped down his forehead. Underwater, the currents tugged hard at his legs, but he plowed forward toward shore, taking huge steps against the pull. Icy daggers sliced across him, but the pain was invigorating.

Gus continued to whip his head around as if searching for the bloody stick. "I'll find ye another one," Rory said. He wouldn't be throwing it in the surf again.

"Your throw led him too deep."

The woman's voice made Rory's face snap up, and he stopped in the water that fell about his hips, just high enough to cover him while balancing Gus's huge, wet body.

The lass from the hill held her green skirts higher and kicked off her slippers to wade a bit into the surf as if ready to help pull his dog to shore. A generous mouth sat in a smooth oval face with a straight nose and rosy cheeks, but it was her eyes that stood out. They were large and blue, the outer edges tipped upward, giving her a magical look, like she was one of the fairy folk who'd given his clan the Fairy Flag so long ago. Her hair was lashed with gold and red and fell forward over her shoulders as she waded toward him.

"Do you need help with him?" she asked.

Rory shifted the large dog in his arms, ignoring the water trying to suck him back out, like he was prey that it hated to lose. "Nay," he said. "If ye come out here, then I'll have to rescue ye, too."

"I can swim," she said with a frown.

"Not with all those petticoats."

He cursed low as the sand and shells shifted under his feet. His frozen ballocks had crawled back inside him. Invigorating as the icy water was, he needed to get out. "I'm unclothed."

"Shall I turn away so as not to embarrass you?"

"Turn around or swoon in awe." He shrugged as

best he could with the one-hundred-forty-pound wet dog in his arms. "But I can't help a fainting lass when I'm helping my dog."

That generous mouth of hers turned up at the corners. "I'd help the dog before a fainting female, too."

Rory stepped out of the sea and lowered Gus onto the shells before trudging to his discarded plaid and belt. The woman hadn't turned away. Did the lass know that icy water made a man's ballocks and cock pull up as if to hide in the warmth of his body? His mouth opened to explain, but he stopped himself before he looked like a fool.

"Daingead." He wrapped himself in his plaid with hardly the right number of pleats, but it would hold with his belt, nonetheless.

"You poor thing," the woman said, and Rory turned to see her crouching before Gus, checking his paws.

"I have salve up at the castle." Rory glanced down at the bloody tracks he'd left on some rocks and the crystallized seaweed and shells. "Ifrin," he cursed.

The woman backed up, studying him from under long lashes. "You live up at Dunvegan Castle?" Her speech seemed more refined, keeping each syllable evident. Blue ribbons crisscrossed her bodice, fitting it to her body, making her gentle curves evident.

"Some of the time," he answered. With his brother and his mistress trysting in shadowed corners, Rory had learned to stay out of the castle and was planning to make a permanent move out to one of the old tower houses.

A small pinch appeared between her brows that

looked like disappointment. "And this is your sweet pup?" Gus plopped down, making it clear he was worn out, and she scratched his head.

"Aye. He used to swim off this beach all the time," Rory said, grabbing his tunic. "But he's getting older."

"What's his name?"

"Gus, short for Angus of the Northern Hills."

She smiled, and her eyes glittered with mirth. "A valiant name for a valiant beast."

"I found him nearly starved and covered in mud on a journey in the northern mountains on the mainland. That was long ago now."

"He was quite fortunate," she said, taking Gus's massive head in both her hands and scratching behind his ears. She didn't seem to care that his dog was filthy and wet. The woman laughed as Gus licked her cheek, and Rory noticed a fine sprinkling of freckles flicked like pale stars across her nose. "What cloudy eyes you have," she said. "You're old indeed. Have you lived a glorious life chasing hares and birds?"

"Aye, he has." Rory turned to jam his cut feet into his boots.

He caught the lass staring at him. Her expressive eyes snapped up to meet his gaze, and he guessed from their wideness that she'd seen the scars on his back from the flaying he'd received compliments of the English king. He threw on his tunic, letting it hang loose.

"There are ointments you can apply to help them fade," she said without a trace of pity, although her face had grown serious.

Even so, he stiffened and studied her. Sunlight played across the streaks of gold in her hair. Her hands looked strong and gentle at the same time. "Ye know about scars?"

She stared at him, unafraid to meet his gaze. So the lass was brave. "Yes," she said. "Some fade, some do not. But I think yours are the kind that fade."

The woman took a full inhale through her nose, the edges of her lips relaxing. "I make an oil with blaeberry, lavender, and rosemary," she said. "To rub in."

She spoke with confidence, her knowledge as bright as her eyes. She wiggled her feet into her slippers and then squatted to kiss Gus's black nose. Still crouched, she turned her face to Rory. "You could put some on his feet, too, although he'd probably lick it off." She turned her face away from Gus's big tongue, and Rory's wolfhound licked her ear, making her laugh and scrunch her neck on that side as if it tickled.

The woman had pretty little earlobes. *Has anyone ever tugged on them…with their teeth?* The thought shot straight to his randy cock, which had most definitely thawed.

She straightened but still smiled down at the dog. "I wager your big tongue gets you into trouble, Gus. My tongue gets me into trouble, too."

The image of her licking an ear rammed into Rory's mind. "Yer tongue?" he said, and she turned back to meet his gaze. His brows rose, and he gave a lopsided grin. "What type of trouble does it get into?" He hadn't felt like smiling for a long time.

She tucked some of her whipping hair behind that sweet ear and huffed. "I meant that I speak before I consider how my words might be construed." She flapped her hand at him. "Like right then."

"I rather like how ye talk before considering yer words."

She pinched her lips into a serious line, but her eyes sparked with humor. "You would be the first person to commend me for carelessly speaking what's in my mind." Her gaze slid to the hill behind him and then back to meet his gaze. "I must go, but first… Are you, by chance, Jamie MacLeod?"

The abrupt change in topic took him a moment. Rory's grin collapsed back into the frown that seemed to have become a permanent feature over the last years. But before he could answer, a bellow from up on the hillside made her spin away.

"Sweet Mother Mary," she said, and Rory followed her gaze to the man standing on the hill above the beach. She patted Gus's wet head and turned away. "Good day to you," she called as she hurried back up the hill, her skirts held higher so she could move at a pace that was as fast as a run but looked like a walk. She stopped, glancing back at him. "I will see you… again, I think." She hurried off, her red-hued tresses flying in the wind behind her.

The lass was bonny, but there was some other quality that tugged at Rory. Perhaps her kindness to Gus or the genuine tone to her words, as if she had nothing to hide. Rory's chest clenched. Madeline had possessed a guileless air about her, and Rory's trust in her had seen her dead.

CHAPTER TWO

"Set your life on fire.
Seek those who fan your flames."

*Jalal ad-Din Muhammad Rumi, 1207–1273,
Persian poet & philosopher*

Walter Macdonald grabbed Sara's arm in a bruising hold. He sniffed with his red nose and screwed up his whiskered face in a grimace.

"Ye smell of smoke, Seraphina," he said, using her full name, which she hated. "And wet dog." His gaze moved to her neckline. "Keep yer dress up else someone will see yer mark. Can't have the MacLeod calling off."

Sara tugged on the neckline near her shoulder, making sure to hide the red swath of skin that curved to her back. The mark had been part of her since birth, never fading. Her Aunt Morag said she'd seen it once on a girl's face, and no amount of poultices nor prayers made it disappear. Sara was grateful her mark ran under her clothing, but what would her husband think of it?

The swath of red across her skin was ugly, and she was ugly because of it. Her father had been reticent about marrying her off, saying that her husband would refuse once he saw her devil's mark. Apparently, Walter Macdonald didn't care what the MacLeods thought of her blemish. She felt her cheeks warm. Hopefully, her groom would look past her ugliness to her usefulness.

Sara glanced over her shoulder but couldn't see the beach. Could the man be her bridegroom, Jamie MacLeod? He'd said it was *his* beach, and Dunvegan sat over the rise to the south. He was handsome and had the chiseled body of a warrior. Her cheeks warmed remembering the taut muscles of his arse and legs as he walked away from her to retrieve his plaid.

"What are ye doing wandering so close to Dunvegan?" her father demanded. "And the fires?"

"I came to see where I'll live," she said. "I didn't know they were burning fields today." She tried to snatch her arm back, but her father held so tightly that she quickly gave up. "If you leave black and blue marks on me, Father, the MacLeods will say you beat me. 'Twill be talked about all across Skye before midsummer."

Walter released her arm, and she rubbed it as she walked slightly behind him, his familiar stuttering gait making it easy for her to keep up. They traversed the narrow cut through the high grasses covering the edge of moorland.

"Who was the man with the hound?" Walter asked. "He could have taken ye, used ye. Then ye'd be no good to marry."

"He didn't seem a threat, Father." And he might be her bridegroom. She thought of him racing in to save his dog, and the flutter of heat that had pooled in her abdomen as he stared at her intently. *Lord, please let him be my groom.*

"If a man's got a cod, he's a threat," her father said. He threw his hand out wide. "This is MacLeod territory, and they are all tricksters and raiders who plunder and steal."

"And yet you are having me marry one," she said, unable to keep the words in. She'd been hearing all her life how all the other clans on the Isle of Skye were worse than Lucifer. How the only way to gain peace was to rule the whole isle.

"Yer husband can do what he likes to ye," Walter said.

Heat prickled up in Sara's cheeks at the horrible notion. "He was saving his dog from the sea." A man who risked his life for something weaker than himself must have a good heart.

"Ye stink from it." Her father grunted. "Stay close to your aunt's cottage, Seraphina. Your wedding is on the morrow, and ye'll do nothing to jeopardize it."

"You think this wedding will bring peace between our clans?" she asked. Her father had longed for conquest against the clans on Skye, especially Clan MacLeod. When Chief Alasdair MacLeod, his old nemesis, had died the previous winter from the sweating sickness, Sara thought her father would attack the MacLeods, not negotiate a wedding.

He stopped and turned to her, holding a finger before her face, his brows raised like two gray clouds floating above his eyes. "I've never found a way into their damn castle, surrounded by water. Ye'll be inside and able to find the Fairy Flag. With the flag we will control the clans. Hell, we could take over England if we wished."

Her father believed in the magic of the banner called the Fairy Flag, which was kept in Dunvegan Castle under the watchful guard of Clan MacLeod.

Legend said it had been given to the MacLeods when their ancestor married a fairy. It was to be unfurled to guarantee the owner of the flag victory no matter how outnumbered they were. But only three times, and Alasdair MacLeod had unfurled it, for the second time, against her father in 1520. Walter was lucky to get out of that battle alive when the tide turned against the Macdonalds.

"I almost had the damn flag in my fingers ten years ago," Walter said and shook his head as if brushing off the annoying memory.

He trudged along a path that went around a spongy moorland leading to the small woods, bright green with ferns. "Nothing can interfere with the wedding, Seraphina. I need ye in that castle. Eyes and ears." He pointed to his narrowed eyes and his ears, which seemed to grow hairier each passing year.

"You want me to steal the fairy flag?" she asked, stumbling over a rock. "I can't possibly—"

"In time," he said, waving off her concern. "In time, when our clans are together, we will march as one under the flag."

Her shoulders stiffened. She'd spent her whole life learning to read her father's gestures and tone. He'd told her brother, Kenan, that he brokered the union for peace. Was he truly trying to put her inside Dunvegan to steal the flag?

"And a lass should be loyal to her father," he retorted, dragging her along. "No matter what that entails."

Should she warn her new husband of her father's possible treachery? She thought of the man on the curving white shoreline. It could be him. Her husband.

A man to whom she'd show all of herself. Her heart fluttered with a mix of worry and anticipation.

The man's skin had been tanned and without pockmarks, but his scars across his back were puckered as if he'd been flayed with a whip. So his skin wasn't perfect, either. Perhaps he was embarrassed over the proof of brutality against him. Maybe it would help him understand how she felt about her own marks.

Sara followed her father along the forest path, but she didn't see the bluebells or daisies. She only saw the golden brown of the handsome man's eyes, like rich amber. Had she heard anything about Jamie MacLeod's eyes? No. Disappointment tugged on the hope that had flared inside.

After an hour and a half of her father's slow pace through a small forest and across a moor, Sara spotted the one-story cottage up ahead. Her Aunt Morag stood on the stoop before the open door.

"Come inside," she called. Five crows stood on a tight line strung between two poles stuck upright in Morag's side yard. They fluttered their wings and cawed. Six more watched from the roof of her small barn. Sara could see why some people swore Aunt Morag was a witch. The long white and silver braid she wore down her back and the otherworldly greenness of her eyes only added to the witchy look about her. She was also clever, brash, and liked to stare at people until they looked away. 'Twas a wonder she hadn't yet been accused.

Walter flapped a hand at the glossy black birds. "Bloody hell, Morag. Yer minions? Devil birds?"

Morag shrugged. "They keep the pixies away." She

tipped her head side to side. "And other troublemakers."

Walter snorted with rare good humor. "Hanging them dead will do the same."

"Dead, they can't pluck your eyes out, Walter," she said, staring at him without expression.

He shuffled his feet in the pebbly earth and gave Sara a small shove toward her aunt. "Found Seraphina with a man on the beach."

The older woman's flat gaze slid to Sara.

"He was saving his dog in the surf, and I sought to help," Sara said with rapid words and a wave to her damp skirts.

Morag's face softened the smallest amount. The woman had been her mother's twin sister, but they were as different as the two colors on a chess board. Where Elspet had been calm and prone to smiling, Morag was known for her tempers. She'd remained unmarried after her first husband died under mysterious circumstances decades ago. Some whispered that she'd poisoned him after he beat her. She'd refused to take another husband after putting the first in the ground, but it was rumored she had trysts.

Witch or not, Sara loved her aunt.

As a child, Sara often accompanied her mother on visits to her sister. She'd flit around in the garden, collect daisies on the moor beyond, or play with her stitched doll by the hearth. Her mother and Morag would speak and laugh for hours while they made tinctures and syrups for curing illnesses and injuries.

After Elspet died, Morag had taken on the role of mother, teaching Sara and her younger sister, Eliza, about domestic duties when they visited. Once, Morag had sat them down to explain the workings of their female bodies, including the parts that elicited pleasure. Eliza had stared wide-eyed. Sara had blushed profusely but found the advice very enlightening. The way Morag explained that a woman could take control of her own pleasure took away any shame Sara had felt about touching herself when she was alone. Their mild mother would never have taught them pleasure was something for which to strive.

Elspet had encompassed all the meek virtues of a lady, whereas her sister, Morag, had been the wild one. Sara often thought that she was more like her aunt than her mother, and luckily nothing like her father.

Only her younger brother, Gilbert, had taken after their father's conniving, arrogant ways. Gilbert tried to imitate his callousness and was already challenging Kenan to be the next Macdonald chief.

"Make sure Seraphina is fresh as a bluebell on the morrow," Walter said, nodding to Morag. "Gilbert and I will be along to retrieve ye for the church."

Sara frowned. "Not Kenan?"

"Kenan doesn't have the stomach for it," Walter said and then met her gaze. "I've sent him back to Dunscaith to make certain no Mackinnon is trying to take advantage of my absence. He can embroider pillows with Eliza if there's no trouble."

"Doesn't have the stomach?" What did that mean? Kenan had regained his strength quickly upon his return from England. Her brother was clever, brave, and deadly with a sword. He trained all the Macdonald warriors.

"Neither Kenan nor Eliza will attend my wedding?" she asked.

Walter flapped his hand. "The lad can't stand to see ye wed off. He's even softer since his return. And Eliza"—her father glared—"doesn't belong here."

Guilt tugged at Sara's middle to mingle with the constant concern for her sister. And Father calling Kenan soft was like calling Sara perfect. Kenan had survived the battle of Solway Moss and journeyed back up into Scotland until he was recalled to stand as a pledge in place of their father.

Aunt Morag tugged her inside her cottage, closing the door on her father. "Come, child. We'll get ye a warm bath, a hot meal, and a shot of whisky."

"Whisky?" Sara asked, studying the sly smile on her aunt's lips.

"Aye." Morag cupped Sara's cheek and smiled, nodding as she stared into her niece's eyes. "'Tis time I told you about how a man should treat a lass on their wedding night. If your bridegroom doesn't know, you can tell him what to do."

Sara stood motionless. "I thought I would lie on my back so he couldn't see the flame across my skin." She spoke with a flippant undertone to hide the familiar pangs of worry. Her groom didn't know of the ugliness hidden by her clothes. Her father surely wouldn't have revealed the red mark that had darkened instead of lightening as she grew. Once she was wed, her groom could do nothing about it.

Morag's lips pinched. "I have a new salve to try on it." She squeezed Sara's hand, because they both knew it wouldn't work.

CHAPTER THREE

"Humiliated by the defeat [at Solway Moss], King James died a few weeks later aged just 30, leaving behind a six-day-old daughter, Mary, Queen of Scots."

Historic-UK.com

Rory held Gus's leather lead so he wouldn't wander off to visit all the people arriving at the thatch-roofed stone chapel in the valley south of Dunvegan Castle. Between the near-drowning yesterday and the dog's bath afterward, the poor old boy was tired enough to sit obediently.

"Must ye bring yer shaggy beast to my wedding?" his brother, Jamie, asked. Jamie was the eldest son and the new chief of Clan MacLeod now that their father had joined their mother buried in the family plot. Today, Jamie would wed to form an alliance with their oldest enemy, Clan Macdonald.

"Gus will help keep the Macdonalds in line," Rory said. His gaze narrowed as he watched a light-haired woman in a low-cut yellow ensemble walk up, dabbing at her eyes. Rory leaned closer to Jamie. "Must ye bring yer mistress to yer wedding? She might be clean, but she'll dampen the festive mood with her weeping."

"Daingead," Jamie said, frowning. "I told Winnie not to come. She's been weeping nonstop."

"She acts like the Lady of Dunvegan even without wedding vows," Rory said. "Of course she's upset. She's been demoted." Rory glanced at his brother. Was Jamie thinking of keeping both his mistress and wife at Dunvegan? Lord help them. Rory would have to move to one of the stone tower houses out on the open moors sooner than he'd thought.

Jamie rubbed the back of his neck. "Brodrick," he called over to his good friend, a commander in Rory's army. "Dissuade Winnie, Mistress Mar, from coming up the path. Tell her I'll find her later during the festivities."

Find her? Tupping one's mistress on one's wedding day was foking dishonorable, but what did Jamie know of honor? "Should I send Gus after her?" Rory asked. "He's never liked Winnie." Nor did anyone else in the household who'd fallen under her glare and waspish tongue.

Jamie laughed darkly, turning away from the scene unfolding up the path with his loyal guard telling the woman that she would have to mourn in private. Winnie's sobs had turned to terse threats against Brodrick's ballocks. Luckily, their old nursemaid and current housekeeper, Margaret Harris, came up and led the woman back down the lane.

"I'm glad ye've returned," Jamie said, switching topics. "I didn't approve of the exchange after Solway Moss." Jamie had remained up on Skye when Rory and their father, Alasdair MacLeod, had honored the call of King James to invade the English borderland.

Didn't approve of the exchange? Jamie was lying, but it was his wedding day, so Rory wouldn't call him out as the calculating liar he was. "Glad to hear it, brother," Rory said instead.

Jamie looked back at him. "Was it hell? Where ye were held at Carlisle Castle?"

Rory looked out at the fresh green grasses and flowers that bent over in the sea breeze that ruffled everyone's hair and tugged at their clothes. He remembered putting his hand out through the small window in his cell to feel the breeze on his fingers, longing for the wind rolling in from the sea. Rory inhaled deeply of the air he would no longer take for granted and looked at Jamie with a wry grin. "'Twas worse after King Henry realized I couldn't be persuaded to pledge him my loyalty."

Jamie crossed his arms, his chin rising defensively. "When Father was there, he was treated well. We thought the same for ye." He looked up at the sky. "And King James forbade us paying for yer return, Rory."

Rory's hand came down on Jamie's shoulder, and he resisted the urge to shake his brother until his head whipped back and forth and he fell on his arse in the dirt. He'd defended his older brother, as was his duty, all his life. But the truth was that Jamie was morally weak and lied easier than breathing. He took after their father that way.

Rory waited until his brother met his gaze before he spoke. "King James was dead within a fortnight after Solway Moss." So, the king had given no orders. Rory's brow hitched in question. It was better than punching him, something he'd continually reminded himself not to do since his return.

"Well, his advisors then," Jamie said, his words coming on waves of defensiveness. "And I thought the mighty Lion of Skye could survive anything."

Rory's eyes narrowed. "I did," he said, his voice a low growl, but he said no more. 'Twas a day to celebrate the joining of the MacLeod and Macdonald Clans, a step to strengthen Scotland.

Their father had died before he could see this momentous day, while Rory was surviving in the dank Carlisle dungeon without provisions or coins to lessen the hell. Even the occasional communication with Scotland had ceased, so Rory hadn't known that his father had died over the winter. He'd been forgotten as if he'd been buried with Alasdair MacLeod.

Rory looked toward the path where a contingent of Macdonalds was striding. "Yer bride comes hither."

"Ye know I'm the one to give that limp to Walter Macdonald," Jamie said with satisfaction, apparently looking at the elderly man and not his bride. Rory would rather look on the man's daughter than the red-faced bastard with the bulbous nose and bushy brows.

The woman wore blue, a shawl draped over her hair as if to protect it from the very wind in which Rory reveled. What foolhardy demands would the woman put on Dunvegan once it became her domestic kingdom? Their mother, Charlotte Sutherland, had been the only woman not to bring trouble to Dunvegan.

"I'm wedding a bloody Macdonald," Jamie said. "Our ancestors are spitting down from Heaven."

"I'm fairly certain Father is in Hell," Rory said, thinking of the people he'd killed. Not in battle, but in fury while meting out punishment.

As the procession came closer, Gus wagged his

tail, his tongue lolling out before he gave a happy bark.

"Your hound wants to gnaw on our enemy," Jamie murmured, but Gus's bark showed quite the opposite. "The Macdonalds are not to be trusted," Jamie continued, "and our scouts say a large number have come onto our territory over the last week."

"Chief Macdonald has as little trust for us as we do for him, so he's brought warriors to safeguard his daughter," Rory said. He'd be more on edge if he hadn't survived those many months with Kenan Macdonald, who also spoke vehemently about desiring peace between all the clans on Skye.

Led by Chief Walter Macdonald, Jamie's bride came down the path, her gaze going right to Gus and then rising to Rory. Her generous mouth curved into a smile.

Bloody hell. Rory's chest clenched like his fists at his sides. *Bloody foking hell.* The lass from the beach yesterday, the one who'd entered his dreams last night, was Seraphina Macdonald, soon to be his sister-in-law.

Chief Macdonald, frowning and gruff, halted before the two brothers. The bride lowered her blue shawl to expose her golden auburn hair where a wreath of spring bluebells sat snug in her curls. The colors made her large blue eyes even more vibrant. Rory was unable to move. Even his breath felt hostage.

She bowed her head to Rory. "Chief MacLeod."

Next to him, Jamie made a strangled noise that ended in a chuckle. "Nay, fair lady. He is my brother, Rory, the Lion of Skye and commander of our vast army. I'm your bridegroom, Jamie MacLeod, chief of the mighty MacLeods of Dunvegan."

Seraphina's smile faded as her gaze shifted to Rory's brother. Jamie smiled at her, although one would have to be stricken with madness to think there was any warmth in it. His gaze slid down her form, not bothering to hide his assessment as if she were a mare he was thinking of breeding. Her lack of smile pinched into a small frown, but she bowed her head to Jamie.

"I present my daughter," Walter Macdonald said. "Seraphina Macdonald, the Flame of Dunscaith, as agreed with your father before he passed."

The woman's gaze snapped to her father at his words.

Flame of Dunscaith? Rory had never heard the name, but Jamie only nodded.

"I am usually called Sara," she said, but no one acknowledged her. Jamie didn't even look at her. He only noticed things that brought him immediate pleasure and ignored the rest. He was making the lass feel like a nuisance, only an object to bring a truce.

"Let's proceed," Jamie said, turning on his heel to enter the church. Even though the lass's father was the one to walk her to meet her future husband at the end of the aisle, Jamie's quick retreat without a word of welcome cast a cold unease despite the mild spring day. One glance at Seraphina showed that the lass was exceedingly aware of the snub. The rosiness in her cheeks from the walk had spread across her entire face, down her long neck, and across the exposed swell of her bosom in splotches that looked like she'd been slapped.

Rory's jaw ached, and he realized he was clenching it. So, the beautiful lass on the shoreline, who he'd thought to seek out after the wedding, was going to be his bloody sister-in-law. Aye, he would have to move to one of his towers as soon as possible. Or at least go on an extended visit to Cyrus Mackinnon in the northern part of Skye.

Gus tugged, and Rory let the lead escape his fingers so the dog could reach her. She looked down, and her smile returned. "You're looking fine and fit today, Sir Gus," she said softly, patting the dog's head before being dragged ahead by her father.

Rory watched her younger brother, the stocky, forever-frowning Gilbert, walk after them into St. Mary's Chapel. The lad's gaze shifted about, taking in every MacLeod with scorn. His cheeks were splotchy, too, as if blood thrummed under his skin. Rory had seen pale men redden before battle as they prepared to fight. But this was a wedding, not a war.

Rory's gaze moved among the guards who'd accompanied them. "Where is Kenan Macdonald?" he asked the nearest member of the Macdonald Clan.

The man watched the dark doorway of the chapel, the strung flowers and twisted hay swinging in the breeze. "Sent back to Dunscaith." The warrior turned narrowed eyes to Rory. "Ye best get inside to witness the union."

Rory picked up Gus's leash and led him inside, unease tightening the muscles of his arms and legs as if, instead of a wedding, he was joining a battle. He rubbed a hand up the back of his neck where a pain was growing to match his sour disposition. The comely lass, who seemed to genuinely like Gus, was destined to end up in Jamie's bloody arms. Hopefully, Winnie wouldn't make life unbearable for her. Maybe he'd leave this very day to visit Cy after a dram of whisky.

Inside the one-room stone chapel, light cast shades of crimson and yellow through the thick, colored glass windows depicting saints. As people filed in, Rory breathed past the unease of the cramped space, courtesy of fifteen months in a small, dark cell.

Three rows of polished oak pews held the small number of guests. Jok, Rory's best friend; Brodrick, Jamie's best friend; and Margaret Harris with her husband, Theodore. Half a dozen MacLeod warriors also entered. The rest of the clan waited near the castle, preparing for the wedding celebration. The Macdonald guests were only warriors and sat or stood in the back. Not even the crone with the crows, who was aunt to the bride, attended.

Seraphina waited with her father before the priest, Father Lockerby, Jamie on her right side. His brother cast a glance at Rory, calling him silently to stand beside him. *Daingead*. So, he could witness the lass who'd invaded his lusty dreams the night before pledging herself to his brother. Perhaps 'twas God's punishment for the pleasure he'd taken in the dream. Her trouble-seeking tongue was certainly at fault. He snorted softly, and the priest cast a frown in his direction.

"I swear before God," Seraphina answered the question of her loyalty and obeyance.

"I swear before God," Jamie answered the question of his protecting and providing for his wife. Love was not mentioned, so the two didn't have to worry about lying before God.

Jamie gave her a kiss that seemed too long. Seraphina's hands dropped to her sides like she was merely enduring it, and Rory looked away. Her father, the Macdonald chief, produced a quill, shoving it into Jamie's hand, breaking the kiss. "Let's sign the document so Father Lockerby can hurry on his way."

Seraphina stepped back, and when Jamie took the book, she wiped the moisture from her lips with a look of distaste. Jamie and Seraphina signed their names. Rory took the quill, glancing at her flowing script. Even her name looked beautiful.

"Go on," Chief Macdonald said, and Rory signed his name, handing the quill back to Walter, who scratched hastily across the parchment. The priest signed it, sanded the ink, and rolled the document carefully, tucking it into his satchel. That was it. Jamie was wed to Seraphina Macdonald, bringing the two largest clans on the Isle of Skye together.

Gus seemed to be the only one happy about it. He wagged his tail and leaned into the bride. Gilbert escorted the priest out of the building, hurrying him along by the elbow until the cleric slapped the eager man's hand off himself to walk out on his own.

"Come along, Seraphina," her father called from the chapel door. When Rory gazed toward it, he realized not a single Macdonald remained inside except Walter beckoning his daughter.

Margaret Harris, his and Jamie's old nursemaid, hastened forward, hugging the frowning bride. "Welcome to Dunvegan and our family." The still-spry woman gave her a genuine smile.

Margaret's husband, Theodore, was one step

behind her and engulfed Seraphina's hand in both his. "We are a rabble, to be sure," he said, "but committed to welcoming ye into our home and hearts."

"Seraphina!" Walter called. "Now!" He was ordering her as if she must still obey him.

"Thank you," she said to Theodore with a tentative smile. She looked like she wished to say more, but her father kept bellowing for her to follow him out.

Jamie laughed at a lewd jest Brodrick made beside him, not concerned that his bride was being ordered to hurry away from him.

The woman's gaze swung to Rory, her blue eyes widening. She blinked, and her brows narrowed. She shook her head, frowning. "Something isn't—"

"Now!" Walter yelled.

Seraphina's gaze was full of... Was it fear? Maybe remorse? She snatched Gus's lead from his hand. "Something isn't right," she whispered and pulled Gus up the aisle.

The wind blew in through the open door, the tang of smoke on it. Was it from the fields that they'd been burning all week? They were acres away from St. Mary's Chapel in the valley.

Rory leaped forward before he'd even registered the danger, never questioning his instincts. He heard Jok curse behind him. Rory reached the door just as Walter Macdonald tried to slam it shut, but Rory got his boot in the crack. Gilbert stood beside his father on the outside with a thick log in his hands. Macdonald guards held torches, the flames twisting and dancing horizontal with the wind.

"Let me go!" the lass yelled out from somewhere beyond, and Gus growled, barking.

"I will finally have Dunvegan," Walter Macdonald called, his voice booming, breaking through the rush of wind and sea. He grinned wickedly at Rory, and his men came forward with the lit torches.

"Gu airm!" Rory yelled in Gaelic, alerting the MacLeods trapped inside the chapel. Pain shot through Rory's foot as a log slammed into it, knocking it back inside. Several toes were likely broken, but it mattered naught. The thump of bodies against the door preceded the hard drop of a bar across the outside. The doors had been open when they came up to the chapel, and no one had inspected to see that iron holders had been affixed to the outside sometime during the night. *Bloody hell.*

"Fire!" Margaret yelled, pointing above at the thatching that made up the roof. Darkness fell inside as planks were slammed over the stained-glass windows running along each side and behind the vestibule. Mallets nailed them into place.

The MacLeods were locking them in to die.

CHAPTER FOUR

"...the noise & crakling & thunder of the impetuous flames, the shreeking of women & children, the hurry of people, the fall of towers, houses & churches was like an hideous storme, & the aire all about so hot & inflam'd."

John Evelyn about the Great Fire of London, 1666

Sara staggered back from the chapel, pulling Gus with her while he barked and tugged to run back to his master, who was now trapped behind the church door. Smoke rose from the wind-fed flames sinking its teeth into the thatched roof.

Muted yells from within were accented by the crackle of the flames and orders from Gilbert and their father to bar all exits, including the windows. Her father meant to burn the MacLeod wedding party alive! No wonder he'd sent Kenan away. Her oldest brother would never have allowed it.

Father Lockerby stared at St. Mary's Chapel with wide eyes beside her, passing the sign of the cross before him. "Heavenly Father, give comfort to those who will perish now. Forgive those who act with such violence against your house of worship."

"We must get them out," she said, shaking the cleric's arm. "They'll die." And there'd be war.

Dropping Gus's lead, Sara ran around behind the chapel. Her frantic gaze slid across the planks nailed over the windows. She didn't even have a chisel to pry them up. Hitting her bouquet of bluebells against one in frustration, she swung around, searching for a way to help those inside. No one was paying her any attention as they stood watching the blaze from the front and waiting with more boards to see if the MacLeods broke through those already hammered in place.

Wisps of smoke leaked out from around the covered windows like gray snakes trying to wriggle their way out. Curses and guttural yells came through the walls. *Mother Mary, help!*

Behind a series of shrubs, Sara spotted a short door in the foundation of the church. *A crawl space.* "They can go under!" With a glance over her shoulder to see no one, Sara grabbed the small iron handle and yanked. The old door swung open, and she ducked underneath to look within. Wooden boards ran above, and uneven dirt sat below. There were also spiderwebs, and something wriggled on the ground. *Don't think. Move!*

The cool earth soaked right through her petticoat and smock to her knees as she crawled under. Footfalls pounded above her, making dirt fall on her head. She sneezed, blinking against the grit in her eyes. Fingers, swiping and clawing through the dirt, found a rock. She rolled over onto her back, held the heavy rock in two hands, and pounded above her face.

Bang. Bang. Bang.

Eyes shut against the falling dirt, she slammed the rock until she heard a *thump* right above her face. "Yes!" she yelled. "Break through here!"

Something over her hit the floorboards, sending down a heavy shower of grime. She coughed and rolled over to crawl backward as fast as she could, pushing her elbows into the mud. Floorboards splintered right over where she'd banged, cracking as the heavy baptismal font fell through. It was yanked back out and hands ripped apart the boards.

The pleasant older woman was the first to lower through. Her eyes were huge in her ash-dull face.

"Duck your head and crawl," Sara called, and Margaret followed her to the barely cracked door.

Sara peeked outside before throwing the door open wide and sucking in fresh air and wind off the sea. Crashing behind her made her jerk around as she stood, watching the roof cave into the center of the stone church. Rushing forward, Sara helped Margaret stand and led her away as coughing men poured out of the little door forgotten between the bushes at the bottom of the church.

Sara watched as each man emerged, but both Rory and Jamie were still inside. "Please God," she prayed. Around them, MacLeods were drawing their swords and rushing to the front of the chapel. Coughing and cursing, they clashed with the Macdonalds while Margaret tugged Sara back from the violence.

"But Rory!" Sara struggled against her.

"Come, milady," Margaret said, but Sara broke away, rushing back to the small door as it flung open wide again. Jamie's head emerged, slid out across the beaten grass and dirt. His eyes were closed, and blood darkened his hair.

"Jamie!" she yelled, grabbing the man's limp arm, pulling him from the hole. Margaret helped, taking his other arm. Through more smoke Rory emerged, crawling out after his brother.

A small sob echoed in Sara's ears, and she realized it was her own. *Thank you, God.* She ran to Rory, her hands wrapping around one thick bicep, desperate to help him stand. Rory straightened, coughing, and Sara backed up as he yanked his sword free of the scabbard at his side. He was covered in sooty ash and debris, his eyes red from the smoke, and he took deep breaths, coughing and spitting. His gaze met hers, and she felt all the air leave her chest.

Brows narrowed, his eyes burned with hatred.

• • •

Betrayal and fury blazed through Rory like the fire rampaging through the chapel. The lion's heart within him roared hot and vengeful. There was no time to check that Jamie had survived the beam falling upon him, knocking him unconscious. Unlike his brother, Rory wouldn't leave a family member behind.

The Macdonalds were murderers, and Seraphina had known what was going to happen. The Flame of Dunscaith? How appropriate. He'd seen the sorrow in her face in the church, had realized it as she pulled Gus's tether from his grasp, not willing to let his dog burn.

Something isn't right. Guilt had tugged at her, made her warn him at the last second. Had she only gone along with the wedding because she'd known her father would release her from the marriage before consummating it? Once again, Rory had fallen for a lass's trick. Hot, thick turmoil roiled inside him.

A man cursed as he thrust his sword at Rory, but Rory jumped back. 'Twas easy to spot the devil

Macdonalds for they were clean of soot, while the MacLeods who'd barely escaped wore tunics covered with ash and dirt, some of them singed from falling flames. But then other MacLeods, seeing the black smoke, raced down into the valley from Dunvegan.

Rory's jaw opened like the maw of the king beast, the rumble coming up from his clogged chest, and his lips pulled back in a snarl. He coughed but kept his teeth bared. His look, full of seething hatred, startled the Macdonald battling him. The slip in the man's concentration gave Rory the opportunity to slash across his chest. The Macdonald fell to the trampled earth. Rory spit out soot and coughed, his lungs aching, and leaped into the bloody frenzy before the burning church.

Where had his defensive instincts for sinister plots gone? Had the beguiling look of a Macdonald lass stolen his prowess? The bloody Flame of Dunscaith! The witch. She'd even bespelled his dog. Gus stood before her barking ferociously to keep everyone away.

Rory spun to see Jok parry the sword of Gilbert Macdonald, Seraphina's younger brother. Was this why Kenan hadn't come? Did he know about the attack and refuse to be part of it? No warning had come from the man who'd worked with Rory to escape Carlisle.

Rory grunted as he turned and dropped low, slicing across another man who'd tried to catch him from behind. "Foking bastard!" Rory roared but heard the wheeze in his words. He coughed again as he kicked the man in the chest, sending him sprawling backward, his chest flayed open and bleeding.

Rory spun around, sucking smoke-tainted wind, and coughed out more clogging ash. He met Walter Macdonald's gaze. "Ye foking monster! Setting a trap to murder at your daughter's wedding." He stalked toward the Macdonald chief as the man held his sword. Rory wiped his hand across his mouth, further dirtying his sleeve with gray stain. "Ye have no claim on Dunvegan," Rory said, "even if Jamie dies."

"My daughter is his wife," Walter Macdonald yelled back.

Look for her, Macdonald, Rory thought. *Turn your attention even for a second.* But the calculating warrior knew better than to take his gaze off the Lion even for a moment, even with Rory coughing.

"They never consummated the marriage," Rory replied. "The contract is void. The union is a farce, and I am very much alive to take over the chiefdom."

"How did ye get out of there?" Chief Macdonald yelled and waved an arm to his men.

"Ye aren't getting away, ye bastard," Rory said, but three Macdonalds ran at him with swords. *Daingead.* While he fought them off, the wily chief limped to his horse, his son dashing off with him on his own horse.

Rory would have given chase, ordered his men to follow and continue the battle, but they were all coughing. Rory felt hot blood washing down his arm and glanced at the bright red of his tunic sleeve where a sword must have nicked him. "Aye, run, devil," he said, watching Walter Macdonald and his son escape. There'd be another time for revenge, and it would be swift and painful.

Father Lockerby stood slack-jawed before the burning church. Rory ran up to him. "The wedding contract, where is it?" The priest pulled it from his pouch. Rory grabbed it and hurled it into the blaze where the fire ate it quickly. He turned back to Lockerby. "The union did not happen. The vows were lies." He waited until the priest nodded his agreement before turning to Margaret, who'd appeared next to him.

"Let me tie this around the wound." She tightened a rag over the bloody slash.

"Is he dead?" Rory asked, glancing past his old nursemaid toward Jamie. Sara crouched beside him, her flower crown holding halfway down her curls.

"Nay," Margaret said, but her voice was grim. "But he's sorely injured."

Seraphina's blue eyes lifted to Rory as she straightened. She blinked and rubbed at them as if the smoke stung.

"She knew," he said, and a wheezing cough followed. He pointed. "The Flame of Dunscaith! 'Tis why ye dragged Gus out," he yelled. The bitterness of soot came up on his tongue, and he spit into the grass.

Her striking eyes narrowed, and her full lips pulled back in disgust. "I knew nothing of his plans."

"The Flame of Dunscaith," he spat. "With a name like that, of course ye—"

"The name is a farce." She shook her head vehemently as her arm threw out to emphasize her words. "I've never heard it before my father uttered it this morn."

"Ye went along with the wedding knowing ye'd be free of the marriage!"

"I knew nothing!"

"The marriage is void, the contract eaten by the

flames," Rory said, glaring at Seraphina. She didn't say anything, but stood, continuing to keep her gaze on him, mud and ash over her wedding ensemble.

Rory's voice rose above the flames and wind. "The Flame of Dunscaith is not wed to any MacLeod."

"There's no such thing as the bloody Flame of Dunscaith," the woman yelled, which brought on a coughing fit. She turned away from him.

She stared at the burning church, proof of Macdonald evil. Father Lockerby walked to her. "Yer father destroyed a house of God," he yelled. "He will burn in Hell." Even though the priest spoke of her father, he raged at Seraphina with his dire prediction.

She stood there, hands fisted by her sides as if ready to defend or attack. Her embroidered blue gown was smeared with mud and soot. The wreath of bluebells was tossed backward, hanging in the tangle of hair with grass and dirt. Smudges of black smeared her forehead, and her bottom lip bled as if she'd bitten it. Stepping back from the heat of the flames and the condemning priest, she turned in a circle as if looking for her clan.

"They've abandoned ye," Rory said.

She wiped quickly at her streaked cheeks. No hysterics came with her tears. She stood straight, hands in fists. "I think he knows I…" Her voice trailed off.

Rory met her eyes with a hard, narrowed stare. Despite her beauty and courage, she wouldn't find the weakness of leniency within him. "Seraphina Macdonald," Rory said, "ye will come to Dunvegan, not as a bride, but as a prisoner."

CHAPTER FIVE

Seraphina – "Feminine form of the Late Latin name Seraphinus, derived from the biblical word seraphim, which was Hebrew in origin and meant "fiery ones". The seraphim were an order of angels, described by Isaiah in the Bible as having six wings each."

BehindtheName.com

Sara watched a woman with light-colored hair, which matched her muted yellow petticoat, wail when she saw Jamie on the stretcher.

"Nay! It cannot be. Jamie. My Jamie!"

Her Jamie? Who the hell was she?

"The Macdonalds did this," the woman yelled, and more people rushed up the hill toward them, men with drawn swords, women with knives in their hands, determined to beat back a Macdonald attack. The wailing lady pointed a finger at Sara. "She did this! A trick to wed our chief and then kill us. 'Tis a Macdonald trick."

A prickling of fear spread through Sara. The hatred on the faces of the villagers felt like daggers being thrown at her tethered body.

"She's called the Flame of Dunscaith!" one of the men yelled.

"Seraphina means fiery one," another cried.

"Throw her in the fire!" came from an elderly woman holding a long knife. The words penetrated Sara's inability to move. She might not be able to run to Dunscaith, but she couldn't stay here.

More people were rushing closer from the town. Loathing and shock tightened their faces as they glanced between the church and Sara. Even if her fiery mark prevented her from being loved, she'd still yearned to be useful in sowing peace. However, the looks from the MacLeods showed she'd failed.

Crows cawed overhead, several landing in a tree in the churchyard as if to watch the destruction. *Aunt Morag.*

Self-preservation pushed her to move. The wind shifted, and the villagers cursed while blocking their faces with their hands and rubbing their eyes at the smoke-sting. *I need to run.* Shedding the granite that seemed to have imprisoned her, Sara clutched her skirts. Her fingers rucked them up to give her slippered feet room to run. She spun away, leaping across the path leading away from Dunvegan. Sharp pebbles bruised the bottoms of her feet, but she didn't have time to have more than a fleeting wish that she'd worn her boots under her gown. Of course, she hadn't planned to be running for her life on her wedding day.

Plan for the worst.

Her mother's words echoed in her ears with the thumping of her blood. The advice couldn't pertain to the nightmare of that day. Her mother would have been struck mute by her husband's treachery.

Damn skirts! Sara lifted them nearly to her knees as her legs battered against the layers of wool and linen. Her heart pounded with exertion and subdued alarm. Panic wouldn't help her survive, so she stomped it down and focused on the copse of trees to the west that sat between Dunvegan and Morag's cottage. It was blurred in her sight because of the smoke burning her eyes.

Would Morag's crow army and strong oak door be enough to hold off MacLeod thirst for retribution? *Rather to die by the sword than the flames.* Legs churning along the road, she ducked off the path across the moor, leaping from hillock to hillock in a run that could break her ankle if she didn't concentrate. Her chest burned, and she spit the soot from her throat, blinking wildly as she kept moving.

She didn't dare look behind her, imagining MacLeods swarming after her like angry wasps after she'd trounced their nest. If only she had the wings that Kenan talked of building.

"Seraphina Macdonald!" 'Twas Rory MacLeod, the man who'd seemed so honorable the day before, so brawny and handsome. But he wasn't her groom. He was the brother, the bloody Lion of Skye, and now more than ever, she was his enemy. She kept her eyes forward on the spongy moor. One misplaced step and she'd go down like a ruined horse. "Ye are my prisoner!" he yelled. The steel in his tone made tingles erupt all over her skin.

"The hell I am." She drew even breaths to dispel the sparks in her periphery, but the soot in her lungs made it hard to draw in so much air.

Hillocks on a spongy moor would slow her pursuer. Even the Lion of Skye would have to walk carefully while she reached the forest where the ground was firmer, and the ferns grew thick around old oaks.

The neigh of a horse came from the road at the edge of the moor. Maybe he wouldn't pursue her. "Leave me!" she yelled back over her shoulder.

She heard coughing and then, "Daingead, I will not."

"Go to Hell," she shouted without looking.

"I'm already there." His words weren't shouted, but they carried over the moor where the remaining morning mist floated in wisps over the green.

Sara's sweaty hands clutched her skirts as she hopped to the swollen, moss-covered hillocks where tiny early-summer flowers reached toward the sky. She trampled them, desperate to get away. Her father had abandoned her, left her to face the MacLeods' vengeance alone. She'd always known Walter Macdonald thought little of her, reminding her of her ugliness all the time, but to abandon her...

She hit firmer ground and charged into the woods. The coolness of the shade felt like a wash of refreshing water over her heated skin. Sweet Saint Mary, she wished she had something to wash the fire from her throat. She coughed again, not bothering to stifle the noise as her gaze shifted around, hunting for a place to hide. Because if Rory MacLeod still followed her, she couldn't outrun him.

Brilliant green ferns and fiddleheads grew thickly to the right. Sara veered into them, realizing that she'd lost both slippers on the moor. The cool mud squished between her toes through her once-white stockings. Gathering her blue petticoats, she dropped to her knees in a bunch of vegetation, ducking flat against the earth. She rolled onto her back and used her hands to pull the ferns overtop of her in an attempt to make them look undisturbed. Wind rustled the leaves overhead. Hopefully, any movement in the ferns would merely look like breezes.

Cool mud pressed through the back of her bodice

and smock. Before the ceremony, she'd plucked even the smallest piece of lint from her ensemble, but now it was all mud and soot. Her breath came in rough gasps from the smoke and the run. Eyes wide, she stared upward at the small patch of blue sky that peeked through the green canopy of tree leaves high above her and the brighter green, feathery fronds over her face.

"Seraphina Macdonald!" The deep voice was close, making her choke on a breath. There was a growl in the tone, almost like the one her father had when he called her full name. 'Twas why she despised it. The name translated to "the burning one" and was given to her because of the fiery mark across her back. Her mother had said she'd been named after the highest rank of angels, but her father constantly brought up her imperfection, the reason he couldn't marry her off to any ally.

She covered her mouth, swallowing against the cough that tickled, pushing to escape. She waited, barely breathing, willing her heartbeat to calm and the rising cough to abate. But it grew despite her trying to suffocate it. A small thud off to the center of the woods made her eyes shift that way, but she didn't dare move. What would Rory do if he found her? Would he run her through with his sword, justice for his injured warriors and Jamie? Who would care for her young sister, Eliza, then?

"Yer tracks stop here," Rory said and cleared his throat. "Come out, Seraphina Macdonald, or I will come in to get ye."

Get her? What did that mean? Kill her? Rip her throat out? That's what Gilbert used to say about the younger MacLeod brother. That he'd seen him bite men during battle, blood running down his jaw, as if he were truly a lion lunging in for the kill.

Rory coughed again. "I have a flask of ale."

It took her a few seconds to get past the image of the man ripping into someone's throat to understand he was offering her refreshment. 'Twas surely a trick. He knew she was parched and clogged with smoke. But she wouldn't allow him to lure her with ale. The cough inside battered against her, breaking through the slightest amount despite her covered mouth. There was no helping it. Her lungs were desperate.

The ferns brushed aside, and Rory MacLeod's face appeared above her, looking down, blocking the patch of blue sky above. His cheeks were gray with ash and dirt. Blood dried along a cut on his forehead and drops of blood speckled his neck. His cropped waves of hair were wild about his head, and his amber eyes were red from the smoke.

Sara gave into the tickle in her chest, coughing hard. It no longer mattered. He thrust his hand out to her. "Take it."

Fury, gut-wrenching disappointment, and a determination to live mixed to shoot through her spine where she lay in the ferns.

He leaned over her. "Take my hand." His order came through clenched teeth. Did he truly bite people with them? They were white and looked sharp.

But instead of taking it, her thumb slid to the outside of her tightening fist. In a movement like the triggered kick of a hare's back legs, Sara's stomach contracted, raising her upward, and her knuckles punched straight into Rory's eye. *Crack!*

"Bloody hell." He reared back, and she was up and leaping through the ferns before the words had left his mouth. The pain in her knuckles was nothing over the satisfaction of surprising the man enough to get away.

Unfortunately, the punch didn't slow him. *Sweet Saint Mary!* He charged after her through the ferns until she felt him right behind her. Instead of yanking her arm or throwing her to the ground, she felt his arms encircle hers, pinning them to her sides as he picked her off her feet.

"Let go." Sara kicked, but devoid of even her useless slippers, her attack did nothing to save her. She twisted with all her might, but he squeezed.

"Stop yer wiggling, woman."

Wiggling? As if she were a helpless worm. But she stilled, realizing her struggles were taking all her energy.

He turned her to face him, his one arm still wrapped around her in a manacle-like hold. She stared into his eyes, gratified to see one pinched closed and swelling.

"Ye were trying to blind me!" he yelled in her face, blinking his other eye as if clearing the smoke from it. There was no overpowering him.

"Go ahead," she said, staring up at him with belligerence despite the shameful tremble that wracked her. "Slice my throat." She'd rather die here in the cool ferns than blistered in a fire. Against the wishes of her rushing blood, begging her to magically grow huge enough to fight him off, she tipped her chin higher, exposing her throat. She looked down her nose to meet his gaze. "May this face, my very eyes, haunt you for the rest of your life, Rory MacLeod."

CHAPTER SIX

"In each fire there is a spirit; Each one is wrapped in
what is burning him."

Dante, 1265–1321, Italian poet

Rory stared down at the woman in his arms. Red-gold
hair tangled in waves about her straight shoulders, the
green ferns behind her in bright contrast. The gentle
tilt of her wide blue eyes and the flush of color on her
cheeks all made her look like a fairy of the woods
who'd been caught by a human. Had she been painted
in his mother's old book of tales, he would expect her
to vanish on the next page, like a will-o'-the-wisp.

Her throat, an exposed length of pale, smooth
skin, lay bare, but it was her piercing eyes that pulsed
through him, as if they looked past his layers into his
soul and found it lacking. If he was bent on killing her,
as she'd prophesied, those hate-filled eyes would truly
haunt him forever. Just like Madeline's eyes, but this
time, Rory could save the lass.

Seraphina's chest rose and fell like a bird caught in
a snare, and he felt her tremble despite her vengeful
gaze. Devious traitor or not, he wasn't planning to kill
her. He wasn't his father. "I'm not cutting yer throat."

"I won't let you throw me in the fire," she said, and
kicked out with one of her bare feet. It hit higher this
time, above his boot, with a good amount of power,
surprising him enough that he glanced down at her

bare toes, toes he remembered from the beach.

"I won't burn ye," he said. "If I release my hold, will ye take my hand?" The warmth of her body was penetrating his tunic. She was soft and full of curves that were incredibly distracting, making his blood thrum with thoughts quite opposite of killing.

"Kill me here or let me go," she said and coughed harder, directly into his face.

He released her but kept one hand manacled around her slender wrist. She was a Macdonald, someone not to be trusted. Yet, she'd been so kind to Gus. "Drink something." He glanced away to cough himself. "The smoke is working its way out of us both." She tried to snap her hand away. "Stop yanking and drink before ye break yer wrist."

The lass frowned but lowered her chin, conceding that he wasn't going to slice her throat. It was a small victory. She turned her mouth to the side, and the deep bark of her cough sounded painful. She'd inhaled a lot of the smoke, too. She still didn't take the flask.

"I'm not going to foking kill ye while yer drinking," he said, the pain in his eye fouling his mood.

"You better not be foking lying," she retorted, grabbing the flask with her loose hand.

Surprise at her mimicked curse nearly made him smile, but this was certainly not a day for smiles. It was definitely a day for swearing. *And whisky.* She lifted the uncorked bladder to her lips and drank, her eyes closing. He watched her slender throat swallow.

How could anyone slice through something so lovely? Memories of another slender throat made his gaze rise back to her face. *Bloody hell!* Ghosts and regret ruled Rory's life.

Relief softened the woman's features, her lips working at the spout. He couldn't look away at the thirst in her face and stance, and the gradual relaxation of her body, her curvy, sensuous body. Her lips were damp and formed the perfect *O* around the opening. The thought of her sucking on something made his cock stir, which was completely inappropriate. She was nearly his brother's wife. He cleared his throat and looked away.

She lowered the flask and handed it back.

"Come," he said, pulling her to walk out of the ferns to the old forest floor, spongy with a millennium of detritus and colonies of moss.

She tugged back, almost digging in her heels like a child. "I didn't know anything about the fire."

"From the lips of the Flame of Dunscaith." Rory dragged her from the woods onto the moor. His dappled silver charger, Airgid, stood obediently waiting on the road beyond. "Do all Macdonald women lie?"

She tried to yank her hand away, but he'd closed his grip tightly. "I told you already, no one calls me the Flame of Dunscaith. 'Twas some sick jest from my"—she sniffed, rubbing her nose—"my damn father."

"Ye've never been called the Flame of—"

"Nay!" she yelled. "He came up with the name after Chief MacLeod introduced you as the Lion of Skye."

His father had given him the name after he'd vowed to protect the MacLeod Clan above all else. Rory was the commander of their mighty armies across the large isle. 'Twas Rory's duty to protect all parts of his clan, train his warriors, and battle their enemies when called.

"I am no flame."

"Ye're named Seraphina, which literally means the fiery one."

He glanced back at her, and even though she looked down to watch her steps on the hillocks, red climbed up into her cheeks. "I prefer the name Sara."

They continued maneuvering across the moor. "I can't go back to Dunvegan," she said. "Your people think I'm responsible for the fire, the attack."

He turned to her at his horse. "Ye truly refute yer involvement in the fire," he said, feeling the raw fury try to ignite within him. How could she not have known? She'd taken Gus's lead.

The reddish irritation in her eyes gave her irises a greenish hue, like emeralds set in her dirt-smeared face. "Oh, I was very involved in the fire." She indicated her ruined dress with her free hand. "I tried to warn you inside the church when I felt something wasn't right. I had no forewarning before my father demanded I leave with him." Her words came through clenched teeth.

"And I was quite involved in saving the lot of you by crawling under a burning church, risking my life to bang rocks above my face on the floorboards and crawling backward before being smashed by the baptismal font." Her voice had risen until she shouted. "Now I can't go home because my father will kill me for interfering, and I cannot go back to Dunvegan or your clan will throw me in the fire. So, my choice is to go to my Aunt Morag's cottage." She threw her arm out in the direction she'd been running. "And have her contact my brother to help me into exile."

"Gilbert?" he asked to provoke her a bit more. He liked how her eyes flashed with fury. 'Twas much better than fear.

"Bloody hell, no! Gilbert is as brutal as my father. And he's only clever enough to be dangerous. I mean Kenan, of course, the man you apparently escaped England with. He said you're honorable."

He reached forward to catch a tear running down her cheek. She jerked her face away. He dropped his hand and studied her. "Ye yell like a wronged patriot being dragged to the scaffold yet weep at the same time."

She wiped a flattened palm over her cheek, but the strength and anger in her face didn't recede. "'Tis an eye problem and no concern."

"Weeping? An eye problem?" He released her wrist.

Her freed hand flew through the air as if she were casting his questions aside because of their miniscule importance. She pointed a sharp nail toward his injured eye. "It looks as if you have an eye problem, too. How would you like a second one?"

Again, his lips felt like turning up if the day had been different. "I've been threatened with tears before from a lass, but not in that way."

Silence sat for a moment, and then as if she were done with their conversation, she whirled and began to traipse away toward the crone's cottage again.

Damn, she was slippery. "Seraphina—"

"Sara!" she interrupted without looking back.

"Sara, we are returning to Dunvegan." He must see if Jamie survived and prevent an immediate retaliation. Thought was required, not pure vengeance.

He'd learned that while held in Carlisle's dungeon, where threats of retaliation led to flogging.

Sara shook her head as she marched away, her hair wreath slipping to the very end of her tresses, bumping against her arse until she yanked it from her red-gold waves. "I'm not fool enough to go willingly back to my torture and death." Mud covered her blue dress, and the smashed flowers sailed through the air as she threw the wreath. Fists tight and barefoot, she strode with purpose like some elfin lass marching to war with only her magic as a weapon.

"I won't let them harm ye." Rory wasn't a youth, just growing into his leadership of the MacLeod warriors, a lad still under his father's thumb. Rory was a seasoned warrior now and commander. If he said she wouldn't be harmed, bloody hell, she wouldn't be harmed. Rory caught up to her easily and grabbed her arm.

She spun toward him, yanking her arm away while bringing her fist around to his face. Only warrior reflexes saved his nose. His large hand wrapped around her small fist caught in the air, and he bent forward. "Ye are coming with me to Dunvegan. Now, put yer claws away, Hellcat."

Her lips pulled back slightly to show perfect white teeth. "You drag me to my death then."

He glared back. "I'm the bloody Lion of Skye, Sara. I command the MacLeod armies. My word will prevent your death."

The tension in her face didn't lessen. "So, my life depends on the favor of a bloodthirsty lion," she said, her voice low.

"If I let ye return home, yer life will depend on the

favor of a bloodthirsty tyrant with no honor," he growled back. "Yer father abandoned ye."

A red hue infused her cheeks. "We have that in common then," she said and spun, continuing to trudge away.

Rory's shackled fury broke free at the reminder of his father's betrayal. In two strides, he caught her around the waist, lifting her from the forest floor. Her medium-sized frame was small compared to his, and he easily flipped her about to set her over one shoulder like he had with his sister, Eleri, when she was small. But instead of happy giggling over his back, this banshee screamed and struck with all her fury.

"Foking put me down! I will kill you as soon as I find a blade! I have a plan to survive on my own. Let me go!" Her words shot through his ears with such pain, he could imagine tiny blades stabbing inside the canals. She nearly slid off his shoulder with her wild squirming, and he felt her hands searching his arse and hips. For a blade, most likely.

He opened his mouth and roared, his charred throat stretching to allow the flow of sound. It did the trick, startling her so he could catch her in a firmer grip.

Recovering quickly, Sara kicked backward, arching her back, twisting like an eel, except instead of being slimy and cold, Sara was warm and pleasantly curved. And she smashed those curves into him in her bid for freedom.

"I take no pleasure in carrying ye this way," he said, his words grinding out. It was mostly true, if he'd stop noticing how gloriously colored and long her hair was, stretching down past the edge of his plaid wrap to tickle the backs of his knees.

"You bastard! I'll...cut your heart out and watch ye choke on it."

"'Tis good ye have a strong will to live."

"You lowly sheep rider! Lucifer is preparing his chains for you in Hell."

She had a humorous way of twisting words into curses, but Rory knew better than to laugh.

"Ye're probably correct," he said. "About the chains, not the sheep rider. My legs would drag on the ground if I tried to ride a sheep."

Using both arms wrapped around her legs, pinning her arms under her, he balanced her on his shoulder. He felt the strain on the slice on the opposite arm where the Macdonald blade had found flesh. Margaret would chide him, but he had little choice.

"Put me down, you shriveled louse!"

He held his tongue, since she was absolutely not in the mood to listen to his good reasons for carrying her back to Dunvegan: wolves across the moor, her murdering father, her brutal younger brother, violent brigands, killing thieves, starvation. Each horrible thought made him hold tighter to her legs. Sara Macdonald and the peace she could bring was too important to lose. And he wasn't ready to lose the most resilient lass he'd ever met.

CHAPTER SEVEN

"On what was once an island in Loch Dunvegan, Dunvegan Castle consists of…a 16th-century tower known as the Fairy Tower, which was built by Alasdair Crotach…"

TheCastlesofScotland.co.uk

Sara's limbs ached with impotent exhaustion, so she draped forward over the neck of the horse the Lion had thrown her onto. As her heart slowed, her gaze followed the patches of small white flowers on thread-thin stems shooting up from the thick clumps of moss as the horse walked along the edge of the narrow road.

She almost wished to slide off under the horse's feet, but being trampled to death was painful. There was also the chance that Rory MacLeod wasn't lying when he said he wouldn't let her come to harm. *Where there is life, there is hope.* Her mother's advice calmed Sara.

Rory paused and came to the side. Sara didn't bother to move. She felt his fingers pry her foot from the stirrup. The saddle tipped as he lifted upward, but she gave him no room in the saddle. *Let him keep walking.*

She gasped as he lifted under her, setting her onto his lap. With a quick wiggling shift, she slid off his crotch to straddle the pommel. But there was no helping her backside pressing into his groin. At least her petticoats bunched between them. "'Tis not decent," she said.

"'Twill be less decent if ye keep rubbing yer arse against my cock."

She snapped her gaze around to face him. His golden eyes were narrowed in challenge, but wry humor played about his lips. Before she could say anything, he looked over her head. "Hold on."

She gasped as the horse lunged forward into a gallop. The beast thundering beneath them was no leisure palfrey but a courser, a war horse. If Rory's arm hadn't latched around her middle, holding her in the seat, Sara may have indeed slid off to her death.

Wind filled her face, and Sara took large inhales to calm her heart. The air no longer made her cough, but as they closed the distance that she'd run, the smell of smoke rode the breeze. St. Mary's Chapel smoldered ahead, its roof having caved in. Villagers stood around it, watching the structure that couldn't be saved.

Gazes turned toward them as they neared, some curious, some hostile. Sara wasn't sure who had yelled to throw her into the burning chapel, so she imagined it coming from all of them. In a show of defiance that hid the quake running up and down her spine, she tipped her chin slightly higher and kept her back straight.

Most of the men who'd escaped the burning church had left the area. The litter holding her groom was gone. Was Jamie still her groom, her husband? Sara had watched the flames hungrily grab the wedding contract, destroying it. But did the priest still consider Jamie and her married? Did God?

Rory pushed them up the incline and through the village to the base of towering Dunvegan Castle. Margaret and Gus, the wolfhound, remained near the side of the castle with several horses tethered there. Rory guided his horse toward them.

When they stopped at the wall, Rory dismounted. Sara pulled her leg over to jump down, but Rory's large hands wrapped around her waist, setting her down without jarring. Gus pressed against her legs, and Margaret came up to her with a drinking bladder.

"Here, milady," Margaret said; the woman's voice was strong and kind. "I'll get ye a rosemary and peppermint poultice to lay on your chest and a steam for ye to breathe once we're inside." She thumped her own chest and coughed. "'Twill help all of us."

Sara nodded her thanks but felt her cheeks heat with embarrassment. "I am sorry for—"

"You pulled me out of that inferno, milady." Margaret waved off the rest of her apology.

Margaret's gaze swung back to Rory. "You opened your wound again," she said, frowning between them. She squinted at Rory. "And your eye is swelling."

"No matter," he said.

Rory issued orders to a few soldiers who wore soot-free tunics, making it evident they hadn't attended the nightmarish ceremony. "Lay the dead Macdonalds out on a wagon bed and deliver them to the nearest Macdonald holding. Morag Gunn."

"The witch with the crows?" one asked.

"Aye," Rory said.

Sara opened her mouth to say Morag wasn't a witch, but she really didn't know. To be associated with her aunt right now wouldn't help her. She looked at the two Macdonald warriors. They were her father's men, but no one she knew.

"Send a message to Kenan Macdonald about this"—Rory waved his hand indicating the smoldering chapel—"atrocity. Let Walter Macdonald know that we are officially at war with the Macdonalds of Sleat. To make peace, they must replace the chapel and compensate us for the attack with two wagons of grain."

Sara knew her father would never give them anything. They were at war. Her heart sank deeper. No matter the brave, cold face she presented, her stomach roiled as if she would vomit. Without his old adversary leading the MacLeods, both Sara and Kenan had hoped a peace between the clans could be settled. But her father had fouled that up completely.

The looming stone castle sat on a saltwater strait off Loch Dunvegan. A ten-foot-thick curtain wall surrounded Dunvegan Castle. Sara had heard her father grumble and curse about the difficulty of getting inside the seat of the MacLeods, and now she saw why.

Tables were set up outside the wall where the wedding would've been celebrated. The villagers had decorated the area with garlands of bluebells and daisies. The flowers flapped in the wind from an arch at the top of the table where two chairs had been set side by side. Food and tankards had been abandoned and chairs knocked over. A doll made of twisted reeds lay in the path as if a child had dropped it when her mother grabbed her to run to safety.

Sara picked the doll out of the path, brushing the dirt from the sewn dress of blue. Yellow and red-dyed wool had been braided and attached to the faceless head. She set it on the table to be found. When she turned back, Rory was watching her. Their gazes connected, and she felt a flush warm her cheeks at being caught doing something so…inconsequential.

Sara turned her face from his and searched the soaring wall for a portcullis or gatehouse. There was nothing but solid wall and a dock at the water's edge. "We must take to the water to enter Dunvegan?"

Margaret answered, "'Tis the only way in or out through the wall."

Sara watched Gus leap easily onto a flat ferry that looked to hold ten large men. Margaret motioned for Sara to follow her onto it. The vessel dipped with the shifting weight as men climbed on board, two of them taking up poles to push them through the water. Thankfully, Gus stood before Sara so that men couldn't press against her front, but she felt someone brush her back.

Prickles skittered along her nape, and she felt breath brush her hair.

"Do not try to escape through the water." Rory's deep voice sent chill bumps down her arms, and her body prickled with awareness. "Men have been known to drown trying to swim."

"I'll be sure to grow wings and fly to my freedom then." Her gaze remained out over the water as the polemen pushed the barge around the side of the massive castle. Only the lapping of water and slight grind of pebbles being crushed by the poles on the bottom broke the silence.

The ferry docked on a spit of land that faced the outlet to the sea. One by one they stepped off to climb the bank to a set of granite steps carved into the steep incline. Gus half ran, half walked up them to bark at a barred gate in the stonewall. Rory remained behind, taking Margaret's hand to help her down with his good arm. He turned back to Sara.

"I can manage," she said, pulling the hem of her skirt higher to find her step. She'd lost both her slippers on her run, and the bottoms of her feet ached with bruises. Rory took her free hand, and the warmth against her cold fingers made her clutch it as he helped her from the ferry. He then turned away, releasing her and striding up the steps. Sara's fingers curled inward as if trying to contain the warmth he'd left against her palm.

Fatigue weighed on Sara, but she paid close attention as she passed through the barred gate through the ten-foot-thick wall and then up another set of narrow steps into the entryway of the castle. One warrior helped Margaret, but no one asked Sara if she needed any, not that she expected it. She was the enemy here. *Dear Mother Mary.* She'd probably be poisoned within three days.

High-arched ceilings of timber buttresses soared overhead in the great hall. Rich tapestries hung on the walls depicting battles, flags, and stag hunts. One showed a man and woman being wed beside a loch that sparkled in the sun.

Another showed the woman handing the yellow Fairy Flag to her groom. There were several legends about the revered flag. 'Twas said a fairy princess wed a MacLeod hundreds of years ago and gave him the powerful flag to protect him and his clan. The flag was still housed somewhere in Dunvegan. Alasdair MacLeod had unfurled the banner in 1520 when her clan almost conquered the MacLeods. Both sides felt the battle had turned in MacLeod favor only because of the magical scrap of silk.

A wooden table ran down the center of the room, and a cluster of chairs and stools sat in a semicircle before a hearth at one end. Jamie must have been carried above because he wasn't in the hall. Margaret issued instructions for medicines, while her husband fretted around her, giving her a goblet and wet rag for her flushed face.

Sara stopped in the middle of the room like a tree rooted in the center of a flooded river as people rushed around her. A bearded man with a hawk-like nose to match a tall forehead hurried across the room to Rory. She felt lost and weak. Her gaze latched onto the strong features of her captor as if he were a buoy.

"Sit down," the bearded man ordered Rory. "We cannot lose ye."

Rory's large form folded into a chair at the table while the man inspected his sliced arm.

"Jamie's in more jeopardy than me, Hamish," Rory said.

"I tended him and will go above after I sew yer arm."

Windows high above allowed in light, and lit beeswax candles in an iron chandelier hung over the table draped in colorful embroidered linen.

Several times a guard or maid nearly ran Sara over but slid past her at the last second without giving her so much as a look. How could she escape from a castle surrounded by seawater?

Half-created scenarios twirled in Sara's mind until the walls around her seemed to wobble. She realized she'd locked her knees and purposely made them bend. She pulled in a long breath but still swayed, the vision of Rory blurring. Perhaps if she swooned, all of this would end. Her eyes flicked closed. Then open. Then closed.

"Bloody hell," Rory yelled, "someone get her a chair!"

Sara felt someone touch her elbow, and her feet moved without her attention. A chair edge hit the back of her knees, making her sit near the low fire in the large stone hearth.

A cup was pressed into her hands. "Drink, milady," a voice said. She looked up into the lean face of a tall, thin man with dark hair and a smile that showed upper teeth that jutted outward. His jaw had little definition, but his eyes were large and concerned. He nodded at the cup, making his hair fall in his eyes. "'Tis a weak honey ale." He gave a slight shake of his head to part the hair so he could see. 'Twas such a quick, subtle gesture that Sara imagined he did it all day long.

"Thank you," she said and took a drink, closing her eyes to concentrate on the soothing liquid.

"I'm Reid Hodges of Lewis," the man said, and she opened her eyes, immediately seeing Rory MacLeod staring at her from his seat. She frowned at him and turned her gaze up to Reid.

Reid cleared his throat. "Mistress Margaret tasked me to look after ye." He gave her a little nod, almost like a bird bobbing its head, shook the hair from his eyes again, and took the empty cup. He turned away to hustle off before she could say anything else. Apparently, he already knew who she was. The hated

Macdonald bride whose father tried to murder everyone on her wedding day.

Margaret had disappeared. Had she gone above to see Jamie? Should Sara go to him, her betrothed or husband or enemy? When she'd met him before the church and realized her fantasies had been about Rory and not Jamie, an unbidden sob had settled inside her chest. Such disappointment had almost made her turn away from the church. Would her father's plans have proceeded if she'd refused to wed? Walter Macdonald would probably have killed her before everyone.

Rory remained sitting at the table, his knees splayed wide, while the slice to his arm was washed and stitched. Sara stood slowly from her chair and walked over, stopping before him. "I should see if I can help…Jamie," she said. "Is he above?"

The elderly man at Rory's shoulder stopped, as well as several others nearby.

"Ye're no chief's wife," said an old man with one eye pinched shut and sunken in. He cut his hand in the air. "Trying to murder yer groom and his family on yer wedding day makes yer vows lies said to God."

"Aye," another man said, stepping up next to the first. "No dowry, no consummation, and an evil plot to murder…" He waved a hand in the air, and Sara noticed his other sleeve was tied under the elbow, his left forearm missing. "Means no marriage. Ye, the Flame of Dunscaith, are our prisoner." His scowl matched the expression of the one-eyed man.

"What John said," the first man said, tipping his head toward him. "And Jamie, bless him, might never wake. Throw her in the dungeon."

Sara's heart thumped hard. The dungeon at Dunscaith Castle was damp, cold, and dark with rats scratching around for food, or bare toes. Gilbert had locked her in there once when they were children when she'd told her father that he'd been sleeping in the barn instead of training. Feeling forgotten and trapped in the space had terrified her.

Rory stood, the needle and string dangling from his arm where the barber-surgeon hadn't finished. Sara looked up into his hard face. Just like when she'd peered up at it through the ferns, she saw questions there.

"Until my brother regains leadership," he said, "ye will remain at Dunvegan."

"In the dungeon?" she asked, squeezing her hands so Rory didn't see her tremble.

He continued to stare into her eyes. It was as if he were trying to read what was inside her head. "Reid, take Lady Sara to wash in the kitchens and then take her to the west tower." Rory never took his eyes off hers. "Make sure she's given food and drink."

"Bloody hell," the man missing an arm cursed.

The one-eyed man snorted. "In my day, she'd have been—"

"Lady Sara is under *my* protection," Rory said, his gaze moving about the great hall and finally falling on the two gray-haired men. "I am the chief of Clan MacLeod on Skye until Jamie wakes, as well as the commander of our armies. Unless…" His gaze moved to the warriors being treated by maids or standing armed about the room. "Unless someone challenges me."

Silence swelled between them. Even the men who

were still plagued by coughing muffled the sound in their elbow pits. No one seemed inclined to challenge the Lion of Skye even with his one arm sliced. The thread of his suture hung from his massive arm as he scanned the quiet hall.

A large warrior with red hair and freckles over his scowling face walked toward him, and for a moment Sara worried he might challenge Rory. But then the man stood beside him looking out in a silent gesture of support. Five others came forward to do the same.

Rory nodded to them and walked back to the barber-surgeon. "Reid, lead Lady Sara to the kitchens." He didn't even look at her.

CHAPTER EIGHT

"Caboc is a rich double cream cheese… The recipe for Caboc dates back to the 15th century in the Scottish Highlands. Mariota de Ile, the daughter of the chieftain MacDonald of the Isles, developed the recipe of Caboc and passed it to her daughter, who in due course handed it over to the future generations."

Cheese.com

Rory fought to keep his gaze on the men moving about the great hall instead of letting it slip to Sara Macdonald. He wanted to clasp her head in his two hands and stare into those glittering blue eyes until he extracted all her secrets.

Had she not known about her father's scheme? Or was she playing the innocent to wheedle her way into their midst? Her dislike of his brother seemed genuine enough, but she'd wed him anyway. Could her father have forced her?

Don't let foolish sentiment hide the facts.

His father's advice was sound even if he'd been a devil.

Margaret said Sara was the one to knock under the church, giving them the idea to smash through the floorboards. Sara led Margaret out, leading the way for the rest of them to follow. Then she'd been abandoned by her clan. Why? Did Walter Macdonald want her to finish his work inside Dunvegan? Killing Jamie and discovering the entrances in the castle so her Macdonald Clan could infiltrate?

Sara had looked at Rory, not Jamie, after the ceremony when her father loudly commanded her up the aisle. She'd whispered to him that something wasn't right, snatching Gus from him.

With Sara following Reid, Rory allowed his gaze to settle on her straight back where pins stuck out of her loose hair. Even muddy, rolled in ferns, and missing her shoes, she walked with grace and dignity through the archway toward the kitchens. She hadn't begged him to leave her in the woods. She'd demanded it and then fought with courage. Sara Macdonald wasn't a meek maid following her father's orders to wed. She was brave and clever.

She could be another Macdonald spy. Rory was surprised Jamie had accepted Walter Macdonald's suggestion of a marriage alliance. Maybe he'd planned to feed his new wife false information.

"There," said Hamish, cutting the string he'd used to stitch up Rory's arm. "Keep it clean. Margaret will likely have a poultice for it."

"Thank ye," Rory said, standing.

"Yer orders?"

Rory turned toward his red-haired, freckled friend, Jok Duffie. Jok had taken over training and command of the MacLeod armies when Rory was imprisoned in England. He'd seemed truly happy when Rory had returned, even though Jamie had said Jok wanted to keep control. More brotherly lies. Rory didn't believe anything that came off his brother's tongue. Even the truth could be twisted.

"Place a watch on the village, all night and day.

Make sure no Macdonald enters." Rory rubbed the back of his neck. "Send a messenger to Kenan Macdonald, telling him what has occurred. I'll meet him at his aunt's, the crow house, in three days' time."

Rory wasn't going to order a slaughtering raid on the day that peace was supposed to be declared. He needed to know what Walter Macdonald intended.

Rory glanced at the archway. And, at present, there was only one person, even if she wouldn't admit it, who might know the plans of the Macdonalds of Sleat.

• • •

Sara held her damp hair in a towel over one shoulder as she entered the square tower room cautiously. There was a single bed against the wall across from a small hearth. She glanced up at the heavy wooden beams of the ceiling.

Reid set the basket of food and flask of ale on a table that looked like it might buckle under its weight and lit the candle from his lantern. "There are sconces on the walls that ye can light from this," he said.

"Thank you," Sara said, but two windows set in opposite plastered stone walls let in plenty of daylight. A rug of dull blue and yellow roses lay across the floor, matching the blue of the quilt on the bed. A dry towel and rags along with a hair comb and tooth powder had been left by a water pitcher and close stool. Several small paintings of landscapes and the sea hung about, making the room rather cozy, but she knew it was a prison.

She swallowed hard, knowing Rory could've easily

ordered her to the dungeon below. Instead, he'd let her wash away the smoke and dirt, and had Reid lead her to a comfortable room.

"I'll return to light a fire in the grate when night falls," Reid said. With one last glance and hesitant smile, the man left.

Sara waited, her eyes closing as she heard the key turn in the heavy iron lock. She was definitely a prisoner. At least until Jamie woke and decided if he'd release her. She wrapped her arms around herself and sat on the bed. Would Jamie retaliate against her? Was he the type to batter women in a rage?

She'd heard whisperings about Jamie's dark ways between the maids back at Dunscaith when her betrothal had been set. But she'd prayed that the rumors were false. Jamie's mistress, however, must be true from what Sara had witnessed of the wailing woman in yellow. At least she didn't look battered.

"But right now, I'm clean and warm," she said. Her brother, Kenan, had told Sara that Rory would help her if she were mistreated by Jamie. The two men had been imprisoned together in Carlisle Castle after they'd been traded for prisoners taken at Solway Moss. *Rory is honorable*. Sara held tightly to Kenan's assurance. Would she lose that help if Rory thought she had colluded with her father?

Sara stood, straightening the woolen skirts of a rose-hued costume that Margaret had found for her to wear. She walked to the basket of food in her matching slippers. The honey ale, probably the same that was to be served at the ruined wedding feast, was cold and refreshing. She drank and pulled out the wrapped cheese.

Caboc cheese rolled in oats was a light-tasting soft cheese that she'd helped make at Dunscaith whenever she hid from her father down in the kitchens. Sara's mother used to say the cheese was first created by her great-great-grandmother.

Sara spread some onto a piece of dark bread and took a bite of the familiar meal. She chewed while she inspected the painting above the table. It was a scene of Dunvegan Loch as if seen from the tower. The paints had been mixed expertly, depicting the hues of a summer day.

Another painting, featuring a field and forest she recognized from the other side of Dunvegan, was crooked, and she adjusted it on the wall. Vibrant greens and sky blue were broken up by a purple haze of flowers on a field, and the little chapel was a gray structure in the distance. She wandered about the room, noticing that each painting was from the vantage point of being up high as if in a tower. But not this tower because she couldn't see the chapel from either of her two windows.

She combed her long hair and spent the next hour nibbling on the mild cheese, thick bread, and a sweet, crisp apple while moving from window to landscape painting to window. The windows weren't locked since there was no fear of her trying to escape down a four-story tower, and she pushed one open. The breeze off the sea blew in, ruffling the curls that had dried around her face. From the window, she saw another tower on the east side of the castle.

Sara blinked as she stared across at the open window in the far tower. "Eliza?" A girl looked out toward the sea, a girl so familiar that a sob caught in

Sara's chest. Long brown hair was captured in a thick braid, leaving wisps about her oval face with its pert little nose and rosy cheeks. She was only twelve and still held that childlike softness.

Cupping her hands around her mouth, Sara yelled across the space to her sister. "Eliza! Eliza Macdonald!"

The girl's face snapped to her, eyes wide, lips parted. *Good Lord!* It was Eliza. Sara leaned as far out of the window as she dared and waved her arm, horror surely on her face at the thought of her sweet young sister being imprisoned in a Dunvegan tower. "Eliza!" Sara had left her safely in their room back at Dunscaith a week ago.

But instead of calling back, the girl pulled the glass window shut. "Eliza?" Sara said, her hands dropping back to the rough window ledge. Why was she imprisoned at Dunvegan? And why had she shut Sara out?

• • •

Sara's gaze moved between Reid and the unlocked tower room door. He was crouched before the small hearth, lighting the night fire. The temperatures still plummeted when the sun began to set as if winter threatened to invade despite the beginning of summer. She'd wrapped the quilt from her bed around herself as she sat by the open window. The window in the opposite tower had remained shut, but Sara had watched it the rest of the day.

She looked at Reid where he crouched by the hearth. "Why is Eliza Macdonald locked in the tower across from me?" Sara asked, her voice stark and forceful in the silence.

Reid jerked, knocking his arm into the ash bucket with a *thunk*. He glanced over his shoulder at her. "Yer sister?" His brows furrowed deeply. "I know of no other Macdonald at Dunvegan."

"Who then is in the opposite tower from me?" she asked, standing.

Reid stood, too, walking toward the door as if in full retreat. "I…I don't know."

"I saw my sister there and demand to know why she's being held." She clasped her hands before her. "I would give her comfort. We can be housed together and thus—"

"I'll tell Sir Rory about yer questions. Please take yer meal," he said, indicating the new basket he'd brought. "Fiona's tarts are most sought after." Reid, breathless and wide-eyed, yanked the door open and ran out. She could imagine him exhaling with relief on the dark landing before running down the tower stairs.

Sara went to the hearth, turned to warm her back, and stared at the door. Reid hadn't locked her in unless she'd missed the deep *click* of the turning key. Had he been too flustered by her questions?

She walked to the door, her hand wrapping around the curved iron handle next to the keyhole. Pressing lightly, the door opened outward into an inky darkness cut only by the soft glow of a lantern that showed the descending stairs. Poor Reid would lose his position, and if he worked for her father, possibly his life for his incompetence. Unless she remained in the room and chided him in the morning.

She closed the door and leaned on it, her head

tipped back. "I'll just visit Eliza in the tower room," she said to the empty room. They'd plan an escape, and then she'd sneak back to her own tower without anyone knowing. There was no chance she could escape the castle over the wall or by ferry without being apprehended. And right now, she had nowhere safe to go. Aunt Morag wouldn't be able to hold Rory's forces off.

Sara's stomach growled, reminding her of the food set on the small table. Fiona's tart called to her. Sara loved confections, and it was too early to roam the castle corridors. She ate, kept the fire going, and monitored the moon moving across the sky. The dim candlelight in the opposite tower window was snuffed out, and Sara stared at the window's shadowed rectangle for a long moment. Why hadn't Eliza responded to her wave? Had she imagined her?

She shook her head, turning from the window. "Oh, Eliza." Sara had taken care of her like a daughter since their mother died years ago when Eliza was only five. Sara struggled with leaving her at Dunscaith, and she sure as hell wouldn't leave her locked up in Dunvegan alone and frightened.

Sara lit the small glass lantern from beside the hearth with a taper. The door handle made no protest as she depressed it, and she peeked out into the faintly lit landing. She stepped to the top of the turning staircase that reminded her of the inside of a snail shell, wrapping around itself so she couldn't see if anyone waited around the corner. Her heart pounded hard.

She'd taken off her under petticoat in hopes she'd move easier and quieter, and she picked up the light wool skirt to step down the stairs. Around and around, she descended, carefully minding her step so she wouldn't fall. There was no rail on which to hold, so she ran her free hand along the rough plaster of the stone walls. Here, too, there were several landscape paintings in oils. She'd paid no attention to them on her way up earlier that day.

Reaching the bottom, a long corridor stretched out to the left that should lead her to the other tower. To the right was another staircase that would take her down to the third floor where the family bedchambers probably sat.

Was Rory asleep down there? She could imagine him lying on his back, naked and splayed across a large bed, his muscles beautifully sculpted in repose.

The lantern splashed yellow light before her as she turned left away from him and her lustful thoughts. A prickle of unease rose up her spine, and she paused. No footfalls. She swung her lantern around, raising it high, but there wasn't anyone in the center of the corridor. Several doorways sat recessed, but she didn't take the time to backtrack. Turning forward, she hurried on, making sure not to thump her heels, alerting someone below of her expedition. Up ahead was another set of circular stairs, running both up and down. She hesitated, glancing down the dark staircase.

"Ye won't find an escape there."

Sara's free hand thumped against her chest as if to keep her heart from leaping free. She spun toward the darkness behind her. Chill bumps covered her whole body, but she kept her voice even. "I'm not looking for an escape."

Rory MacLeod walked out of the shadows from

down the hall. Her lantern cast him in a golden glow, which made the scar peeking out along his hairline stand out in white contrast. Today's treachery had added another one to his arm, and his one eye was still swollen and had blackened. His frown was fierce, and he crossed his arms over his chest, his feet braced. Even though he looked ready for battle, Sara didn't feel the need to retreat.

"Ye taking a wander around the castle then?"

Sara thought of her sweet sister's face in the window, and ire licked up inside her like fire climbing a brittle wall. She took three steps forward to stand before Rory's menacing stare. He was as tall as her older brother and broad through the shoulders. When Kenan had returned from England, he'd seemed thin. If Rory had grown thin in prison, he must've eaten gustily when he'd returned to Skye to fill back out to the mountain before her.

The man seemed to be some type of magnet pulling Sara, and she took a step closer. "I'm finding my sister, you…brute." She gestured toward the other tower stairs. "Locking her up here at Dunvegan." Her voice had risen, and she lowered it. "I don't know how or why you have Eliza, but she needs to be with me, not locked up alone and threatened. She's only a child." The thought of her younger sister being terrified twisted like a snake moving under her skin, making her restless. It snapped the strange tether she'd felt toward the mountainous man.

Rory didn't even blink. He'd washed. His short beard was clean and combed and framed his frowning mouth. The darkness cocooned them in the corridor, making it feel as if they were the only two people in the whole castle. For long seconds, they stared at one another, neither of them moving. Sara found herself trying not to blink, either, as if their contest of wills could be won or lost over eye movement. Her heart hammered.

Unable to stand it any longer, Sara drew her empty hand up and flicked her fingers outward right before his eyes as if she would poke them. He blinked and caught her hand in his large, strong clasp.

"Ha," she said softly and let her mouth relax into a wry grin. "You aren't a granite statue after all. Even the mighty Lion of Skye blinks." She turned away to continue toward the other tower, but he kept her hand, preventing her. The touch sent a sizzle of awareness up her arm. A warmth infused her chest, rising into her cheeks.

He didn't squeeze her hand, making her bones bite together in pain like Gilbert did, but she couldn't pull away from the grasp, either. She tried to ignore the warmth of it, the strength in it, but she couldn't, not when the man was so close to her.

Turning back, her gaze slid up his chest to meet his stare. "Release me." Her words sounded loud in the silence.

His lips parted as if he wished to say something. They looked soft, kissable. She blinked, pushing the traitorous thought away. "I do not cower before brutes, nor do I put up with ruffians."

"Survival at Dunscaith must have been difficult then." He continued to hold her hand like a manacle. Had Kenan told him of their home life? How Sara had taken over the running of the household after her mother died but had to fight for every little freedom she could devise for herself and her sister?

"I must see my sister," she said, feeling her flush turn from ridiculous attraction to embarrassment.

His brows pinched, making a *V* above his nose. "Yer sister isn't here."

She poked his chest and was reminded of a granite wall. Had he even felt the small assault? What would he do if she rested her palm there? Her hand curled into a fist at the thought, dropping. "I saw her in the window." She pointed the same finger at the dark staircase.

"Ye think yer sister is imprisoned in our tower?" Even the dratted man's voice was a lush rumble. *Fool! I'm his prisoner.*

"What?" she asked, her mind momentarily blank.

"Yer sister is not here."

She frowned, her ire at her ridiculous thoughts making her words snap even more. "I don't believe you."

"That doesn't change the fact that ye are the only Macdonald at Dunvegan."

What game was Rory or the MacLeods playing?

Sara hadn't realized they were locked in another stare until Rory raised his hand and flicked his fingers out before her eyes. She blinked and slapped his hand away. "Stop that."

"Ye started the game," he said, shrugging. The small rise of his broad shoulders muted the look of fury in the stony facade he wore so easily.

"'Tis not a game." Sara whirled around, and this time he released her hand. The sudden disconnection made her feel adrift in the sea of darkness. But she brandished the lantern before her and charged forward, lighting the ascending steps as she climbed. His heavy footfalls followed behind. "Do you have the key?"

"Aye."

She climbed the narrow, chiseled steps, around and around. His silent presence behind her, as if he questioned her judgment, made her cheeks heat.

At the top, Sara stopped before the door, her breath coming fast. *Rap. Rap. Rap.*

Movement on the other side shot a knowing excitement through Sara, and she gave Rory a smug grin. She'd caught him in a lie. "I knew someone was in there."

"I never said the room was empty."

CHAPTER NINE

"It is your concern when your neighbor's wall is on fire."

Horace, 65–8 BC, Roman poet

Rap. Rap.

"Eliza, 'tis me, Sara." She gave Rory a stern look. "Don't frighten her," she said, her brows high and her eyes snapping.

Rory leaned over Sara, and her breath caught as his body pressed against her. He was warm and hard, dwarfing her with his masculinity. He smelled of clean linen and leather with a hint of something else, a spice.

He looked down at Sara as he spoke. "Eleri, ye can let us in. Lady Sara would like to meet ye."

"Eleri?" Sara asked but pivoted to the door when the key turned in the lock from the inside. It opened inward, and Rory lifted his gaze over her head.

"I apologize for waking ye, Eleri."

Sara's focus turned to the wide-eyed, pale face staring at her from the open door. "You're...Eleri?"

The girl looked exactly like her twelve-year-old sister, except this person was shorter and wore her long hair in a plait instead of wrapping it up in rags before bed to encourage curls in the morning. The girl's illuminated oval face floated in the darkness.

"I wasn't yet asleep," the girl said, pulling her braid

over one shoulder to finger the ends. Her voice was similar to Eliza's but slightly lower in pitch.

She melted backward into the shadows of the room. Rory climbed past Sara and pulled her inside the tower room with him. It was the same square-shaped room as the one Sara had been given.

Rory strode to the hearth to kindle it, filling the room with more light. Under the earthy scent of herbs, the acrid tang of paints and mineral spirits loosened Sara's nose. She sniffed and rotated in a tight circle. The room was full of paintings; some hung on the walls, but many more leaned against them all the way around the space. An easel was set on spindly legs near the window, and a picture of Sara's tower sat upon it.

Sara set her lantern down and walked across a plush rug to stand before the girl. "You are not Eliza Macdonald." She could see that now, but the similarity was eerie. "Who are you?"

The girl smiled. "Eleri MacLeod." She tipped her head. "I saw you earlier in the window." She pointed at the wet canvas. "'Tis you. See?"

"The landscapes in my room," Sara said, bending to inspect her miniature portrait in the window on the easel, and glanced back at her. "You painted them?"

Eleri nodded. "Do you like them?"

Sara nodded back. "Very much. You're skillful." The little portrait had captured the highlights of sun on her cheeks and hair and the shadows in contrast.

Eleri beamed and clasped her hands together in obvious pleasure.

Sara looked between her and Rory. "Who are you?" And why did she look identical to her sister?

The girl walked over to Rory, and Sara saw her uneven gait. It was as if her legs weren't the same length, making her hobble. Eleri took hold of Rory's hand. He smiled at her and placed an arm over her shoulders like a protective cape of chainmail. Eleri smiled up at Rory. "I'm Rory's sister."

Sara's eyes opened wide. *Sister?* "I don't…understand," she said. "You look exactly like *my* younger sister, Eliza. How's that possible?"

"We're not siblings by blood," Rory said, but didn't remove his arm from the girl.

"I was a foundling," Eleri said. "My parents didn't want me because of my crooked spine." She said the words with a straightforward tone as if she spoke about a cottage that leaned instead of a child who'd been cruelly given away. "Chief MacLeod—Alasdair MacLeod," she corrected, "allowed me to live here." There was a coolness in her eyes as if the memory wasn't particularly warm.

She was so small next to the commander of the huge MacLeod army, but she didn't seem frightened of Rory, even with his scars. 'Twas like the lion and the lamb. A lion with the most interesting tawny gold eyes.

Eleri's hands came together as if in prayer before her lips. "Perhaps Lady Sara's sister is my sister," she said and looked up at him before turning her gaze back to Sara. "I would be your sister, too."

Could Eleri and Eliza be twins like their mother and Morag?

"We will ask Morag what she knows of this," Rory said.

"My aunt?" Sara asked, her brows pinching.

Eleri nodded, stifling a yawn. "She brought me here as a bairn."

Morag had never mentioned her to Sara. Why? Had Sara's mother known that her sister had taken Eleri away?

"We should let ye sleep, El." Rory led her back over to her bed, and in the firelight, Sara could see that one side of the girl's back protruded like a hump.

Eleri smiled with a look of tired excitement. "I'd like to hear about someone who might be my sister." She pulled her legs into the bed and looked at Rory. "Do you have your key to lock the door when you leave?"

"Aye." He kissed her forehead and lifted the covers up to her chin. "Sleep well."

"Can I come down for the morning meal?" Eleri asked, her words hesitant. "Or is Lady Mar still here?"

"Ye come down any time ye wish," he said. "And if Winnie is here, she'll be nursing Jamie."

Eleri turned toward the wall, snuggling down under her blankets. Sara noticed that the girl didn't ask about Jamie's health. And Winnie? Did the woman make Eleri feel unwelcome in her own home? Irritation itched inside Sara.

Sara followed Rory from the room. She remained silent as he produced a key and locked the girl inside. She held her breath as he slid past her, nearly touching her. Without a word, she followed him down and into the vacant corridor. When they reached her own tower steps, Sara's hand curled around his bicep. It was granite beneath her fingers. "The door is locked to help her feel safe at night," Sara said. "Not to keep her a prisoner."

He turned to face her, the wall sconce flickering light and shadow across his face. "Aye."

Sara's breath became shallow as her heart thumped. "They must be twins. They look exactly alike except for…the curve in her back."

"The bend was obvious at the time of her birth and has worsened over time," Rory said. "She prefers to stay hidden when Winnie's about, and my father encouraged it. Jamie, too." He frowned. "I do not."

Rory continued to stand directly before Sara, keeping her there between the wall and his body. But she didn't feel trapped. Sara knew that particular feeling well after living with her father and younger brother. No, this was a protected sensation, a warmth. "She was brought during the night as a newborn. The dark stump of a cord sat in her navel."

Sara cleared her throat. "Why would Morag take her from Dunscaith to bring her here?"

Rory breathed evenly, and she waited, feeling a flipping of her heart at his nearness. She'd never been with a man, standing against a wall in the dark, all alone. And she'd never known a man as mesmerizing as Rory MacLeod.

"I don't know." Rory's brows lowered and his nostrils flared. "But I won't let her return to Dunscaith regardless of her lineage."

• • •

Rory studied Sara's smooth features in the shadows where they stood at the base of the spiral stairs. The low light made her pupils take up her entire eyes. 'Twas disarming, the emotion she allowed him to see. Disarming in its honesty. *Honesty or a good act.* He'd been fooled before by a beautiful Macdonald lass.

"My aunt wouldn't steal away Eliza's twin." Sara's words tumbled out like a rockslide, fast and sharp. She lifted her hand from his sleeve to thump her palm against his chest, leaving it resting dangerously close to his heart.

He cleared his throat. "Perhaps the crow witch felt she could cure her back."

Sara frowned. "My aunt is not a witch." She thumped his chest. "And my mother would never have sent her bairn away, even if the child had a crooked spine."

"I wasn't privy to…the event. I was a lad of seventeen."

"And why would your mother take in another's child as her own?" Sara stared up at him with disbelieving eyes.

"My mother died when I was fifteen. She wasn't here."

Sara's gaze slid to the darkness behind him. "I was thirteen when Eliza was born," she said. "I remember…" She shook her head. "I wasn't in the room while my mother labored, because I was taking care of Gilbert who was dashing about in the great hall. Aunt Morag helped her through the birth. No one mentioned twins."

One of Sara's curls curved like a thin vine down her cheek. He knew she'd washed, and her hair had dried through the day into waves that fell down her back nearly to her hips. It was hair he could wrap around his hand, fisting it gently while he kissed her.

He inhaled slowly, reaching for that slightly floral scent that seemed to emanate from her skin. *Good bloody Lord.* He shouldn't be thinking about how soft her lips looked, either. He forced his gaze to settle on the dark wall above her head.

"Don't you have anything to say?" Sara asked. "Morag and my mother are twins. It runs in families. Eliza and Eleri must be..." She thumped her palm against his chest again, barely taking a breath. "I have another sister," she whispered.

He frowned, leaning toward her. "But she was raised as a MacLeod, and like I said before, Dunvegan is where she will stay."

Sara blinked, but instead of leaning back or lowering her gaze like most people did when his tone grew dark, she leaned forward, staring hard into his eyes, eyes that were said to be unnatural. The closeness brought the floral scent to Rory's nose.

"I would never wish anyone to go to Dunscaith," she said. Even though the words were softly spoken, a steely conviction ran through them, anchoring them there as if she would never change her sentiment.

He nodded, accepting it as truth. Rory stepped away from Sara, so her palm dropped to her side. The withdrawal of the warm contact left a chill in its place. "Does Eliza have a crooked spine?"

Sara shook her head. "Not that I've noticed, although now I want to run my hand down her back to be sure." She followed him away from the wall. "We must bring Eliza here. She's unsafe at Dunscaith, especially since I'm gone."

"Kenan will care for her."

"Father sends him on campaigns and raids all the

time, across Skye and onto the mainland."

Kenan Macdonald had been taught like Rory that everyone apart from his own clan were interlopers on Skye. But Kenan had worked with the other three Highlanders to help them all survive and escape England. A loyal brotherhood had formed from it. Rory rubbed a thumb absently across the scars on his palm.

He glanced over his shoulder at the empty corridor and stairs leading down and then pointed up the spiral staircase. "I'd not have people overhear and gossip. 'Twould hurt Eleri."

Sara spun around, took the lantern he'd set on the floor, and climbed. Rory reached around her to take it. "I don't want ye to trip and barrel me down the stairs," he said.

"I doubt I could knock down a mountain." She looked back but let him take the light.

Did she think him invincible? No man was, and this strange warmth that her touch had kindled in him made him feel weaker. Perhaps Sara had inherited some of Morag's unnatural powers. He frowned, holding the light high so she could see where to place her slippered foot. At the top of the stairs, they paused outside her room on the small landing.

"My door…" she said and cleared her throat as she pushed it open. "I managed to work the lock open with my hair pins."

He stared at the back of her head as she walked inside. Was she lying to save Reid? Or did she tend to lie? Sara didn't know Rory had told the man to leave her door unlocked so Rory could follow her if she chose to escape her room.

"Now," she said, pacing across the floor, "why would Morag give Eleri to Clan MacLeod?"

Rory walked past her to the hearth and crouched to add more peat to her fire. "The curve was evident at birth. Perhaps yer mother thought Walter Macdonald might order the bairn left to die if he saw her deformity."

He set the poker down and straightened, turning to lean back against the wall. "Morag brought her here, and since my mother was already passed, Margaret, the lady ye helped out from under the church, raised her."

Sara shook her head. "But why would your father allow that? Taking in a Macdonald, especially a girl and one with…a medical concern."

Rory crossed his arms, his hands in his armpits. "I don't know. My father wasn't kind." Like a chief, he was firm in his convictions, and his hatred of the Macdonalds ran like molten rock. "'Tis possible my father realized whose child she was and thought he could use Eleri against yer father."

"My father doesn't know of Eleri's existence." Her eyes glittered in the flamelight. "I need to ask my aunt about her. Morag doesn't provide information unless asked. I just never knew to ask."

"Ye can ask Margaret, too. She may know something."

Sara sat on the bed. "Jamie," she said softly and tilted her face up to Rory. "How does he fare?"

Did she care for his brother? The man didn't deserve her tender thoughts. "A beam grazed his head as it fell," Rory said, "which is why he's unconscious. There's a deep cut and large bump on the side of his head. He also suffered a lot of smoke in his lungs, which he isn't clearing with coughs. There's a definite wheezing sound when he breathes."

Sara blinked, her face tight with sadness or regret. He couldn't tell which.

"Hamish says he could die or live. 'Tis up to God now," Rory said, pinching the bridge of his nose for a moment.

"Should I go care for him? Try to get him to drink or clean him? Like a wife would."

The thought of Sara hovering over Jamie, washing his body and murmuring prayers for his recovery, twisted inside Rory. The woman had no idea what type of person she'd wed. How he didn't deserve her prayers and certainly not her tears.

"Nay," Rory said. "Ye'll stay away from my brother."

Her face hardened, her large eyes narrowing. "Because you believe I was privy to my father's plot." She stood up from the bed, her hands fisting at her sides as she paced toward him. "That I will kill someone unconscious, even after I helped pull him out from under a bonfire."

Except for Eleri, who was always mild, and Margaret, who held her tongue more than most, Rory had no experience dealing with lasses, at least not ones who challenged him. Sara had no aversion to staring him in the eye and almost snarling. Passion, that's what Sara Macdonald was, a tangled ball of restrained passion. What would happen if he cut the twine holding her together? Would she explode?

"Perhaps ye decided not to condemn yer soul by killing innocents in a house of God," he said, "but have since realized that Jamie MacLeod deserves to die."

Her fist struck out at him, but he caught it. His earlier injured eye winced as if remembering her pointy knuckles. They stared at each other for a moment. "Ye're easily provoked."

"And you insult as easily as blinking." She yanked her hand back from his grasp and crossed her arms. "I would not murder a man I swore to live with before God. And I don't go along with vicious plans to kill innocent people." She flung her other hand out toward the door. "I am done discussing anything with you."

Rory sucked in a large breath through his nose. Her reaction seemed genuine. *Madeline seemed genuine, too.* He pushed the thought away. "I'll send paper and ink up in the morn. Ye can write to your brother or father, whichever ye think will release Eliza to be yer lady here at Dunvegan."

Her shoulders relaxed, and she sat on the edge of her bed, suddenly looking tired. The anger leaked from her, leaving the lovely woman he'd met by the sea. He wanted to pull her into a hug and assure her that both sisters would be safe.

Don't be tricked by a bonny lass. They're the most dangerous.

His father's words were echoed by Jamie and Jok and any of the warriors who'd witnessed the treachery behind a woman's smile.

Nay. Rory would never fall for that kind of subterfuge again.

CHAPTER TEN

"The blood of the fallen Macdonalds of Sleat and
MacLeods of Dunvegan has painted centuries of
Skye's history red. During the late 16th century, as an
offering of peace to end the long feud between the
two clans, MacLeod chieftain, Rory Mòr, offered his
sister's hand in marriage to
Donald Gorm."

IsleofSkye.com

"Where is Sara?" Kenan Macdonald's voice boomed
as he jumped down from his horse outside the squat
cottage that stood alone on the moor. Fluttering
crows squawked in agitation behind him as if defending Morag Gunn's territory.

The man was as large as Rory, with dark hair
streaked with bits of red and a slightly crooked nose
from having it broken by the butt of a musket in
Carlisle Castle's dungeon.

"She's not here," Rory answered and stepped away
from Airgid, who was tied loosely to a hitching post.

Kenan drew his sword, lips curled back in fury.
Rory pulled his own sword, meeting him, their sword
blades clanging together. They stood on opposite
sides, Kenan glaring at Rory as if he'd personally ab-
ducted, assaulted, and killed his sister.

Kenan gritted his teeth. "Where is she?" They
pushed equally against one another.

Did Kenan really think that after what they'd gone through, Rory would bring harm to his sister? Anger licked up inside him, but he gripped it tightly, although the animal fury must have shone in his eyes because Kenan blinked. In a warrior so fierce, it was the most surprise Rory would get from Kenan.

"She's safe," Rory said, his words like a growl. "Unharmed, warm, and well fed."

They stared through the crossed swords for several breaths. Rory lifted his empty hand, spreading his fingers wide, palm facing Kenan so he could see the scars, the scars that should remind Kenan of their loyalty to one another. Kenan's gaze moved to it, and Rory instantly felt him relax his forward press. He raised his own scarred palm, and the two clasped hands, palms together. "The Brotherhood."

"Thicker than blood," Rory answered.

Kenan stepped back, sheathing his sword. His hands went to his wild, mussed hair. "I've been sick with worry." He looked at Rory, dropping his hands. "She's the best person I know." He shook his head. "She had nothing to do with Father's scheme."

Rory studied the man. He looked honest in his frustration and concern. "Yer father called her Seraphina, the Flame of Dunscaith."

Kenan's lips opened, and he paused in the pacing he'd begun. "She hates Seraphina, because it means fiery one."

The woman did have a fiery disposition, but it gave her strength.

"The rest is a concocted name." Kenan cursed, shaking his head.

"My cottage is neutral territory, so come inside,"

Morag called from where she leaned against her front door eating a handful of shelled nuts as if she were watching a theatrical production. "Out here, you're disturbing my birds." Glossy black crows swooped to catch a handful of nuts Morag threw up into the air for them.

Kenan tied his horse to Morag's fence next to Airgid. Rory walked inside, nearly bumping his head on the low ceiling. He scanned the tidy two-room cottage, its walls a white plaster over stones. Bundles of herbs hung from the low rafters under a thatched roof, and a lime-ash floor was swept with a few small rugs placed about.

Morag moved with such grace it seemed she floated. The difference between the youthful walk and her braid of silvery white hair was jarring. Stopping by a hearth made of fitted gray stones, she took up a long iron spoon to stir a pot of stew like some witch in a fable. He wouldn't be surprised if there were frogs and poisonous mushrooms in it.

"She isn't being kept in Dunvegan's dungeon, is she?" Kenan asked. "She hates dank, dark places." The two warriors stood slightly bent so as not to knock their heads.

"Nay. She's in the west tower room," Rory said.

Kenan's face looked tormented. "And she suffered no harm from the fire or battle afterwards?"

Rory shook his head and watched relief soften Kenan's features.

"I am indebted to ye," Kenan said. "I should have realized my father's trick in sending me away. And then he swore that ye had killed Sara."

No wonder Kenan had started this meeting with

an attack.

Rory wouldn't tell Kenan about the furious thoughts that had scalded his mind when he first saw Sara standing there beside the flaming chapel. Or how she'd thought he would slice her throat, leaving her to bleed amongst the green ferns.

Rory cleared his throat. "Jamie is still unconscious, but the surgeon is hopeful he will wake. Either way, yer sister should not wed him."

"She can't return to Dunscaith," Kenan said. "My father blames her for foiling his plans to take over yer clan." He stretched his bearded jaw as if it ached. "He will never agree to peace."

Rory's hand came down on his shoulder. "My father was a warring bastard, too. But then he saw fifteen thousand Scots defeated by three thousand Englishmen at Solway Moss because our troops didn't trust each other. I think 'tis why he made Jamie promise to try to unify the Isle of Skye with his dying breath." Jamie had also told Rory that their sire hadn't mentioned him at all the night when he succumbed to his illness.

"And when yer brother suggested the wedding," Kenan said, "my father used Sara to get close to ye."

Morag swore. She'd taken a seat at the table where a single candle stood lit before her. "Walter Macdonald will use anyone who can advance his plans. He's a selfish cur." She looked at Kenan. "Your mother thought she could change his wicked ways, but she couldn't." Morag shook her head. "He treated her better than most, at least at the beginning, but he wouldn't change. Vengeance taints his blood and heart."

How many Macdonald and MacLeod lives would be saved by the death of that one man? Someone needed to send Walter Macdonald to the grave, and it couldn't be Kenan. Patricide would be asking too much.

As if reading his mind, Morag swept a hand toward her shelves of little clay pots. "'Tis easy enough to get rid of Walter Macdonald." Some pots must hold poison.

Kenan's face snapped toward her. "Ye would kill your brother by marriage?"

She shrugged her slender, straight shoulders draped with a gray woolen shawl. "He likely killed my sister."

Rory stared at the woman in silence. He didn't trust her and her witchy ways.

Kenan rubbed a fist against his forehead as if it ached. "Ye have no proof of that, Aunt." From his weary voice, it sounded like an old argument.

She moved her hand in the air. "You pray to God every day without proof of Him. I believe Walter killed my sister without having seen it. 'Tis wisdom and my clever mind that sees what happened." She offered a grim smile.

"Will Jamie treat Sara as a traitor when he wakes?" Kenan asked, changing the subject. "Is that why she shouldn't marry him?"

"Jamie has a suspicious heart," Rory said. "It may not be enough for my housekeeper and several of my men to swear that Sara helped to free us from the fire."

Kenan stepped closer. "If my sister is in danger, bring her here, and Morag will send for me."

Morag grinned. "My birds will protect her." She sounded so sure of the black-winged battalion that circled her cottage.

"I'll send word to ye if 'tis needed," Rory said to Kenan. "Right now, she's safe. Sara has a key to her chamber, so she can lock herself inside. I have the only other key hidden away."

"I could take her to stay with Cyrus Mackinnon," Kenan said as if contemplating his next steps.

Rory's brows rose. "Is that wise? The man's a rogue." The idea of the charming warrior prowling after Sara made Rory's stomach sour. *Bloody hell.* Cyrus might offer for her right away since her marriage to Jamie had been annulled.

Kenan's mouth pinched closed, and his tongue slid over his teeth. He exhaled. "If Sara is safe at Dunvegan, 'tis best she stay there. Bring her here only if she's thrown in the dungeon or persecuted for the fire."

"I'm acting chief while Jamie recovers," Rory said. "I won't let her come to harm." The thought of Sara being in pain, or even her face pinching in fear, made Rory's temper rise. She'd been so brave when he'd caught her in the forest, even exposing her neck for his blade. The woman had remained unbroken after all these years at Dunscaith under her father's thumb. To see her come to harm under Rory's watch would be an atrocity.

"Many thanks for seeing her innocence in this," Kenan said, rubbing the back of his neck.

"Before ye go…" Rory pulled Sara's letter from where it was tucked into his belt and handed it to Kenan. "From Sara."

Kenan nearly ripped it open in his haste in breaking the seal and read. Rory watched him closely. He didn't know what Sara had written but knew it must involve Eleri and Kenan's little sister, Eliza. When Kenan's gaze snapped to Morag, Rory knew the letter did indeed describe the twins.

"Elspet Macdonald had twin bairns," Kenan said, the words slamming against the walls of the cottage. His eyes narrowed at his aunt. "And ye stole one."

Morag moved to the window where several crows hopped on a wide ledge. Pushing it open, they flapped and settled back down. She set out some pieces of dried fish for them.

"Answer me," Kenan ordered.

She turned, leaning against the window casing, and her piercing green eyes opened with apathy, feigned or real. "They were twins, but one had an obvious curve to her spine. Walter Macdonald would have been furious the bairns were lasses to begin with. I knew if one was not perfect in his eyes, he would neglect or kill it outright." Her gaze softened as she kept Kenan's gaze. "Your mother was wise in the ways of her husband, his anger and whims and cruelties. She wouldn't allow harm to come to the second bairn and asked me to carry her away to safety."

"Safety with our enemy?" Kenan asked with disbelief.

Morag looked first at Rory and then at Kenan. "Safety with the bairn's true father, Alasdair MacLeod."

CHAPTER ELEVEN

"Against love's fire fear`s frost hath dissolution."

William Shakespeare

"My paints are under my bed," Eleri said, excitement in her tone as if they were going to a festival rather than down in the great hall to paint. The poor girl must truly feel imprisoned up there.

Sara lifted the edge of the heavy quilt and pulled a wooden box out, opening it. Eleri gasped behind her. "Not that one."

The open box held a folded swath of yellow silk. *Holy Mother Mary!* Sara knew immediately that it was the Fairy Flag. Did Rory know his clan's biggest weapon was hidden under his adopted-sister's bed?

Without a word, Sara closed the box and pushed it back under the girl's bed, retrieving the other one. Sara lifted it, meeting Eleri's wide eyes with a reassuring smile. "Let's see if we can carry everything in one trip."

After Eleri made certain her door was locked, they carried the girl's painting supplies down to the great hall: a canvas, metal spatulas, a palette, and one of two wooden boxes out from under her bed, a treasure trove of paints. Sara placed one foot before the next while her mind whirled with worry and surprise. Neither of them broke the silence down all four levels of the castle. Reaching an empty great hall,

Eleri laid her canvas and roll of spatulas on the cleared table before sitting. Sara set the box of paints down, along with rags. Gus pushed underneath to lie at their feet.

Sara felt Eleri's cold hand cover hers. "You mustn't tell anyone," Eleri whispered, not looking at her. "About the flag."

Sara took her hand in her warm ones, rubbing it. "I won't, but Eleri…" She waited for the girl to look at her. "It should be locked away. 'Tis too dangerous for you to be the one guarding it."

Eleri shook her head. "No one comes up to see me, and I keep my door locked. It makes me…useful."

Sara's heart clenched at the word, and she squeezed the girl's hand. "You don't have to be useful to be here, Eleri."

"Jamie won't be able to use me to form an alliance with my bent back." She pulled her hand from Sara's. "I feel better when I'm useful."

Well, hell, Sara could understand that only too well. She'd agreed to wed a stranger to be useful.

Eleri pulled a few vials out of the paint box. "I use madder root for deep red browns. The blues could be better, but the Azur of Acre costs too much, more than gold leaf. I use azurite instead. 'Tis blue enough for my work."

Sara would talk to Rory about moving the Fairy Flag and Eleri's skewed view of her position at Dunvegan. Jamie had made his adopted sister feel like a burden. Anger tightened her forehead.

Eleri's movements with the metal spatula were confident as she scraped the dabs of paint around. She seemed to have a natural talent, which had been honed with hours of practice.

"If I'm ever commissioned to paint something of import," Eleri said, "I will request the brighter blue." Using a dull blade with yellow and a bit of madder root pigment, Eleri sliced the paint across the canvas to create realistic petals on a bouquet of spring wild-flowers.

Voices from the entry archway filtered into the great hall. "Well, she *is* called the Flame of Dunscaith," came a man's croaky voice.

Both Eleri and Sara looked up, Sara's heart tapping faster. That bloody name would see her dead.

A snort was followed by, "Alasdair would have figured out that Macdonald bastard's plan before Jamie said 'I do pledge.'"

Around the corner came the two elderly men who were said to be Rory's mother, Charlotte Sutherland's, cousins, John Sutherland and Simon Sutherland. Decades ago, they'd come with Charlotte when she wed Alasdair MacLeod and remained on Skye. From what Margaret had told Sara, they'd counseled Alasdair and Charlotte on everything from relations with England to the types of puddings to be made for Christmastide. John had lost his forearm, and Simon had lost his eye, in battles against the Macdonalds.

The men paused when they saw her sitting with Eleri. Simon's one good eye rounded. "What are ye doing out of yer tower room?"

Gus stirred and stretched out from under the table. His nails clicked as he trotted over to sniff the two men.

"Ye shouldn't be down below," John said, gesturing with his remaining hand toward the stairs.

"Lady Sara said I could come down," Eleri said, starting to gather up her paints.

Sara rested a hand over hers, halting her. "They mean me, not you." At least she hoped that was true.

"Oh." Eleri stilled, but her eyes remained large and unsure.

Simon glanced around. "Where's Rory?"

"Are there no guards here?" called John.

"Rory said I was allowed to come below," Sara said. "I'm not a prisoner."

After a pause, Simon said, "Since when?" They seemed to take turns talking, and it took them a moment to remember who spoke last.

Sara pulled the iron key to her room from her tied pocket. "Since Rory gave me this."

John looked at the ceiling as if beseeching God for assistance. "Giving a Macdonald the run of Dunvegan?"

"She'll set us aflame by nightfall," Simon said.

"That name," Sara said over their grumbling, "the Flame of Dunscaith…" She shook her head. "My father devised it outside the church. I've never been called it before."

John's unruly brows rose to his thin hairline. "Well, ye're being called it now."

"By every MacLeod and their allies." Simon threw an arm out, waving it around as if pointing to people outside the layers of thick stone walls surrounding them. His sewn-shut eye stretched as if trying to match his wide other eye.

"I'm not a flame of anything," she said, frowning. "Are you two fueling these lies? Jamie won't like his...betrothed slandered with lies." Did the two old men respect their new chief enough for her mild threat to make an impact?

"Jamie won't mind what's said about ye if he dies," John said.

"And ye aren't his bride or wife. The contract was burned in the fire," Simon said with a deep nod. "Ye'll be blamed along with yer evil father if"—his voice rose—"Jamie is struck dead."

"Jamie is struck dead?" came a screech from the archway, and the blond woman that Reid had told Sara was Winnie Mar ran into the room, clutching her hands. "My Jamie died?"

Gus barked ferociously as if some sea creature had slithered up the steps from the loch and broken through the barred gate to enter Dunvegan, bent on ripping them all apart.

"Nay, lass," John said, his voice booming in the sudden quiet as Gus took a breath before he continued barking.

"Only if he *does* die, she will be blamed." Simon pointed at Sara.

"You traitorous bitch," the woman screeched, and Sara saw Eleri flinch.

Sara stepped before Eleri and next to Gus, her hand resting on the dog's head to calm him. It was a natural, practiced stance that she'd used at Dunscaith to protect Eliza from her father or Gilbert's cruelty.

Winnie's fingers bent as if they were claws ready to scratch Sara's eyes out, and the mistress charged. Protecting Eleri and the old dog, Sara's response was as involuntary as a cat protecting its kitten from a hawk swooping in with talons bared. Arm pulled back, Sara took a forceful step forward.

Crack. Sara's fist, thumb outside her clenched hand, smashed into the woman's nose. Pain erupted in Sara's hand, but she followed through with a swipe of her leg. Even though the skirts hindered her, she'd learned to compensate with a swipe so hard it could trip Gilbert. It definitely knocked Winnie Mar off balance as she screamed, hands going to her nose. She fell with a deep thud on her arse, her yellow petticoats billowing out around her.

Sara leaped back from Winnie when the woman's legs began to churn wildly in the bright layers of fabric. Eleri had both hands over her mouth, eyes round as full moons. John and Simon clung to each other in horror and then jumped apart as if realizing their cowardly embrace.

Margaret came running into the room. "What's going on?" she yelled and stopped by Eleri, pulling her against her bosom as if to protect the girl.

"She attacked me!" Winnie called. "Grab…" Her order trailed off on a groan. "My nose!"

"Grab yer nose?" Simon asked.

"I'm not touching it," John said, but everyone ignored the confused men.

"*You* attacked *her*, Mistress Mar," Eleri said from Margaret's arms.

Sara's heart thumped in a delayed response to the threat, and three guards ran in from two different archways. Winnie wailed, although it was slightly muted from her hands around her nose.

Margaret left Eleri and hurried to Winnie while one of the guards pulled the squawking woman up from the floor. Margaret handed her a rag from a pile

Eleri had on the table. "Hamish is here. He can set it for ye."

"Set it?" Winnie screeched. "'Tis broken?"

"Fetch Hamish from Jamie's room," Margaret said, and a guard jogged off.

"What are ye doing here, Mistress Mar?" Margaret asked.

"Being attacked!" A dot of red grew on the outside of the white rag as Winnie's nose bled through it.

Margaret led her to a chair at the table. "Besides that?"

Eleri quickly grabbed up her half-finished flower portrait as if Winnie might destroy it. The girl looked at her paints but moved away, deciding to abandon them rather than getting within reach of the banshee.

"To see Jamie." Winnie's gaze sparked with venom as they settled on Sara. "And I saw this traitor roaming free in the castle." She gestured toward John and Simon. "They saw. She's vicious! Throw her in the dungeon pit."

The dungeon was a pit? Good lord! She looked at Simon and John. "If you try to put me in a pit, you'll get a bloody nose, too."

John rubbed the back of his neck and looked quite uncomfortable. Perhaps Winnie didn't have as many allies willing to lie for her as she thought. But before either one could add credence to her depiction or reveal her as a liar, rapid boots sounded on the steps leading up from the dock.

Rory tore into the room, his sword out. "What the bloody hell is going on?" His voice hit like shards of glass, but Eleri didn't jump. Instead, the girl's shoulders relaxed despite her brother's scowl. His sweeping gaze settled on Sara but then turned to Winnie, who loudly expounded on Sara's evil, unprovoked attack and subsequent need for flogging, imprisonment in the pit, and eventual death.

Sara leaned toward Eleri. "You can go upstairs if you want."

The girl shook her head. "I'm a witness to what happened. I won't leave you."

Sara smiled in thanks. The girl, who reminded her so much of Eliza, made Sara's heart swell. "You're very brave."

Rory held up a hand to stop Winnie's tirade. "Margaret, if ye would, take Mistress Mar up to Jamie's room where Hamish can stop her nose from bleeding."

"Certainly," Margaret said, taking Winnie's arm to help her stand. "Jamie is still unconscious but holding his own." She led Winnie toward the stairs, the banshee's muffled complaints fading as she climbed.

"Where'd ye learn that?" John asked Sara, his eyes narrowed.

Simon then made a fist, punched the air, and swiped his leg as if tripping someone. "Do ye use it on that sire of yers?"

Sara looked at the men. "I...use it against Gilbert when he gets angry enough to strike."

They both stared at her for a long moment, and then John's wrinkled face relaxed into a half grin. "That big oaf would topple like a sack of grain off the back of a wagon hitting a rut in the road."

Simon hit John's good arm gently. "I can see that fool boy spread out on the floor with blood coming from his nose and his slight sister," he indicated Sara, "standing over him, fists in the air."

John and Simon looked at her expectantly, as if waiting for some word about her battle conquests. Sara crossed her arms. "I suppose that's happened a time or two."

John cackled. "I knew it."

"Ye've got a fighting spirit, lass," Simon said. His smile pinched into a half frown. "Must be from your father's blood."

"Nay," John said, shaking his head. "Walter Macdonald is a coward bent on using trickery. Seraphina Macdonald punches straight forward." He threw a punch at an invisible foe. Their kind words made her feel lighter.

Rory's piercing gaze softened, and he looked down at Eleri. "I'm happy ye came down from yer tower." He led her toward the steps while carrying her paint box under his other arm.

"Lady Sara asked me to, and we came down together."

Rory glanced at Sara. Their gazes met, and he gave a small nod in thanks. "Come along, Lady Sara. I have news for both of ye."

Sara followed him and Eleri into the alcove toward the stairs. "News? Have you heard from Kenan?" Sara asked.

"I saw him today," Rory said without turning.

"What?" The word flew from her lips like a dagger, and she ran after them, carrying Eleri's dirty spatulas and palette. "You met with my brother and didn't take me?" She wanted to grab Rory and shake him, but her hands were full.

"I didn't know if someone would follow him," he

said. "Gilbert or yer father." Rory indicated for her to climb up the winding staircase behind Eleri. "I will tell ye above what I found out."

Sara's gaze was judging and hard. He met it like an unmoving boulder. Had she imagined the warmth in him the night before? "What am I here?" she said. A glance over Sara's shoulder showed that the girl had already climbed ahead. "Am I a prisoner? Someone to be used against my father?" Sara asked. "Because he won't care what happens to me." She swallowed at the truth. *Sweet Mary.*

Why had she just given Rory that information? But he must have realized that when her father rode off without her. "Or…am I a weak woman you've taken pity on, letting me stay under your protection?"

Rory's gaze never wavered, and, once again, his amber eyes almost mesmerized her. She blinked, waiting for his reply.

"There is nothing weak about ye, Sara."

The compliment surged warmth through her like a sunburst.

He took the paint palette from her hand, setting it down, and gently opened her fingers one by one. Her stomach flipped as his thumb brushed against the center of her palm. He turned her hand over, inspecting the broken flesh on her knuckles from where she'd hit Winnie.

"I'll have ice chipped from the block in the icehouse, and Margaret will bring it up with a poultice," he said, bending his head to look closer at the wounds.

Sara couldn't breathe as he held her hand, gently caressing the center of her palm underneath as the fingers on his other hand touched the unbroken skin around the cuts. Rory MacLeod was a hard warrior through and through, but as he stood there caressing her skin, his touch was gentle, almost reverent. "Thank you," she whispered, raising her gaze from her hand to his face. It held a pained, searching look.

"I'm going to keep climbing," Eleri called from above, and Rory drew back, leaving Sara's hand to hover between them. She dropped it.

"We're coming," Rory said, picking up the palette. He nodded toward the steps for her to continue.

She adjusted the supplies she held with her other arm and turned. With each step she took, her hips moved naturally side to side under the two layers of petticoats. She could feel Rory's gaze burning into her back.

There is nothing weak about you, Sara. The respect in the words, in his tone, made her pulse thrum faster, shooting the heat from his touch down into her abdomen. What would it feel like for his fingers to trail like that over other parts of her body?

Sara turned down the hallway that led to Eleri's tower, and they proceeded in silence, but she felt Rory's gaze on her the entire way. It wasn't warm like a sunray but more like the sizzle of a lightning bolt touching down, leaving its little scorch marks across the landscape of her back. Everything about Rory MacLeod was intense, including his scrutiny.

Sara released a breath, the familiar concern about her ugliness washing cold through the heat. *Ye're ugly, girl.* Her father's words had been slurred with whisky. *I can't even use ye to form an alliance with an ally else they send ye back.* His words had etched themselves inside her as if done with jagged glass. But he'd easily agreed to her wedding with an enemy.

At the top of the tower steps, Eleri produced a key, and Sara and Rory followed her inside. The room was cold because the fire had died, but Eleri tossed on a block of peat before going to her bed to perch. Both women looked at Rory, but Sara couldn't help but think about the flag underneath the bed. It made her squirm.

She crossed her arms. "What news do you have? Did you ask Morag about Eleri and my sister, Eliza?"

He nodded. "Aye." Rory's gaze turned from Sara to settle on Eleri, and his face relaxed into something close to a smile. "Ye do have a twin sister."

Eleri's mouth opened with a little gasp. She blinked, her palm cupping the side of her face. "A real sister, by blood?"

"Aye."

The girl bounced up off the bed with overwhelming energy. "I have a sister, a twin sister."

Sara smiled at the joy that exploded out of her as if she had too much to contain in her slender body.

Sara looked back at Rory. "How did they come to be separated?"

"Morag said yer mother, mother to both of ye, Elspet Gunn Macdonald, knew that her husband would…not be accepting of a bairn with an issue with her spine. He'd already lamented that he wanted a third son and not another daughter. So Morag took ye, Eleri, away from Dunscaith. Yer twin sister, Eliza, remained."

Eleri's smile reached every part of her body as if passing right over the rejection. Sara certainly believed that she'd have suffered under her father. Sara suffered his taunts, and her infirmity was hidden under clothes.

"I've always felt like I was missing something or someone," Eleri said. She turned to Sara, clasping both her hands. "I have a twin sister and you, another sister. Does she paint? Does she look like me? I wonder if she likes sweets as much as I do."

Sara laughed lightly. "She draws, looks exactly like you, and, yes, she loves sweets."

"I can't wait to meet her."

"There's more," Rory said, and they both turned to him, still clutching hands. Rory frowned, his arms crossed over his chest.

Sara tipped her head, her heart picking up pace at his stony face. "More?"

He looked at Eleri. "Yer mother is Elspet Macdonald and yer father…" Rory caught his chin in his hand and rubbed it thoughtfully. "Yer father was Alasdair MacLeod." His gaze slid to Sara. "'Tis why Morag brought Eleri here to Dunscaith and why my father kept her."

Sara's jaw dropped open, and all breath halted inside her. She stared at Rory for a long while and swallowed, standing slowly. "So…my mother and your father…had an…assignation?"

Rory nodded. "And Eleri and Eliza came from it."

Sweet Saint Mary! Her stomach twisted into knots. "Does my father know?"

"Kenan wasn't sure."

But when Sara thought about the neglect and almost cruelty her father exhibited toward Eliza, Sara grew certain. "He at least suspects. Ever since…" Sara pulled her hand from Eleri's and held both cool palms to her cheeks. "A couple years before my mother died, he became more incensed, angrier for no apparent reason. I thought perhaps it was because she seemed so sad and started ailing."

"Is he cruel to my sister?" Eleri asked, and Sara could see the moisture gathering in her eyes. Sara drew a clean handkerchief from the pocket tied under her outer petticoat and set it into Eleri's hand.

"I was there to protect her," Sara said and glanced at Rory. "Until I was taken here."

"Kenan will bring her to Dunvegan," Rory said.

"When did your mother die?" Sara blurted out. Her mother would never have tried to break up another marriage.

"Nearly fifteen years ago."

"So before Eliza and Eleri were born?" she asked.

Eleri nodded solemnly. "I never met her."

"She died a year before Eleri was born," Rory said. "I did the calculation when Morag told us. My mother was dead, and Elspet Gunn must have met my father at the Beltane Festival both our families attended in 1531 on the mainland. 'Twas a surprise that both MacLeods and Macdonalds were present."

"I remember it," she said, thinking of the boys who'd competed, remembering the one with watchful, golden eyes. Rory had won most of the contests, and Kenan had considered him his greatest adversary in competition.

"Morag said she helped yer mother see my father because Elspet was in a loveless marriage," Rory said.

Sara's heart ached for her mother, remembering the tears that she tried to hide from her children. How she'd poured her love into them, even Gilbert when he tried to act exactly like the always-grumbling man she'd married.

"Somehow, Father found out," Sara said, thinking of the yelling and occasional bruises her mother endured toward the end of her life. Sara felt the ache of unshed tears. Elspet Gunn Macdonald had been a light so bright in Sara's life that when it went out, Sara had fallen into a chilled darkness and remained there for the last seven years.

"Did he beat her?" Eleri asked.

Sara exhaled, sitting beside the girl. "Not where I saw, but I think he did."

"I will say a prayer for her soul," Eleri said.

"I will, too." Sara looked at Rory. "Will Kenan tell Eliza?"

"I believe so."

She nodded and continued to stare outward. "As long as he doesn't tell Father or Gilbert."

"Rory?" Eleri asked, looking at him. "You are my half brother." He nodded. She looked at Sara. "And you are my half sister." She nodded.

Eleri pointed to the two of them. "Does that make you two brother and sister?"

CHAPTER TWELVE

"[In medieval times] a double birth was treated with
suspicion, with the mother often accused of adultery
or even witchcraft."

Artuk.org

"No!"

"Nay!"

Sara and Rory yelled out at the same time. The
loudness of their protests made Eleri's eyes widen.
"No," Sara repeated, her voice tempered. "My parents
are completely different from Rory's parents."

"Same with Jamie," Rory said.

"So, you can still marry Jamie?" Eleri asked, looking at Sara.

The thought swelled like bloat inside Sara. Marry
Jamie after he nearly died in the church on their wed-
ding day? Even if he wished to when he woke, Sara
couldn't do it. "I…we won't marry, though," she said.
She slid a finger over the cuts on her knuckles where
Rory had touched, and she felt his gaze.

"Why not?" Eleri asked.

"He won't want to after what he's gone through
because of my clan," Sara said. It was the safe answer,
because the truth brought her back to a pair of amber
eyes, eyes that she felt sure watched her now.

Rory exhaled. "'Twould not be safe."

The words sent prickles of unease along Sara's

nape, and she raised her gaze. "Not safe?" Sara's stomach churned with nausea at the thought of Jamie touching her, but was he truly dangerous?

Rory crossed his arms, his legs braced. "Jamie is suspicious even without a reason. He won't be easily swayed to believe in your innocence in the fire. 'Tis not safe now for ye to marry him."

The tightness of fear made her stomach flip. "The annulment will stand." Sara wasn't about to jump from an abusive father to an abusive husband.

"Will you tell me about my mother, Sara?" Eleri asked. The sadness retreated somewhat. "I know nothing about her."

The wistful emotions behind her quiet words made Sara miss her mother, Elspet, all the more. "She was lovely and kind and liked to paint, too."

Eleri smiled broadly. "I love to paint." She hugged Sara. Eliza smelled of wildflowers because she pressed the fragrant ones and slid them amongst her smocks. Eleri smelled of oil paints with a hint of baked biscuits.

The girl tipped her head back to smile up at her. "I'm so glad we're sisters"—she glanced at Rory—"and brother."

"Even though Lady Sara and I are absolutely *not* brother and sister," Rory said.

"Of course," Eleri said, tipping her head. "Although, we could pretend."

Sweet Mary. "I don't think that…" Sara didn't look at Rory. "I don't feel that way about Rory." Especially after he'd held her hand before the steps. "But I can certainly be your sister."

After promising to think of tales she could share

of her mother, Sara walked out the door and Rory followed. They waited together on the dark, silent landing until they heard Eleri lock her door. Without a word, Sara stepped evenly down the stairs, but her heart beat like a sparrow's wings as she listened to Rory's tread right behind her.

At the bottom, he caught her arm, turning her to him. Several seconds stretched before he spoke. "In what way *do* ye feel about me?" he asked. His deep voice teased her, and the words, his question, opened a valve within Sara like a fluttering of leaves on a summer tree.

You are ugly. Her father's words overrode Rory's, and they sounded like her own voice after she'd believed them for years, repeating them and trying to accept them. What good would it do to draw closer to Rory, think of him as anything but her brother's friend? "I…I don't know," she said. "It depends on so much."

"That's thinking," he said, closing the gap between them. "I asked how ye feel about me."

"Feelings are changeable and not dependable." Her words sounded breathless, and she swallowed.

"Ye had distasteful feelings about my brother even though ye went through with marrying him." He was close, the wall at her back. "Did ye hope yer feelings would warm toward him?"

A sizzle of irritation knifed through her, and she frowned. "The only feeling I had toward Jamie MacLeod was obligation and hope that I could help forge a peace between our clans, and, from what you've said, that wouldn't have changed."

"And ye do not feel…brotherly toward me?"

She'd think he was trying to make her

uncomfortable for fun, but he didn't wear any type of grin. What did she feel for him? She wasn't about to reveal how she'd imagined kissing him. How she'd dreamed of him, wishing that they could just be two villagers meeting on the beach.

"No," she answered.

"How do ye feel then?"

She exhaled. "I feel safe with you," she said. "I suppose that is trust."

"But not in a brotherly way," he continued the thought.

"More as a friend." There. A friendship wouldn't be mortifying, and it wasn't brotherly. "I trust you as a friend." She smiled, happy with her non-answer.

But he didn't smile back. "Trust shouldn't be given lightly, Sara. I can't say that I truly trust anyone."

"Trust is crucial to a fruitful marriage," she said. Her cheeks grew hot when she thought how that must sound with her taking a leap from friendship to marriage.

"I won't marry." Rory shook his head.

Sara's brows pinched. "You won't marry because you can't trust a woman enough to love her?"

He stared hard at her. She knew his eyes were golden, but in the shadows, they looked obsidian. "Love is a fantasy. I deal with reality and solid things, not something as intangible as the emotions a bride would demand of me."

"And yet you ask me how I feel?" The warmth from moments before had slid away from her. "When you feel...what? Anger, revenge?"

He raked a hand through his trimmed hair. "Feelings are complicated."

"Everything is complicated," she said, not bothering to hide her anger. "My father tried to set everyone on fire. Your clan thinks I was part of it. I was wed for less than an hour to a man who is dangerous, you don't trust anyone, I have unbrotherly feelings toward the bloody Lion of Skye, and I don't know if you're my captor or my…friend."

He watched her as she breathed heavily from her short tirade. "Unbrotherly feelings of…friendship?" he asked again.

She didn't say anything but pressed her hand against her flying heart. Her chest rose and fell as if she'd run up the stairs.

He took a step closer until she felt his legs press her petticoats. The torchlight splashed across his face, his brows pinched in a mix of questioning and what looked like pain. "Or…" he said, his hand rising to her cheek. She almost felt it brush her skin but then he stopped, letting his hand hover in the air. "Or are your unbrotherly feelings more heat?" He leaned forward, and her breath stopped as she felt the brush of his lips against her ear. "Hot like a flame?"

Sensation ran through her as she listened to him inhale as if smelling her, and chill bumps rose across her, pearling her nipples.

"Rory!" Footfalls shot through Sara, making her jump back from Rory, hitting against the wall.

Rory turned, his large body standing before her like a shield. "Jok?" he called, and the footsteps reached the top of the stairs leading down below.

The warrior with the flaming red hair and beard burst into the corridor. "Bloody hell, Ror, where've ye been?"

Sara peered out from beside Rory, and Jok's eyes grew wide as he looked between them both.

"What is it?" Rory demanded.

Jok seemed to shake off his surprise. "Jamie is awake."

CHAPTER THIRTEEN

"The Four Elements were believed to be the building blocks of creation. All things which exist are believed to have these Four Elements within them. It has always been understood that the Elements refer not to the physical substances of air, fire, water, and earth, but to qualities represented by them."

SacredWicca.com

Rory strode down the corridor, Sara on his heels. *Unbrotherly feelings.* Every instinct he depended on had screamed at him in that dark corridor that she ached for him as much as he ached for her. And there was nothing wrong with simple carnal pleasure. He wasn't betraying his oath if he gave into the heat he was feeling if Sara felt the same.

The memory of Madeline Sinclair's, nay, Madeline Macdonald's treachery left Rory's skin prickling as if his father had slapped him. *'Tis the fault of yer weak, foolish heart that made her death necessary.* But Rory's father was dead and surely in Hell. Alasdair MacLeod couldn't slice Sara's throat open, letting her bleed out in front of his horrified son. And Rory was a grown man now who knew better than to lose his heart to a woman.

Rory tried to shake off the dark thoughts from that hellish fall day ten years ago, the gulls crying above on the currents of wind. The crimson of her blood on her pale skin. He wouldn't think of it. He hurried with Sara to Jamie's room.

Jok caught his arm, letting Sara hurry forward. "What the hell did I step into?" Jok said, his eyes accusing. "Ye were dallying with Jamie's wife?"

Fok. Rory pushed Jok's shoulder so that he flattened his back against the corridor wall and stared hard in his face. "Sara Macdonald is not Jamie's wife, and she's stated plainly that she will never marry him."

"Sara *Macdonald*," Jok said, emphasizing her clan name. "Ye can't trust a Macdonald woman. Ye know that better than anyone."

"I don't trust anyone," Rory shot back, his face tight with a restrained snarl. "And I don't have to explain anything to ye."

Jok raised his hands, surrendering, and swallowed as if Rory had changed into a lion right before his eyes. "I just don't want…ye to lose the respect of yer clan again, Ror. It took years for—"

Rory shoved away from him and strode down the corridor toward his brother's room, his mind spinning and his blood pumping as if for battle.

"How dare you come here!" The screeching voice pushed Rory into a run. Winnie Mar stood barring his brother's door against Sara. "You tried to murder my Jamie and attacked me." The woman's nose had stopped bleeding but looked swollen, and dark bruises had spread under her eyes.

"I'm an emissary for peace between MacLeod and Macdonald Clans," Sara said.

"You're an assassin. No one trusts you. Jamie surely doesn't." Her words had grown shrill again.

There was that bloody word again. *Trust.*

If Sara produced a sword from the folds of her costume, Rory wouldn't be surprised. Her look was menacing, displaying her inner strength. "I am the daughter of a clan chief, an invited lady to Dunvegan, and I have no problem adding to your injuries."

Rory felt the tension in his mouth relax. There was a lot of fight in Sara despite being beaten down by her father.

Winnie's eyes narrowed until they were only slits framed by long lashes. "We will see who stays at Dunvegan and who is either banished or thrown in the dungeon pit to drown with the high tide." She whipped around to stride down the corridor and around the corner.

Sara waited until she was down the hall before turning her anger on Rory. "A pit? You have a pit where people can drown if the tide is high? That's barbaric. And don't say it's less barbaric than burning someone in a chapel." Even soft, her words were clipped and icy.

"Ye may come in," Hamish said in the doorway.

When neither Rory nor Sara moved, Jok walked between them, his big body like the barrier he thought Rory should erect against the Macdonald woman. Jok entered the room, leaving them staring at one another.

"The pit is not used often, and no one is left to drown," Rory said. His hand went out to the door. Sara turned, and he followed. Hamish stood with Margaret on the far side of Jamie's large bed. Two maids changed the water in the pitcher and tended the hearth. The heavy curtains at the windows were pulled back to allow in more light.

Jamie wore his nightshirt and was propped up with many pillows. Had he heard the exchange in the hallway? He frowned as Sara walked toward him.

She curtsied gracefully when she reached the side of the bed. "I'm pleased you're awake, milord."

Jamie's face was pale as skimmed milk. A bandage covered the stitches Hamish had put in his head, making his usually combed hair stand on end. He seemed to press into the pillows at his back as if they held all his weight. His eyes were red-hued and narrowed as he studied Sara.

Daingead. Rory glanced at the door. What had Winnie told him about Sara's involvement in the fire?

"Ye, Lady Seraphina, Flame of Dunscaith, tried to kill me and my family on our wedding day." Jamie's words were rough as if he had coarse wool down his throat. "Macdonalds are demons that should be wiped from God's earth."

Rory glanced away, annoyed. Jamie was as dramatic as ever.

Sara took a step backward, her face flaming, and everyone in the room stiffened.

"Like I told ye, Jamie," Margaret said, her face set in a scold like when they were lads, "Lady Sara saved us by leading us out from under the chapel. Mistress Mar was not there to witness her heroic actions and is swayed against her because of her affection for you."

But Jamie kept his pinched stare on Sara as if Margaret's words had been swept away by a receding tide before they could flow into his ears. He raised his hand in the air, one finger crooked, beckoning Sara to him. She obeyed, making Rory draw closer.

"Lady Sara tapped under the floor with a rock to show us where to break through the floorboards," Rory said. "She led Margaret through and helped pull ye out, Jamie."

Jamie never looked at Rory but kept beckoning Sara. "Come to me, bride," he said.

"Ye're not wed," Rory said. "The contract was burned, and Father Lockerby agreed the union was null."

Sara stepped up dutifully despite the anger in Jamie's tortured face. "We are not wed," she repeated. "Milord, I am glad you are—" Sara's words cut off in a soft gasp as Jamie's hand snapped around her wrist, capturing her like an iron manacle.

He stared into her surprised face. "We *are* wed, Sara," Jamie said. "And I will make it binding by foking ye as soon as I can rise from this bed. Ye can't get away from me."

Horror widened Sara's eyes, and it struck a chord that vibrated right through Rory's center. "Bloody hell, Jamie!" He grabbed Jamie's hand with both of his and worked his fingers loose, letting Sara pull away. The red blooming on the skin of her wrist showed the force his brother had inflicted. If he'd been at full strength, he could have snapped her bone.

Margaret shook her head, frowning with her own shock. "Jamie, she is a lady. You cannot speak—"

"She's no lady," Jamie said, staring right at Sara. "She is my murderous wife who I will punish for her betrayal. Rory, have Father Lockerby draw up a new contract."

"I won't wed you," Sara said.

Jamie drew back his hand as if to strike her.

"Jamie!" Rory yelled, easily catching the weak swing. "She won't be threatened into marrying ye."

"Then she will leave," Jamie said, sinking into his pillows as if the violent effort had drained him of all energy. "Seraphina Macdonald is banished from Dunvegan." His gaze found Sara and he stared into her eyes as he struggled to draw even breaths. "Or she will burn."

· · ·

Morag poured the lavender seeds she'd harvested for soapmaking upon the table in her cottage. Her weathered hand smoothed the grains into a flat circle of pale purple, and she inhaled the soothing fragrance.

*Tsk*ing lightly, she took a moment to study the back of her hand. One's hands showed one's age, the years of toil they'd endured. "We all get old," she said. "If we're lucky." Her twin sister hadn't been fortunate enough to develop wrinkled hands. The hollowness of regret and loss gnawed her stomach, and she breathed past it.

Morag set her fingertip at the top left corner and dragged a diagonal line down, then repeated it on the opposite side to form an *X* through the tiny flowers. It made four quadrants like large pie wedges: north, south, west, and east. In the north, she set a chunk of salt crystal. On the left or west quadrant, she placed a small silver cup of water. In the east quadrant, she set a white feather.

"And finally," she said, "fire in the south." She moved the white beeswax candle to the bottom quadrant. With it she laid a single red-hued hair she'd plucked from Sara. "The flame." She bowed her head. "Let the Celtic goddess of Fire, Brigid, protect Seraphina. Earth Mother, Gaia, help me bring strength to our isle. Protect the elements and make them strong and united. Guide me as your helper in this realm."

Morag passed her hands over the circle, feeling the warmth of the flame as she did, and prayed for several minutes. Sighing, she lowered her hands to her lap. She had much work to do to save her isle.

CHAPTER FOURTEEN

"…and upon this the Clitoris cleaveth and is tied, which being nervous, and of pure feeling, when it is rubbed and stirred it causeth lustful thoughts…"

Jane Sharp, 1671, The Midwives Book or
The Whole Art of Midwifry Discovered

Are your unbrotherly feelings more heat? Hot like a flame?

Rory's words played about in Sara's head as she sat on the edge of her small bed. They strummed through her like a vibrating chord to tease that very flame he'd detected within her.

He wanted her, maybe as much as she desired him. But he'd said he didn't trust anyone. Could he come together in pleasure with a woman he didn't trust? Morag said physical love could be different for different people. Sometimes, it was an act to find pleasure and had nothing to do with the heart. To Sara, trust lived in the heart.

Sara worried at her bottom lip. Could she do that? Be with someone without throwing her heart into jeopardy? Her aching body screamed yes, but her mind wasn't so sure.

With a huff, Sara pulled her robe over her smock and unlocked her door, peering out into the darkness of the landing. It was late. She'd woken from a dream that had left her aching in carnal frustration, and now her mind wouldn't let her fall back under its spell.

Sara slipped from her room and down the tower stairs. She held her breath, but no one moved out of the shadows. Pushing past the niggling disappointment, she continued down two more flights. Apart from an occasional snore or creak behind a door, everything in Dunvegan was quiet.

Perhaps she truly wasn't a prisoner. She had a key and no guard. Despite Jamie's cruel words today, those two facts made her a guest. Someone would surely stop her at the gate if she tried to take the ferry across. Although, Jamie had ordered her to leave. The man was mad if he thought she'd marry him now. The bruise on her wrist was still tender even after Margaret had wrapped a poultice around it.

Sara stopped in the great hall, considering, but turned down another corridor away from the gate. She couldn't leave Dunvegan in the night, in her robe, without saying farewell. Morag's was too far to journey to alone at night on foot.

Margaret had brought Sara through the castle earlier to the kitchens to tend her cut knuckles and blossoming bruise, and Sara had noticed a garden beyond. She hugged her robe tighter and hurried through the shadowed corridor. A few sconces guttered, their flames scarcely alive.

The sound of even breathing met Sara when she entered the kitchen. Fiona, the gruff cook who wore her hair plaited in two braids coiled atop her head, slept on a thick pallet near the hearth. She rolled her curvy bulk over, pulling her blanket to her chin.

The kitchen walls were plastered with bright white, and someone had painted a flowering vine along the wall where it joined the ceiling. Bunches of dried herbs hung from the exposed beams like at Aunt Morag's cottage, and a door opened out into the culinary garden inside the thick Dunvegan wall. The glow from the hearth helped Sara maneuver without hitting anything as she crept through the tidy space. She lifted the bar from the door with silent care, setting it down, and slid out into the garden.

Fragrant aromas of rosemary and oregano greeted Sara as she walked down the pebbled path between bushy, well-tended herbs. At the far end of the garden stood two trees, and a swing dangled from one of the thicker limbs. The chilled air helped cool the ardor in her blood as she filled her lungs with the freshness of the night. The half moon peeked from behind drifting clouds, illuminating the crushed white stone paths. Sara's slippers crunched as she hurried toward the swing.

Her hand flitted along a lavender bush, and she plucked a stem, holding it to her nose. It smelled of her mother, because Morag always added it to the soap she'd made for her. What must Elspet have felt having to let one of her little daughters go? Sara's heart squeezed.

Sara sat on the wooden swing. Her feet dangled above the grass, and she leaned back to make it move. The breeze tugged at her hair, and she was glad she'd left it down to drape her shoulders, keeping her warmer.

Eyes trained forward, she walked her feet back, releasing into a low swoop. The breeze felt refreshing in her face.

Movement. Sara's breath halted, and she tried to

stop her swinging by dragging her toes. The kitchen door opened. The light from the hearth fire was blotted out when a tall figure emerged and closed the door behind him.

By St. Mary's tears! Jamie wasn't well enough to walk outside, was he?

But the figure's gait was brisk and strong with health. "Rory?" she asked, her voice just above a whisper in the vast darkness.

"Aye."

Sara released her breath and leaned back on the swing. Her hands clenched around the ropes on either side.

"What are ye doing out here?"

She pushed her toes against the grass again. Even though fear had dissipated immediately, her heart still thudded. Rory had followed her. And now they were alone, in the dark, and she was in her sleeping smock and robe. Desire prickled through her despite the bracing coolness of the air. "How did you know I was out here?" she asked.

He stopped beside her, his broad form creating a giant's shadow across the garden wall. "Ye answer a question with another question."

"Does that annoy you?" She hoped her voice sounded casual, playful, to hide the fluttering breathiness afflicting her.

He released a soft bark of laughter at another question and walked behind her. Sara forced herself to take a long, even breath.

"I heard someone walk past my door," Rory said, his voice so close she imagined she could feel the warmth of his breath. "Someone light on their feet. So

I followed and waited outside the kitchen thinking ye might be hungry."

His hands pressed against her backside, lifting her way up. She gasped, clutching the ropes, and then he released, stepping aside. Sara swooped down, her toes skimming the wet grass, and he pushed her again. In the darkness, it was as if she were flying, and a pulse of panic surged, reminding her of her aversion to heights.

"Not so high," she said as her legs came even with her head on the upswing. He let her swing back and forth a few times without pushing.

"Ye didn't come downstairs to eat then?"

The swing slowed, and Rory gave her a slight push to keep her going without her having to kick her legs.

"Did you push Eleri out here on the swing?"

"I will answer yer question after ye answer mine."

She inhaled the breeze until her head swam. "I couldn't sleep, so I came out to find peace."

Rory pushed her gently a few times before speaking. "I used to swing Eleri out here when she was a wee lass." Rory walked out before her, letting the swing slow to a halt. With the moonlight peeking past the border of a moving cloud, she could see the hardness of his frown. "With Jamie awake, it isn't safe to leave yer room when everyone is sleeping."

She swallowed, her throat tight at the memory of her fear when she saw Rory's shadow. "I didn't think he could walk about in his weakened state."

"He'll improve quickly now that he's awake and can eat and drink."

She slid off the seat and looked up into the sky where sea mist grew into fog, muting the moonlight.

The dampness of the fog prickled against her cheeks, and she knew her hair would curl wildly from it.

"The fog's coming in," she said.

Rory inhaled. "The air is fresh with it."

"Not like the fettered air of prison."

He stared down at her, his eyes dark in the shadows. "I dreamed and prayed to breathe the clean sea air of Skye again."

Sara remembered the festering slashes on Kenan's back when he'd returned from England, and his nose swollen from a bad break. Rory must have suffered the same, although he seemed to have recovered. His arm muscles bulged against his sleeves, and she still remembered his chiseled legs and tight arse when he'd walked naked to retrieve his plaid on the beach.

What would it be like to touch that toned flesh? His skin would be warm, his body tight with power.

"Come," he said.

"Come where?"

He pointed down. "The wind is blocked closer to the ground." He pulled the long sash from across his chest, shaking the wool out. The other end of the woven swath was caught by his belt, keeping its pleat in the wrap around his waist. "'Tis big enough."

Rory sat on the grass, apparently not minding the cold damp against the flesh above his boots. He threw the sash out from him and leaned back on his palms. "'Tis like a picnic but without food."

She let out a small laugh, staring down at the swath of wool. "That would be called sitting on the ground."

"Probably fewer ballads written about it, but 'tis still fine."

She pulled the sash wide and lowered to sit on it. Rory leaned his head back to stare at the sky. Sara did the same, watching the layers of barely lit fog slide over them, descending inside the wall. "It looks like ghosts."

"'Tis like God snapping out a blanket to let it float down over us," he said.

"The Lion of Skye is a warrior *and* a poet."

He sniffed in what could have been a laugh. "I'd make a poor poet."

"Why?"

His head came up and he met her with a serious expression. "I don't rhyme."

Sara laughed and any remaining unease faded.

They sat side by side, leaning their heads back to stare at the damp ribbons of fog. "Dunscaith is by the sea, too," Sara said, "but I've never sat watching the mist like this." The truth was that it wasn't safe to wander at night there, either.

After a moment he said, "Why couldn't ye sleep?"

She turned to Rory's profile. His eyes were open, looking up. She could give him part of the truth. "I worry about Eliza, about what my father might do next." She sighed. "About your people still wanting to burn me alive and about Jamie hating me and wanting me to leave when I have nowhere to go."

Rory's face turned to hers, and her gaze traced the edges of his strong jawline. His words were low like a deep caress. "How about I take half that worry so ye don't have so much to carry?"

"Worry doesn't work that way," she said, unsure if he was jesting.

He kept his gaze on her. "'Tis clear that Jamie isn't

right in the head and won't listen to reason, so I'm in charge of the clan until he improves. I won't let Jamie, yer father, or the villagers harm ye, and we have Kenan working to bring Eliza here."

His assurances were sound, but Sara couldn't tell him that what was really keeping her from sleeping was him. The way his amber eyes met hers with intensity that warmed her to the core. How she kept repeating his words about heat, trying to weigh if they were some trick.

"Perhaps…I would sleep easier with a weapon."

He leaned closer, and she could make out his grin in the darkness. "Ye seem to have a fine weapon here." His warm hand clasped hers where it sat in her lap. "Who taught ye to punch?"

His thumb slid across the thin poultice tied over her knuckles and up the back of her hand. It caused a shiver to slide through her. It was like the touch in the corridor, reverent and tentative, and she could imagine it running along other parts of her body.

"Kenan," she said. Should she hold Rory's hand back or let him hold hers like some stunned bird he'd pick up from the yard?

"Why?" he asked, the lightness gone from his tone. His thumb stopped its caress, but he continued to hold her hand.

"Gilbert is a bloody arse who…plays tricks on me." Her hand fisted within his hold.

"What type of tricks?"

Her other hand flipped in the air. "Throwing me in the sea, locking me in the dungeon, tripping me, especially when I was younger. So I learned to punch him and anyone who threatened me. It usually surprises them enough to let me go."

"Ye certainly surprised me."

"You still carried me away," she said, sounding surly.

"If I carry ye back to yer room…because 'tis unsafe to be out at night, will ye punch me?"

The thought of Rory MacLeod carrying her back to her room, to the bed there, relit the dry kindling Sara had been trying to smother within. "Are you going to carry me away right now?" She kept her tone light.

"I'm thinking about it. Will ye punch me?"

"Perhaps," she said and caught the slight gleam of his white teeth in the dark. "And then will you bite me, Lion of Skye?"

"Nay." His mouth tipped in a grin and moved close to her ear so that she could feel his breath stir against her hair, making her stomach flutter. "Unless ye want me to."

The spark at her ear sizzled. It spread down her neck and through her body like lightning sparking a tree and lighting the darkest night.

Her words came easier under the thickness of the mist and shadows. "Why would I want you to bite me?"

"Some lasses like a nibble."

Sara tried to remember what Morag had told her about physical love. She didn't remember biting being part of it.

"So it…doesn't hurt," she said.

He didn't laugh, but she still felt her cheeks burn and appreciated the coolness of the mist falling on them. "Nay," he said, his voice low like he was imparting a secret, "that type of bite is a little capture of skin between my teeth that is soothed quickly with a kiss and touch of my tongue."

He'd done this to other women. His words painted an image that annoyed her until she replaced the face of the woman with her own. "'Tis not the type of bite you do in battle."

"I rarely do that, either," he said, "but the threat deters most."

"The…nibble and other things," she said, "where exactly do you do that?" Her curiosity shot off more lightning, making her legs shift together.

Rory took her arm and placed a finger on the inside of her elbow. "Here." His warm pad stroked her skin.

She held her breath as his hand rose to her earlobe, pinching it gently. "Here," he said, the word coming on a low exhale. His finger slid slowly down her neck, setting tiny bumps popping up on her skin. "All along here."

Her nipples peaked in anticipation, but his finger stopped at the base of her throat, warm against her cool skin. "And lower," he said without moving it.

"Lower?"

"Aye."

She almost groaned when he removed his finger, but then he bent his mouth to her ear. "I could nibble and lick a path around yer breasts and the hard pearls of yer nipples, Sara." His accent was rougher, deeper as if he, too, were affected by his words and the images they painted. They were no longer about some phantom lover, but about her.

"I'd love the skin over yer stomach and the rise of

each of yer hip bones."

Sara could imagine his warm mouth working its way down her body. His words stroked her like she imagined the brush of his fingers and lips would do. Even the edge of his white teeth could slide against her sensitive skin, teeth able to cause pain, but he would use them for pleasure.

"Anywhere else?"

"Aye," he said but still didn't touch her except with the whisper of his breath at her ear. "There is a sensitive spot between yer legs, lass."

"I know." She felt the nub throb as if nothing would calm it.

"Ye've…touched it?"

She nodded in the dark. "I want to touch it now." She felt heat flush up her neck into her face. She wanted Rory MacLeod to touch it. The thought sent a pulse of wet desire between her legs.

Rory murmured something that sounded pained. She felt him shift, his hand going down into the shadows. Was he stroking himself? The heavy jack and ballocks she'd seen briefly when he'd walked out of the sea? Without the icy seawater, was it hard and standing upright like she'd seen one night on the Macdonald warrior with a maid in the barn?

She'd watched them from a back stall, and the sight and sounds had shot an achy heat through her.

Rory groaned lightly. "'Tis indeed dangerous out here for ye, Lady Sara Macdonald."

Lady Sara Macdonald? Her full name put distance between them. He pulled back from her. "I'll escort ye back to yer room."

For a moment, she did nothing, the ache pulsing in

her rooting her to the ground.

"If ye stand," he said, nodding to his sash trapped under her.

"Oh." The flush that had shot through her body now rose into her cheeks.

Heart hammering and face aflame, Sara stood and backed off his woolen wrap. Rory rose and tucked it better into his belt, flipping the end over his shoulder. The two of them walked in silence through the kitchen past the snoring cook. He didn't take Sara's hand but escorted her up the flights of steps without a word. So many steps. The burn in her thighs helped tame the fire inside her, but his nearness on the small landing before her door made it flare.

"I'll listen for ye to lock yerself inside," he said.

She looked into his eyes that she could once again see in the light of a wall sconce. The flame from it glowed in the amber pools. "Will you come inside with me?"

There was a pause so long that she startled slightly when his voice broke the silence. "I am a warrior, not a...not a man to woo a lass. And ye're a maiden, not a widow looking to relieve an ache."

Sara felt her jaw tense. "Maidens can ache, too."

"I'm also not a scoundrel, Sara," he said, his words rough.

"And I am not a whore, Rory." Her words followed his same inflection. "But I *am* truthful and not ashamed of the heat inside me." She opened the door to her room. "I have no need for my maidenhood, and I ache." Her words were soft but sounded loud in her ears as she stared into her dark room "Life is too short to ignore it."

She turned toward him and let her robe part. The thin white smock dipped down along her collarbone. In the darkness of her room, he would not be able to see the ugliness across her back. The shadows made her bold. Sara slid one hand up from her abdomen, her body alive even under the touch of her own fingers, and she lifted under one of her breasts.

Rory's gaze followed her movement, hunger in the set of his jaw. His lips parted, and she caught sight of the tip of his tongue touching his bottom lip. Her heart thumped at the surge of want that slight movement caused. He'd come to her, pull her into his arms, kiss her, touch her. He wanted to, maybe desperately. She could see the lustful strain on his features and the rise of his jack against his plaid.

His hands braced on the lintel of her doorway, stretched over his head. His muscles bulged like he was stopping himself from stepping in. His gaze raked her, and he swallowed hard. "My honor is stronger than my want."

He turned and walked down the staircase.

CHAPTER FIFTEEN

"[Hippocrates (460-375BC)] was the first who
invented devices based on principles of axial traction
and three points correction for
correction of curvatures of the spine and
the management of spinal diseases."

NCBI at NIH.gov

Ye're ugly.

Her father's words slithered around inside Sara, biting her. But Rory hadn't seen the ugly red marks across her back. And he wanted her. Sara knew it, had seen it, had heard it in his words out in the garden.

Did he think she'd seduce him to win MacLeod secrets? He'd admitted he trusted no one. Her stomach unclenched. That was better than rejecting her because of her fiery marks.

She huffed and descended the tower steps two days after Rory had left her cheeks flaming in her dark tower room. She hadn't even had a chance to talk to him about hiding the Fairy Flag somewhere else.

"Are you ready?" Eleri asked, walk-running down the corridor from her own tower.

Sara retied her cape strings that had already loosened and smiled. "I am." She took Eleri's gloved hand, and they made their way down the steps and across the great hall while Eleri chattered on.

"I wonder how much we look alike. And you said she draws. Maybe she can draw something, and I can fill it in with my paints."

The hall was empty except for John and Simon, who nursed tankards while they played a game of chess before the hearth. Eleri waved to them but continued to talk. They waved back and nodded to Sara. She nodded back. 'Twas as if they thought better of her after she'd punched Winnie and admitted doing the same to Gilbert. Or they pitied her for Jamie's brutality and horrifying threats. The whole village was talking about it from what the maids told Sara.

They continued down to the ferry where Reid waited to help them cross safely.

"Thank you," Sara said, smiling at the nervous man. She hadn't had a chance to ask him about himself. "I expected to have to pole us across myself."

"'Tis my responsibility to look out for ye," Reid said, his face growing red.

"Is it?"

"Aye, milady. I will be your steward while ye're here." Reid strained to push the long pole into the muck under the water. Slowly the ferry moved from the edge of Dunvegan. Eleri and Sara exchanged a look. The girl wanted to help Reid push the pole, too, but he'd have taken offense.

Sara cleared her throat. "Margaret said you're from the Isle of Lewis."

He walked along the edge of the ferry, keeping them moving. "Aye, milady, but there were more opportunities here on Skye."

"When did you come to Dunvegan?" she asked, tilting her head. The man was fidgety, and she wondered if he'd been tormented for his slight figure and nervousness. Perhaps that's why he seemed vaguely familiar. Her friend back at Dunscaith, Beatrice, had the same way about her.

"Three years ago, milady, and I'm happy to be of service." They bumped into the land on the other side.

"You're doing a fine job," she said, giving him an encouraging smile. He turned away from her to tie the ferry to the dock.

He glanced behind him at the crunch of gravel under hooves, and she lifted her gaze.

Sara gasped. "Lily!" Holding her skirts, she hopped off the ferry and ran to her white horse who walked from around the thick castle wall.

"Rory thought she was yours," Jok, Rory's red-haired friend, said. He led Lily and another horse while Brodrick led Rory's gray charger and a smaller horse out.

"This is so exciting," Eleri said as Jok helped her mount the short mare and handed her the reins.

Sara stroked Lily's sleek white neck and hugged her. She'd been well cared for in the MacLeod stables.

"We should ride." Rory's voice sent a jolt through her, and she pulled away from Lily to see him standing behind her.

She tamped down her surly questions about his avoiding her, gathered her petticoat with one hand, and put her toes into the stirrup. But then Rory's hands caught her around the middle, and he lifted her up into the saddle. Before she could inform him in a haughty voice that she was certainly capable of mounting herself, he walked away to his own horse. She huffed instead.

Sara patted Lily's neck, and the mare tossed her head as if happy to be riding out again, her mistress on her back. Sara ignored the glances of the villagers as they rode through the village, because most of them wore hostile frowns. Instead, she watched Rory riding his dappled gray charger. As they rode by the burned chapel, she was reminded of why he hadn't given in to the fire between them. She was a Macdonald, daughter of the devil.

Sara and Rory flanked Eleri, and Jok rode behind. "Who do I have to thank for taking such good care of Lily?" Sara asked.

Jok trotted up next to her. Fiery red hair was cut short to show a rugged jawline under a short beard and mustache of the same color. A profusion of freckles covered his pale skin. "I did," he said. "Thought she might bite me at first." Jok grinned at Lily. "But she gave me a sweet nibble instead."

Sara's inhale caught, and she coughed into her hand.

"Excuse me," Rory said, his voice strangled. He pressed his mount into a run.

They watched him gallop, dust flying up behind him. "Maybe he's scouting ahead," Eleri said.

"Looked a bit like the devil was chasing him," Jok said, frowning.

Sara exhaled slowly and wondered if horns were sprouting from her head.

The three of them followed Rory at a fast pace under heavy clouds and made quick time through the woods to her aunt's cottage.

"Eliza!" Sara called as their party halted before Morag's cottage. Black crows fluttered their wings at the disturbance but didn't leave the stone wall that ran around the cottage.

The door swung open, and her oldest brother, Kenan, ran out. "Sara!"

He lifted her down from Lily and swung her around in a hug. "Bloody hell, Sara," he said and kissed her head. "I worried I'd lost ye in Father's mad plan." He shook his head, fury sharpening the lines of his face. "He's getting worse all the time."

"I'm well." She looked behind him when he set her down. "Where's Eliza?" Sara's heart felt too low in her chest. If Eliza was there, she'd have run out with Kenan. "We've brought Eleri." She gestured toward Eleri who had dismounted with Jok's help and smiled as Morag bowed to her. Morag straightened and touched the girl's back, keeping her smile as she spoke quietly to Eleri.

Kenan exhaled, his gaze drifting to Eleri. "Och but she does look very much like Eliza."

Sara's fingers curled into her brother's tunic as if to shake him. "You left Eliza at Dunscaith?"

"Father won't allow her to come," Kenan said.

Her stomach clenched. "Why not?"

Kenan touched the bandaged poultice across her wrist. "What is this?" He turned a hard gaze on Rory.

"Jamie woke," Rory said. "He was not…forgiving about the fire."

Jok crossed his arms. "He banished Lady Sara from Dunvegan."

Kenan glared at Rory. "Ye allowed this—"

"'Twas unexpected," Sara cut in, her hand flapping at the unimportant question. "Why won't Father let Eliza come?"

Kenan continued to stare at Rory as if he battled inside on whether he should inflict some penance on him for Jamie's actions. Sara stomped her boot down on his toe.

"Bloody hell, Sara," Kenan said, wincing, and turned back to her. "He says ye don't need a lady's maid since ye didn't wed."

Sara huffed and strode past him to enter the warm cottage. She dropped into a wooden chair, resting her face in her hands. The fragrance of lavender filled the whitewashed room. "Oh, Eliza. How could I have left you there?"

"Ye didn't have a choice," Rory said. "And the wedding was supposed to bring an end to this bloody feud." It was the most he'd spoken to her since the night she'd been mortified with his rejection. She looked up from her hands but not at him.

Kenan had followed him inside. "And if ye're to leave Dunvegan, at Jamie's order, Eliza shouldn't go there anyway."

"She's not leaving Dunvegan," Rory stated.

Jok flapped his hand at a crow that had gotten too close and ducked inside. His frown moved to Rory. "She's not? Jamie ordered—"

"Sara is not leaving Dunvegan."

Morag and Eleri walked inside hand in hand. Her aunt frowned at Jok. "Dunscaith is unsafe for any woman or girl." Morag led Eleri to the hearth before turning to the room. "Walter Macdonald is a menace to this world." She held her hands palm to palm and touched the tip to her lips as if she were in prayer. "If only Elspet had realized his vileness, she would have poisoned him before he pushed her."

Jok swore under his breath.

Sara's face jerked up to stare at her. "Pushed?" Sara said, the word coming out on a gasp. She looked from Morag to Kenan. "Did you know this?"

Kenan exhaled. "Aunt Morag has discussed it with me, but there's no proof Mother didn't fall on her own."

Or jump, Sara thought, thinking of the misery her mother had endured.

"Get him drunk enough and he'll admit it," Morag said. "Bring him here, and I'll do what my sister couldn't bring herself to do."

"Is Father vile enough to murder his wife?" Sara asked.

Morag's gaze turned to Eleri, and the girl's eyes widened. "He...found out about me?" Eleri said.

Rory strode to her as if he could protect her from the knowledge. He brushed her hair from her face. "Ye take no blame in his foulness."

"There was a Macdonald spy at Dunvegan," Morag said and looked at Rory. "A young woman named Madeline who got word to Walter about Elspet and Alasdair and about the girls." She kept her gaze on him.

Madeline? Had Sara heard that name before?

Rory's face tensed and paled, but he crouched before Eleri, whose face was wide with guilt and ghastly fear. "Ye were a bairn of two years, El. Ye're not at fault, neither ye nor yer twin."

"We need to get Eliza out of Dunscaith," Sara said, standing with an urge to ride to Dunscaith that minute. "He may snap and take his revenge out on her."

"She's locked in her room," Kenan said. "Guarded as if he suspects we plan to take her."

"From a mere request to have her as a lady's maid?" Jok asked.

"An overreaction," Rory said.

Morag flicked her hand. "Not to a madman."

"And Gilbert is supporting him?" Sara asked.

Kenan tipped his head to the side, narrowing his eyes. "I think he questions his actions silently, but so far, he does whatever Father tells him. When Father dies, I'm sure he'll challenge me for the chiefdom." Kenan stood with his feet braced.

Sweet Mother Mary. Eliza must be rescued from the civil war brewing at Dunscaith. Sara exhaled long. "If this spy told Father what she suspected back when the twins were only two years old, and he hasn't harmed Eliza in the last ten years, she should be safe for a bit longer. Even if I'm not there." Her last words grew soft because she didn't know if they were true.

The fire crackled in the hearth as wind whistled around the corners of the snug cottage.

"Is he planning any other attacks on Clan MacLeod?" Rory asked.

"He hasn't said."

Sara walked over to slide an arm around Eleri. "Find out, Kenan. In a way that won't make him hold tighter to Eliza. See if there's a way to sneak her out without open bloodshed."

Her brother nodded. "I'll return immediately. The longer I'm away from Dunscaith, the less I can protect her."

He stepped before Eleri and bowed, making her blush. "I look forward to speaking with ye over a longer visit, sister."

She curtsied, the bend of her back making it look awkward, but she smiled. "I'd enjoy that." Her smile faded, and her hands clasped before her. "Please tell my sister I long to meet her and I think of her often now that I know about her. I'll paint a portrait of us together when she comes to Dunvegan."

"I will." Kenan smiled and then turned to Sara, his momentary brightness fading to gray. "Stay away from Jamie MacLeod." He glanced at Rory and then back to her. "If he harms ye again, I will kill him."

Sara huffed at the boast. "Which will increase the blood feud." She shook her head. "I can take care of myself. Don't wage war against him on my account."

Kenan looked at Rory, and Rory lifted his hand where Sara saw bright scars across his palm, just like the ones on Kenan's palm. Rory clenched his hand into a fist and brought it silently to his chest. "I will make certain Sara isn't at risk."

"My sisters come before the brotherhood." Kenan's face took on the granite hardness of a mountain.

"As does my sister," Rory said.

Sara looked between them. "Brotherhood?"

"And Jamie?" Kenan asked, his gaze still narrowed.

"And Gilbert?" Rory countered.

The negotiation between the two Highlanders was full of history and manly posturing. Sara willed herself not to interrupt despite her need to send Kenan on his way to Eliza. It was bonds like what the two men had forged in England that might bring their clans together.

Kenan made a fist with his own scarred hand and brought it to his chest. "Our brothers are poisonous to peace."

"Agreed," Rory said, and Kenan nodded as if that was enough to reinforce each other's loyalty to this brotherhood they'd formed.

"Excellent," Morag said, a smile on her unnaturally smooth face. A flapping at the window made Jok jump, his hand going to his sword. Morag glided to the window to see her crows and peered upward. "Clouds are moving in, and my bones feel rain coming. Perhaps a storm." She rubbed the knuckles of her right hand. "You will stay the night."

Kenan shook his head. "There's a friendly homestead several hours south of here." He glanced out the same window. "I'll beat the rain and be sooner back to Dunscaith with Eliza."

"We should go, too," Rory said. "Ye haven't room for four horses in your stable."

Eleri's gaze darted to Morag. Their aunt nodded, and Eleri looked back to her brother. "I…Mistress Morag says she knows some exercises that can lessen the pains in my back."

"She can stay the night," Morag said. "I could teach her to prevent the twist in her spine from worsening. Come back tomorrow or the next day to fetch her."

"She also paints." Eleri pointed at some stretched canvases in the corner under a wooden shelf of clay pots and brushes. "And weaves reeds and grasses."

"'Tis not safe," Rory said.

"Please," Eleri said. "I've longed to escape Dunvegan for a bit."

"The bars I have for my door will prevent anyone from entering," Morag said. Her smile widened, showing straight teeth. "And my crows are known to peck eyes from faces."

Eleri went to Rory. "Please, brother. 'Tis an adventure, and I feel perfectly safe."

Rory looked at Jok. "Ye will stay with them tonight."

"But ye will be…alone," Jok said, glancing at Sara.

At the word, Sara's stomach flipped.

"We'll be racing back to Dunvegan," Rory said, frowning at his warrior and friend.

"And I'll smell like a pot of lavender flowers by morning," Jok said, letting out a breath. He looked at the crows who bobbed their heads down so they could look in the window. "If we manage to keep our eyes, we'll return to Dunvegan in the morn."

Rory gave Eleri a quick hug. "Take care, El."

Sara tied her cloak tightly around her neck and noticed Jok looking at her. He turned to Rory. "The weather could turn vicious."

"We'll ride faster than the storm," Rory said.

Sara opened the door, and a great wind blew into the cottage. It rustled the bunches of rosemary Morag had hanging from the beams and whipped the lavender smell about with the earthy aroma of coming rain. "Faster than the storm," she said with a huff. "I predict I'll be wet and hot tonight." Her cheeks warmed as her tongue once again moved without thought. "Hot from the frantic riding." Even that sounded impure.

Jok coughed into his fist while Rory stared at her. Morag chuckled.

Were they all thinking carnal thoughts? Only Eleri

looked unimpressed as she inspected Morag's paintings.

"Go on quickly," Morag said, shooing her out the
door. "The Flame of Dunscaith shouldn't get soaked
by rain."

The rain smell was heavy and fragrant. "The name
is a farce," Sara called back.

Morag shrugged. "Walter may have created the
name on the spot, but you'd be wise to use it to its full
advantage."

Sara hurried after Rory out of the cottage. Several
crows hunkered down under a covered perch over
Morag's well. Jok jogged over to his mount, leading it
and Eleri's spry mare to the small stable behind the
dwelling.

"Lily dislikes storms." Sara slid her hand down the
mare's neck. The horse's nostrils flared as she sniffed
the air, and her ears flitted backward.

"We could take Jok's horse back," Rory said.
"Leave Lily in Morag's stable."

"She'll become crazed and escape, fleeing across
the spongy moor until she catches her hoof and
breaks her leg. She needs to come with me to your
sturdy stables."

Sara quickly checked the girth and face straps on
the mare. "There now, Lily, let's run a race back to
Dunvegan." The horse tossed her head as if agreeing.

Hoisting herself up, Sara flung her leg over the
saddle before anyone could help her, bunching her
petticoats upward to allow the straddle. Jok spoke low
to Rory, his face etched with concern. Rory shook his
head, his features hard, and spun away, striding to
Airgid.

Rory mounted and called to Eleri. "Get inside behind the barred door." She waved and ran inside.

Sara followed as Rory surged forward to fly down the path that cut across a hard-packed moor before the forest. Sara could feel the slight tremor in Lily's body and stroked the horse's long neck whenever she tossed her head.

They rode for half an hour in a slow run next to each other, Lily's nostrils sucking in even breaths. With the dark clouds racing in, twilight was falling quickly. The mist turned to light rain, which turned into a deluge of cold water. Sara threw her hood over her head and raced, the drops hard stones against her face. Rory kept right behind Lily's flying tail.

They had almost another hour to ride. Even with their cloaks being made of fulled wool, they'd be soaked through if they continued in this windy gale toward Dunvegan. Misty clouds descended with the rain, giving an otherworldly appearance to the moors stretched out before them. The mist rose and fell with the sheets of rain as if they battled against each other.

"Sara," Rory called, and she looked back over her shoulder. He said something but all she heard was "Dun Beag Broch."

A bolt of lightning zigzagged down from the angry sky about a mile off, cutting through the clouds and rain like a blast from a vengeful Zeus in Greek mythology. Sara yelped with the deafening crack of thunder.

Lily squealed with terror, her front hooves churning upward as if fighting off the god himself. "Sweet Saint Mary!" The slippery reins yanked out of Sara's hands.

CHAPTER SIXTEEN

"Dun Beag is a wonderfully preserved Iron Age broch standing on a hillside… The broch probably stood around 10m high (roughly 33 feet). The double walls are roughly 3.5m (12 feet) thick, with a stair passage built into the thickness of the walls."

BritainExpress.com

Sara's heart leaped as she clung to her mare with arms and legs, refusing to fall off. Her hand grabbed the pommel, her other arm squeezing along Lily's damp neck. *Hold on! Hold on!* The words became a mantra through Sara's mind. If she fell from her terrified mare, she might be trampled if she didn't die immediately from a broken neck. *Hold on!*

Lily's hooves hit the muddy trail, and she took off in a wild gallop. Sara fumbled to find a good grip on the pommel, and her legs gripped the saddle as hard as she could. She threw back her hood to better see the darkening landscape that flew by as Lily ran wild across the road.

"Lily, Lily," Sara called, trying to soothe her frightened horse with a calm voice. But the lightning shooting to the ground cut through any last threads of Lily's courage, sending her racing in a rain-blind panic.

Would God strike Sara dead for not wedding Jamie, for not stopping her father's murderous plan? Should she be doing more to garner peace between their clans? *Sweet Saint Mary!* There was no time to think about God's wrath. Not with Lily frantic and the slippery reins slapping against the horse's legs.

Sara leaned forward over Lily's long neck, her fingers spread and stretching to reach the flapping thin straps of leather. Thunder grumbled like a rolling stampede, punctuated with *cracks* of violence shooting down from the heavens. The rain sliced down like small daggers, cutting across Sara's cheeks. The smell of rain and mud filled her every inhale as she clung with desperation.

"Push her east, left!" Rory's voice called from behind her. "Go left!"

Sara wiped the rain from her eyes, trying to remember the landscape before them. If Lily deviated to the right ahead, running blind onto the spongy moor, she'd break an ankle, throwing Sara and crippling her dear sweet horse.

Rory's charger surged up on Lily's right side. Any time her frantic horse veered that way, the gray nudged her back. Sara continued to stretch for the reins, but holding onto the slick saddle was becoming harder. The muscles in her thighs burned despite the cold.

Crack! Another lightning bolt cut across the sky as if it were intent on cracking the world in half. Which might be what Lily thought was happening. She neighed in a high-pitched cry, her eyes wide enough to show the whites, and veered left onto the hard-packed meadow and away from the bog. There were still hillocks that could trip her, but at least the ground was firm.

"Hold on!" Rory yelled above the wind as he

surged again beside them.

Rainwater dripped down Sara's neck to seep under her bodice. The cold met the heat from her body, clashing to send shivers racing over her skin. She squinted against the rain's assault on her eyes, making it nearly impossible to see where they were headed. A hill rose before them with some type of stone structure. A tower?

Rory's horse cut before her, and Lily neighed in fury and fright. It slowed her and gave her someone to follow. With Rory before her, Sara lay completely across Lily's neck, and her fingers caught the slippery reins. She knew better than to try to pull her frightened horse to a stop, but Sara's frantically beating heart eased with the return of some control.

Lily tossed her head but didn't surge around Rory's charger.

"Slow, Lily," Sara called, stroking her horse's rain-darkened neck.

The terrain inclined, and little by little, Rory slowed his horse, which slowed Lily. As they climbed to the top of the hill, a circular tower perched before them. Rory's charger led Lily around the curved wall that soared upward.

Brochs were tower houses that had been built long ago but were still used. This one looked intact although no light showed from the window openings cut into the thick outer walls. Flat gray slate had slid off the roof to litter the yard as they approached a wooden door.

"...inside before...thunder makes her bolt," Rory yelled over the deluge, some of his words washed away.

Lily's footing slipped in the mud, making Sara gasp. But she followed Rory's horse, stopping only when he paused before the door. Lily drew in huge inhales and shook her mane, neighing. The terror in the sound tugged at Sara's heart.

She held tightly to her reins and patted the horse's neck with thumps meant to distract her. Cold and wet as if she'd leaped into a freshwater pond, Sara fought the desperation that made her want to sob.

Rory leaped down from his horse and threw the outer bar off the door, pushing into the tower. Ducking her head, Sara strained to see inside, but a wall of darkness blotted out any light. Rory reappeared. "Follow Airgid inside," he called and led his horse in through the door, the horse bowing his head to enter.

"Sweet Saint Mary." If Lily weren't frantic, Sara would dismount and lead her in, but she was afraid the frightened horse would bolt. She pushed her heels into Lily's flanks, and the horse stepped quickly after Airgid. She quivered, neighing as she dipped her head to enter under the stone lintel. Sara flattened over Lily and still the back of her head and shoulders scraped along the stone overhead.

The space between the inner and outer wall was the length of her horse and they soon walked through to the inner circular room. 'Twas too dark to see how big it was.

"Stay on yer horse," Rory said. "She can't trample ye there. I'm lighting a fire so we can see."

"Seeing would be good," Sara said. There were no windows cut into this bottom floor even though she'd seen them higher on the outside of the outer wall.

Sara lay over Lily, using both hands to stroke her neck, sluicing water off her.

The sound of pissing overrode the wind outside. "Is that you?" Sara asked. She could also hear flint being struck and saw a spark in the inky blackness.

"I don't piss like a waterfall," he said. "'Tis Airgid."

"Lovely," she said but sent a prayer of gratitude for the shelter as thunder cracked outside again. Lily trembled like leaves flapping in a gale. "'Tis well with us," Sara soothed.

The spark of fire grew enough that Sara could see Rory's face, in a golden glow, blowing gently on a pile of dry wool cupped in his hands where the flames reached tentatively into the air.

The light showed a fire circle in the middle of the broch, and Rory strode right to it. Luckily that wasn't where Airgid had soaked the bare dirt ground. Remanent coals from old fires sat in the center, and dry wood and a pile of sticks encircled it.

"Thank God there are supplies."

"Thank me," Rory answered. "I keep the brochs equipped and from going to ruin for such a purpose."

"Storms?"

"And wolves," he answered, crouching low to set the wool in a small pile of twigs already arranged in the center of the firepit. He blew gently, feeding the tiny flame so it could grow, catching on the wood and peat squares.

Sara never ventured from Dunscaith at night when wolves roamed, hunting for a meal, and she avoided storms. For those who had no choice but to be out, the broch was a sanctuary. The fire grew, burning away the shadows, and Sara pushed upright on Lily's back. The horse's trembling subsided with the light.

The room was circular and open to the top where the wind blew around what must be a covered opening to allow the smoke out. Even with the thunder vibrating outside, the tower felt snug, impenetrable.

Rory returned from closing the outer door. "The walls are ten feet thick," he said. "There are rooms within them and a staircase. We can leave the horses here in the middle and sleep in a room above."

"Sleep?" she asked, glad he couldn't see her flush.

Rory crouched before the fire, blowing gently, feeding it with his even exhales. He tipped his face to her. "We can't go out in this."

Sara didn't say anything because Rory was right. She'd never be able to get Lily back out with the sharp thunder and sparking veins of white lightning through the sky.

Rory stood and brushed his hands together. "Jok won't say anything about us not being with them tonight. Neither will Eleri. We'll ride to them in the morning and return to Dunvegan together."

Wind lashed around the roof, catching between the layers of slate around the smoke hole to whistle mournfully. Sara pulled her sodden skirts over to one side and dismounted. She plucked at her wet bodice, her smock sticking to her damp skin. The chilled air clashed with the heat radiating from her body from the frantic ride.

Rory added more kindling he'd left piled next to the fire. The flames flickered upward, splashing light on the walls like orange and gold tendrils reaching for the pointed ceiling.

"Are provisions hidden about the place?" she

asked as she picked up a taper in a wooden holder near the doorway. She walked to the fire, crouching opposite him to light it. The hem of her wet petticoats would soon turn muddy.

"Some oatcakes in my satchel. I have two buckets tied above out windows to collect rainwater, and I have a flask of ale." He stood, taking a leather pouch from his hip to hand to her.

Sara took it, and their fingers touched briefly. The sizzle that went through her lit her body like the lethal lightning outside. She tamped the sensation down. Another rejection would make the night unbearable.

The ale was cool on her tongue, and she took two big swallows, willing the sizzle to subside.

"There should be dry blankets in the bedroom on the upper level," Rory said. He pointed to an alcove where the staircase must be hidden.

"Bedroom? Is there only one?"

His eyes were dark shadows in the low light as he looked at her. "Aye. Only one. 'Tis yours. I can sleep in a storage room or upstairs corridor."

Sara lit the lantern. She lifted her heavy petticoat and stepped into the alcove, the back dragging behind her. Darkness was so thick it seemed to seep from the stone walls encasing a narrow staircase that turned gently with the curve of the tower wall. She took a full breath and climbed, leaving below the fire, horses and their piss, and the Highlander, whom she must expel from her constant thoughts.

Her fingers slid along the rough stones that weren't plastered, although the mortar was intact and didn't crumble under her touch. The broch was sturdy, but the heavy darkness made the walls feel unstable, and Sara's pulse became a drum beat in her ears as she climbed the chiseled steps.

She reached a flat landing and followed the corridor with her lantern held aloft. Doors sat open, and the first room was empty except for a chest against a wall and a glassed window big enough to crawl through. The next two rooms were completely empty, one with a window bricked in. It felt like a tomb, so she hurried on. A room seemingly opposite the stairwell had a bed, big enough for two. She exhaled. It was better he didn't want to be intimate with her.

Ye're ugly. No man who sees ye will wed ye. Her father knew how to wield insults and expressions like a sharpened sgian dubh. She would spend the night alone in this bed, ignoring the storm that swirled in her body at the thought of Rory. 'Twas better that way.

Sara stepped inside and halted. The window was also large and open to the wind, which tore about the room, making the flame in her lantern dance despite the glass surrounding it. Something in the far corner moved, and she gasped. Sharp angles of black shadow reached upward along the stone wall, and Sara screamed.

CHAPTER SEVENTEEN

"The ancient Greeks and Egyptians described a mythical bird called the Phoenix, a magnificent creature that was a symbol of renewal and rebirth. According to legend, each Phoenix lived for 500 years, and only one Phoenix lived at a time. Just before its time was up, the Phoenix built a nest and set itself on fire. Then, a new Phoenix would rise from the ashes."

BirdNote.com

The scream above rent the stillness inside the heavy, thick walls of the tower house. Rory caught a burning stick out of the fire and surged into a run toward the stairs.

"Sara!" he yelled as he leaped up two and three steps at a time, following the curve of the wall. "Sara!" Could someone be in the tower? It had been locked from the outside when they arrived.

"Rory!"

He heard her boots clacking on the stone corridor. She ran around the curve, her face turned away as if she sought something chasing her.

Rory opened his arms at the last second as she ran into his chest. She would have bounced off him, falling into a heap of wet skirts, but he wrapped his arms around her back, holding her to him.

Despite the chill in the air, made worse by their

rain-drenched clothes, heat shot through Rory, heat he'd been denying for days because he wouldn't be tricked by another Macdonald. But Sara felt right in his arms, fitting perfectly.

"What is it?" he asked, pressing her back against the wall. He turned outward, his sword raised to the darkness pushing in on both sides of them. Anything dangerous would have to get through him and his sword before reaching Sara.

"I…I don't know," she said, her words riding the gulps of air she pulled in. "'Tis in the bedchamber in a corner. I couldn't see it, only movement of large shadows against the far wall."

"The door was barred from the outside." He'd fortified the old ben himself when he'd returned from England, thinking he might move into it once Jamie married.

"The window was open," she said, "or someone could have locked him inside."

"Him? Did he speak?"

He felt her fingers curl into his tunic. "No," she said.

Rory tried to focus on the darkness and not how her fingers gripped him as if she clasped sheets in pleasure. He cleared his throat and gave thanks for the darkness that could hide his rising cock. "It could be an animal."

"That doesn't make me feel much safer."

His mouth relaxed into a muted grin. "Ye can return down the steps to the horses, and I'll—"

"I'm staying with you," she said, and for a brief moment he let the words take on a different meaning, a more permanent meaning, and his chest opened for a moment before he slammed the door on the possibility.

I don't get close to lasses, he thought. Not since Madeline. He'd kept his oath to his father for ten years. *Father's dead.* But, once again, he was dealing with a Macdonald lass, and she was the daughter of his greatest enemy. Even if he wouldn't trust her, Rory wouldn't let anything harm Sara.

Rory threw his flaming stick into a holder attached to the wall and grabbed Sara's hand. She clutched his hand back as if it were a normal action.

Holding his sword out before them, they moved together down the corridor to the bedchamber door where she'd left her lantern. Sara bent, picking it up, and they entered the room. Rory's shadow slid across the walls with the lantern's illumination from behind, making him look giant. He'd used the same technique to make shadow stories for Eleri on the nursery walls when she was young.

"Show yerself," Rory said, his voice booming out without forewarning.

Sara bumped into his back. "Sweet Mother Mary."

"Friend or foe?" Rory called. Silence. "Which corner?" He kept his gaze sliding along the walls around the room.

"The far left. By the wooden trunk."

Rory continued to scan the entire black space. Sara came up beside him, holding the lantern high. Then he saw it.

A pointed shadow moved along the wall, the tip bobbing slightly. "Let me hold the light higher," he said, and Sara gave him the handle. The higher light made the sharp shadow diminish down the wall, and he walked toward the trunk.

Blinking, its bill turned toward him, the beast spread its wide wingspan. The orange and red flame reflected against the paleness of its feathers as the wings extended, perhaps to look as large as possible against a predator.

"A phoenix," Sara said.

With the bright coloring from the flames in the absence of all other light, the creature certainly looked like the mythological bird that burned and was born again from the ashes.

"A heron," Rory said, lowering the lantern. "And a frightened one at that."

The large bird flapped its angular wings, becoming as large as it could.

"She must have come in through the window to evade the storm winds," Rory said.

"A she? You think it's female."

He looked down at her. "The only phoenix I know is a lass."

Confusion on her features smoothed, and he watched the gentle upturn of her lips. The simple gesture relaxed his gut. "I'm not a phoenix rising from the ashes," she said.

"Och lass, but ye just might be." Their gazes held as he regarded the woman before him. Soaked through, her hair plastered to the sides of her head, cold and abandoned by her father, Sara still exuded strength as if nothing could keep her from rising again.

The creature flapped its wings, and Rory returned his sword to its sheath. "She's frightened of the storm."

"And us." Sara sighed. "Poor animal. This wind is full of vile strength," she said, her voice soft and empathetic. As if to prove its lethality, thunder cracked a second after a lightning bolt illuminated the night outside the window. Sara shook her head. "'Tis dangerous for bird, horse, or human tonight." The heron slowly lowered its wings, pulling them back in against its slender body as if responding to her calm voice.

Rory's stomach grumbled, and Sara cast him a reproving look. "Don't sound hungry in front of her," she said. The flame cast a golden glow over Sara's features. Bloody hell, she was lovely.

"I'll stop sounding hungry when a roast or basket of apples and tarts flies through that broken window."

"We aren't eating her."

Rory chuckled. "Our phoenix here has a champion." He nodded to Sara. "She's safe tonight, from the storm and my gullet."

"Let's leave her be." She pulled Rory to follow her out of the room. "The horses need to be untacked."

He held the lantern high as they descended, and he listened to her boots hit each step. "Ye're a brave woman," Rory said when they reached the bottom.

"I screamed and ran from a bird."

"But once ye start to defend something—Eleri, Gus, yer frantic horse, and the phoenix—ye become a warrior."

"There's no such thing as a phoenix," she said in answer to his compliment. She didn't take praise well. Maybe she wasn't used to receiving any.

Rory set the lantern down and dodged around a pile of fresh horse dung to reach the fire. He pulled his tunic off over his head and set it to dry by the flames before going to his mount. "'Tis a better story to say it was a phoenix seeking protection from the Flame of Dunscaith, Seraphina. Instead of a heron who sought a way out of the rain."

Sara stroked her horse's face as she unbuckled the thin straps there. "First off, there will be no story told to anyone."

"Eleri would love this adventure. Would ye deprive a child from a great tale?"

"Bloody hell, Rory. You don't want people to think we've…that we're…"

"Eleri won't tell anyone, and she won't think that we acted improper."

Sara watched him. "What will Jok think?"

So, she'd caught the warning Jok had tried to bludgeon him with before they left Morag's. Jok remembered the disaster that befell Rory the last time he'd trusted a lass, a Macdonald lass at that. And his friend had sworn he wouldn't let Rory do it again. Even ten years later, Jok was taking his oath seriously.

"I'll tell him about yer horse bolting," Rory said. Jok would never betray him.

She crossed her arms. "He doesn't like me. Why?"

Jok had made his opinion clear as they were leaving Morag's. *Jamie banished her. To calm the people and prevent the Macdonalds from attacking, saying we've taken their lady, she needs to go. Do not let a woman ruin ye again, Rory. Winnie swears that Sara's a spy, and the villagers agree with her.*

"'Tis complicated," Rory said to Sara, "but Jok's loyal to me. He'll think better of this situation if we tell him about your phoenix."

"Very well," she said, her hands finding her hips,

"we can tell Eleri a large heron took refuge with us from the storm, and we thought it looked like a phoenix."

"And that it came for protection from the Flame of Dunscaith."

She stepped to the side to lift the stirrup over the saddle and unbuckled the girth strap. "I am not a flame of anything."

"Then Seraphina, a fiery angel."

"And I'm certainly no angel."

She looked like an angel or a fiery goddess with her long, flowing waves of auburn hair and large blue eyes. When they were in the sunlight, they had flecks of gold in them, almost making them appear green. And they usually looked serious and watchful as if humankind was unpredictable and always treacherous. She was a goddess on guard.

And possibly a Macdonald spy.

He watched Sara struggle to pull off her saddle, but she managed and walked with it, clutched before her. He carried his own saddle over to the table along the far wall.

"I think the name Seraphina suits ye," he said. "Ye have fire and courage, strength and compassion like an angel."

"I…" Her gently arched brows pinched together but then she looked away, breaking whatever tether had held them. "I'm an ordinary woman."

"Ye saved us from the fire even against yer father's plans, even when ye've likely been raised to believe MacLeods deserve the fires of Hell."

She brushed her hands together to rid them of dirt. "As a child, I was told MacLeods drown kittens, puppies, and infants."

Annoyance tightened his face. "I'm fairly sure even Jamie hasn't drowned any newborn bairns."

"As I grew, I was told MacLeods steal and kill without provocation," she said.

They stared at one another across the glow of the lantern, darkness around them giving the area an otherworldly feel. "And did ye believe what ye were told?"

She searched his eyes. "No."

Rory tipped his head, his shoulders relaxing. "Ye're clever."

Her brow rose. "Actions are to be believed, not words, especially not words from my father's foul mouth."

"Beautiful, kind, and clever." The words fell from his lips before he caught them.

She blinked. "And yet you haven't spoken to me since…the night of the garden. Since you made it clear you can find no pleasure with me."

His face snapped to her, his mouth dropping open. "What?"

She waved her hand. "But there's no need to punish me further by barely talking to me. It makes everything more difficult."

"I'm not punishing ye."

"No? Then you're worried perhaps that I will…try to kiss you if you talk to me?"

"Ye don't worry me."

They both leaned against the table in the low light of the fire in the middle of the room. The horses munched on oats he'd left in buckets for them. Thunder still boomed outside, but his gaze remained on her lips.

"Then why the avoidance for two days?" she asked. "The silence on the ride to Morag's?"

Rory rubbed a hand down his face; the weight of his determination, like a bag of grain around his shoulders, was slipping. "My strength is waning."

She poked a finger into his bicep. "Your strength is intact."

He exhaled. "I mean my resistance to ye." He adjusted his cock beneath his wet plaid and turned to her.

"Your resistance," she repeated. "As if I'm a corpulent tyrant English king who has bargained to release you if you'll give in and swear your fealty to me."

"Bloody hell, Sara." His hands lifted to settle at the back of his head. "I dream about ye…"

"Dream?"

"Aye."

"About casting me away, throwing me in a burning church, or—"

"Nay." The word cut in like a bark from a vicious dog. The silence stretched. Only the crunch of the horses and a swish of their tails broke the silence.

"I dream about you, too," she said. Her soft words thundered like the lightning outside, vibrating through him.

"About punching me?"

A slight smile curved her mouth. "Not exactly." She pushed herself up onto the low table to sit, reminding him of a carefree lass at a festival, her legs swinging. "Tell me about your dream and I'll share mine."

Thunder rumbled around them, their cave of darkness blocking out the world, blocking out his oaths. As he looked at her, the beauty of her open expression pulled at him. He drew in a big breath, and it seemed to push honest words from his mouth. "I dream about ye thrashing in pleasure as I...taste ye." He kept his eyes on hers. She didn't even blink. "About us rutting together in a meadow, me behind ye, yer luscious breasts hanging before ye."

Her lips parted as he spoke. "I dream of ramming into yer wet heat from every angle and ye holding my cock between yer lips. And those dreams bombard me while I'm awake. I can hardly think of anything else, and every touch ye inflict on me makes the chains holding me back weaken."

CHAPTER EIGHTEEN

"I never see thy face but I think upon hell-fire. These
violent delights have violent ends and in their
triumph die, like fire and powder
Which, as they kiss, consume."

William Shakespeare, Romeo and Juliet

Rory's words coiled through Sara, pushing her fear of
rejection underneath to be trampled like in a wild
stampede. All concerns about her marks were forgotten there in the dark, the world shut out. The tempest
beating at their shelter was a mirror to the tempest
swirling within her. Only the heat, the pooling ache,
mattered.

"Show me these dreams, Rory," she said. "Make
me thrash."

His nostrils flared as he sucked in a full breath. He
looked like a chained beast, his honor keeping him
back.

Heart hammering, Sara slid off the table to stand
before him. "Teach me to rut with you in those ways
and to taste you."

"Sara," he groaned.

She lifted his fisted hand and worked the fingers
open, laying his palm over her thudding heart. Only
the passion in his intense gaze kept her brazen. She
slid his palm down from her heart to her breast. She
wanted him too much to care about propriety.

With a groan much like a growl, his mouth dropped to hers, capturing her words and lips. Tunic off, Sara's hands rose to clasp his wide shoulders, stroking down to his granite biceps. Her mouth opened under his, and their kiss turned wild, burning away the rest of the world.

She shivered, and Rory broke the kiss, pulling her to stand before the fire. "Ye need to be rid of these wet clothes," he said. She agreed but worry about him seeing her sent an icicle through her heat. But he wouldn't see her mark in the inky darkness.

Slowly, she wriggled out of the jacket and began to unlace the ties of her bodice. Rory kissed her again, his fingers replacing hers as he tugged her bodice open. She lost herself in the warmth of his kiss, the damp smell of him from the rain and the spice that was uniquely Rory. The ties of her petticoats loosened, and she felt the wet layers fall away. Rain heavy, they thumped on the ground, pooled around her feet. He broke the kiss to lift her out of them to set her on a flat rock embedded in the dirt right before the fire. He snatched up her clothes, laying them over the table to dry.

The muscles of his bare back moved with reserved strength under the scars from his time at Carlisle. Seeing them made her blink past an ache in her eyes. Perhaps…he might understand her own marks, her shame.

When he turned back, he paused, taking her in before the fire. The light shone around her, warming her back nearly to burning. Her fingers rose, and she plucked the ties of her stays, loosening them until the contraption slid down her hips to the dirt floor.

"Ye're lovely, lass," he said, staring at her.

She worked off her soaked boots and then slowly untied the bow at the top of her smock to widen the neckline. Sara lowered the edge of the smock until her breasts came out into view, her nipples like rosy pebbles in the light of the fire. The chill of the room and Rory's ravenous look made them pearl tighter, and her hand rose to cup one, lifting it.

Rory murmured low, something that sounded like reverence, and quickly unbuckled the belt holding his wrap around his narrow hips. The pleated fabric dropped to the dirt floor. The fire shone on his glorious body, his powerful erection against his abdomen. Lines cut like a *V* across his lower abdomen under the ridges of stomach muscles as if pointing to the base of his cock. He was glorious.

He moved to stand before her and cupped her cheeks. "I want ye with every ounce of my blood, lass. But one word from ye, and I'll step away."

"I only want you to step closer," she said. Her words were meant to tease, but the emotions running through Sara were too intense for anything light. Wind and rain slashed about the tower as if trying to get inside to them. She could barely hear it over the thudding of her heart.

He lowered back to her lips, kissing her with such intensity, Sara felt the inferno inside her sliding down to her abdomen and between her legs. He kissed a path along her jaw to her ear. "Ye are fire, Sara," he said.

"And I'm burning for you, Rory." Her hands sloped down his back to his naked arse, making him groan low, a vibration coming up from deep within him like a crypt being wedged open.

Behind her, Lily snorted, reminding Sara that they were down with the horses. She must have stiffened because Rory cursed. Without a word, he picked Sara up. Her smock was around her waist as he traipsed across the dirt floor, leaving the fire behind as he climbed with her up the stone steps to the rooms above.

Blood surged through Rory as he strode with Sara along the upstairs corridor lit by a single torch he'd left up in a sconce. He paused, unsure where to go. The comfortable bed with the bird or into a dark room without a bed?

"Daingead," he said, striding into an empty room. He set Sara's stockinged feet down. "I'll be right back."

• • •

Naked, Rory ran out of the room and into the bed-chamber. The bird in the corner startled, its wings flapping. Ignoring it, his muscles bunched as he yanked the heavy down tick off the bed and dragged it along the floor, its blankets still hanging onto it.

He pulled it through the door of the other room. "Sara?" he said, unable to see her in the shadows. The sconce flickered in the corridor, its light barely reaching inside.

"I'm here," she said.

He dropped the mattress near the glass-paned window. Lightning lit the room, and he saw Sara standing for a second, but the image would be etched into his mind forever. Naked except for her tall, gartered stockings, her body had been lit with silver light. She was curved and soft, her breasts full and her hips flared. Her hair was drying into waves that reached down to her hips.

A carnal fire washed through him, and he strode to her, taking Sara into his arms. "Ye're cold." He pressed her against his warm body.

"Only on the outside."

He wrapped around her, feeling her stomach slide against his stiff cock. He groaned, keeping her before him as he guided them to the mattress on the floor. "Privacy and comfort," he said as they tumbled into the sheets and blankets that he'd left the last time he'd been there.

She turned immediately into him, her leg hitching over his hip to bring the crux of her legs against him. "Mon diah," he said, lifting under her round arse to slide her along his length. She moaned, and he knew he'd found her sensitive nub.

"I ache," she said, moving along his leg.

A brilliant flash of lightning from the window lit Sara's face, her eyes half open and her lips parted as if she already felt ecstasy.

"Ye're exquisite." He pushed her back into the soft mattress, his hand sliding down the length of her body. His fingers moved between her shifting legs, and she thrust toward them. He moved over her mound, lower until he found the wet heat he was hunting, sliding in as she moaned. Fingers exploring and stroking, he listened in the darkness as her breathing quickened. She moved with his hand as if they were mating, and his cock throbbed, begging to replace his fingers.

She was an angel, a goddess, and his gaze fastened

onto the lovely face he could make out in the dark. Lightning struck outside, a crack that lit the room. Her head was thrown back, exposing her long pale neck, and he froze as the image of a dark slash seemed to cross it.

"Nay." He pulled his hand from her heat.

"No," she said on a gasp.

He hugged her to him, taking in big inhales to wrestle control back from the lusting fire burning away his thoughts. "Sara, lass. I cannot… I made a vow."

Her breathing was as labored as his. "A vow? Like a priest?"

"A vow to look out for my clan above all else."

"And lying with me would jeopardize your vow?"

"Something like that." *Fok! I can just bed her. It doesn't have to mean anything.*

"I don't understand."

His thumb found her cheek in the dark and slid across it. "I can't think straight lying naked in the dark with ye."

"Then don't think. Feel."

Rory jerked when he felt her cool fingers wrap around his straining cock. The sensation was an added spark to the inferno already smoldering within him. Vows turned to ash as her hand moved up and down his length, clasping him like her body would. But he craved the warmth of her inside.

"Do you like that?"

With a lamenting groan, he threw off the shackles of his conscience and leaned down, kissing her open mouth. The smell of Sara, the heat of her against him, the smooth feel of her skin… He only wanted to revel in it.

"Feel how wet I am," she rasped against his mouth as she continued to stroke him with one hand.

He dipped his face to her nipple, sucking it into his hungry mouth, his teeth grazing the peak. She moaned loudly as if unafraid for anyone to hear. There was no one there to hear, to judge him, to haunt him. His hand moved back to her mound, only to find her own fingers there, rubbing the outside.

"Aye, lass," he groaned as he imagined the sight of her pleasuring herself. He'd make sure to watch her when they had light. His fingers entered her again, and she whimpered, her body clenching around him.

Thunder boomed, imitating his throbbing. He wanted to make her as frenzied as him, so he continued to suckle and nibble her breasts while he worked her flesh inside. Rising back to her panting mouth, he kissed her and whispered, "I want to taste yer heat."

"My heat," she breathed.

Rory moved his knee between her legs. He almost spilled himself right there, and he took a few breaths to rein in control.

He moved down the bed, hovering over Sara's shifting body. In the low light he could see her fingers moving over her crux. Kissing a path up her soft inner thighs, Rory inhaled the musk of her woman's scent. "Aye." He dipped in to taste her. She gasped above him in the dark as he loved her with his mouth, and then his fingers. Rory lost his mind to the animal part of him, smelling her desire, listening to her moans.

Her fingers wrapped in his hair, and he imagined the picture she must present with her head thrown back against the pillows as he loved her. "Oh God, yes!" she yelled, and he felt her core contract around his fingers.

Before any other thoughts could overtake him, he slid up her body. He lifted under her sweet arse, spreading her wide. She was so open to him, and he pressed the head of his cock to her heat. She gasped as he thrust into her.

He groaned at the wet heat surrounding him, reveling in the feel of her tight body still clenching from her first release. He braced his arms around her head. Breathing heavily, he kissed her jawline over to her ear. "Does it…hurt?" he asked, willing himself to remain still, holding her there imprisoned in his embrace, impaled into the bed. He'd never taken a virgin before.

"No." She pushed her pelvis against him and reached around to squeeze his arse as she ground into him. He withdrew, thrusting back into her willing body. She cried out with open-mouthed pleasure, loudly enough to be heard over the thunder. In and out, he thrust. Her fingernails, scoring his back, added more spark to the blazing fire within him.

Her moans grew louder until once again he felt her fly apart. With another deep growl, he joined her over the edge of reason, spilling within her.

CHAPTER NINETEEN

"Love is a smoke made with the fume of sighs."

William Shakespeare

Sara stared at the man sleeping beside her. He hadn't moved when she'd crept from the bed to use the privy and retrieve a bladder of drink. She was back with him, naked under the blanket, and let her fingers slide along her own form.

It was the same body she'd had since she'd become a woman, but somehow it felt more sensitive, as if it craved more nibbles and heated kisses. No wonder the maids at Dunscaith talked nonstop about passion.

The shadows retreated from the pre-dawn light, and she could make out more of Rory's features. He breathed evenly, but his brow pinched as if he were dreaming of misadventure instead of tupping her. It didn't mar his handsome face, though. Watching his parted lips made her remember where he'd put them on her, how they'd driven her wild with lust, kissing and licking and nibbling her flesh.

She cupped and squeezed her breast, gently pinching her own nipple as she watched Rory sleep. He faced her with one arm raised over his head, the large muscles in his bicep relaxed. He must train daily to keep his body ready for war. He was the Lion of Skye, renowned for his battle fortitude. The small nicks along his broad chest gave testament that he'd seen many battles, probably half of them against the Macdonald Clan.

I made a vow. What type of vow would stop him from doing what he did with her last night? He was no priest. He wasn't married to someone else. When she'd asked the kitchen maids at Dunvegan about Rory, they hadn't said he was celibate. Rory MacLeod was more than able to bring molten pleasure to a woman.

Sara's legs shifted at the ache building once again, and she reached down under the blanket to touch her sensitive spot. She wasn't ashamed of feeling passion. Aunt Morag had told her about the pleasures of the flesh years ago. Morag told her to find the spots on her body that felt good and kindled passion. They were built into a woman to compensate for monthly bleeding and the pains of childbirth. Apparently, Rory knew all about these pleasure spots, too.

Sara continued to touch herself, and her blood quickened. Her gaze roamed over Rory's muscular chest, light brown and blond hair lying across it so different from her smooth skin. Rory MacLeod was all man, sturdy, powerful, and built to protect. Built to love a woman. *Built to love me.*

She tugged gently at the blanket, releasing her breasts from the top to lie along the edge. She continued the circular rub between her legs, feeling the restless energy stoke higher. Her lips parted with her breathing. Would she bring herself to her release right there before him? The thought was scandalous, which made it even more thrilling.

Rory's breathing changed, and his lips closed, opening again as his eyelids rose. He stared at her face, and then his gaze dropped to her breasts. The nipples were hard, and Sara imagined him taking one rosy peak into his mouth.

"Sara?" he said, rising onto one of his elbows. He ran a large hand through his hair, staring between her face and her perched breasts. "Ye are a bloody siren," he said, and his mouth relaxed into a smile.

"I'm either a siren or a phoenix," she said, her words light with teasing. "I can't be more than one mythical creature."

"Oh, I think ye're both." He leaned toward her, kissing her gently before backing up to study her eyes. "To make me forget about everything but this heat between us." His words were a mix of teasing and something a bit darker. Regret? It couldn't be regret.

She pushed the blanket down her body while she reclined on one side, keeping her back turned away from him. In the harsh light of day, she wasn't ready to let him see her back.

Sara set her hand on her breast, pinching the nipple before sliding serpentine down between them, over the gentle swell of her stomach to the curls between her legs. The flush of heat, from his gaze and from her audacity, infused her face, but she kept going. Parting her legs, she let him see her touch herself, knowing how damp and ready she was.

"I ache again for you."

"Good Lord." He moved toward her. The first touch of his hands on her skin made the fire within her surge. The blanket shifted down past his narrow hips, and his jack stood up proud and powerful like last night.

Her hand wrapped around it, and he groaned. The

sound and sight sizzled through her, making her shiver in anticipation. She inhaled through her nose, pushing against his shoulder so that he sank back into the downy mattress, and she followed him. Straddling him brought the open crux of her legs in contact with the base of his shaft, him completely under her.

"Dia math," he rasped out, his hands clutching her hip bones as she sat upon him, her breasts revealed in the dawn, her hair draping over her shoulders. "Ye're wet already." His words caused more flames of pleasure reaching up within her, consuming her.

She moved against him. "I was thinking about this before you woke."

He reached forward to rub across her aching nub, and she lifted her breasts in her own hands, plucking at her nipples and feeling the zing stretch taut through her.

Sara leaned over him, letting her red-gold hair fall around his face like curtains. She flattened upon his hard body and kissed him, slanting her mouth against his. She rubbed him with her body below, and he growled into her mouth. His hands explored her back. Could he feel the slightly raised marks? Her birthmark didn't hurt. For a moment, she thought he was tracing it, but then his fingers slid lower to press into her bare arse, helping her find a rhythm against him. He wasn't inside her, but the pleasure built so fast from that simple act that all thoughts of what should happen gave way to primal instinct.

He reached around and below to touch her nether lips from behind. "Exquisite," Rory said against her ear as she slid back slightly onto his fingers, a gasp coming from her. "Ye are hot, lass, like molten honey."

She spread her legs so that her knees fell open on either side of him, letting him explore her. Rory drew one of her peaked breasts into his mouth. The suction tore through Sara, and she moaned.

"Aye, Sara," Rory said as he raised his lips back to hers. "Take yer pleasure." He helped her rock faster along him, his hands on her hips as she ground against him, building the intensity.

Sensation pulsed in Sara, rising higher. When he pulled the other nipple into his mouth, it was enough to make her soar over the edge, and she moaned deeply, her eyes squeezed shut as waves of hot pleasure snapped through her like wildfire.

He rolled them over, so she lay on her back. Rory's hands found her legs spread. He set her heels on each of his massive shoulders. Then he plunged inside her, stretching her, piercing her with sensation. Even her toes flexed where they bobbed in the air as they perched.

With a growl that filled the room, he pulled out and plunged back into her. "Oh God, yes!" Sara answered. Leaning over her, his arms flanking her face, Rory kissed her, their mouths wild against one another.

He set a fast and deep rhythm, and her limbs became weak as she met his thrusts. She was completely malleable to whatever he wanted to do to her. *Trust*, she realized, as she gave herself over to Rory completely. She trusted him.

"Yes," she breathed.

He increased the speed of his thrusts while he rubbed against her. All of Sara's senses were awash in Rory. His smell and heat and taste, the feel of his hands stroking her, and the sight of him laboring over her with beast-like intensity. It was savage and full of sizzle.

They grew higher, and he increased his pace. Shivers of lust and heat spiraled up and down inside Sara until she felt the edge once more.

"Oh God!" she yelled out, feeling her pleasure overtake her.

"Aye, lass," Rory rasped, joining her, filling her once again.

For long minutes they moved together, their bodies riding the waves of pleasure until they began to ebb. Sara tried to inhale, but the weight of Rory made it difficult. He must have noticed, because he wrapped his arms around her, capturing her legs with his to roll them over to their sides.

They lay face to face, legs entangled. Sara took a full breath, raising her hand to cup Rory's stubbled cheek. She looked directly into his eyes, studying the darker flecks in his golden-brown irises. She opened her damp lips to say something but couldn't think coherently yet.

He traced a finger along the curve of her hip and slid it around to her back. It took her a moment to realize he was stroking her mark. They stared at one another, and her heart picked up speed again.

"'Tis nothing," she said. "Something from birth. It doesn't spread to anyone like a sickness."

"Can I see?" He leaned forward and kissed her mouth before pulling back. "I've seen all other parts of ye."

Her cheeks warmed. "I...I would not sully the morning with my ugliness."

His brows pinched. "I have scars from being flayed open on my back, Sara. Do ye think less of me for them?"

"Of course not, but I don't want...I would not have our time ruined."

Only a man bound to ye by God through marriage would risk touching ye. Despite Morag's insistence that Sara's marks were not contagious and didn't make her ugly, somehow the words of her father resounded in Sara's mind. They plagued her along with his disgusted look when he'd made her mother strip her down as a child, inspecting her before he sought a marriage alliance with her.

Even though she'd been young, perhaps ten years old, her parents' argument about the red marks across her back had made it clear that she would never be desirable, making her useless to her father. He'd married her off to the MacLeods anyway, not caring how hurtful her new husband's rejection would be to her.

Sara's stomach tensed as he waited, but then he grinned. "No matter," he said, kissing her again. He held her face as he spoke. "I know every inch of ye is beautiful, Sara."

It wasn't true, but the man was too honorable to force her to show him. Weakness from relief made her sink into the pillows.

He rolled off his side of the bed, and she watched his muscles flex as he stretched. "I'll check on yer friend." He walked out of the room, and she was struck again at how beautiful his body was, even with the scars across his back. But they were different, inflicted upon him. She'd been born imperfect.

He came back in, his cock heavy but relaxed. "She

has flown away."

"Probably once the storm let up," she said, pulling the blanket up over her body and pushing out of the rumpled nest they'd made on the floor. In the daylight now flooding the room, Sara felt vulnerable and hurried over to her discarded smock.

Rory looked out the window. "We should return to Morag to get Eleri."

"To intercept them so we can return together?"

He turned back to her, and she looked pointedly down his sculpted body. "Probably not like that."

He glanced down and then rubbed his temporarily sated cock, lifting his gaze to grin at her. "I'll get our clothes from below." His gaze dropped to the sheet she held around her.

A smear of red showed proof of her taken virginity. It was like a flag of surrender, surrender to lust and pleasure.

"I'm…" She began to apologize but stopped. "Should I wash them?"

He walked over to her and pulled her gently into his arms. "Ye honor me, Sara. Leave them here. I'll bring fresh linens another time. No one comes here but me."

She nodded against his chest and stood back. "We better go if we want to reach Morag's before they depart. She'll insist on cooking them food before they leave."

"Then we have a chance." Worry tightened his face. Perhaps she had indeed read regret in it before. He said he would never trust anyone, especially a Macdonald. There was some history she didn't know about. Had this woman, Madeline, made him distrust all women? As possible repercussions and reality broke through the haze of their time in each other's arms, Sara wondered if Rory would regret what they'd done. Sara would never, but *she* hadn't broken a vow.

• • •

Rory couldn't help but watch the way Sara's red-gold hair waved out behind her as she galloped up the path. 'Twas like a cloth of shining silk when the sun glinted upon it. And he'd stroked it, inhaled it, fisted it in his clenched hands as he lost himself in the heat of her body. Would she regret losing her maidenhead to him?

The thought soured the memory, and he pushed it aside. No man would set her aside because she wasn't a virgin, no man worthy of her. But that soured in his gut, too.

I'll marry her. The thought thundered through Rory. *Bloody hell.* If riding wasn't as easy to him as breathing, he might have fallen off Airgid. Marry his brother's almost-wife? A Macdonald that Jok and most of his clan worried was another Macdonald spy?

Jamie would rage against the idea of his brother marrying Sara, someone he considered a traitor. He'd remind Rory of his vow to his father, to his clan, that he would never endanger them again. Would marrying Sara endanger Clan MacLeod? Jamie had sought her hand.

Sara glanced back over her shoulder, and a smile played upon her lush lips. Och, but he wanted to kiss her again, kiss her right there on the moor. He would have kept her locked away in his tower all day, slowly convincing her to reveal her back to him. He'd felt the raised skin. It seemed serpentine across her lovely straight back. If it had been a scar, he'd find the bastard who'd hurt her. But it was a birthmark, one that she worried over. He'd watched the stiffness overtake her when they'd briefly talked about it.

Rory nudged Airgid to speed ahead, coming up next to Sara on the wide path. Together, they slowed to a walk as they saw Morag's cottage in the distance, smoke rising from the hole in the thatched roof. Jok's and Eleri's horses were tethered out front as if they were preparing to leave.

"What do we tell them?"

"That we took refuge at Dun Beag Broch with a phoenix and two horses who shite all over the inside. Between the smell, the flapping bird, and the wind and thunder coming through the broken windows, we got little sleep and need sustenance and comfortable beds."

She laughed. "Very unromantic."

"And ye slept in the bed and me on the floor in another room." He would cut off any of Jok's questions with the lie before he could utter them.

Sara nodded, exhaling. The lass didn't look like she liked to lie, either. She couldn't be one of Walter Macdonald's spies, no matter what blood rushed through her veins.

Dismounting, Rory strode around Airgid to lift Sara down. He knew she could dismount on her own, but he wanted to touch her again. His hands clasped around her waist, and it just felt…right.

She stared into his eyes as he lowered her before him. Hers were blue, the type of blue that reminded him of warm summer days with dark flecks in them like wildflower seeds.

"Rory!" Eleri's voice came from the opened door. "Thank God on high." She ran out of the door and into Rory as Sara backed up. "I feared…"

Rory hugged his sister, feeling the familiar hump in her back. His gaze dropped to the ground. The mud was churned up as if many horses had recently traipsed there. His body tensed. "Who came here?"

Jok strode outside, and Rory could see Morag sweeping her floor within. "Brodrick," Jok said, "and six MacLeods sent by Jamie." Jok's narrowed gaze fell on Sara.

"Why?" Sara asked, striding to the door. "Bloody hell!" she yelled. "They ransacked your home!"

Rory dropped his arms from Eleri but kept her hand as they hurried after Sara inside. It looked as if the storm, or at least the great wind, had torn through the two-room house, turning things upside down. Bedding, including the tick filled with straw, had been thrown upon the floor. Clothes were tossed from chests and the one wardrobe. Crates of unwashed wool were scattered about, their contents lying in puffs of dirty white and black across the crisscrossed ropes of the bed and the table in the back room.

Rory turned to Jok. "They were looking for something."

"Something small?" Sara asked, righting the wooden box that held Morag's paper, quill, and ink. A leather bag of lavender flowers was upturned, fragrant buds all over the table.

"The flag," Jok said.

"Wee shites, all of them," Morag muttered.

Sara looked between Jok and Morag. "What flag?"

"My flag," Eleri said, her cheeks red, "the one I guard in my room at Dunvegan."

Rory felt her words like a punch, all breath leaving him at once.

Eleri turned tear-filled eyes to Rory. "Someone took the Fairy Flag. Jamie says it was Sara."

Rory struggled to swallow. He felt Jok's gaze shredding along his chest as he stared at him and then at Sara as if he could tell that they'd tupped, more than tupped. They'd explored nearly every part of each other, teasing out moans and gasps and delicious, wicked words.

"Sara does not have the flag," Rory said, staring back at Jok.

Jok looked at Sara. "Did ye hide it somewhere? Around Dunvegan? Or hand it off to someone else?"

"Neither!" she blurted out, her eyes flashing with anger. "Why would I do that?"

"To give to yer father," Jok said.

"I despise my father."

"But ye love yer clan," Jok continued.

Memories of a similar inquisition ten years ago pulsed within Rory's mind with every hard thump of his heart. Dunvegan searched, the castle and the village turned upside down with it. The flag being found in a cottage Rory knew well, where he'd lain with his first woman, Madeline, the woman he thought loved him.

He remembered his father pointing a finger in the face of the woman who had taught a young Rory about physical pleasure. But Madeline Sinclair had been a Macdonald spy, her mission at Dunvegan to steal the Fairy Flag for Walter Macdonald.

CHAPTER TWENTY

"There is a tradition that should the MacLeods be in
peril in battle they can unfurl the Fairy Flag and they
will then be invincible. But the magic will only work
three times, and it has been used twice in the past."

Historic-uk.com

The Fairy Flag was the most powerful weapon on
Skye, perhaps in all of Scotland. For generations, the
kings of Scotland had demanded it from the Macleods
of Skye, but it had never left their clan. 'Twas said that
the ancient cloth could be unfurled and flown over
battles to ensure victory, but only three times before
the magic was depleted. It had been used twice before
to save the MacLeods. Afterward, it was secreted
away to some safe place under guard at Dunvegan
Castle.

"I did not take the Fairy Flag anywhere," Sara
said, each word succinct.

Morag sniffed indignantly. "That blaigeard, Jamie
MacLeod, sent his men to tear my place apart."

"And they didn't find it?" Rory asked, glancing at
Sara.

By the devil! He thought she'd stolen it. Sara shot
him a frown, her ire instantly flaring high within her.
"I didn't take it from Dunvegan. I haven't even
seen…" She pursed her lips, stopping the easy lie. "I
saw it under Eleri's bed in a box when I was hunting

for her paints."

"Is it my fault 'tis gone?" Eleri asked, sitting on the edge of a righted chair.

"Nay," Rory said. "Ye keep yer door locked. And ye haven't told anyone about it?"

Eleri shook her head, giving Sara a worried glance.

"Brodrick said ye didn't return last night to Dunvegan." Jok's red brows rose as he looked between Sara and Rory.

"The storm made Lady Sara's horse bolt," Rory said. "We had to take refuge at Dun Beag Broch."

"With a phoenix and frightened horses fouling the floor," Sara added. Sara looked at Rory, as if silently nudging him to lie about their sleeping arrangements, but he said nothing.

"A real phoenix?" Eleri asked, clutching her hands together, her eyes wide. "Was it burning up to be reborn from the ashes?"

"Phoenixes are myth," Jok said, a pinch in his brow.

"'Twas a gray heron that happened to look red in the light from a lantern," Rory said, pushing his fist against the pain that had started in his forehead.

Jok looked back at Sara. "Is the Fairy Flag at Dun Beag Broch?"

"I haven't seen it outside Eleri's room," Sara replied with a glare.

She sat down in another righted chair next to Eleri, pulling her long hair to one side.

"You're hurt," Morag said, coming up to her swiftly, her fingers going to Sara's neck.

Holy Sweet Mother Mary! Had Rory left a bite mark on her neck? "'Tis nothing," Sara said, trying to pull her hair back across it.

"A bruise of some sort," Morag said, and Sara could hear the question in her voice. But she spun around. "I have a poultice for that," Morag said, leaving her to find it across the upended room.

"A bruise?" Jok said. "On her neck?" His words held accusation, and Sara saw him looking at Rory.

A small hand slid over Sara's on the table, and Sara looked up to meet Eleri's concerned eyes. The trust and sympathy Sara saw there made her own eyes tear, and she blinked to clear the watery sight.

"It will be found," Eleri said. "Don't worry."

"Brodrick is out looking for us?" Rory asked from near the door. His hand clasped the back of his skull. "And he knows we weren't here last night?"

"We should go back to Dunvegan," Jok said.

"If Jamie MacLeod thinks Sara stole his Fairy Flag," Morag pointed a finger at her, "he will throw her in the pit."

"The pit with the icy water in the bottom?" Sara asked but everyone talked over her.

"If she stays here," Rory countered, "his warriors will find her."

"Are they not loyal to you?" Morag asked, her brow raised.

"I've trained them, but they spoke oaths to my father and Jamie."

"I could run," Sara said, not liking to be spoken of as if she weren't in the room and responsible for her own actions. "But then I'll look like a thief." She stood, crossing her arms, and paced the littered floor. "I'll go back to Dunvegan and tell the truth that I don't have this lost flag."

"Stolen," Jok said, tipping his head. "Not lost. 'Twas locked in a box under Lady Eleri's bed. The box is gone."

Sara threw her hands wide. "Where on me do I have a box or a flag?" She dropped her arms and flipped up the hem of her skirt to show her underpetticoat. "Nowhere. And Rory, you can give proof you haven't seen me with either."

Rory's gaze slid to her, and what she saw hit her like a thunderbolt. Suspicion. He wasn't sure. Did he think she'd seduced him last night to distract him from her true purpose? Her breaths were shallow, her cheeks growing red, as if she were guilty.

"Aye," he said, but then exhaled with a voice tinged with defeat. "If Jamie is in his right mind, he'll believe me."

Morag snorted. "He's never been in his right mind."

• • •

"And then Mistress Morag told me to hang from a bar that she hooked across two of her rafters," Eleri said. They rode back through the woods on MacLeod land that led to the burned church and on to Dunvegan. "It felt good, pulling my back straight." Eleri shrugged. "I mean, I know it didn't straighten it, but it felt less curved. After that, she showed me how to tighten the muscles around my spine. She says if I do the exercises every day, the pain will lessen, and my spine might straighten some."

His sister, or half sister as he now knew, was more excited than he'd ever seen her. "I didn't know ye live in pain, El," Rory said.

She sat on her horse, who walked even with Airgid. "'Tis a constant ache, sometimes worse. I try not to think about it." Her voice got small. "And I don't want people to see it."

He knew she'd been made to feel lesser because of it. Even though his father had been kinder than most to Eleri, he hadn't taken her to festivals or introduced her to visitors. Now that he was dead, Jamie encouraged their sister to stay in her tower. Winnie Mar had told Jamie he should send her to a nunnery, that Eleri was a burden he should cast away. Could Sara have suffered a similar discouragement?

"Good people see yer beautiful smile and eyes, Eleri," he said. "Yer wit and cleverness, yer talent for capturing the world with your paints. The people who pass over those things and only see your back are not worth knowing."

He heard her sniff, but she didn't rub an eye or turn around. "Thank you, Ror," she said, using his old nickname.

Sara rode Lily next to them on the path, Jok bringing up the rear. The white mare's ears perked and turned as if sensing danger. She was still agitated from last night's storm. Airgid kept his head up and alert as usual, but Rory was also tense as if his warrior instincts had been triggered. Were Brodrick and his men close? He'd hoped to reach Dunvegan before their group so it wouldn't look like they'd been forced by them to return.

"I think Lady Sara is a good person," Eleri said, her sweet face looking past him to where Sara rode on his other side.

Rory glanced at Sara. Had she heard Eleri's assessment? The regal woman stared straight ahead over her horse's ears, but a softening in her lips made him think she had.

"I believe ye're right," Rory replied, and Sara's gaze shifted to his, connecting for a moment. It was a brief joining, but he thought he saw relief. His chest tightened as he looked forward. Did he really believe it? She was a Macdonald woman whom he'd obviously lost all control over, and now the Fairy Flag was gone. 'Twas like he'd jumped back in time to ten years ago. Jamie would surely see the similarities if he knew what had happened between them at the tower. Rory's brother wouldn't hold back from raking him through fire with his condemnation and rage.

The horses clopped along the pebbled, hard-packed road under a cloud-heavy sky. The morning had broken with sun, but it seemed another storm was moving in. The stillness felt heavy with only an intermittent breeze to push through the trees flanking the path. Breaking from the woods, they rode in silence past the blackened chapel. Rebuilding wouldn't begin until the anger had smoothed into acceptance, which, if nudged, could build into hope for a peaceful future.

That was Rory's goal on Skye—peace. And a strong Scotland.

Over the rise of the hill, Rory caught sight of Jamie on the bank before Dunvegan's curtain wall. MacLeod warriors filled the streets before him, swords at their sides, and some villagers held crude weapons as if they might be heading to war.

"Daingead," Rory swore beneath his breath.

"Mother Mary," Sara said beside him while Jok

followed up with a more colorful curse involving an otter's odiferous ballocks.

Jamie held his fist in the air, making Rory wonder if he were still too weak to lift his sword. "Right now, that bastard Macdonald," Jamie called, "who burned our church and almost yer chief, might have our most powerful weapon, the Fairy Flag." The deep rumble of discontent followed this speculation. "As we saw in my father's time when he unfurled it when we were outnumbered in battle, the flag will bring victory despite the odds."

Jamie's gaze landed on them, and he threw an arm out toward Sara. "Stolen by my traitorous bride."

Everyone turned to look at their small party riding up on the scene. Glares and curses flew through the air. In a swift movement, Rory dismounted and lowered Eleri to the ground. "Find safety, El," he said and moved in front of Sara.

"Lady Sara does not have the Fairy Flag," Rory called back, his voice reaching over all the protest. His eyes narrowed as he scanned the men he'd trained, good men who'd only had Jamie to listen to for a year and a half. Had he poisoned their minds with his suspicions and hatred?

"She's already given it to her devil of a father," Jamie retorted, making the rumble swell again.

"She never had the flag nor the box containing it," Rory said, ignoring the niggling worry that he had no way of knowing if this was true.

"'Twas held safe under our sister's bed in the tower room," Jamie said, "and now 'tis gone. The only person visiting our sister was Lady Seraphina Macdonald, spy and enemy to our clan."

Jok came up next to Rory as Sara dismounted. Both men stood before her like shields in case Jamie ordered someone to shoot an arrow. Jamie had whipped the MacLeods before them into a frenzy.

"We've been visiting Morag Gunn of the glen," Rory said, his tone stern but even. "Anyone could have entered Eleri's room and stolen the box."

Jamie snorted. "The only traitor we have within our clan is she." He stabbed a finger in the air toward Sara.

"I have taken no flag nor box," she called out, her voice strong and unwavering. "My aunt's cottage was searched with cruel, destructive force, even while your own sister was in residence."

Rory couldn't see Sara's face, but he imagined the tip of her chin and the flashing of fury in her blue eyes. Her lips, so soft and kissable before, were probably pinched in tight anger that she tried to hold back. Her tone was hot with unleashed wrath for slandering her name and morals.

Sara held her arms out wide. "Search me. Search my room." She dropped her arms. "Your accusations are to throw blame off someone within your own ranks." She pointed a finger along the rows of men and even the women who stood staring at her audacity.

Most of the village had come out to Jamie's rallying cry. Margaret and her husband weren't present, but Reid Hodges was there, standing to the side, shuffling his feet, worry etched deeply into his pale face.

"Throw her in the pit until she admits her crimes!" Winnie yelled, her waspish tongue confident.

"Nay." The word snapped out of Rory almost like

a growl, and he let his lips curl back in disgust. "The chief of the MacLeods will not be ruled by his mistress, and a mistress who's been evicted, too."

"Go fok your horse, Rory MacLeod," Winnie called back. "Or go back to England where your loyalty has been bought. Perhaps you stole the flag to send to King Henry!"

'Twas a worry of the Scottish nobles that those kept in England would be swayed to Henry's side of whatever the current conflict was between their countries. Since the beginning of time, rulers had tried to control the entire isle, south and north, east and west: England wanting autocratic rule of Scotland and Scotland doing whatever it could to keep the greedy monarchs out of its territories while fighting amongst themselves to rule.

Rory's men knew he hated the bloody king of England more than most since being starved and left to rot in Carlisle dungeon, but a few others stared with questioning accusation in their eyes. Rory ignored Winnie. "We will enter Dunvegan." He motioned to the ferryman. "Join the discussion inside, brother."

"Why?" Winnie said. "So you can persuade your chief that the serpent in our midst is only a sweet apple? One would think you'd have learned your lesson about Macdonald spies years ago."

He narrowed his eyes at her. She knew about Madeline's treason? Even if she hadn't been there, most of the onlookers had, and someone must have told her.

Sara's voice rang out with authority. "To discuss the whereabouts of the missing flag with those wise enough to understand the issues instead of throwing wild accusations about to incite unrest and panic." She stared directly at Winnie. Without waiting for any reply, she led her horse to the ferry, where she spoke to two eager children whom Reid had beckoned over to take care of Lily.

Jamie stood on the table that had been left before the bank where the wedding feast would have taken place. His face was red and contorted, but he climbed down and strode to the ferry. Sara had boarded the flat barge and stood, looking out the front, chin tipped higher with dignity. It made her perfect neck look long like that of a swan. And then Rory saw a different neck—long and pale and sliced across, blood dripping from it. He inhaled slowly, slamming a lid down on the memory.

Jok, Reid, Jamie, Rory, Eleri, and Sara moved across the water in silence. At the small dock, the two elderly men stood waiting.

"Ye didn't send the barge back across," Simon said, glaring with his one good eye.

John waved his stump of an arm in the air. "Did ye think I was going to swim across to ye?"

"Keep close to the Macdonald woman," Jamie said to the two guards standing on the dock.

Sara snatched up her petticoats. "I have no intention of swimming away."

"But ye might set the tapestries ablaze, Flame of Dunscaith," Jamie said and reached for a soft curl of red hair stretching down her back, rubbing it as if testing its softness.

Rory's fists clenched into murderous weapons at his sides, but then Jamie released the curl, and Sara hopped over the narrow gap off the barge. She climbed evenly up the steep steps into Dunvegan's entry, Simon and John trailing her while they whispered together, stopping now and then to rest.

Simon turned his head to Rory as they entered the castle. "Did he tell ye the Fairy Flag is gone?"

"Aye."

"Right out from under yer sister's bed," John said. They all walked into the great hall, boots clicking on the stone floor.

"Did everyone know the flag was there?" Jok asked.

John shrugged. "Now they do."

"Such an uproar, like none since that other Macdonald woman stole the flag." Simon nodded, fixing his one good eye on Rory. "Ye remember that, don't ye, lad?"

What an idiotic question. How could he forget the frenzy of fury grabbing hold of the villagers as his father held Madeline before them, describing how she'd betrayed them as a spy for Walter Macdonald?

"We had to turn everything upside down in the castle then, too," John added and sat down on a bench pulled back from the table. "Winnie Mar was screeching about Lady Sara, and Jamie was—"

"Enough," Jamie said. "Ye two never hold yer tongues."

Jamie was an arse, but he'd never disrespected their mother's cousins before. The two men looked at one another with grim expressions and stared at him in silence.

Margaret walked into the hall from the kitchen corridor and opened her arms to Eleri. Eleri hurried over, letting the only mother she'd known comfort her from the confrontation beyond the castle walls. Margaret tried to lead Eleri away, but she shook her head. "I would be here to support Lady Sara."

"Bloody hell," Jamie yelled, making Eleri jump.

Eleri drew herself up, but Rory could see her breathing quickly. "Lady Sara had no flag nor box on her when we left Dunvegan yesterday."

Jamie narrowed his eyes at her enough that Margaret took a step before her charge, her lips pinched.

"Has the village been searched?" Rory asked.

Jamie stood with his hands propped on his hips in agitation. "Brodrick led a search yesterday."

"A search of the outlying farmsteads is underway," one of the guards, Barnaby, said. "Although if the flag was taken days ago, it could already be in enemy hands."

"Foking hell!" Jamie's curse cut through the tension in the great hall like a honed blade through sinew. "I need the Fairy Flag back! I need it to conquer the bloody Macdonald Clan once and for all!" His words snapped out with some spittle, but he didn't seem to notice or care.

"The lad's bloody loud," John said, and Simon nodded, sniffing.

Jamie pointed to Sara. "I will wed ye and conquer your clan. Dunscaith and its Flame will be mine."

"Nay," Rory said at the same time Sara spoke.

"I won't marry you, Chief MacLeod, and Dunscaith, under the leadership of my older brother, will never fall." Her words were calm as if she stood with a battalion of support surrounding her. But the opposite was true. She was alone except for Eleri who stubbornly refused to be led safely above.

Jamie strode toward her, and Rory leaped forward, lips pulled back in a silent snarl. He wouldn't let Jamie, or anyone, harm the brave woman standing without so much as a shield to protect her from violence. Ten years ago, he'd just become a man at eighteen years old when Madeline was condemned, but now he was a seasoned warrior, the Lion of Skye.

Jamie's bent fingers rose to grab Sara by the neck like a pair of talons, but Rory shoved his arms away, placing his larger body between them. Jamie faltered slightly, even under the reined-in force that Rory had used. "Ye will not touch the lady," Rory said, staring into Jamie's glare.

"Ye protect her, a Macdonald, daughter of our enemy who tried to murder us on my wedding day? A Macdonald spy?" He shook his head. "Did ye learn nothing before? Women, especially Macdonald women, cannot be trusted."

"And yet ye were going to marry her," Rory said.

The side of Jamie's mouth pulled upward in a wry grin. "To keep my enemy close, I could send false information to her father."

"A failed plan," Sara said, "since I tell my father nothing."

As if he'd been waiting for a line spoken in a play to herald his entrance, Brodrick strode through the archway from the stairs leading up from the ferry. His steps were clipped and forceful. Jamie whirled around, spotting a folded fabric in his hands.

"Ye found it!" Jamie yelled. "The Fairy Flag."

"Where was it?" Simon asked.

But Rory knew instantly that it wasn't the fabled flag held sacred by his clan, and all of Skye. For one thing, it wasn't yellow.

John shook his gray head. "That flag is white. A flag of surrender?"

"Is Walter Macdonald surrendering?" Simon asked, but everyone ignored the ridiculous question.

"'Tis not the Fairy Flag, my chief," Brodrick said, his gaze flickering to Rory and beyond to Sara before returning to Jamie. His face pinched with condemnation, but then he bowed his head to Jamie. "'Tis a bed sheet I found at Dun Beag Broch."

Rory's hands fisted at his sides. *Bloody foking hell.*

Jamie's brows gathered. "The tower house that Rory's determined to outfit as his own little castle?"

"Aye," Brodrick said, holding the folded rectangle from two points so that it dropped down as if he were unfurling a real flag. "I believe 'tis where the Lion of Skye and the Flame of Dunscaith took refuge in the storm last night. Alone. This was in the bedchamber."

Across the bleached white of the sheet were smears of bright red blood.

CHAPTER TWENTY-ONE

"A little more research led me to Ambroise Paré,
whose 1573 treatise on 'monsters and marvels'
includes the description of popular techniques,
known since the time of Galen, for creating false
evidence of virginity by inserting a fish bladder filled
with blood into the vagina, so that the sheets on the
wedding bed would be stained with the necessary
proof."

Elizabeth C. Goldsmith, WondersandMarvels.com

Sara felt the muscles under her skin turn to stone.
Even if the devil and England's King Henry suddenly
walked arm-in-arm into the hall, she wouldn't have
been able to move. Only her heart continued to prove
she lived, pounding in her chest so hard that bruises
would surely mar the inner wall.

John sucked in a breath through his large nose.
"Daingead," he muttered.

"What?" Simon asked, opening his one eye larger.
He lowered his voice. "What is it?"

Sara could try to deny they were all staring at the
remnants of her maidenhead, say that it was her
monthly flux having taken her by surprise. She might
die from mortification but 'twas better than admitting
she'd given herself to Rory only days after she'd wed
his brother. But the blood looked different, lighter,
brighter, a beacon of her lost innocence. Would men

know such things?

She couldn't bring herself to look at Rory. He'd said he'd broken a vow for her. Did his brother know of this vow? Did the others in the room?

Jamie turned slowly on his heel, his hard gaze passing first to Rory and then to Sara. He opened his thinned lips, but Sara found her voice first.

"I fell running away from Phoenix, the heron that surprised me inside the tower, bumping my head and cutting it. The wound must have bled."

"Show me this cut," Jamie said, his words a mix of subdued anger and triumph as he stared at her.

"The back of my head under my hair." Sara's leaden arm moved under the heavy stare, her fingers touching the back of her head. "'Tis mostly healed already." She swallowed past a lump of dryness in her throat. If one was to place the sheet back onto the bed, the smear would be too low to have come from her head, but the sheet had been balled in a corner, so there was no way for Brodrick to know which side had been toward the headboard.

Sara probed the back of her head. "I didn't…use a pillow." Could she scratch herself with her fingernail now to cause a wound?

"Ye'll wake with a crick in yer neck if ye don't prop it on a pillow," Simon said, rubbing his own neck. He looked at John. "I use two, filled to popping with goose down."

John shook his head. "Too high will also put knots in yer neck."

Rory kept himself between Sara and Jamie as if daring his older brother to try to get past him, like some childhood game and not a provocation of civil war. Brodrick and Jok also moved in closer.

Margaret dropped Eleri's hand and traipsed over with a brusque stride as if she wore impenetrable armor walking through a battle. "I will check that the wound isn't tainted," she said, her fingers brushing Sara's aside. Sara held her breath as the woman parted her thick hair, looking for a crusty wound.

For several seconds, Sara stood as if balanced in a tree. Jamie like a wolf underneath, waiting for her to fall, and Rory as the most powerful beast ready to tear his clan apart, and all of Skye with it. For that's what would happen if the MacLeod Clan broke between brothers. The other clans would take sides, and old rivalries would turn into all-out war.

"An abrasion, which has almost healed," Margaret said with a perfunctory nod. "Scalp wounds can bleed quite a bit, even if the cut is superficial." She stepped back. "I will send up an ointment for it to make certain it doesn't become tainted."

"Do ye remember when that careless lad pushed me at Samhain years ago and I hit me head on the corner of the barn?" John said. "My head bled like I'd been brained with a battle axe."

"Ye were drunk and ran into the barn," Simon said.

"Bloody hell, no," John protested. "That lad…" He moved his hand around as if grasping for a name. "Martha's boy. He was running after kittens or some such and clipped me."

"Well, ye were also too drunk to stand up by yerself," Simon said.

"But I bled like I was brained." John looked at Jamie. "So, aye, scalp wounds do bleed a great deal."

Margaret placed her arm through Sara's and led her away from the middle of the great hall. "Come along with Lady Eleri and me, and we will let the brothers calm themselves down until they are once again civilized men. Then they can devise a plan to find the flag." It was obvious Margaret was more than a mere servant because no one moved to stop them.

Reid leaped forward to follow, his slender build and rapid movement making him look like a hare pushing off through tall grasses to escape a predator. "I can be of assistance, Mistress Margaret."

"Master Reid," Margaret said, "go to the kitchens and have hot water brought up to both towers. Ladies Eleri and Sara will want to wash. And fetch my ointment against taint. Cook Fiona will know where I keep it."

"Aye." Reid nodded and veered off down a hallway as the ladies began to climb the stairs.

They rounded two turns of the spiral staircase when Margaret broke the silence. "I do not hear a battle below." She let out an exhale and shooed Eleri forward when the girl stopped above them to look behind her down the stairs. As Eleri disappeared around a turn, Margaret glanced back at Sara. "Either Jamie has never seen virgin blood on a sheet or he's smart enough not to challenge the Lion of Skye."

Sara felt heat prickle into her cheeks. But Margaret turned back around and continued to climb without waiting for a response.

• • •

Rory watched his brother carefully as they stared at

one another across the short distance. Perspiration dotted Jamie's upper lip along the edges of his mustache, and his hands balled into fists.

"The Flame of Dunscaith is mine," Jamie said, his voice rough. "She's my bride." Each word was emphasized. Everyone, including the two old advisors who rarely held their tongues, remained silent.

"The union was annulled within minutes of the vows," Rory said. "By Father Lockerby so her family would have no claim to Dunvegan if ye died."

"And ye took her," Jamie continued as if Rory hadn't spoken. "Ye lay with my woman."

"Mo chreach." Simon leaned into John's ear.

"She is not yer woman," Rory said. "Sara is her own woman, married to none and able to choose—"

"Ye foking bastard!" Jamie yelled, lunging at him with a frontal assault.

Rory sidestepped easily and caught Jamie around the chest, hauling him before him, his arms pinned to his sides like he did when they were children and Jamie lost his temper. "Calm yerself and see reason. Sara won't marry ye. Ye attacked her when ye woke, blaming her for her father's murderous plan. And ye have no kind feelings for her. Ye didn't even look at her when she walked up to the chapel."

"She was part of her father's plan!" Jamie said, seething and struggling to break Rory's hold. Brodrick took a step forward, but Jok put his arm out to stop him. Jamie's faithful man was strong and cunning in battle and had always remained Jamie's closest friend.

"Nay," Rory said near Jamie's ear. "Her father keeps her and his eldest son, Kenan, ignorant of his treachery."

"She's a liar," Jamie said, spitting with the force of his words, "and a whore."

Anger welled up inside Rory, and he jerked Jamie around to stare him in the face, holding him by the shoulders, his fingers curling to bite into him. "Watch that tongue of yers, brother. 'Twill lead ye to pain." Tension rolled through Rory's muscles, preparing him. For what? War with his own brother? Hadn't Jamie already started it when he left Rory to die in that hellhole down in England?

"She's fooled ye," Jamie said, his words full of venom. "A Macdonald who has infiltrated Dunvegan and stolen the Fairy Flag, exactly like Madeline. When she died, ye made a vow not to trust a woman again, especially not a Macdonald woman."

"I didn't vow not to tup them," Rory said and was thankful Sara was no longer below to hear the callous declaration. When they'd come together, there had been a trust between them. She'd trusted him not to harm her despite his strength, and he'd…he'd trusted she wasn't a Macdonald spy distracting him and seducing him to be an ally.

The smallest trickle of unease slithered inside Rory, but he stomped it back with determination. "Sara led us out of the burning church. She saved ye and me and all of us trapped in there. She risked her life and has ruined any chance of returning to Dunscaith."

Jamie stared hard into his eyes, convinced of his opinion. "She led ye out of the church so ye would trust her. And now, fool brother, ye lust for her, too." He shook his head, stepping back from Rory's reach as if he'd regained his composure and command. "Ye are so easily led by yer cock."

Jamie looked at Brodrick. "Put her in the dungeon pit."

The dungeon of Dunvegan was a pit that dropped down thirteen feet, the last six being nothing but hard stone. It sat on the other side of the kitchen, so the smells of roasting meat could reach the prisoners while they starved to death. Icy water leaked in at the bottom with the tide, giving the occupant three to twelve inches of water to stand in.

"Nay," Rory said. "Keep her in the tower."

Jamie's lips hitched in one corner like he was laughing at Rory's foolishness. "Let the Macdonald chit choose. My bed or the pit."

John and Simon both stood up. Simon's mouth hung open, and John shook his head. The guards who'd come in with Brodrick stood behind him with Jok facing all three.

Rory's voice remained even despite the hardness of his jaw. "The dungeon is for murderers and traitors, not women who have taken charge of who they lie with."

The words turned Jamie's grin into a glare. "She's a whore, and ye're a traitor to yer clan for foking her. Ye deserved to be left with the English!"

Crack! Rory's fist connected with Jamie's foul mouth with all the power of an exploding cannon. The impact lifted Jamie off his feet, throwing him backward to flop flat on his back. If it was war Jamie wanted between brothers, 'twas war he would get.

"Ror!" Jok yelled out his name, and Rory spun in time to see Brodrick lunge toward him. The guttural yell that came from Rory as he met the warrior filled the vaulted room like the roar of the lion. For a moment the battle was only between Brodrick and Rory. Jamie's personal guard was as large as Rory and had fought well beside him while Jamie remained behind a line of defense whenever they engaged in battles or raids.

"Traitor to yer clan!" Brodrick yelled, throwing a fist toward Rory's middle, but Rory jumped back, avoiding the punch.

Jok blocked two other guards, saying something that made them halt and watch. Brodrick swung again, but Rory ducked and caught him in the gut. Who would be the first to draw a blade? It wouldn't be Rory, not in his own hall against his own clansmen.

Out of the corner of his eye, Rory saw Reid hustle back into the hall, yelp, and run back out. Margaret's husband, Theodore, stood against the wall, holding an iron fire poker before him as if to fend off anyone who might come his way. Rory delivered another punch to Brodrick's middle. The man jumped back before Rory's fist could swing upward into his jaw.

Brodrick threw his meaty arms around Rory, wrapping him in a brutal hold, but Rory had an elbow free and thrust it into Brodrick's face. "Bloody hell!" Brodrick yelled as blood gushed from his nose, and he dropped Rory. With a shove, Rory sent the man backward where he tripped over a stool and fell next to Jamie, who had pulled himself up.

Jamie glared at Rory and yanked his sword from its sheath. "Well, brother," he called, "'tis come to this."

"Stop!" The voice cut through the cursing and

sound of swords sliding free of their sheaths. "Stop, right now!"

Rory turned, his hands still empty of steel, to see Sara Macdonald, still in her wrinkled, water-stained clothes, standing inside the archway, Reid hopping from one foot to the next behind her. Her red-gold hair draped her straight shoulders, and her graceful arms were held out to her sides as if she was encompassing the room like a queen.

Her gaze moved from Rory to Jamie, a mix of horror and anger tightening her lovely features, truly giving her the look of a vengeful queen or a fire goddess. "I won't be the spark to burn through this clan."

Rory still slid his sword free as Jamie took a step closer.

"No!" Sara called again. "Do not battle each other."

Jamie snorted and resheathed his sword. He raked his hand through his hair as if he'd just jousted in the lists instead of battling his own brother. "She'll be locked in the pit."

"Her tower room," Rory demanded. Disgust at his pompous, scheming brother twisted tightly in Rory's stomach.

"She can be locked in my bedchamber," Jamie said.

"Are ye trying to die today, brother?" Rory stared hard into Jamie's narrowed brown eyes. They were dark like their father's and looked beady as a rat's.

Jamie words were harsh. "Very well, she'll be locked in the tower while ye, brother, find that bloody flag."

CHAPTER TWENTY-TWO

"One fire burns out another's burning,
One pain is lessen'd by another's anguish."

William Shakespeare, Romeo and Juliet

"I won't be the cause of a civil war," Sara said aloud as she paced in her locked tower room. With her window open, she'd heard the sound of riders heading out to search for the flag and knew Rory had been with them. Across from her, Eleri waved from her own tower window, and Sara waved back, trying to look cheerful. Jamie had ordered Sara locked away alone.

Rap. Rap. Rap. Sara spun toward the door as the lock turned and it swung open.

"Lady Seraphine Macdonald," Brodrick said, "ye will accompany me."

"Where?" she asked, but he came forward.

Outside the door, Reid hopped nervously from foot to foot. "Oh, Lady Sara." He worked his clasped hands before him. "Chief Jamie has ordered ye to the pit."

She stared, her stomach dropping inside her. "Rory—"

"Isn't here," Jamie called from what sounded like the bottom of the steps.

Brodrick's cheeks had turned red. "Please don't make me carry ye."

Sara spoke through gritted teeth. "He will punish

you when he returns."

Brodrick swallowed hard, looking away. Dark circles surrounded his eyes from the break to his nose.

She had no weapon but what God gave her, and teeth and fingernails wouldn't do too much to this warrior. She grabbed her heavy cloak, throwing it around her shoulders, and followed Brodrick out of the room with her chin held high.

At the bottom of the stairs, Jamie studied her. "Ye can choose the pit or…my bedchamber."

Reid gasped softly, and Brodrick stared at his chief as if he hadn't thought Jamie would truly resort to rape. But the gleam in the chief's eye told Sara quite plainly that he would take anything his younger brother had claimed, including her.

"I choose the pit," she said firmly, holding his stare with blatant disgust.

He frowned, and for a moment she worried that he'd force her to his bed anyway. But then he waved a hand at Brodrick. "Throw her into the pit then." Jamie walked away, his boots cracking against the floorboards. "Ye might change yer mind when the tide comes in."

"Rory will know he can't trust his brother."

"He already does," Jamie answered without looking back.

Reid trailed her as she followed Brodrick, sniffing every few seconds like he had an ague. They entered the bowels of Dunvegan where a dampness hung in the cold air. The smell of old fruit and vegetables emanated from several root cellars.

When they reached a square cut into the rock floor, Brodrick threw his torch into a sconce bolted to the wall. "There's a ladder," he said, and Sara looked down at a rope ladder attached at the top by two iron hooks. "Climb down."

"So, throwing one in is against your conscience, Brodrick," she said, "but making a woman choose to be raped or climb down into an icy wet hole underground isn't?"

Brodrick didn't answer.

"Oh, Lady Sara," Reid said.

She looked at the nervous man. "Let Mistress Margaret know about this." He nodded and hurried off.

With a resigned sigh, Sara hitched her petticoats up to find secure footing. At least she was wearing her boots and not slippers, although they hadn't dried since last night's ride in the storm. Her feet were damp and cold already. Brodrick didn't hurry her but waited quietly as she stepped down each rope rung. "It won't fall off the hooks, will it?" she asked him when her face was even with the edge.

"Nay, milady, 'tis secure."

"Secure but treacherous," she murmured as the floor disappeared, and she continued down into darkness. She hesitated at the bottom, not wanting to step off into the inches of water.

"I need to pull the rope up," Brodrick said.

"God's teeth," she swore and finally stepped into the icy water. It soaked quickly through the leather of her boots. "'Tis better than a slimy devil's bed," she said and stared up at the square-cut hole eight feet above her head.

"When Rory finds out about this, it will be civil war," she called up as the rope was hoisted out of her reach. "The blood of your clan will be on Jamie's and your hands, Brodrick."

"There's quite a bit of blood on Macdonald hands, too." Brodrick walked away from the open hole.

Thank God he hadn't covered the top. She wrapped her arms around herself, pulling the cloak tighter. The dank moisture on the stone walls made Sara feel damp despite the dry warmth of the woolen garment. She lifted one foot from the water at a time, but the cold permeated up through both her legs. Even though the hole above was a four-foot square, the prison below opened into a rectangle so that a prisoner could lie down flat about eight feet across. Not that she would lie down in the water.

"Sweet Mother Mary." She leaned back against one wall.

Long minutes passed when, somewhere above, a door opened. Slow footfalls came down the chiseled stairs leading to the corridor above her. She watched the open square, listening as whispers grew closer.

"Don't fall in. Ye'll squash the lass."

"I'm not going to fall in. Ye're the one with one eye who can't see how far away something is. Stay against the wall or crawl across the floor."

A face appeared over the square-cut hole. 'Twas John Sutherland. And then Simon Sutherland's face joined his. "Bloody hell, she *is* down there," Simon said, holding a lantern over his head. "Are ye well, lass?"

The bright light made her squint like the one-eyed man. "Well enough."

"See," John said, "she's sturdy."

"Are yer feet wet?" Simon called down, trying to

keep his voice both soft and loud enough to carry.

"Yes."

"Sorry for that," Simon said. "But we brought ye food and drink."

"Because that cold water will suck the life right out of ye," John said.

Simon hit John's shoulder. "Don't worry her about that. Hold on to me while I lower this down."

A pulley was already rigged with a rope above the pit, and they lowered a basket slowly down into the hole. Sara caught the edge with stiff fingers, pulling it into her arms. She opened the bladder first and took a long drink of the sweet, weak ale. Wiping her mouth, she looked up. "Thank you."

"No good reason to put a lady down there," John said.

The sound of the door opening above made their faces snap to the left in unison. "Bloody hell," one of them said, and their faces disappeared.

"Lady Eleri?" John said and lowered his voice. "What are ye doing here?"

"'Tis no place for a lady," Simon added.

Eleri's face appeared over the square hole. "Which is exactly why I'm here."

"I'm holding onto yer ankle, lass," one man said. "Don't fall in."

Eleri's young face was pale as she squinted, trying to see down in the hole. "Sara?"

"I'm here. Simon and John brought me some food and drink."

Eleri glanced over her shoulder. "Thank you both." And then she looked back. "I have a blanket and well…"

"Ye brought her a stool?"

Eleri looked down. "In case the water gets higher with the tide. The stool is to stand on."

"Clever lass," Simon said, holding the lantern over the hole. "We'll lower that first so ye can get it under ye, Lady Sara."

"At least ye won't be standing in the water anymore," John said.

The three of them worked to lower first the stool and then the blanket that Sara wrapped around her and over her head. With the stool, she could even crouch down without getting wet. "Will the tide come up much higher?" she asked, seeing the reflection of Eleri's lantern in the water under her.

"I'm not sure," Eleri said. Sara could see her shaking her head. "But I won't let you drown."

Certainly, the water wouldn't come that high, would it? Sara traced a finger down the water stains on the stone that came up to her shoulder.

The door above opened again. All three heads disappeared, and she could hear muted footsteps as they ran down the corridor, perhaps to hide in one of the storage rooms. Without the lantern, the only light above was that of Brodrick's torch in the sconce, which barely reached Sara. She hid the basket of provisions under her cloak.

A light broke the shadows above, and Margaret's face appeared over the hole. "Milady? Are you well?"

Before Sara could answer, Margaret jerked upward as the other three trotted out of hiding.

"What are you all doing here?" she asked. "Lady Eleri, this isn't a safe place for a lady."

"Lady Sara is stuck down there," Eleri said.

"What did you bring for the lass?" Simon asked. Sara could see him in the light of a second lantern.

"I…I thought a tart from the kitchen would be cheery," Margaret said.

"A single tart?" John said. "She'd starve on one measly tart."

"And a warm brew to fight the chill." She reached up to attach a smaller basket to the winch.

"A single tart," Simon grumbled. "We gave her a piece of venison pie, bread, and butter. And drink."

"She's only been down there for an hour," Margaret said.

Sara couldn't help the smile that played along her lips, and she rubbed the muscles of her neck that ached from looking upward. "Thank you all," she called up as she caught the basket, unhooking it, "but I don't want you to get into trouble."

"Pish," Margaret said. "Jamie's gone to bed, and Brodrick knows better than to cause trouble with me." The woman carried a fierce rod of authority when it came to protecting those she felt were slighted.

"Is the ladder still up there?" Sara asked. If the water continued to rise, she would need more than a stool to stay dry.

Four heads swiveled left and right and then looked down together, shaking. It would have been comical if things weren't so dire.

"No ladder," Margaret said. "Brodrick must have taken it after lowering you. I can find it, though, take it from him if I must."

Simon snorted and leaned his head down a bit into the hole. "The woman knows the right amount of poison to put in one's supper to send him to the privy for the night."

Margaret smacked his arm. "I don't poison people, ye old goat."

Even though Sara was standing on a stool in icy water down in a stone hole, her neck aching from staring up, these four people warmed her. "You all can go now. I'll eat and drink and lean against the wall in this warm blanket and keep my feet dry on this stool. I will be well enough for the night, and then Rory will return."

"Is there nothing else we can do?" Eleri asked.

Sara peered up at her. "Please write a letter to my brother, Kenan, explaining this mess and asking him to help locate the flag."

Margaret nodded. "Aye, we will do that." She leaned away and stood, helping to pull Eleri up.

Eleri's hand fluttered in farewell. "We will be back with more food and drink later."

"We sent her down plenty," John grumbled.

Simon's face appeared again. "And if ye need to use the privy, release it in the water."

"Good Lord," Margaret said.

"Dear Mother Mary," Sara said, ignoring the mead that was winding its way down to her bladder.

With several grunts and groans, the two elderly men helped themselves up and followed the ladies out of the underground corridor. Sara listened to their footsteps fade as they returned above to the land of light, springtime warmth, and freedom. Carefully, she lowered her backside onto the provided stool, and hooked her boot heels to the thin rung under it. Wrapped in the thicker blanket, she leaned against the wall.

She sighed. Where was the damn flag? She hadn't taken it, but it made sense it had been stolen by a MacLeod enemy, the most obvious being a Macdonald. Did her father have Macdonald spies within Dunvegan? Wouldn't he or she have made themselves known to her? Perhaps not, fearing she'd be loyal to her husband or, when the marriage was instantly annulled and she was captured, that she would give information over when tortured or thrown into a damned icy pit.

Sara pulled the blanket tighter around her face to keep more heat from escaping. Resting her chin on her hands propped on her knees, she closed her eyes. Nestled there, she let her mind wander back to before dawn, to when Rory held her against his hard body and hot naked skin.

With her head bent, she inhaled, remembering the feel of him. He'd been all over her and within her, and they'd truly been one. She shivered as she recalled his lips skimming along her, teasing and kissing her. Even if she had everything else taken away, she'd always have the memory of their time in his tower together. He'd thought her beautiful. She drifted to sleep wrapped up in her blanket and the sweet memory.

Her mind was adrift in darkness when she startled. Blinking, she couldn't focus on what she was seeing. *Where am I?* She didn't move, her arms locked around her legs despite the protest in her lower back from being hunched. The distant glow of torchlight filtered down from above, and Sara realized she was surrounded by dark stone.

The pit.

She straightened on the narrow stool, arching her back. Footsteps faded along the corridor. "Is someone there?" she called, her face tipping up to see the square-cut hole. Her inhale stopped when her gaze slid down the stone, her eyes settling on the wall across from her.

The ladder.

Someone had thrown the rope ladder down into her prison.

CHAPTER TWENTY-THREE

"Keep a little fire burning; however small,
however hidden."

Cormac McCarthy, 1933–2023,
Pulitzer Prize–winning Author

Sara shifted carefully, balancing on the seat of the stool as she got her damp boots under her. Keeping her feet in the middle of the seat the best she could, she used the wet wall to help her stand. A glance below the stool at the torchlight, reflected in the water, showed the tide had come in and the water level was close to the rung she'd hooked her heels onto. She wobbled and gasped.

Leaving the blanket in the lake around her small island, Sara realized the basket with provisions had already sunk. She reached the rope ladder. Tugging on it, she felt that it held fast and began to climb. Her toes hit the wall at each level, and she wiggled them to get her foot safely on top of each thick rope rung. It took time to climb with the rope flat against the wall, and she struggled, scraping her knuckles on the rocks as she pulled herself higher.

Who had lowered it? Would Jamie throw her back down if Rory hadn't yet returned?

Her muscles ached from the hours of sitting down there in the cold. Pulling with her arms and pushing down with her toes, Sara's head reached the top, and she peeked over the edge. The corridor was empty and dark except for the one torch flickering in its sconce on the wall. Both relief and worry tangled inside her with no one there.

Sara pushed with her toes. Chunks of dirt and mortar loosened, dropping down to plop into the water at the bottom. She used her hands to inch herself along the floor on her stomach while her feet continued to push against the rope ladder until she could wriggle out enough to get her knees under her.

I will not think about the grime on the floor. Please, God, don't let there be rats.

Scrambling up, she brushed her damp hands on her petticoat and looked around, her heart pounding with the effort to climb out. Where should she go now? *To the privy.* But after the privy? To her tower? To Eleri?

Should she hide somewhere and wait for Rory to return or try to get across the water to the village? Could she find Lily and ride to Morag's?

Her head spun, and she climbed the steps leading to the main part of the castle. She passed a small window that allowed air into the dank passage and saw that night had descended. Rory must still be out hunting down the flag. Jamie's actions would start a civil war at Dunvegan.

At the top of the stairs, Sara hesitated briefly, peeking out a crack in the door. If she hadn't a need for the privy, she might have watched longer, but she hadn't wanted to piss in the pit. The closest privy was at the end of the great hall in an alcove.

The vaulted room was cast in thick shadows with the fire burned down to embers. Hurrying across the empty room, Sara stopped when she heard a low growl. "Gus?" she said, and the large dog shot up from his spot by the hearth. His nails skittered over the stone floor as he circled her, licking at her hands and snuffling against her skirt streaked with moldy grime from the walls of the pit and the floor of the cellar corridor. He followed her to the privy.

"Wait here."

His tongue hung out of his gray snout, and his backside thumped on the floor as he sat. She closed the door, not bothering to find a taper. Gus's tail swished along the floor outside the door. The click of his nails faded as he moved away.

"Good dog," someone said. It sounded like Theodore. "Guarding the hall, are ye."

"'Tis good," Margaret said, "since most are gone hunting the flag."

Theodore walked with her as they passed the privy. "They won't find it," her husband said as their steps faded down a corridor.

How could he know that? Was he merely speculating, or could he and Margaret be involved somehow? Sara shook her head in the darkness. She couldn't believe Margaret would let Sara take the blame for it. Her heart squeezed. Who could she trust?

Sara relieved herself as she listened to Gus's nails click back to her door. He snuffled at the crack. "Almost done," she said, trying not to feel heartsick at the possible treachery.

Grrrrr. A low rumble came from Gus, and then his nails scratched on the stone floor as he pivoted, running away from the privy.

Sara stopped herself from calling his name when

she heard footsteps enter the hall.

"Go. Get back." It was a woman's voice, full of annoyance. But it was so soft, Sara wasn't sure who it was. Could it be a maid or Eleri? Cook Fiona? It wasn't Margaret, and Eleri would have sounded kinder. Winnie?

Sara's thumb paused on the little latch that kept the door shut. Her curiosity was subdued by her worry that the woman would sound the alarm, and Sara would end up back in the pit. When the woman's slippers faded, Sara cracked open the door, jumping slightly at the dark form waiting for her. Gus's large head lifted, his ears perking up as much as they could in their floppy way. It looked as if he smiled.

She stepped out, stroking the giant head of the wolfhound. "Who was that?" But he only licked her hand in response and trotted after her as Sara tiptoed back out of the hall. She stopped in the alcove that led to the dock and listened. The faintest sound of a door opening came from below, and a slight breeze kissed her cheeks.

Sara exhaled, feeling suddenly extremely tired. She looked down at the sludge across her gown and longed for a bath and fresh clothes, or at least a clean bed. Her toes were damp and probably wrinkled in the wet boots. "Come along." She beckoned the dog to follow.

Holding a taper, she climbed, growing more tired and winded with each step. Gus followed her up the turning tower stairs without them running into anyone. Any guards must be out looking for the flag. She cursed when she opened the tower door. Everything in the room had been gone through, her wedding trousseau spread out across the floor. Velvets, linens, and silk smocks had been heaped beside the chest she'd brought from Dunscaith.

"Too tired." She undressed, changed into a fresh smock and robe, and fell onto her righted mattress. Gus settled down next to the locked door as if he planned to stand guard. "Good dog," she said and let the weight of sleep take her over. Dreams of Rory and then of a great Phoenix turned darker to nightmares about being locked in cold pits where icy fingers reached for her, and she pushed deeper into her blankets.

Bam! Bam! Bam! "Is anyone in there?"

Gus's bark filled the tower room with deep warning, and Sara jerked upright in the bed. *Where am I?* She blinked, her half-asleep mind catching up quickly. *The pit. The tower.* Gus continued to bark over the sound of keys clanking. Sara only had a moment to pull her robe tight and stand before the door swung inward to reveal Brodrick MacLeod.

Brodrick's face was red with exertion as if he'd been running about, and his hair stuck out at angles. She glanced toward the window and saw that the sun had only recently risen.

"Sara Macdonald," he said, his lips pulling back in a quiet snarl.

Gus sniffed around him but had stopped barking.

"I'm not going back into that hole," she said. "Lock me in here until Rory returns with the flag."

Somewhere behind Brodrick, voices bounced between people and footsteps hastened. What was going on? Were they under siege? Would Kenan rush in to save her, bringing Macdonald armies?

Brodrick's heavy breaths slowed enough for him to speak. "Did ye do it?"

Had she climbed out of the dank hell hole of the Dunvegan dungeon? "Not without help," she said, "but don't blame anyone else. I would've figured out how to win my freedom, eventually." Despite their assurances, Sara didn't want the elderly men, Eleri, or Margaret to be punished for her escape.

Brodrick's jaw dropped as his brows rose. He drew his sword, and Gus began to bark at him, backing up before Sara as if choosing her side in a battle.

"Is she up there?" a woman called. It sounded like Margaret.

Brodrick ignored the question and kept his gaze directly on Sara. "Then I arrest ye, Sara Macdonald, for the murder of Chief Jamie MacLeod."

• • •

Rory stretched his arms overhead to work the kinks out of his shoulders. The familiar aches of sleeping on the ground were easily remedied, and he lifted his saddle that had served as his pillow. "'Tis already past dawn, Airgid," he said, settling it onto his horse's back. "Ye let me sleep too long."

Rory had continued toward Dunscaith until darkness made the chance of missing his prey too great. He bit into his oatcake while holding another flat on his palm for Airgid to lip off it.

No tracks.

He exhaled, wiping his horse's slobber on the rag that hung from his belt. Jok and Rory had traveled far apart, but within sight of one another, looking for fresh tracks of someone stealing away the Fairy Flag, but neither of them had seen any.

Should he continue to Dunscaith, knowing Sara's father was the source of the likely thief? Or should he return to defend Sara against his brother who seemed more interested in punishment and blame than finding the damn flag?

Rory had hated riding south away from Sara, leaving her alone to deal with the repercussions of their night together. Her warmth and the softness of her skin had marked him. Rory could almost smell the freshness of her rain-damp hair, the slight floral scent in its heavy layers. How he'd raked it out from her beautiful face like a radiant sun across the bed they'd shared. She had a constellation of freckles across her nose and summit of her cheeks, and her lips were the perfect instruments to show her desire and give him pleasure.

He threw some cold water from the burbling creek onto his face and rubbed roughly through his hair. "Bloody hell," he said, thinking about Sara locked away in the same castle as his brother. He'd never known his brother to brutalize women, but he hadn't seemed in his right mind since the fire.

Jamie had never thrown the memory of Madeline in Rory's face before, reminding him of his foolish, youthful choices that almost destroyed their clan. There had been insinuations and reminders, mostly from his father, for Rory to keep his oath to protect the MacLeod Clan over everything else. But the strength of his oath had weakened after a year and a half abandoned in a stinking English cell. Abandoned by the very clan he was to protect. Loyalty to the MacLeods above all others didn't fit inside Rory like it used to. It was like a warped sword unable to fit easily into its scabbard.

Walking along the bank, his eyes scanned the ground, but there were still no tracks to see. This was the regular route to Dunscaith on the Sleat Peninsula, and riders would let their mounts drink somewhere along here. "Unless they're purposely hiding." He looked east where Loch Duagrich sat in more mountainous terrain.

"Fok." The curse shot out of him, making Airgid's ears twitch. There was no way to tell if someone was stealing away his clan's fabled weapon. Airgid finally lowered his head to drink when Rory squatted to refill his two flasks, shoving them into the bag tied to the saddle. A light morning breeze blew northward, and he paused at a rhythmic sound.

Airgid snorted, his ears twitching again. "Ye hear that, too." Rory threw his boot in the stirrup and mounted, bringing his charger around to the open moor, watching the gentle rise south of them. A rider emerged, flying along the dry path across the moor.

"Siuthad!" Rory yelled, pressing into Airgid's flanks, and they turned to intercept. But as soon as the rider with one smaller passenger saw him, they turned his way, slowing.

"Hail, Rory MacLeod." Kenan Macdonald waved an arm over his head while he held a young woman before him on his mount. They waited for Rory to reach them since the road was firmer than the surrounding moorland.

"What news?" Kenan asked.

For a moment, Rory stared speechless at the girl before Kenan. "Lady Eliza?" Rory asked.

The girl smiled, and she looked so much like Eleri that the cool morning breeze sent a chill along Rory's shoulder blades. "Pleased to meet you, Sir Rory," she said, "the Lion of Skye. I see why they call you that. Your eyes are such an interesting color."

"Sara?" Kenan asked.

Rory turned to him. "The Fairy Flag has been stolen, and Jamie has decided Sara is the guilty thief. He's imprisoned her. Do ye have the flag?"

Kenan was shaking his head before Rory finished. "But my father acts as if he does."

"How so?"

"He's preparing for war from the looks of it but won't say a word to me." Kenan's face pinched in annoyance. "He's decided I'm a traitor for working with ye and the others to escape England."

"And he's not my father," Eliza said, a sternness in her voice. "So Kenan helped me leave."

Kenan waved his hand to get them walking again toward Dunvegan. "When I realized he was planning some type of siege or attack and wouldn't tell me," Kenan said, "I decided my loyalty is with my sisters." He squeezed Eliza before him. "Half sisters and whole sister."

Rory kept even with Kenan and Eliza. "We'll go together to Dunvegan then," Rory said. "If ye didn't see yer father bragging about the flag, he doesn't have it yet."

"But he thinks he'll get it soon," Kenan finished.

Rory huffed. "There's no way for us to find the thief out here on the moors unless they follow this safe road, which is the quickest."

"Bloody hell," Kenan said, rubbing his jaw, which

was covered with a trimmed dark beard. "I should return to Dunscaith to watch for the flag." He pulled his sister halfway around to look in her eyes. "Go with Rory to Dunvegan. Ye'll be safer with Sara."

"But he'll punish you for helping me," Eliza said, her eyes round as she looked over her shoulder at her brother.

Kenan made a grim face. "He can try, but the men are loyal to me. I will be well." He looked out at Rory. "Go with Rory. The Lion of Skye is one of the most honorable men I've ever known."

Rory's chest expanded with the honor his friend bestowed, which also made him feel guilty about tupping his sister. If Kenan knew, he'd call him a scoundrel and try to knock him to the ground or skewer him. Jamie had gone into a rage at the knowledge, Brodrick ready to attack Rory, too. Even Jok questioned Rory's actions. But when he thought of Sara, her soft skin flushed with pleasure, he couldn't bring himself to regret his actions.

He cleared his throat. "I'll keep Lady Eliza safe."

She reached out to Rory. "Let us off then, Sir Lion, and make sure my sisters are safe at Dunvegan." Eliza might be timid due to her circumstances and youth, but she had Sara's courage. Rory lifted her over.

"I'll bring word and the flag, if it turns up at Dunscaith," Kenan said and raised his palm with the four scars. "I swear it."

Rory held his own palm aloft. "And I swear I won't use it over Clan Macdonald if ye're leading yer clan, Kenan."

Kenan nodded and turned his horse around to break into a gallop south.

• • •

Jok appeared in the small doorway of the tower bed-chamber beside Brodrick. "Ye are not to touch her," he said to Jamie's frowning guard.

"Dead? Jamie is *dead*? How? Where?" Sara stuffed her feet into a pair of silk slippers. "Does Rory know?"

Brodrick strode into the room toward the small table next to the window, Jok right behind him. Brodrick grabbed a letter sitting there, half unfolded, the seal on it broken. "What is this?"

Anger mixed with confusion and something she didn't want to admit was relief. A man was dead, but he was a man who'd had her choose between an icy pit and rape. She shook her head. "I've never seen that letter."

Brodrick took a long time holding it. Not many knew how to read. Sara walked over. "Let me see it." She took the folded paper from his rough fingers. Last night, she'd sneaked in without a taper and had fallen into her bed exhausted. It must have been sitting on her table.

Sara's breath caught as soon as she saw the famil-iar Macdonald crest on the wax seal and her father's scrawl across the page.

Seraphina, my stolen daughter.

> *Your orders are plain and imperative. Follow through and return home in triumph. Bring the Fairy Flag to Dunscaith so we can win decisively over our foes. And if you rid this world of your*

bridegroom and the Lion of Skye, I will grant you and your sister, Eliza, Dunvegan Castle and its vast territory. If you fail me, Seraphina, Eliza will be reunited with her mother before Christmastide.

Do not fail us.

> Walter Macdonald, Chief of the
> Macdonalds of Sleat

Brodrick and Jok stared at her. She could try to lie about what it said, but they'd know it soon enough.

"May I?" Jok asked, and she handed it over to him.

Brodrick glared at her. "I can read enough to know your father ordered ye to steal our flag."

Jok looked up from it, meeting Sara's gaze, his eyes hard, mistrusting. "When did ye receive this and how?"

She shook her head. "This is the first I've seen it. Someone left it here in my room. 'Twas unlocked when I came up last night."

"After ye escaped the dungeon," Brodrick said, his tone clipped, "and murdered our chief."

He reached out to grab Sara's arm, ready to haul her away, but Jok stepped before her. "Let the lady dress and come down to the great hall. We must send word to Rory and hear what the surgeon says about how Jamie died."

"Poison," Brodrick said. "There's a bowl of soup by his bedside."

Sara searched his face. "You cannot be sure there was poison in the soup."

"The fiend dropped these around Jamie on the bed." Brodrick held up a bright white mushroom.

"'Tis a Destroying Angel mushroom."

"Sweet Saint Mary." She sent a quick prayer for Jamie's soul.

"Aye," Brodrick said, a white pallor slipping over his features. "And he vomited and…worse in his bed."

"I haven't been near the kitchen," Sara said. "How could I have poisoned him?"

"I will guard this door while Lady Sara dresses and then lead her below," Jok said.

Brodrick's glare at Jok was hot. "If anything happens to that letter or if Lady Sara disappears, ye're a traitor to Clan MacLeod." He turned on his heel and strode out the door, leaving it gaping open.

Sara sank onto the edge of her bed. "Do you know where Rory is? Someone needs to tell him."

Jok glanced at the door and lowered his voice. "Did ye…?"

"No, Jok, I didn't poison Jamie." Sara lifted her head.

"And the letter?"

Sara exhaled. "Someone dropped the rope ladder down into the pit for me last night. I climbed up, used the privy, and came directly up here with Gus. I had no light to give me away and didn't see the letter."

He blinked twice, Sara focusing on his blue eyes with reddish eyelashes. "Rope ladder," he said. "Jamie put ye in the pit after we left?"

"It was either the pit or his bedchamber. I chose the pit."

He rubbed his face. "Daingead. Rory is going to kill J—" But then he stopped because someone had already done it.

CHAPTER TWENTY-FOUR

"What medicines do not heal, the lance will; what the lance does not heal, fire will."

Hippocrates, 460–370 BC, Greek scientist

Rory thundered down the path past the charred ruins of the chapel. He heard Eliza murmur something and saw her make the sign of the cross before her. Surely, Kenan told her about the fiery destruction and mass murder attempt.

But seeing the blackened walls and shattered stained glass of the roofless structure was jarring. It looked almost like the Devil himself had plodded through the one-room chapel, scorching where his hoofed feet had stomped.

The soaring gray form of Dunvegan castle loomed ahead, and before it, warriors and villagers were gathered. Rory slowed his horse. "What the bloody hell is going on?"

"Something bad," Eliza said.

He agreed. Several women dabbed at their eyes or whispered with condemning frowns, and the men looked ready to draw swords, their faces red and hands fisted. Rory came to a stop near the ferry to Dunvegan's entrance. "What goes on here?" he asked as several of his men came forward, Barnaby catching Airgid's bridle.

The man looked up with a pinched face. "'Tis said

the chief has died, murdered."

The words hit Rory like a gale. To the onlookers, he took the news stoically. Inside, his heart pounded. "How?"

Barnaby glanced at Eliza. "Pardon me, Lady Eleri," he said. "Bashed head."

One of Rory's warriors, Edgar, shook his head. "I heard poison."

"Nay," Barnaby argued, "'tis said there was a bloody mess to clean."

Henrietta Blounce stepped forward from the middle of the group of spinners and fullers she helped. She spat on the ground, and her full bosom heaved with anger, her gray hair pulled into a painfully tight bun at the back of her head. She was also the local midwife and unofficial leader of the female population in the village. "The evil deed was done by the Flame of Dunscaith," she yelled.

Sara? What did Jamie do to her? Had he raped her? Attacked her, and she was forced to fight him off? Fury surged through him like an out-of-control fire sweeping across a brittle field.

Rory dismounted, pulling Eliza down right after him. "We need to go on the ferry to the entrance," he said, trying to keep the bloodlust out of his voice. Her cape would hide that her well-known hump was missing. She said nothing but hurried along, letting the villagers think she was his sister, Eleri. No one questioned him about her riding home with him. Perhaps it was the look of fury in his eyes that kept them silent.

Edgar and Barnaby hurried along with him to the ferry. "Did Jok return?" Rory asked.

Edgar nodded. "Early this morn."

Rory leaped off the ferry and took Eliza's hand, helping her jump the gap.

"Oh," she gasped as she looked up the steep incline of steps into Dunvegan. "Go on." She shooed him. "I'll be right behind you, just a bit slower."

His worry about Sara spurred him forward, and he took the steps two at a time, finally running through the open gate and into Dunvegan.

Gus spotted him immediately when he strode into the great hall and met him at the archway. His barking mixed with loud wails echoing around the room, although it came from only one source.

"She killed him! She'll poison us all," Winnie Mar yelled. "Throw her in the dungeon pit again! Or burn her."

Brodrick held Jamie's mistress who tried to lunge toward Sara, her fingers curved like claws to scratch Sara's eyes out.

Sara, on the other hand, stood calmly in a simple blue gown, her hair down, and her face pale. But she didn't back away or cower from the accusation. Eleri, Margaret, and Jok stood next to her. His mother's cousins, Simon and John, sat at the table between both parties as if watching a joust.

Simon spotted him and rose, pointing. "The Lion of Skye returns."

John stood slowly. "He's not holding the Fairy Flag."

"I can see that," Simon said, frowning. "Did ye leave it on yer horse?" he asked, his voice raised to reach over Winnie's loud weeping.

But Rory was looking at Sara. Her brow rose

slightly in question. Did she also wonder if he'd found the flag? He gave a small shake of his head.

"Daingead," Simon said. "That bastard Macdonald must have it."

"We're doomed," John added and flashed an annoyed glance toward Winnie. "Shut off yer yowling, woman."

"My brother is dead?" Rory said over Winnie's sniffles. Sara gave a small nod. Was there sorrow in the pinch of her brow? Guilt?

His two men and Eliza walked in behind Rory, and Sara's gaze slid past him. Her mouth opened on a little gasp, and she clasped her hands as if sending up a prayer of thanksgiving to God. Her face, which had been perfectly masked, changed through a range of emotions: relief, worry, joy. Everyone stopped making noise, even Winnie, as they stared at the girl who was nearly identical to Eleri.

Eleri stared at her twin from across the hall, and Margaret's hand flattened against her mouth, her eyes wide. Simon opened his one eye as large as he could, his head swiveling back and forth between Eleri and Eliza. "John, I'm having a brain attack." His hand went out to grasp his friend's shoulder, but then he plopped back onto the bench. "I knew it. I'm dying."

"There's two of them," John said.

Simon turned his good eye to him. "Ye see…two of Lady Eleri? Ye're dying, too."

"Eliza." Sara dashed across the hall. As she passed, Winnie flapped her arms at her like a person stretching through a set of iron bars to tear into their captor, but Brodrick held her back. Sara gave no notice. She caught her sister in her arms, hugging her. Sara squeezed her eyes closed, resting her chin on the top of Eliza's head, as if she were nearly overcome.

Eleri clung to Margaret, tears on her cheeks, her eyes wide.

The scene squeezed Rory's chest. He hadn't intended for the lasses to meet with a ghastly death marring the happy reunion. But at least Sara knew Eliza was safe from her father's brutality. The relief on Sara's face was almost joy.

"Kenan brought her," Rory said, walking closer to them. "I met him several hours out from here. He returned home to see if the Fairy Flag shows up at Dunscaith."

Sara's eyes opened, meeting Rory's gaze, but she didn't release Eliza. "Is something going on at Dunscaith?"

Eliza pulled from her arms. "Father is preparing for war even though he won't admit it to Kenan. Troops gathering. Swords and arrows being readied." She shook her head. "Kenan said he saw Gilbert carrying cauldrons up for flaming pitch."

"Did she say war?" John asked.

"Hold yer tongue, woman," Simon said, striding over, his arm going out to Winnie. "I can't hear what's being said."

John followed. "Too much to keep up with, and that woman is a banshee."

"Jamie's dead!" Winnie yelled again, and Simon put his fingers in his ears, glaring back at her.

"We all know," John said and leaned into Simon. "'Tis not fair." He stuck his finger from his remaining hand into one ear. "I can still hear her."

"I'm telling ye," Simon replied, "carry a bit of wool

with ye to stuff in the other side."

"'Tis not like I know when she's going to be cater-wauling," John grumbled.

Rory walked to the center of the room and held out his arms. "Everyone, hold their tongues." He looked at Winnie. "If ye need to grieve loudly, return to yer cottage. Edgar can row ye ashore."

Winnie sniffed and bared her teeth at Sara. "I will stay to see her get what she deserves."

Rory exhaled. "Then keep yer mouth shut. If ye can't do that"—he lifted his gaze to Brodrick—"hand her off to Edgar." Rory turned away from Winnie's fury-laden frown to look at Jok. "We'll go up to Jamie's bedchamber in a moment. First..." He beckoned Eleri closer.

His sister ran over to him. "Eleri, I wish it was under better circumstances, but this is your sister, Eliza." He beckoned to the other twin, and she walked over with Sara holding her hand. "Yer father was Alasdair MacLeod and yer mother was Elspet Gunn Macdonald."

Winnie gasped. "Was Jamie nearly wed to his own sister?" She stared at Sara.

"Nay," Rory said. "Jamie's and my parents were two completely different people than Sara's parents. Eliza and Eleri are our half sisters." He looked at Margaret. "Could ye look after them and find a room for Eliza?"

"I would very much like to," Margaret said, and Rory thought he saw tears in her eyes. She smiled as she rounded the girls up like a mother hen.

"Now," Rory said. "Jamie." He strode toward the stairs with Jok and Brodrick, who had made Winnie sit down with Edgar standing guard. John and Simon had apparently recovered from their shock because they hurried on with them. When Rory reached the steps, he turned back to the hall, his gaze settling on Sara. "Lady Sara, I'd also like a word with ye."

She picked up her skirt hem and walked toward him, her slippers giving little taps on the stone. With red-gold hair draping her shoulders, she looked like a legendary heroine stepping out of an ancient tapestry. And like the characters in most tapestries, her face was emotionless.

He wanted to pull her into a room alone, smooth his thumb over the soft skin of her cheeks, and ask what Jamie had done to her. No bruises bloomed on her lovely face, but they could be hidden under her clothing, like what she was hiding on her back. She stopped before him, and he studied her eyes. "Are ye hurt?" he asked, his voice low, although those near him could still hear. "Did Jamie do anything to ye?"

"No," she said and tipped her head, glancing away. "He put me in the pit." She wrapped her arms around herself as if she could still feel the dank, cold stones pressing in on her.

"He said he wouldn't, the bloody shite," Rory said, his words cutting.

"Ye shouldn't speak ill of the dead," Simon said.

"He's a bloody shite, alive or dead," Rory said. He'd been placed in the dungeon pit several times growing up. 'Twas his father's favorite way to remind him he was forgettable. He knew how cold and wet it was. One was dead down there without food lowered, and if the tide came too high, the prisoner could drown.

Rory squeezed Sara's hand. Again, he wished they were alone.

"Tell him," Jok said, looking at Brodrick.

Brodrick cleared his throat. "Jamie let her choose between the pit or his bedchamber."

Rory's nostrils flared. "And she chose an icy pit."

"Yes," she said.

"So, she was angry at him," Brodrick said as if this gave her motive.

Rory led Sara through the corridor toward Jamie's room. "Cause of death?" Rory asked.

"Poison mushrooms," Brodrick said. The man, his brother's only friend, sounded furious with the extra heaviness of sorrow.

"The villagers think his head was bashed in," Rory said. Anyone could use poison.

Jok came even with his strides, handing him a folded letter with a broken wax seal. "This was found in Lady Sara's tower bedchamber this morning." He looked at Sara. "Milady was also there, asleep, and says she hadn't seen it last night when she…when she made it to her room in the dark."

"She climbed out of the pit," Brodrick said as if this spoke of her vileness.

"Presented with a rope ladder," Sara said, "I challenge even you, Brodrick, not to make use of it when stuck down there all day."

"She shouldn't have been put in it to begin with," Rory said.

"And Rory…" Jok said, waiting until he looked at him to speak. "No one has confessed to dropping the ladder down to her last night."

Rory stopped, turning to look at her. "Ye didn't

see who threw the ladder down to ye?"

Her lips pinched as she returned the frown Brodrick trained on her, but her gaze slid to Rory's. "I don't know. I'd fallen asleep and woke only to hear them climbing the stairs to leave the underground corridor."

Brodrick huffed. "One doesn't fall asleep in icy water at the bottom of a pit. And she admitted that she'd killed Jamie when I confronted her this morn."

"I did not," Sara said.

"I asked if ye'd killed him, and ye said that ye'd done it but not alone."

She shook her head, a look of angry confusion on her face. There were dark smudges of weariness under her eyes. Had she been given food and drink yet today?

"You didn't say killed him," she replied. "I thought you'd asked if I'd escaped the damn pit, which I hadn't done alone since someone threw a rope ladder down to me."

"And there's a stool down in the hole, and a blanket," Simon said, "so she very well could have fallen asleep leaning against the wall on it."

"And a hearty basket of food, drink, and one tart," John added.

Everyone turned to stare at the two old men who crossed their arms. John shrugged. "Thought ye should know it all."

The details were piling on top of each other. Brodrick pointed at the letter forgotten in Rory's hand. "Read it."

"'Tis my father's handwriting," Sara said, her voice calm. "And, again, I hadn't seen it before Brodrick woke me. 'Twas dark, and I had no taper or lantern."

"The seal was broken," Brodrick said with a sneer.

"That means nothing. Anyone could break a seal, leaving it in my room, making it look like I'd read it."

That was true, but as Rory read the damning letter, his gut tightened.

If you rid this world of your bridegroom and the Lion of Skye, I will grant you and your sister, Eliza, Dunvegan Castle and its vast territory. If you fail me, Sara, Eliza will be reunited with her mother before Christmastide.

He swallowed. Walter Macdonald's orders were clear, as was his threat against Sara's cherished little sister. Tucking the letter into his sash, Rory turned on his heel to continue down the corridor. He didn't retake Sara's hand. Jamie was dead, and Sara had an excellent reason for killing him. She hadn't yet known that Eliza was on her way to Dunvegan.

Rory stopped at the door of his brother's bedchamber, his hand resting on the carved wooden frame. *Bloody hell.* Could Sara be guilty? If she admitted it, would he understand? Pardon her actions? *I swear to protect Clan MacLeod above all else.* His oath blared through his memory.

Brodrick came around and opened the door as if Rory was waiting for someone to do so. The room was cold since no fire had been stirred, and two maids silently hustled around with dirty bedding. Reid Hodges stood near the window, hopping from one foot to the next like he did when terribly nervous.

Hamish sat in a chair before a squat table where he examined the contents of a soup bowl, bits of it on a large handkerchief. He looked up from his task. "Rory."

But before he could say anything else, Sara gasped, and Rory's gaze swung to his brother. Rory's breath halted at the shocking sight.

"Holy Lord Almighty," Jok screeched.

John grabbed Simon's arm, staggering. "Unnatural."

"My head," Simon said, his hand flattening against the side of it as if he were indeed experiencing apoplexy.

Jamie's lips were parted and his eyes open. He blinked at them all staring at him, but then his gaze shifted to Rory. "Welcome back, brother."

CHAPTER TWENTY-FIVE

"[The Destroying Angel mushroom] contains deadly amatoxin poisons. Effects are seen 8 to 24 hours after ingestion and include vomiting, diarrhoea, and severe stomach pains. There
may be a deceiving period of improvement
before the second effects of liver
and kidney poisoning occur."

WoodlandTrust.org

Sara stared at the man reclined on at least four pillows in the bed, and it took her a moment to inhale. "You're…you're alive."

Jamie didn't move anything but his eyes, which were bloodshot and slightly yellow. "Ye've failed in yer murderous mission, woman. Let yer father know he'll never succeed in his evil plans."

Sara shook her head and looked at Brodrick. The large warrior's mouth had fallen open as if his jaw had unhinged from his skull. "You said he was dead."

Brodrick looked from Jamie to the surgeon to Rory. "He wasn't breathing. There was vomit and… was as if his bowels had emptied." He nodded to the maids who had bundles of bedding at their feet.

Hamish Gower stood and exhaled, holding up a mushroom from a stack he had on the table. "I added a chemical to the white to see if this specimen is Destroying Angel or Fool's Mushroom."

"Both are toxic," Rory said.

Hamish nodded sourly. "Unfortunately, the prognosis is the same."

"Death," Jamie said with a sneer, and Brodrick pulled up a chair to sit near him as if to give comfort.

"'Tis a Destroying Angel mushroom. I thought it was another equally fatal mushroom because the Destroying Angel doesn't grow until midsummer. But this has been dried, probably from last summer." He sniffed it and grimaced. "And it also has the smell of old meat."

"Did he die and come back to life?" John asked. The two elderly men had moved closer to Jamie, staring at him like he was some creature returned from Hell.

Simon passed the sign of the cross before him, his other hand sliding down from its spot on his head.

Jamie swore under his breath and closed his eyes. When he did so, he looked dead with his pale, yellowish skin.

Hamish set the mushroom down and walked to the water pitcher in the corner to wash his hands. "He likely fell into a false sleep as the poison began its attack on his organs." Hamish turned, drying his hands on a rag as he looked at Rory. "But from the state of the chief's eyes and skin, I'd say this is a temporary improvement." He shook his head. "There's no cure now that the poison has been taken up by the blood. It will ravish his liver and kidneys."

Jamie sputtered softly as if he laughed. "'Tis a cruel jest for a man to feel improved only to hear those around him verify he will die quite soon. Dying quickly would be more agreeable."

The maids hurried out, bundles of linens wadded up in their arms. The smell of excrement and vomit still fouled the room, and Rory went to the windows, swinging them open.

Reid moved slowly toward Sara. "Can I do anything for ye, milady? Ye look pale."

Reid looked pale himself, and his hands shook so much that Sara thought about leading him to a chair to sit down. "Thank you for your kindness," she said, "but please take care of yourself."

He gave a nod that could have been a shallow bow. "Thank ye, milady. I think I will…" His words trailed off, and he walked silently from the room, swaying slightly as if the weakest wind would knock him down.

"Master Hamish," she said, and he looked at her. At least he didn't glare. Sara nodded to the pile of mushrooms. Morag had taught her all about edibles to be found and poisonous plants and mushrooms to avoid. "Is it true the poison takes hours to make a person ill at first?"

The man nodded gravely. "Aye, 'tis why survival is rare. By the time the victim suffers ill effects, 'tis too late to have him purge."

"How many hours?" she asked, unwilling to let them know her knowledge.

"At least six hours and often longer before stomach cramps begin," Hamish said and looked to Jamie, who had opened his eyes. "When did you first feel sick, milord?"

"After my last meal before bed last eve."

Hamish began to scribble the information down on a bound stack of paper. How wonderful for him to get such important data from a talking corpse. "That would be about eight last evening," the doctor said.

"I was already down in the dungeon by noon that day," Sara said. "And before that, I was absent from Dunvegan, nowhere near Jamie."

The doctor looked up. "The poison could have moved slower through his system. Up to a full day between ingestion and first symptoms."

Rory nodded and rubbed a hand over his head. "The evening before," Rory said, his words quick, "Sara and I were stuck in the storm away from Dunvegan."

There was relief in his tone. Had Rory thought she'd poisoned his brother? That she'd lied about reading her father's directive and had acted upon it while he was away?

Her jaw felt numb, and her hand pressed against her heart with a breathless feeling.

"She could've poisoned his food before she left," Brodrick said. "Placed it in something he was *going* to eat."

"We eat the same stew he does," John said. "And we aren't nearly dead." He patted his chest with his one hand.

Simon pulled the lower lid of his one eye down. "Does it look yellow, John?"

John stared hard into Simon's eye. "Perhaps."

"Yer eyes, too," Simon said.

Hamish walked over, looking at the skin of their arms and into their wide eyes. He shook his head. "Ye don't look abnormally yellow."

Sara's relief allowed her to exhale. Thank God the two old men hadn't been affected.

The men looked at their arms, holding them next to each other as if in reference. "Are ye certain, doctor?" John asked.

"We could be poisoned," Simon said, aghast.

"Aye," the doctor said.

"Aye?" John said, his brows shooting up to his thin hairline. "We could be poisoned?"

Hamish shook his head. "I was saying aye to John. I'm certain neither of ye look poisoned."

Sara turned back to Rory. "I didn't see that letter from my father, and I didn't poison anyone. I haven't been alone anywhere I could gather mushrooms."

"Like I said, they were dry." The doctor tipped his head toward a pile on the table, but his voice was free of suspicion. "Someone scattered these around him."

"And put the open letter in my room, knowing I would get out of the pit by way of the lowered ladder," Sara said. She'd heard people in the great hall when she was using the privy. Margaret and Theodore and then another who padded away on light feet.

"Jok," Rory said, "gather a few men to question the kitchen staff and the maids. Find out where everyone was over the last thirty-six hours." The man nodded and left the room. "Brodrick."

"Aye," he said, standing straighter.

"Go to the village and let the people know Jamie is still alive, for now, and he was not bashed in the head. See if anyone knows anything about the mushrooms or saw someone unusual going in or out of Dunvegan. Set a second guard at the ferry."

Brodrick nodded, squeezed Jamie's shoulder, and traipsed off.

Simon and John stood straight. "We can help inspect the staff," Simon said.

Rory nodded but held up a hand, stopping them. "And get some lads to drag up the things from the dungeon pit and send for Father Lockerby." They hurried off, leaving the doctor and Sara with him in Jamie's room.

"What would you have me do?" Sara asked, more than ready to leave the foul-smelling room. And she wanted time to think.

"Find yer sisters and make certain they're safe."

"Are you...staying here with him?" She glanced toward Jamie who seemed once again to sleep, his breaths so shallow they were hard to discern.

"There's little time left, and I would have words with him." Rory glanced at Hamish. "Alone."

Sara walked to the door as the doctor gathered his bag of chemicals and notes. Rory sat in Brodrick's chair. He glanced her way, and her heart pounded. His bent brows and hard mouth made his face seem full of questions. And one of them was, did she want his brother dead enough to act on it?

• • •

"Fok the timing," Jamie said, his eyes partly closed. "Ye know she's killed me for her foking father." He was weak but not too weak to shoot venom with his words.

Rory exhaled through his nose. "She saved us from the fire."

"A trick to get her in Dunvegan to find the flag." Jamie rubbed a hand down his yellow-tinged face. "Ye watch. The Flame of Dunscaith will try to kill ye, too, and then her father will ride in and take Dunvegan, the Fairy Flag flying above his head."

Rory's gut twisted inside his already taut body. Dread nearly swallowed him, testing all his convictions about Sara. If she were just another lass, someone not related to the MacLeods' greatest enemy, would he question her truthfulness?

Rory leaned forward to rest his elbows on his knees, ducking his head to rub the ache at the back of his neck. Someone must be setting her up to look guilty. Otherwise, Rory was making the biggest mistake of his life. Madeline had taught him that he couldn't trust his instincts when it came to women.

I was only eighteen. She was the first woman I tupped.

Rory leaned back in the chair he'd been sitting in for the last few hours, trying to get as much information out of his brother as he could before he died. For there was no chance of him surviving, and soon, if the doctor was correct, Jamie would start vomiting and shiting himself again, falling into unconsciousness before dying. It would happen sometime within the next three days.

"I'll be careful," Rory said.

"Don't eat anything she hasn't tasted first."

This was ridiculous. If he was foolish enough to believe a second Macdonald woman, perhaps he deserved to be poisoned. "What? And wait six to twelve hours before I know 'tis safe after she eats it?" Rory asked.

Jamie grunted.

"I will have the foodstuffs searched and refreshed," Rory said. "No one should die this way." Not even his cruel brother who'd left him to die in an English dungeon. Although, he'd threatened Sara. Maybe Rory should bash Jamie's head in to end it quickly.

"I knew when I saw her that she was a traitor," Jamie said, licking his dry lips.

Rory held a cup of watered-down ale to his mouth, and he sipped. "She had nothing to do with the chapel fire." He'd decided he was certain of at least that. Scrutinizing his memory, Rory knew that she'd looked alarmed, surprised, and had tried to warn him. "Like ye've heard, Sara led Margaret out from underneath and then went back to help drag ye out."

Jamie stared at him for a long moment. "Ye like her."

Rory said nothing because he more than liked Sara. After their night together, he couldn't stop thinking about her. The way she'd let him see the pleasure on her beautiful face. The way her body had wrapped around him, pulling out fiery, carnal sensations he didn't know he could feel. She'd been so open with him, except for her back. Maybe the fact she was hiding a part of her body made him worry that she was hiding more. Or maybe he thought of her constantly because he was merely curious. And she was tantalizingly luscious.

"Aye," he said finally. "I like her."

"The same way ye liked Madeline," Jamie said and closed his eyes. "And that saw her dead."

"Sara isn't like her," Rory said, steel in his voice despite the evisceration going on in his gut.

Jamie's eyelids cracked open. "She is exactly like her."

"Madeline had wheat-colored hair and—"

"I'm not talking about how she looked," Jamie said. "But what she did. How she stole the Fairy Flag. How ye let her fool ye into thinking she loved ye." His head moved as if he were shaking it. "Ye've always been a fool, Rory. I thought Father taught ye a lesson about Macdonald lasses when he sliced her throat in front of ye."

Flashes of that horrid day coalesced in Rory's mind. Pale Madeline hauled out before the villagers, her long, thin neck exposed as Alasdair MacLeod yanked her head back. Rory had thought himself in love. But then she'd stolen the Fairy Flag for Walter Macdonald. She was a Macdonald spy.

Her eyes had sought Rory, eyes full of tears and remorse. *I am sorry*, she'd said, and the truth that she'd been using him had slammed into him. Rory had still tried to reach for her, but Jamie and Brodrick had held him back as his father spoke. *Her blood is on yer hands, son, for allowing her to trick ye.* Spittle flew from Alasdair's mouth, his eyes wild, and then…then he'd sliced a blade across her throat.

Jamie was still talking. "Ye vowed that day to protect Clan MacLeod above all else. And never ever to trust a woman, especially a Macdonald. Have ye forgotten that?"

How could he? It haunted him. He looked at Jamie, stared into his yellow-hued eyes. "I merely…" He couldn't say it.

The vow. He'd broken the vow, and the Fairy Flag was gone, and his brother had been poisoned. "I just foked her, Jamie. I've broken no vow." The words were bitter in his throat and made his stomach feel hollow, as if the twisting had reduced it to nothing. He hated himself for the lie. Because being with Sara Macdonald was so much more than a night of pleasure.

"Good," Jamie said, his eyes closing. He sighed long, and Rory almost thought it might be his last breath. But then he spoke. "Father will be foking irate I let a Macdonald kill me."

For a long moment, Rory sat there in his self-loathing, hating the words he'd said about his night with Sara. And hating himself because they weren't true.

Jamie opened his eyes again. "Father said nothing about bringing ye home from Carlisle. 'Twas as if he'd given ye up, and so did I." Jamie looked away. "Perhaps I will meet him in Hell for that."

Rory's chest clenched even harder. His father, the murderer. Rory shouldn't care about Alasdair's abandonment, but he did. If Rory hadn't let Madeline trick him, would his father have tried harder to get Rory released? Would he have at least sent coins for Rory to buy some food, comfort?

A deep groaning sound emanated from Jamie's bowels, and he grimaced but kept talking. "After his death, I'd plans to send a ransom…eventually, once my leadership had been fully accepted by the clan." He opened his eyes to look at Rory. "I know ye hate me for leaving ye there."

"Are ye asking for my forgiveness?" Rory asked. Or was he confessing because he was afraid for his soul?

Jamie closed his eyes. "Perhaps."

Anger tightened Rory's lips. His brother couldn't

even apologize for leaving him to die in an English prison. "Then, perhaps I forgive ye." But there was no mercy in his rough voice. The tether that had bound Rory's loyalty to Jamie had been severed.

Rory thought of the three men who'd been left with him to rot at Carlisle, all of them from the Isle of Skye, their beloved home. Instead of feeling adrift, all four of them had formed a brotherhood themselves, apart from their clans that had forgotten them. They now held Rory's loyalty, not Clan MacLeod.

Bloody hell, the foul room stunk. "Rest well," Rory said and stood, but Jamie had drifted back to an uncomfortable sleep. If Jamie's pain got much worse, Rory knew which artery to slice to end it fast—his father had taught him when he was eighteen.

CHAPTER TWENTY-SIX

"Chess, as we know it today, was born out of the Indian game chaturanga before the 600s AD. The game spread throughout Asia and Europe over the coming centuries, and eventually evolved into what we know as chess around the 16th century. One of the first masters of the game was a Spanish priest named Ruy Lopez. [He] advocated the strategy of playing with the sun in your opponent's eyes!"

Chess.com

Clutching the scrap of parchment sent to her, Sara walked lightly through the shadowed corridors of Dunvegan. *Come alone to the library.* The library was on the second level past the chief's room where Jamie held on to his quickly slipping life.

Had her father sent poison to the untried chief through a traitorous servant? Why then would he send a note ordering her to do so? Whoever placed it in her room was probably the assassin who was trying to make her look guilty. She'd felt Rory's weighing glances during supper several hours ago.

They'd had a freshly cooked venison stew that Brodrick had supervised. All other bread and stews had been thrown into the sea, and Cook Fiona was being watched by a longtime guard while she and one other maid, who'd been retained, kneaded and baked everything new. Still, everyone ate in silence, absorbed in inspecting every bite they took.

Sara continued down the corridor, hoping the note was from Rory. She wanted to talk to him and hear him say that he knew her to be innocent, because his looks had been hard, grim, and questioning.

Jamie's door opened as she neared, and Father Lockerby walked out with Hamish. They were both shaking their heads. "He's received last rites," the priest said, his lips pinched thinly.

Hamish nodded. "There's not much else we can do except clean up the mess." He nodded to Sara as she walked by.

Should she stop and inquire after her once bridegroom? Did it make her look guilty and unconcerned if she didn't? She paused, turning to the men. "Father Lockerby." She nodded to him. "Master Hamish." Another nod. "Thank you for the great care you are giving to Chief MacLeod, his body and his soul."

"'Tis our duty, Lady Sara," Hamish said but gave her a small smile.

Father Lockerby stared at her with piercing, judgmental eyes. "I will be staying at Dunvegan for the next few nights, Lady Seraphina, if ye seek a confession."

Her heart, which was already pounding from the note she clutched in her hand, stuttered. "My confession?"

"I don't believe ye've cleansed your heart and mind since before yer wedding," the priest said. She remembered the awkward meeting inside the small confessional that sat at the back of Dunscaith's small chapel. How she'd told him her nervousness over marrying the son of an enemy, and Father Lockerby had reminded her she must do her duty as a daughter of Eve and suffer through any torment Jamie might bring down on her. She'd been so furious, she hadn't confessed anything else, including her wish for the priest to be sent to an abbey far away where he'd have to remain silent for the rest of his days.

She loosened her jaw enough to speak. "When I sin again, Father, I will seek out a priest to confess."

His wiry brows shot up. "Do ye have the conceit to think ye have not sinned in the eyes of God since we last spoke?"

Being unmarried and sliding naked into Rory's arms was surely considered a sin, but there was no way she was going to tell this grumpy old priest about how he brought her to an ecstasy she hadn't known existed. She forced a small smile. "I'll pray on it, Father." She turned away before he could ask her anything else. The man slammed judgment on his flock like an ax cleaving logs, and most came away bloody.

Her fingers curled around the short note. It'd been waiting on her bed when she'd returned there after checking to make certain the twins were safe and tucked into the large bed they insisted on sharing in a room on the second level. It was as if they'd been missing a part of themselves their whole lives and longed to stay together now.

A gentle smile touched Sara's lips as she thought over how Eleri said she'd teach Eliza how to paint, and Eliza said she'd assist Eleri with the stretching exercises to help her back.

"Ye look content." The voice came from the shadow-filled room as she walked into the library.

Sara's hand went to her chest in surprise. "Holy Mother Mary, Rory."

Rory stood to the side of the doorway. He stepped out of the shadow and shut the door behind her. A fire snapped on a low grate in the hearth, splashing an orange glow over a chess board set upon a table between two chairs.

"Apologies." His voice still felt like a caress over her skin. It was the way he lowered the force of it, as if he were a lion relaxing in the heat of the sun. "I was choosing a book," he said, holding up a copy of *The Odyssey*. "In case ye didn't come."

She tipped her head. "I had a choice?"

His brows pinched the smallest amount as if he wondered if she were jesting. "Aye."

She held up the note. "It wasn't obvious." They hadn't been alone since Jamie's poisoning two days ago. Sara had waited rather impatiently in her tower room for him to come to her, but she'd been left alone. "Am I here for an inquisition?"

He let out a heavy exhale. "I want to talk with ye, Sara, without everyone listening in." He went to a narrow table against the wall, set the tome down, and poured some wine into a glass goblet. He set the glass on a small table next to the other chair where he'd already set a silver cup for himself. "I thought we could play a game."

She narrowed her eyes but walked over, lowering to perch on the edge of the chair. "Chess?" She didn't love the game but would play if he asked. "I prefer Merrills."

"I know a game that ye haven't played before."

"Its name?" she asked, watching him pluck the carved pieces from the chess set, placing them in a basket that sat under its table.

"Tha no chan eil."

Sara tilted her head, holding his gaze. "Yes or No? That's the name of your game?"

He nodded.

She huffed slightly through her nose. "Sounds like an interrogation, not a game." At least he didn't seem quite as rigid as he had at supper.

Rory picked a lion off the chess board, and she realized the pieces weren't the normal pawns and rooks. He held it up to her. "There are playing pieces so 'tis a game."

The shadow of his usual handsome grin touched his mouth, and she remembered how those lips had felt against her skin. A throb pulsed suddenly between her legs, and she snapped her gaze to the pieces instead.

Half were stained a dark red and polished to a shine. The other half were a pale natural wood that had also been polished. She picked up a bird, studying it. "They're all animals." The pawns were carved fish standing up on their tails. The artist had even spent time cutting little notches to look like fish scales on each of them. The rooks were stocky elephants, their trunks turned back along their bodies as if shooting water. The bishops were tall animals with long necks, painted with spots. She held one up. "What is this?"

"An animal with long limbs found on the continent of Afrika. 'Tis called a camelopard."

"And the knights' horses are striped," she said, picking one up.

"Also found on the plains of Afrika. They are stockier than horses, and all of them are striped black and white."

"Have you visited Afrika?" she asked, leaning closer to study the magnificent carvings.

"Nay, but my father's brother sent this to us when he sailed back from there on a trading ship. He had fantastical tales of the people and animals, like nothing here."

"Of course, the king is the lion," she said, holding up her red piece. The lion sat upright with majestic dignity. His large paws propped his powerful chest before him, and a full mane billowed out around his face. He was carved so intricately that the mane almost looked soft.

"Of course." Rory grinned as he watched her Was he trying to read her mind? Pick out indications she could be a liar, a Macdonald spy like Jamie accused? Rory's gaze was like a sun shining on her with intensity, making her heart pulse faster as if to cool her.

She picked up the queen. "A phoenix?" Even though the bird had been carved with its wings closed and a long beak, the red coloring indicated the mythical creature.

"A stork," he said. "There are several varieties in Afrika."

"Are they red?"

"Uncle said there are birds of wondrous colors there, but the piece was colored red for the game."

She set it down softly in its painted square on the board. "I shall call it Phoenix then."

She sat back and crossed her arms over her chest. "And you use a chess board and pieces to play your

Yes and No *game*?" She stressed the last word so he knew that she wouldn't be tricked into an interrogation. She should probably be angry that he wanted to question her, but she'd been waiting for it. Rory was soon to be the next MacLeod chief, and he had a duty to discover the traitor at Dunvegan, a dangerous traitor who could strike again.

"Aye," Rory answered. "But not all the pieces. Only two, one for me"—he held up the pale lion—"and one for ye. Ye can choose."

Sara held up the red phoenix. "It seems fitting."

"I thought ye might choose her," he said, setting the other pieces gingerly into the basket.

"Like the one in the tower." Did he think about that night as much as she?

He set his lion at the top of the board. "Yer phoenix can sit anywhere along yer side."

She set her bird opposite his across the board as if they were preparing to battle. *Appropriate.* Sara's hand squeezed in her lap. "Now what?"

Rory took a sip from his cup. Good Lord, the man was handsome in a kingly way. It was more than his thick hair and amber eyes that gave him the look of a lion. It was the way he carried himself, all restrained power and easily released might, like a taut bowstring. The scar along his hairline showed that he, like the king of the Afrikan plains, had fought for his life and won.

"We ask each other questions or give a statement that can be answered in the affirmative or negative."

"Interrogate each other."

"Once again, 'tis a game," he said, lifting his lion and wiggling it back and forth in the air.

"Then how do I win?"

She'd win if she convinced him she was innocent of all the conjecture swirling around Dunvegan.

He smiled. "The one who reaches the other side of the board first loses. If the response to what I say is aye, ye move yer phoenix forward one space. If the answer is nay, ye move yer piece to the side one space."

"Can we occupy the same space?"

"Aye," he said, "but there's a penalty."

She narrowed her eyes. "What type of penalty?"

"Chosen by the player who is already in the space, but examples are…" He looked up to the wood plank ceiling. "Ye must place the next move standing or ye must take a sip of whisky or remove the pins from yer hair." He nodded to the bun Eliza had fashioned on top of Sara's head.

"You've constructed this game from flimflam," she said, crossing her arms under her breasts. "Why don't you ask me questions, and I'll answer once again that I don't know where the Fairy Flag is, and I didn't poison Jamie."

Rory nodded, his grin gone. "Aye, I could." He looked up to meet her eyes and she saw something there that curbed the cutting words on her tongue. Something sad. "I could," he repeated, "but I don't want to…interrogate ye, Sara."

They stared at one another over the board, the fire crackling beside them. She sighed and passed her hand across the board. "So, a game instead."

His grin came back. "This way, ye can ask me questions, too. And since ye're a guest here and a lady, ye may ask first."

"And you'll move forward one space for yes and one space to either side for no?"

His smile widened and he went to move his piece in answer.

"That was not my question," she said, her voice rising. "Merely a clarification before we start."

"Then ask yer question, milady," he said, his voice teasing. It made her want to smile, too, but she didn't because this was really an interrogation, which meant he didn't trust her. He'd told her early on he didn't trust anyone, so this shouldn't feel as heartbreaking as it did.

She sipped her wine and set it down. "Did you create this game yourself?" she asked, and Rory moved his lion forward one space, meaning that the answer to her question was yes.

"Ho now!" she said in triumph. "I knew it."

He grinned at her outburst. "My turn. Yer favorite tart is blaeberry with crumbs on top."

Her lips fell open, and she blinked at him. "How...? You asked Eliza, didn't you?"

"Is that another question?"

She moved her red phoenix one space forward, the bottom tapping down with her annoyance. "No, because 'tis obvious you asked her."

From the number of squares across, Sara had six other answers before she made it across the board and lost. Not that she really cared about winning this game that wasn't a game. But perhaps it was time to confirm some things she thought were true about the man across from her.

It was her turn. "Did you know who I was on the shore when we met? The day before the wedding?"

Rory moved his lion one space to the side, so they were no longer lined up. *No.* "Did ye know who I was?"

She moved her phoenix over one space in the opposite direction, and he took a drink. The way he didn't take his eyes off her while he sipped was heated, as if by tasting the amber liquid he was tasting her. The throb turned into a sizzle that zigzagged through her like lightning hitting the ground.

She shifted in her seat. "Is your favorite drink whisky?"

"Hmmm…" He picked up the cup again and stared down into it. "That depends on a lot of things. If I've recently woken, 'tis warm mulled wine. After training or battling, 'tis ale. When I find a free-flowing spring, fresh water."

She waved a hand at him. "Right now, is your favorite drink whisky?"

He moved his lion forward, and she smiled. She could ask him obvious questions and his lion would have no choice but to move quickly across the board. But then she wouldn't learn anything about him, and she wanted to know more about this man who heated her dreams at night and thoughts during the day.

"Yer soap has the essence of flowers in it," he said.

Sara tipped her head. "That isn't a question." She took a sip of the red wine. It was sweet and slid down easily.

"It doesn't have to be, but I'll be more specific. Is the flower in yer soap…bog myrtle?"

She moved her piece to the side. "'Tis twin flower. Morag collects it and puts the scent into soap. She prefers lavender in everything, but I like the lightness of twin flower."

His mouth curved. "I think 'tis my favorite scent."

His words brought a warm flush up her chest into her neck. She glanced down. As much as her body responded to Rory's every glance and sweet comment, there were questions nagging at her. She met his eyes as she asked her next question. "Am I innocent of my father's plan to burn you all alive in the chapel?"

Sara held her breath. It seemed Rory took a long time to move his lion forward, indicating "yes," but she released her breath when he did. He thought her innocent of at least that.

He took another sip and set his pewter cup down. "Ye hide a mark on yer back, something ye didn't want me to see that morning in the tower."

Looking down, she slid her piece forward one, but she didn't plan to elaborate. She thought of the scars on his back on the shore. "Were you flogged at the prison in England, on your back?"

He slid the lion forward. Despite the grin curving his lips, his face had hardened, and she wished she could take the question back. Her brother didn't like to speak of his time under King Henry's thumb, either.

"Ye suffered while living at Dunscaith," Rory said. The man preferred statements to questions.

She wished she could refute it, but she wouldn't lie. She slid the animal forward one square.

Rory's nostrils flared slightly, and all remnants of his grin were gone. "I'm sorry for that."

"It helps one realize where they stand within one's clan."

He frowned. "Something I learned while

imprisoned in England is that family loyalty can be broken. That overcoming obstacles together can form a stronger bond."

Kenan had said something similar when he'd returned, thin, weak, and with a hardness about him, especially when he interacted with their father. Walter Macdonald had seen it immediately and cut Kenan out of all his plans, involving Gilbert as if he were the oldest instead of the youngest son.

It was her turn to ask. She touched her forehead close to her hairline as she stared across at his scar, the one she'd actually run the tip of her tongue along that morning in the tower. "Is that a scar from a battle?"

He slid his lion sideways toward her phoenix. "Was a skirmish with my brother, not a battle."

The fire popped, making her look at the flames. When she looked back, he was studying the board as if they played a real chess game.

"Ye stole the Fairy Flag," he said.

She frowned and slid her phoenix to the side toward him as if challenging the ridiculous notion. "No."

She could be lying, but his broad shoulders relaxed. He believed her? At least he wanted to. He lifted his gaze to her. The flaring fire in the grate made his amber eyes look more golden like the beast on the Afrikan plains.

Morag used to say not to ask questions you did not want the answer to, but Sara must know. She swallowed. "Do you believe I poisoned your brother?"

Without breaking his stare, he moved his piece. She didn't want to cut the tether between them, but to breathe again, she must know the answer. She looked down.

CHAPTER TWENTY-SEVEN

"[Maternal Impression] phenomenon describes a belief that birthmarks result from the marked child's mother having some sort of strange or frightening encounter during her pregnancy... Japanese tradition held that a pregnant woman who gazed into a fire would give birth to a child with a 'burn mark.'"

TheList.com

Sara's lovely lips parted as she looked down at the board, and he watched her inhale. Her gaze slid up to him again. "You don't think I poisoned him?"

He shook his head. "Nay." It wasn't a lie. The timing didn't work unless she had help and despite what Jamie said about her tricking them into trusting her, she'd pulled Jamie out of a burning church, thus barring her safe return to her home. Rory might not trust his own abilities to read duplicity in others, but facts spoke louder than guesses.

"Well," she said, gathering herself, "I'm glad for that because I *didn't* poison Jamie. I think someone is trying to make me look guilty."

"Another indication ye're innocent," he said. He'd said as much to Jok when he'd insisted that Rory interrogate Sara *for the good of the clan*. Rory had agreed but would do it his own way, giving Sara a chance to do the same to him.

Rory tipped his head toward the board. "We occupy the same spot."

She dropped her gaze to see both animals pushed together, half in the square and half out. "Since you chose to move that way, I say that I make you do something." She flapped her hand at him.

"We both do something," he countered.

"Like what? We both stand on one foot while we move next?"

He remained back in his seat in the most non-threatening posture he could put on. "Show me yer back, Sara."

Her spine straightened as if it realized it would be on display and sought to stand at attention. "My back?"

"The mark ye've hidden from me." He did lean forward then, his head tilting slightly. "I wish to know every inch of ye." His words were smooth like the whisky he sipped, and he didn't even blink, not wanting to give her a chance to break the tether between them. He hadn't started this concocted game to ask to see the mark. But he'd decided to trust her despite Jamie, Jok, and a village full of people who remembered him being duped by Madeline. And he wanted her to trust him.

"I want to kiss every part," he said, his voice low and even. "Kiss, and lick, and nibble."

A flush rose into her cheeks, and those lush lips parted again. "I don't believe anyone has ever said something so…lustful to me before."

His grin turned into a smile. "I seem to remember some lustful words between us in the tower."

Her flush intensified. Och, but she remembered. Words, wicked and tantalizing, spoken between them as their bodies moved together, sliding and grinding. "You remember?" she asked. "From the coolness you've displayed since our return, I thought you'd pushed it from your mind." Her words were soft, just above the crackle from the flames in the hearth.

"Despite everything bombarding us, those words are etched inside my skull." In truth, they played through his mind every night when he'd taken himself in his own hand. Her breathy commands to touch her inside, to tease her into moaning.

She shifted in her seat as if the glorious crux of her legs ached, too.

"And what, would ye have me surrender to ye?" He nodded to the two pieces on the board. "Now that ye know my price." Would she ask him to make her moan again? To tease her until she exploded with passion?

"Then I would see your back, Ror," she said, using his shortened name.

He tipped his head. "Ye already have."

"I would see it here, now."

Rory stood and pulled his sash from his shoulder, letting it hang from the wrap around his hips. Keeping his gaze locked on Sara's eyes, he yanked his tunic off over his head. Her gaze slid down his chest like a caress against his skin until it fell on his jack jutting forward under the wrap. With her gaze still on him, his hand cupped it, and he slowly adjusted it through the wool. He saw her swallow.

He turned around, letting her see the two lash marks that had scarred over. They weren't the type of scars a man could boast, so Rory stood there rigidly. Three of the four Skye prisoners had the two lash marks, given by the captain in charge of Carlisle dungeon. Only Ash had been practically deformed by the flaying he'd received when captured trying to escape on his own.

Would Sara actually let him see whatever was on her back? Of course, he wouldn't force her. He heard the scrape of wood and looked over his shoulder.

Sara slid the bar over the door, locking it against anyone trying to enter. When she turned back to him, she nodded to it. "So no one walks in to find you half naked."

He didn't care what people saw but Sara would if she complied. She walked up to him. "Do they hurt?" She lifted her hand, and he turned his face back to gaze unseeing at the wall of books opposite him.

"The ridges can get irritated and scratched open easily, but they don't really." His inhale caught as he felt her cool finger touch the rough, raised lines across his back where he knew her own fingernails had left light score marks.

"You're fortunate they didn't become infected."

He pushed the thought of Ash's bloody slices away and concentrated on the feel of Sara's fingers on his skin. His most imperfect part of him. "Fortunate? Aye. Fortunate we were given a means to escape when we worked together."

She walked around to the front of him, standing close as she looked up into his face. "Kenan mentioned items sewn into blankets." She shook her head. "But none of you know from where they came."

He shook his head, his fingers rising to catch a curl that slid along her cheek. It was so soft, and he knew that if he inhaled near it, he'd catch a faint whiff of twin flowers. He tucked the curl behind her delicate ear, which he remembered teasing with his teeth before. His cock remembered, too.

"I had skeleton keys which we used to open the cell door and the dungeon door and another gate."

"Kenan had gold coins," Sara said, and he watched her lips move. They were so soft. His cock twitched again as if trying to escape his woolen wrap.

"Can I see yer back?" he asked before she did something like lick her lips and make him forget everything else except the heat he knew lay between her legs.

She stared into his eyes for a long moment. "'Tis a birthmark, not a scar. No one has beaten me."

Rory was certain she'd been harmed in other ways. "Were ye told it made ye…less?"

His sister, Eleri, had been made to feel shame for her curved spine, despite having nothing to do with it.

Her gaze dipped to his throat. "By some. Most don't see it. I keep it hidden." She looked back up. "But my husband would see it, and I had hoped…"

Hoped Jamie wouldn't have condemned her for something she'd been born with? If his treatment of Eleri, ordering her to stay up in her tower, was any indication, Sara would have suffered bound to him.

She took a full inhale and slid her short jacket from her shoulders. Her fingers pulled the pins from her stomacher and plucked the ties of her blue stays, which laced down the front with white ribbon. Quickly, it dropped away, leaving her in her smock up top and her petticoats below. The neckline was tied together at the base of her throat. He itched to help her, but kept his hands fisted by his sides. The heat from the fire behind him, and the fire rising within, made him hot even though he wore only the wrap around his hips and his boots.

Her skirts swished as she turned around, and she shrugged her straight shoulders until the linen fell away from the soft skin there. He remembered kissing that rise of shoulder, inhaling at the base of her neck, and sliding his cheek along the creamy skin. But the stiffness in her stance was a barrier she'd set, one he'd respect. So, he waited as she moved those beautiful naked shoulders a bit more, widening the opening of the smock so that the white undergown fell farther down her back.

The red stain, her birthmark, stood out like fire against the paleness of her skin. It stretched downward in a swath of deep crimson that curved into the middle of her back, reaching down into the folds of fabric at her waist. It covered a third of the pale landscape of her back.

• • •

Sara's breath felt stuck between her ribs. The coolness of the room made chill bumps rise over her skin. Sweet Mary, the bumps would just make the mark look worse.

"Does it pain ye?" he asked, his voice soft behind her. He didn't touch her except with his gaze.

"No. Sometimes I think 'tis more sensitive, but…" She shook her head, the bun feeling wobbly like her legs. She forced herself to breathe evenly.

She felt his fingertip at the peak of the birthmark. It dragged along an edge down until the waistband stopped him. The edges weren't crisp, the patch of red-hued skin feathering into the smooth skin around it like a swath of river feeding the flanking vegetation. She'd viewed it in Morag's polished glass the night before her wedding, but it hadn't lessened or faded over time.

She looked over her shoulder at him, studying his reaction, but he kept his emotions in check. The coolness in the room reminded her of the yearly inspections her father demanded to see if it had faded, making her stomach twist. But the mark only ever darkened. "'Tis ugly. I know."

"Nay." He held her gaze. "It curves like, well like a flame." He laid his palm against the skin and followed the slightly raised patch down her spine. "'Tis as if ye are the beautiful and mysterious Celtic goddess of fire." His voice was deep, a tumbling rumble. He lowered his lips and gently kissed the peak of the flame several inches below her nape.

Sara's heart leaped at the sensation, and she felt tears swell in her eyes. Was this acceptance? Even Morag had fought to lessen the stain, to rid Sara of it.

Rory's hand slid up to grasp her shoulder, his thumb reaching inward to stroke the stretch between shoulder and base of the neck. She shivered at the sensations penetrating her skin, shooting down through her. A gentle kiss touched the spot before trailing slow feathery kisses to return to her birthmark.

"Ror," she whispered, an unspoken plea within it.

Rory bent his knees, lowering inch by inch, kissing the flame down her back. The flame born to her, etched into her, marking her as different, unworthy, and ugly. But it didn't seem to bother him.

When he reached the waist of her skirts where he could go no farther, he stood, and Sara turned to face him. Her pale, full breasts were exposed, the nipples hard. But Rory just looked into her eyes.

Unshed tears swelled there, one overflowing to slide down her cheek. Her instinct was to wipe it away, but he leaned in, kissing it away from her cheek. He stroked her face. "I would flay everyone who has told ye ye're ugly, Sara." The flash of beast-like rage caught her breath.

She stepped into him, her peaked nipples brushing the light hair of his chest, and she captured the back of his neck. His gaze slid to the paleness of the underside of her upper arm. He took a moment to kiss it. "So soft."

"'Tis one of my best features," she said, holding her arm out.

The anger in Rory's gaze softened, and he grinned. "I think ye have many of those features, lass. Soft little secret places that I will taste." He leaned forward, his lips brushing hers. "Every. Single. One."

A shudder ran through her, sending a pulse down through her core, making it ache for his touch. She pressed into him which made the swell of her breasts rise up, the softness such a contrast to his hard chest. "May I love ye, lass?" His face came closer, his lips lightly touching her ear. "Make ye moan and thrash, my lusty fire goddess."

Sara released his neck, pulling three long pins from her bun. She let them fall to the floor as her hair tumbled down, tickling against her bare back. "Yes, Rory MacLeod, Lion of Skye. Make me moan and thrash."

With a charged groan, he grabbed her to him, his mouth descending to her lips. She opened with an immediate, wild response, the longing she'd felt over these days making her reaction urgent and intense. His hand raked upward through her mass of hair to hold her head in his palm, guiding her and holding her steady as he plundered the softness of her mouth. He tasted of whisky and desire, of heat and need. The tinge of wine on her own tongue mixed with his taste into the most delicious flavor she'd ever known.

His hands stroked down her bare back, his fingers tugging eagerly at the ties of her petticoats. She pulled the end of his thick leather belt that held his plaid pleated together. Her hand grazed his straining cock through the wool, and he growled. She loved his response to her. He'd seen her back and still responded with need. She did it again, this time cupping her hand around him through his wrap in a stroke.

Sweet Mother Mary, he was large.

His answering groan was fire to her soul, eating her up in the most pleasure-filled way possible. She was no longer a maid and was ready to explore more ways to find wanton pleasure. Her passion was already growing into an inferno, and it was glorious.

Her heavy outer petticoat dropped, leaving her in only the thin red under petticoat. With each layer lifted from her body, she felt lighter, freer. His mouth lowered to capture one of her nipples as his fingers caught the petticoat, raising it to the back of her knee.

"Oh my God, Ror," she gasped as he sucked hard on her peaked nipple.

His fingers licked a trail up her thigh, hitching the petticoat as he rose, kissing her neck. The heat from the fire behind her prickled against her bared skin. It mirrored the heat raging inside her. Sara threw her head back, giving him access to every bit of her skin.

His fingers stroked down over her backside, farther, seeking the heat between her legs. As he neared, her thighs parted, giving her silent permission. His mouth left a damp trail of kisses and nibbles to her ear. "Are ye wet for me, Sara?"

She answered with a soft moan.

"Aye," he murmured. "Och but lass, ye're all hot honey."

"Oh yessss," she hissed out when he sank two fingers into her primed, pulsing flesh.

From the sounds, she knew she was slick with desire, desire for him. She panted as he moved inside her, but then he withdrew. Before she could complain, he lifted her, carrying her to the chair, kicking the table out of the way. She heard the lion and phoenix fly off and tumble across the thick rug underneath and onto the wood floor beyond.

Rory perched her in the chair and knelt before her, a wicked smile on his lips as he watched her. Sara palmed her own breasts, pinching the nipples, her lips parted as she stared back into his eyes.

He rolled up her red smock until her legs were exposed, her thighs spread apart in the chair. "Remember this?" he said.

"Oh God." Her heart leaped in anticipation as he bowed his head.

He wrapped his arms around her hips, holding her to his face. Licking and nibbling, loving her with his mouth and fingers. She moaned as fire raked through her blood and squeezed her own breasts as he poured pleasure into her below.

She felt her body tense around his fingers.

While pleasure rolled through her, Rory lifted her from the chair, turning her to lean against it. Body contracting, her fingers curled around the back of the chair. He threw her skirts up her back, and she spread her legs, knowing the sight must be driving lust into Rory. She was open and slick with need. She glanced over her shoulder when he grasped her hips.

Rory was hard and straining, his face intense with dire need. Never before had she seen anything so primal. It sent another jolt of want through her, matching him.

"Yes, Ror, now."

He thrust into her, filling her completely, her still pulsing body gripping him. Sara threw back her head, and he thrust again and again. His arm held around her stomach, arse slamming back into him. Eyes closed, she felt his fingers reach around to rub her still roused body as he continued to thunder in and out of her from behind. For long minutes, they moved as one, undulating and colliding. He slammed into her so hard, her thighs hit the chair, sliding the piece of furniture across the floor.

Suddenly, her feet left the floor as Rory's arms wrapped around her stomach, carrying her toward the wall. He set her down facing the wall, and she braced against it as he continued to thrust up into her. He bent over her back, his mouth at her ear where he growled low, and she shuddered at the intensity in his voice. "Yer body wants me. Moving inside ye."

"Yes," she answered on an exhale. "I'm so full."

His fingers moved outside her, rubbing her into a

frenzy of sexual need. "Yes, yes!" she called, and her body clenched around his cock as she peaked again.

Rory's lips nibbled at her ear, his growl turned into rasping words. "Ye are mine, Sara. Mine, marked and filled. Do ye understand?"

"Yes, oh God yes," she answered, passion still wrenching through her.

With one mighty roar, he exploded within her, his mouth resting in that space between her neck and shoulder. Body tight and pulsing, he filled her, and they continued to move, riding the waves of sexual oblivion that washed away the world around them.

• • •

Sara woke slowly, stretching, feeling the softness of the sheets brush her naked skin. She blinked and saw she was alone, the bed beside her cool. Her gaze went to the pointed, whitewashed ceiling.

In the tower.

Tugging the blanket and sheet higher to cover her breasts, she rose on one elbow.

Alone.

From the look of the sun coming in the windows, it was well past dawn. Of course, Rory had gotten up, and probably hadn't wanted to wake her. Sara slid her hands down her sensitive body. She ached in all her well-loved parts. Even her nipples were sensitive after rubbing along the thick rug the second time they'd come together in the library.

She smiled thinking of the wickedness that had made her sink to her knees on that carpet first to take him in her mouth, giving him the same type of pleasure he'd given her. When he could stand no more, he'd pressed her down on the carpet, first face to face, and then on her stomach from behind. She'd felt him kiss her back along her birthmark before he draped over her, plunging into her willing, open body. The crux of her legs pulsed at the memory.

Rap. Rap. "Lady Sara," Margaret called through the door.

A deep flush rose up Sara's neck, and she pressed against the throbbing once more before pushing out of bed. Her fingers snatched up the fallen robe, and she threw her arms into it, tying it around her waist as she called, "One moment, Mistress Margaret." Raking fingers through her hair, Sara hoped none of Rory's passionate nibbles showed on her skin like the one she'd gotten in the tower. She clutched the collar of the robe up higher as a precaution and went to the door, opening it.

Margaret stood there with four maids behind her, and two men holding something large between them. "What is all this?" Sara asked, standing aside as Margaret lifted and carried a bucket of water into her room, walking to the hearth where only cinders remained. All seven of them breathed hard from climbing four floors with their burdens.

"Sir Rory ordered you a bath, milady. Upstairs instead of in the back of the kitchens."

Two stout men carried in a narrow wooden tub that she'd be able to sit in to wash. Setting it down, they helped the maids with the buckets of water, pouring them in.

"Let the two on the fire heat up and pour it in the cold water," Margaret said, setting the iron poker back against the hearth. She'd added two peat squares to the glowing embers.

"I…thank you," Sara said, her cheeks warm. "I told Ror…Sir Rory that I was cold yesterday morn. 'Twas considerate of him to think to send me a hot bath."

The others marched out, but Margaret turned her direct gaze on Sara. "Of course," she said, walking forward to set a bar of soap in her hand. "And he says you like essence of twin flowers in your soap." It wasn't so much the words but the inflections that told Sara the older woman knew exactly why Rory had ordered her a hot bath.

"And this liniment can be used on any sore muscles." Margaret set the small bottle in her other hand. Her brows rose. "External muscles only."

Sara's lips parted, but the only words that she could muster were "thank you."

Margaret nodded and pointed to a tray one of the maids had set on her rumpled bed. "Enjoy your bath and break your fast. The girls are already asking for you." She looked back over her shoulder at Sara. "But I told them to let you have your rest." She smiled wickedly and stepped out onto the landing.

Margaret started to pull the door shut and then bent. "A note." Without looking at it, she held it out for Sara, who set her soap and liniment down to take it.

"Thank you," she said.

Margaret nodded with a smile and shut the door while Sara broke the seal.

Come see me this morn. Jamie

CHAPTER TWENTY-EIGHT

"It is your concern when your neighbor's wall is on fire."

Horace, 65–8 BC, Roman poet

Rory whistled lightly as he climbed the steps from the dock. He'd been called away that morn right after he'd asked Margaret to send up a warm bath to the tower room. He should ask Sara to move down to a room on the same floor as his. He'd rather have her in his own room, but he knew she would never agree to be his mistress.

Once his position as the new chief of the MacLeod Clan of Skye was firm, he'd ask her to wed. He'd already sent a message to Father Lockerby requesting a dispensation for marrying his brother's wife since their union was annulled within minutes of being blessed. Without consummation, the marriage wasn't valid.

Gus barked at the top of the steps in greeting, and Rory scratched his head and smiled. "I agree, old fellow, 'tis a glorious morn." He'd thought that the moment he'd opened his eyes to find himself curled around Sara in her small bed in the Tower Room. They'd ended up there after the library so she could gather a fresh smock and clean her teeth. They never made it out.

He chuckled as he walked into the great hall.

"Good morn," he called to Jok and Brodrick. "And to ye two." He nodded to John and Simon, who seemed to live in Dunvegan now. Did they ever ferry across to their own cottages in the village? Maybe they were sleeping in one of the spare bedchambers. 'Twas fine with him.

Jok's brows rose. "Was that ye whistling coming up the stairs?"

"Perhaps," he said and muted his smile. After all, his brother was still deathly ill, and the Fairy Flag was missing.

"Did ye find the damn flag then?" Simon called from his spot at the hearth.

"Nay," Rory said, his smile disappearing on his exhale as if a cloud had covered the sun.

John knocked Simon with his one arm. "I tell ye, Walter Macdonald is right now rigging it up on a staff to fly over himself when they march to Dunvegan. Its magic will multiply his forces by ten."

"My scouts haven't reported them riding off their territory," Rory said and sat at the table.

Brodrick crossed his arms, his usual frown in place. "I didn't expect ye back so fast. Was there nothing amiss at the mill?"

The millhouse on the Allt Beag River ground all their grains into flour. 'Twas powerful, and farmers from across Skye came to use it.

Rory uncorked the bladder of ale he'd been drinking off, which had come from Fiona's guarded stock. "Nay," he said and took a long swallow before looking back at the man. "The millstone wasn't cracked that I could see. I spent time inspecting the wheel buckets while I was there, and the gears and the hopper, but the whole process was running smoothly, churning out finely ground oat flour. Randal Grant was red-faced furious that someone reported a problem to me without informing him first."

The informant had sent an anonymous note that morn. Rory thought they hadn't signed it because the person worried over being blamed. That was probably why they hadn't informed Grant.

Rory studied Brodrick's tired features. He'd been spending the nights with Jamie, guarding him as if the assassin could do more damage. "How fares my brother this morn?" Rory's tone had lowered. He still wondered if he should end Jamie's suffering with a well-placed slice to his throat. "Is Hamish with him now?"

Brodrick shook his head. "He saw him right before dawn and was called away to help with a difficult birth the midwife worried over."

"Henrietta Blounce worried?" Rory asked. The older woman never called in the barber-surgeon to help her. Only women, trained by herself, were permitted in the birthing rooms in the village.

Jok shrugged. "I know Reagan and Aiden are expecting a bairn soon. Perhaps Aiden is worried and called for him."

"Unless she's lost her mind," Rory said. "Henrietta will be sending Hamish right on his way when he gets out to their cottage. Poor man will probably need a shot of whisky after her tongue lashing."

"Jamie seemed a bit improved this morn," Brodrick said.

"Improved?" Rory asked. Hamish had told him that Jamie's skin, urine, and eyes were turning a darker yellow.

"He said he wanted to talk to someone and sent me away," Brodrick said.

"When was that?" Who did Jamie wish to speak with? Winnie? The woman hadn't been around much since the first day, as if she couldn't handle the noxious smells in the room despite the windows being thrown open. Could he want to talk again with Sara? Or see Eleri? Had he learned about Eleri's twin and wanted to meet Eliza?

Brodrick glanced toward the steps. "I left him nearly an hour ago." He nodded at Rory. "Someone should check on him now."

Rory stood. "Ye look exhausted, man. I'll check on him."

Brodrick stood, too. "I need to get my pallet from his room." So he'd been sleeping there.

"Do ye need help cleaning him up?" Jok asked and nodded to Margaret, who'd come from the kitchens.

"Probably," Rory said.

"Maybe we should say our farewell now," Simon said, following them. "The priest gave him last rites, so he could go anytime now."

Rory exhaled as he led the small procession. A person certainly didn't need last rites to die.

"Hamish said he was improved," Brodrick insisted.

John hurried to keep up, his gait wobbling side to side, almost like a duck. He shook his leg. "'Tis fallen asleep."

Rory stopped before his brother's door and inhaled the cool, relatively clean air of the corridor before depressing the handle, the weight of onlookers at his back. "Let me first see—"

The door swung inward, and the sight before him stole the rest of his words.

Sara stood beside Jamie's bed, holding a plump white pillow in her hands. With a gasp, she whirled toward him at the door, and Rory saw bright red across the linen of the pillow. "Rory. I found him—"

"What is this?" Brodrick yelled as he rushed past Rory into the room.

Heavy goose down pillows were scattered across Jamie's bed, and Brodrick ripped the pillow from Sara's grasp. Rory crossed to them in two strides, steadying her. Distress tightened her shoulders, and her face was pale as the bleached sheets encasing the pillows. He pulled her into his chest as he looked down at his brother.

"Bloody hell," he said when he saw Jamie. His eyes were open but there was no life in them. Blood dried under his nose, which looked crooked, broken.

Beside them, Brodrick jabbed the pillow in the air. "She smothered him! Broke his nose even when he was already in pain."

"No," Sara said, pushing out of Rory's arms. "I found him with the pillow over his face."

Simon and John crept closer to the bed. Simon leaned in, centering his good eye on Jamie's face. "Aye, he's dead now."

John poked Jamie, but he didn't move. The elderly man pointed at the pillow that Brodrick clasped. "And he was alive when that pillow broke his nose, or it wouldn't have bled so bright."

Jok moved around the room, looking under the bed as if the culprit could be hiding there.

Rory rubbed his forehead. "Why would someone kill him now?" If someone meant to relieve his suffering, they would have sliced his throat or given him a quick-acting poison. Jamie had suffered.

Brodrick dropped the pillow. "He must have known something that the murderer"—he scowled at Sara—"didn't want anyone to know. Maybe he guessed who the poisoner was and was questioning her about it."

Sara kept her gaze on Rory. "This note was left outside my bedchamber door this morn." She handed the folded paper to him. "Margaret can attest to it."

Jok looked over his shoulder as he read. "What did he want to see ye about?"

"I don't know," she said, her lips tight. "He was like this when I got here."

"Ye killed him because he knew ye poisoned him and was going to tell Rory," Brodrick said, his voice sharp with conviction. His face snapped to Rory. "She's poisoned the chief. She's stolen the Fairy Flag." He pointed a finger at her while staring hard into Rory's eyes. "She's turning ye against yer own clan just like Madeline."

"Madeline?" Sara asked. "Who is Madeline?"

Rory looked to Jamie lying there in the rumpled, stained bed, so gray and diminished in death. Hot prickles moved under his skin up his neck into his jaw. Jamie didn't even look like the warrior Rory had known, the hotheaded, disloyal brother he'd grown up with. The one who'd made him give the foking vow never to trust a Macdonald woman again. The one who'd left him to rot down in England, even after their indifferent father had died, giving Jamie the power to act.

Who would smother him, killing him quicker than the poison? Who besides Rory? Who besides Sara?

Hamish Gower bustled in. "Henrietta Blounce is a cold, frustrating—" His words choked off as he viewed Jamie. "Well, Hell," he said and began to perform a basic examination.

Rory saw Reid standing wide-eyed in the entryway. He bit his bottom lip until Rory thought he saw the red of blood there. "Master Reid," Rory said, "please escort Lady Sara up to her room while I deal with this…assault."

He met Sara's gaze for a moment. There were questions in her eyes, but at the moment, Rory was devoid of any answers. She walked out the door in front of Reid, and a chill fell over Rory. As soon as Reid pulled the door closed behind him, everyone started to talk.

"She smothered him, broke his nose," Brodrick said.

"Could she do something like that with those thin arms?" Simon asked.

John grabbed a pillow with his one intact arm and pressed it against himself. "The feather pillows are heavy. I could do it if Jamie didn't fight."

Jok grabbed Rory's arm with a tight grip. "Ye're the new chief, Rory. Ye have to set an example."

Rory rounded on him. "An example? What do ye mean? Do ye want me to haul Sara out front and slice her throat? Let it bleed out before everyone and make every last MacLeod swear to never talk to a Macdonald again? Is that the example ye speak of?"

Silence fell within the room.

Simon and John looked at each other, shaking their gray heads as if this was all a pity.

"Ye questioned her last night?" Jok asked.

"Aye," Rory answered, leaving his game method and subsequent night of hedonistic pleasure out of his explanation. "And I'm convinced she has nothing to do with this." He threw his arm out toward Jamie's body, Hamish moving silently around him.

"She's wily," Brodrick said, "and has fooled ye." Disappointment weighted his words.

Rory's heart thumped hard, anger licking up inside him. "I have not been fooled." His words were a low warning, hiding any doubt that might be snaking up within him. His glare centered on Brodrick and then slid to Jok, the man he trusted the most, his closest friend.

Jok held up his hands as if trying to stop Rory from charging. "We are merely saying… Ye've only known Sara for a couple weeks if that, and she seems to have…changed ye."

She had. She'd brought hope to him that their clans might one day be united against the real enemy, England. She'd freed him from the guilt of Eleri being tucked away and feeling like she wasn't worthy. She'd finally trusted him enough to show him her back even though it was obvious she felt lacking because of the marks. Her vulnerability had lowered his resistance to trusting her. She'd done all these things, and she'd made him happy. How long had it been since he'd felt a lightness inside? He closed his eyes. *Ten years.*

He opened his eyes to take in the stares of the four men around him. "I will not kill her, even if she took the flag and smothered all of ye."

"Well, fok," Brodrick said, crossing his arms and jamming his hands in his armpits. "She's foking fooled ye."

"Hold yer tongue," Rory shouted over him. "Or I'll slice it out of yer screaming mouth."

That shut them all up. Even Hamish cast an uneasy glance his way.

"I am the chief of Clan MacLeod," Rory said, his voice hard. "If ye want to challenge me, do it, Brodrick. Otherwise, keep that bloody tongue still."

"No one said kill," Jok said, his words even.

"I did," Brodrick said.

Rory yanked his sgian dubh out of its sleek holder at his belt and took a step toward him. Jok stepped between them, two hands bracing Rory's chest to stop him from cutting Brodrick's tongue out.

"I didn't say kill," Jok said, "but she has to leave Dunvegan."

CHAPTER TWENTY-NINE

*"I wish I could give you a taste of the burning fire of
love. There is a fire blazing inside of me.
If I cry about it, or if I don't, the fire
is at work, night and day."*

*Muhammad Rumi, 1207-1273,
Persian poet & philosopher*

Sara paced in her tower room. Who the hell was
Madeline?

The door was unlocked, but she knew Brodrick
and two more of his men walked the corridor below
as if she might attempt an escape.

"Why would you smother him when he was already poisoned?" Eliza asked. She and Eleri sat
together on Sara's bed.

Eleri clasped her hands in her lap. "They say she
either became enraged by his accusations or that he'd
found proof she'd poisoned him and stolen the Fairy
Flag. That she'd taken up the pillow to still his tongue
before he could tell anyone."

"They?" Sara asked. "Who is saying this?"

Eleri looked at her with worried eyes. "Brodrick,
Barnaby, some of the women in town. I'm sure Winnie
Mar is circulating the condemnation, too."

"She was Jamie's mistress?" Eliza asked her twin.

Eleri nodded. "And she's not a nice person."

That was being kind. Winnie had been nothing but

a waspish banshee since the moment Sara had seen her when she walked up to St. Mary's Chapel for her wedding. And from what she'd heard from Margaret, the woman had treated Eleri like an unwanted embarrassment.

"Eleri, do you know who Madeline is?" Sara asked.

Eleri scrunched her face as if thinking hard, but then shook her head. "No. I don't know someone named Madeline."

Rap. Rap.

All three of them looked at the door. Were the guards coming to drag Sara away, throwing her back into the pit with ice-cold water? Quickly, she threw her feet into her boots and grabbed a cloak.

"You don't think…" Eleri said, her eyes round.

"What?" Eliza asked.

"The dungeon," Eleri said.

Rap. Rap. "Sara. Can I speak with ye?" The sound of Rory's voice released the rock-hard knot in her stomach, and she walked to the door, pulling it open.

Rory leaned his arm against the low lintel, his face grim. "Sara," he said, his eyes searching her face. Her stomach flipped. 'Twas as if all his unspoken questions flowed out of his face, his eyes, mirroring the questions in his heart.

Prickles of anger sparked anew within her. She'd said that she was innocent of smothering and poisoning and stealing the bloody flag. What other questions could he have if he believed her? None. So Rory didn't believe her.

She stepped aside, and Rory bent to walk in, straightening. "Can I speak with yer sister alone?" he asked the twins. It was a question, but Sara had no doubt that it was an order. It had only been two days since Jamie was killed, and Rory already wore the authority of a king as he stood there in his white tunic and plaid wrap, the thick leather belt showing his narrow waist that she knew was all muscle.

He might not wear a crown of gold like a king, but it was clear in his stance he was now acting as a leader, chief, someone who must act on behalf of his clan, and not her lover. And to most of the MacLeod Clan, she, a Macdonald, daughter of their greatest enemy, was dangerous. But not Rory, not after their last night together when she revealed her back to him and he'd kissed the thing she hated about herself. He trusted her, didn't he?

The twins slid off the bed. Eliza even bobbed a curtsey to Rory on her way to the door. The action made Sara's hands fist, not in anger at her sister but at the authority he exuded. The door shut with a *click* behind them.

Sara swept an arm to indicate the room. "I have no chessboard for you to play your game."

"This is no game. People are calling for yer execution."

Her hands gripped together, and she swallowed. "But you've told them I had nothing to do with all this."

The silence that followed thumped hard in her chest, and Sara was torn between fear and fury. "Dammit, Rory. I've told you the truth. I did *not* poison, nor kill, nor steal." She paced to the hearth and then back, stopping before him to stare up into his eyes, her hands fisted in frustration. "And who the hell is Madeline?"

His gaze flitted to the fire that gave Sara no warmth because she was cold in her bones.

Sara glanced at the wooden beams of the ceiling, remembering. "She's turning ye against yer own clan like Madeline." She looked back at Rory. "That's what Brodrick said."

Inhaling, Rory's face turned back to her. "She…" He swallowed. "I was eighteen when she came to Dunvegan saying she was running from a grisly old suitor in the north of Scotland. Being a young warrior full of notions about chivalry, I wanted to help her. She said she loved me."

"You were lovers?" Sara asked and tried not to care. It was ten years ago.

"Aye, but I also thought we would marry." He rubbed his jaw that held several days' growth of beard. "Then the Fairy Flag was found in her satchel that she'd packed as if to leave. She was a Macdonald spy sent by yer father."

Bloody hell. Sara cursed her father and how one man's greed for power could hurt so many.

"And during the six months she lived here," Rory continued, "she gathered information for him, and had finally found the flag hidden in Jamie's bedchamber."

"Jamie's?" Sara asked.

Rory's mouth was tight. "To search his room, she seduced him."

"But you were to blame?"

"My father knew she was my lover. He said I'd told her things that she carried to Walter Macdonald. That it was my fault for trusting her. So before me… and the village…he slit her throat."

Sara's hand rose to wrap loosely around her own throat, her lips parted. "Good Lord, Rory."

"And Jamie called for me, before everyone, to vow never to trust a woman again enough to divulge MacLeod secrets, especially a Macdonald woman."

"Your vow," she said. He'd talked of not breaking a vow when they were alone in the tower house. She'd teasingly asked him if he were a priest. She looked at him. "And Jamie was still willing to marry me?"

"He would marry ye," Rory said, "have begotten children on ye, but he would never have trusted ye even if it was only I who swore before everyone."

A mantle of shame covered the kingly one he'd donned. Sara walked closer to him, and her hand slid across his jaw and cheek. "Rory," she said, viewing the torment in the amber of his eyes. "I am not Madeline. I *am* a Macdonald, but I am not a spy to steal information or your flag or your brother's life. I came to Dunvegan to help forge peace between our clans."

She shook her head. "I have no desire to help my father take over Skye. Dammit, Rory! If it came to that, I'd desire war against the Macdonalds, against my father." She threw her arm wide as if toward Dunscaith.

She turned back to study the hard mask he wore. Dark circles had appeared under his eyes since Jamie had been suffocated in bed. Rory stood tall despite the vicious personal attacks he was probably enduring, his counselors and people condemning him for his inability to judge her without bias. How many times over the last two days had Rory had to protect her from angry revenge-seekers?

He cleared his throat, taking her hand. "There are

those saying they saw ye sneak away with a wooden box under yer arm." He stared at her hand as if memorizing the lines across the palm.

"Who said that?"

He shook his head. "Jok and Brodrick both said they've heard villagers talking about it."

"The same villagers who spread that Jamie's head had been bashed in?"

He released her hand as he exhaled, and she crossed her arms over her chest like a shield against the doubt in his eyes.

"You don't trust me."

He crossed his arms, too. "I don't trust myself to know if...I'm being lied to."

"That woman, Madeline," she said, "she really cut your soul to pieces, Rory."

He didn't say anything for a long moment and walked over to stare out the window that looked upon the other tower where the flag had been hidden. "I won't let them hurt ye," he said. "Ye were raised to hate us, and yer father was using Eliza to persuade ye to act."

Sara blinked. "You think I gave myself to you to seduce you into letting your guard down so I could steal the flag or give my father information in exchange for Eliza?" Her voice was soft, a trembling river of words hiding the dangerous depths of anger and despair below the surface.

"I'm saying it makes sense, and nothing else does. There are no other enemies amongst us."

"You don't know that." There were spies within clans. Numbness spread through her, and her heart felt like it was turning to gray ash, breaking apart and falling into nothingness.

"I trusted you enough to show you my back."

He looked away as if gazing upon her was too painful. "I won't let them harm ye," he repeated. "But I wanted to let ye know what was going on. How 'tis unsafe for ye here."

Her heart jumped into a quicker pace. "Eliza?"

He shook his head. "She's my father's daughter, like Eleri, and she wasn't here when things began to happen. No one has said a single word against her."

Relief suffused Sara's chest for a quick moment, only to be dulled by the rest of this nightmare. Sara had trusted him, had felt the trust growing between them was enough to break down the prejudice between their clans. But who was she to break apart a feud that had been honed over centuries? She'd truly need to be one of God's seraphim, a fiery angel flying down from Heaven, to conquer such bloody history.

And she was not.

She was merely a woman who dropped the armor around her heart and was now paying the price of that foolishness. Sara lowered to sit on her bed and stared across the room at the wall. "Thank you for the warning." She was proud her voice didn't shake. Her fingers curled into the blanket under her.

"Food will be brought up for ye," he said.

She continued to stare before her, feeling only the center of her chest hollow out. When she heard the door close, Sara fell sideways and buried her face in the sheet.

Her tears flowed hot and silent.

CHAPTER THIRTY

"My drops of tears I'll turn to sparks of fire."

William Shakespeare, *Henry VIII*

Sara,

Since I secreted Eliza out of Dunscaith, Father has treated me like a traitor, but the warriors refuse to act against me. We have an uneasy peace between us. Gilbert is often by his side and the two of them bend over the map of Skye and stop speaking if I come close. Gilbert has tasked the blacksmith with making sure every warrior's sword is sharpened, and the farrier is checking the shoes on every horse at Dunscaith. A catapult has been erected and brought to the bailey as if it will be carted over land.

I think Father is going to war against the MacLeods.

Be safe. Your loving brother, Kenan

Sara looked from the letter in her hand to Jok standing in the doorway of her room. The seal hadn't been broken, so it hadn't been read by anyone else. "Does Rory know I received a letter from Dunscaith?"

He nodded once, suspicion in his eyes. Nothing about the freckled, red-haired warrior was soft or humorous as he waited. Had Rory told him to wait for some reaction from her? Did he expect her to give him the letter to read?

"Kenan doesn't mention the Fairy Flag," she said. "If my father has it, he's not bringing it out yet." Which seemed odd, but he might be worried if he unfurled it or held it up, that would be the third time even if he wasn't marching into battle.

Jok said nothing, just stared at her. Sara exhaled. "I don't know what to do."

Jok crossed his arms, his legs braced. "Ye need to leave Dunvegan."

Her face snapped up to his. "I do?"

"I'll help ye leave, milady. Get ye out safely."

Her lips parted as her heart, which she'd thought was ash, somehow squeezed tighter like an overripe fruit giving way to rot. Was this what Rory wanted? For her to go away?

She swallowed hard, willing the tears swelling in her eyes not to fall. "It isn't safe for me to ride by myself at night," she said, glancing at the darkening window.

"I'll escort ye across on the ferry at dawn," Jok said as if the plan was already in place. "Your horse will be ready."

She looked at Rory's closest friend. "Jok, do you think I'm a Macdonald spy like Madeline? That I seduced Rory to steal the flag?"

She watched him shift in a numb type of haze. His lips opened for several seconds before words came out. "I know only that Rory must have the faith of his people to be the chief. That he cannot have whispers behind his back, milady."

She turned toward the hearth. After a long moment, she heard the door click as Jok left. Her jaw hardened as anger swirled into the place where her heart had shriveled. "I'm going to find that foking flag," she murmured. "And I'm going to…" *Stick it up Rory's arse.*

She sniffed, wiping her nose. She imagined her riding up with Kenan next to her and dropping the unfurled flag in the dirt at Rory's feet. Then she would turn around and ride away from him forever.

· · ·

"I was tasked to look after ye," Reid said, "and that's what I will do." He nodded, his lips pursed tightly.

He stood before Sara and her horse, Lily, at the edge of Dunvegan Loch. Rory had been nowhere in the castle when Sara had descended from her tower room. She didn't dare wake the twins to say goodbye. Eliza would want to go with her, and it wouldn't be safe.

No one had been in the great hall as she passed, except for Gus whom she'd kissed and shed a tear for. Rory hadn't even come to her room or met her outside to say farewell. The treachery was another dagger in her already ragged heart. One would think with so many piercings to the vital organ, she'd have dropped dead. But, amazingly, she'd woken during the early hours when Jok had knocked on her door.

Jok now held Lily's bridle. "The man was waiting here when I brought yer horse out, milady." He nodded at Reid who stood by a bay horse, fully saddled.

"'Tis my own mount," Reid said. "And even if ye

say I must remain here, I'll still follow." The man had two large satchels tied to the back of his horse and a rolled blanket. He looked ready for a journey, one from which he may not return.

Sara was too tired to argue, and the man had been loyal from the start. She nodded. "Very well then, Master Reid. I'll appreciate the company."

He smiled, his shoulders relaxing, and mounted. "This is Jasper."

"My horse is Lily." Sara lifted into the saddle, shoving her boots into the stirrups. She reached down for the bundle that Jok handed her.

"Food and drink."

Sara looked down at him. "Guard his back, Jok. I was not the danger here, and I fear that the true assassin isn't finished."

"I'll lay down my life to protect him, milady," he said, his serious words coming out like a binding oath.

She glanced up at the massive stone fortress that was still a black form in the ebbing night. "He'll need a friend. Someone he can…trust." The last word almost didn't squeeze from her tight throat.

"And here." Jok held a pouch out. "Coins for passage to the mainland and beyond if needed. From Rory."

She stared at the heavy-looking coins. Mainland? Rory didn't just want her gone from Dunvegan. He wanted her gone from the Isle of Skye. She forced herself to breathe and sat straighter, turning her face away. "Tie it to my satchel."

When he did, she pressed into Lily's sides to move forward, but then Sara turned her in a circle. She raised her gaze to Dunvegan, and there on the roof, tall and broad, stood Rory. He didn't raise his arm or nod or do anything to show warmth. Sara shivered at the hardness in his face, the determined look of choosing lies over her truth.

She stared back, her heart seeming to quiver in her chest as if stuck on its normal thumping, because nothing was normal or as it should be. *I don't trust anyone.* And he never would.

Sara turned Lily, sitting up tall like a queen in a procession, and rode out of town. Reid remained slightly behind. She viewed the waking village from behind a watery veil as tears welled up in her eyes.

Henrietta Blounce stood outside her cottage door, hands on her ample hips. Her frown was meant to eviscerate Sara as she departed.

But Sara was already empty. Her joy and hope had bled out under Rory's cold gaze from above.

• • •

Morag's crows scattered from the yard as Sara pulled her horse to a stop, quickly dismounting. She untied the coin purse off the satchel. The heavy weight of so many coins felt like a boulder, threatening to pull her underwater. She turned toward the door and called out, "Aunt Morag, 'tis Sara."

Morag opened the door. "Seraphina," she said, glancing at Reid dismounting next to Lily. "What's happened?"

"So much." Sara walked into her aunt's open arms.

Morag wrapped her in a warm, secure hug. "Damn the breakers of hearts." Her words dripped with vehemence.

"He thinks I stole the Fairy Flag and poisoned his brother," she said against her.

"Jamie's dead?" Morag asked, her hand sliding down Sara's arms, pulling back to look into her wet face.

"Yes, poisoned first and smothered when he was taking too long to die."

Morag's face pinched into a hard frown. "And they think you did this."

"Most of the villagers do, but I was here and in the Tower with Rory overnight when Jamie must have ingested the poison."

"But Rory let you go anyway," she said, her eyes narrowing.

She nodded then tilted her head. "Do you know about a Macdonald named Madeline who stole the Fairy Flag ten years ago?"

Morag glanced at Reid and pulled Sara into her cottage, shutting the door before he could follow.

"Yes," she said, leading her to the table so she could sit. "Sorrowful tale. Alasdair, in a fit of rage, sliced her throat."

Sara dropped the coin bag with a *thunk* on the table. "They all think I'm another Madeline, there to trick Rory into giving up his clan to the Macdonalds."

"Nonsense," Morag said, picking up the bag, weighing it with her hands before dropping it back down.

Sara huffed and stood to pace across the floor. "I think my father has the Fairy Flag, though, even if I don't know how he got it. He's planning to wage war on the MacLeods. Kenan has gotten Eliza to Dunvegan, and Rory says she's safe there."

"He wants you to leave. But where?" Morag asked, glancing out the window.

Sara turned, and her gaze went to the commotion outside where Reid was shooing off some overly interested crows. One swooped down at him, and he ducked, running back to stand next to his horse.

"I can't stay at Dunvegan. I'm returning to Dunscaith to get the Fairy Flag back."

Morag pivoted, piercing her with sharp eyes. "Walter will kill you, no matter that you are his true daughter. Don't lie to yourself that he won't."

Sara closed her eyes for a moment. "Kenan is there. He will help me."

Morag's hand clasped like a manacle around her wrist. "As soon as you arrive, he will take you prisoner before you can even look for the flag."

At least Dunscaith's dungeon wasn't a watery pit. "I have little choice," she said. "And I must do something. I'm not a hider."

A grim smile pulled Morag's lips into a thin line. "No, you're not a hider. You're braver than my sister." She caught Sara's cheek in her palm. "You're made of fire, Seraphina. 'Twas why your mother named you after the great angels, a fiery warrior of God."

Sara smiled. A splinter of laughter broke from her lips. "I was a newborn when she named me. It was because of the birthmark on my back that looks like fire."

Morag shrugged. "That, too." She took Sara's shoulders and squeezed as if trying to push her encouragement into her. "But you're also a flame of light and truth, and full of bravery. Your mother is proud."

Her words made Sara's eyes ache again. "I won't let my father tear me apart, too."

"You're the Flame of Dunscaith," Morag said and gave her a firm nod. She released Sara to go to a large clay jar on her shelf. Something clattered inside as she tipped it, and an iron key fell into her palm. She returned and held it before Sara's face. "It opens almost any door." She put it in Sara's hand and curled her fingers around it. "In case you must escape."

A yelp drew their gazes to the window. Outside, Reid flapped his arms with a look of panic pinching his face as the crows dived down at him. He covered his head with one arm and pranced around, his thin, long limbs looking rather spider-like.

Morag tilted her head. "Now, who is this person with you?"

• • •

The journey to Dunscaith would take two days. As they rode along the snaking river, neither Reid nor Sara voiced the worry that her father and Gilbert might meet them with an army marching north along the known trail. But as she crested each hill, Sara held her breath.

Exhausted and hungry, Sara followed Reid to a squat structure made of stone that was used by sheep farmers in the winter. It was dry if not warm, and Reid had brought more foodstuffs than she had, sharing them. He also walked to the river to haul fresh water for them to wash. Sara watched Reid add a couple thin, cut tree limbs he'd brought in one of his big satchels to the fire.

"Thank you," she said when he handed her a bladder of fresh water.

"I would see ye safely home, milady."

She frowned, glancing up at him. "I might be imprisoned when I get home." She could just leave Skye, but, no, she'd find that damn flag, or at least try. Let Rory see how bloody wrong he was about her.

Reid crossed his arms, gripping himself as if he were cold. "Master Kenan will keep ye safe."

Sara bit into a piece of cheese. "Do you know my brother?" Her voice sounded gravelly from disuse since she hadn't spoken since leaving Morag's.

Reid opened his mouth twice but closed it each time. He turned to the doorway. "I'll be right back." He headed out into the night. The man was nervous by nature, and riding into enemy territory must be adding to his discomfort.

"I'll get his damn flag," she whispered in the empty hovel. And then what? She'd have to leave Skye. The thought made the pit of her stomach grow hollow again. Not that she was sad to leave Dunscaith, but leaving Eliza, Eleri, and Kenan would be hard. And leaving Rory... *I won't think about it.*

She wiped at the few escaped tears with such force one might think she was slapping herself. *I won't cry for him, the man who cannot trust.* "That's it. I'll pity him." He'd certainly hate that.

Her sorrow hardened to stone. Fury was strength and sorrow was weakness, and right now she needed strength. Bloody hell! She'd saved Rory's life in the chapel by crawling under when the whole thing could have collapsed on her and knowing that her father would take revenge on her for ruining his plans. She'd shown him the flaming birthmark on her back, had let him touch it, kiss it. She'd trusted him, but he hadn't trusted her.

"Dammit," she muttered, shaking with anger. "No," she chided and wrapped the blanket around herself, rolling to her side before the fire. *I won't think about him.*

They started out early the next day, and by noon they broke through the tree line into the far reaches of Macdonald territory. Her father's scouts were there even if they weren't seen.

"Please let Kenan be here." Her prayer was caught in the wind tugging her hair out behind her. Reid kept his horse even with her, and his face was pinched with intensity.

Sara slowed her horse to a walk, and Reid followed suit. She looked over at his earnest face. "Turn back, Reid. Ride home to Dunvegan. There's nothing but torture and death at Dunscaith for a MacLeod."

His face reddened. "I will stay by yer side, milady."

She shook her head. "You will die, Reid. I won't have your blood on my hands."

He swallowed and then sniffed, glancing outward toward the castle perched on the edge of the sea before them. "My mother was a Macdonald, Lady Sara."

She stared at him. "But you've been with the MacLeods. You said you came from Lewis." Confusion made her speak quickly. Was no one what they seemed?

"I've lived in many places and not at Dunscaith for...some time."

"Then you're still in danger, Reid."

He smiled sadly at her. "We're all made to die, milady, and I would do so doing something worthy and honorable." Lips pinched, he glanced away from her, looking back at his bulky satchels tied to Jasper.

Sara sighed. "You're brave, honorable, and true."

His face snapped back to her, his eyes wide and tortured as if she'd slapped him. She watched him swallow hard before looking forward.

Ahead, several Macdonald scouts entered the path leading to the castle. "He'll know we are here now. May God keep us safe."

"Amen," Reid murmured.

They rode the rest of the way in a rolling canter, and Sara watched as the warriors swarmed out from the walls surrounding Dunscaith. Like Kenan had said, there was a catapult next to the wall with dozens of ropes tied to it. It was ready to roll toward Dunvegan, but her father hadn't yet started his campaign.

If she could only find the flag before then. At best, she'd escape with it, returning it to the MacLeods. At worst, she'd destroy it so her father couldn't unfurl it.

Perhaps I should let Father use the damn flag against them.

The thought made her stomach sour. There was anger and then there was dishonor, and Sara would never cross that line.

As they clopped along the winding path through the village, curtains fluttered in windows and frightened people peeked from cracked shutters. Did they think she was bringing war to their village? Sara felt like yelling, "I'm trying to stop a war," but instead, she kept her gaze forward and her back straight. She'd grown up with these people, danced around the may-pole with them and walked between Samhain bonfires together. Had her father poisoned them against her?

One window sat unshuttered, and she saw her friend, Beatrice, looking out at her with a mix of fear and sorrow on her face. Sara met her eyes but couldn't speak. Beatrice fidgeted there, her hand raising halfway to give a little wave. Sara mimicked the gesture, riding on.

Sara guided Lily over the bridge, under the portcullis, and into the bailey of Dunscaith Castle. Reid followed, keeping Jasper behind her. She concentrated on remaining still and expressionless when her father, flanked by Gilbert, walked out of the keep. Where was Kenan? Her stomach tumbled.

"Why are ye here?" Walter asked, his eyes narrowed.

"Sara!" Kenan called as he jogged up from behind her. Her eyes closed briefly in relief, and she exhaled some of the tension she'd been holding. He lifted her down from Lily's back and wrapped her in a hug. "'Tis not safe for ye here," he said near her ear.

Behind them, Reid dismounted, going to his largest satchel. Did he think to unleash some type of weapon? She should have warned him not to. If he, a MacLeod, brandished a weapon before the simmering anger of the Macdonald chief, her father would have him shot through with an arrow with a mere incline of his head.

"Let go of her, Kenan," their father called. "Present yerself, woman, to yer chief and father."

With a squeeze, Kenan released her, and they walked forward together.

They stopped several feet before Walter and Sara spoke. "My betrothed at Dunvegan is dead." Sara kept her expression stony. "I have no place there."

"So ye return here?" Gilbert asked, his deep voice tinged with accusation. "When ye're a traitor to Clan Macdonald?"

"I am no traitor."

"And where is Eliza?" Gilbert continued.

"Safe with her…" She glanced at her father. "With her twin sister who was raised at Dunvegan."

"What the bloody hell," Gilbert said, his face swinging toward Walter.

Walter walked closer, and she was grateful that Kenan stood beside her. She saw Reid come closer out of the corner of her eye. Her father's face was red, spittle on his lower lip. "I had them locked in that chapel," Walter said, not even bothering to show a response to the truth about Eliza. "The smoke would've taken them within minutes, the whole leadership of Clan MacLeod wiped out in one bloodless plan." He threw his arm out as if wiping away a meaningless fly. Bloodless? Perhaps, but deadly and dishonorable.

Sara saw Father Lockerby standing behind. His narrowed eyes rested on all of them, judging them as if he truly were God, ready to hurl them into Hell.

Sara focused her gaze on her father. "By burning a house of God?" She shook her head. "'Twas dishonorable."

Walter continued as if she hadn't spoken. "Ye gave them a way out and actually helped drag them to safety!" His voice had risen so that by the end, he was shouting. "Saving those I had already condemned. In so doing, ye've brought war to Dunscaith."

"No, Father," she said. Her arm swung out to indicate the catapult they both knew was on the other side of the wall. "Your actions have brought war to our people."

Walter raised his massive fist and swung it toward her face. Sara had time to squeeze her eyes shut, anticipating the jaw-breaking pain. But it didn't come. She opened her eyes to see Kenan forcing Walter's hand down. Gilbert slid his sword from his sheath.

Kenan's hand remained wrapped around their father's fist, but he turned his gaze on his brother. "Put that away, little brother, or know I will slice yer arm off today." And maybe his head. He didn't say it, but Sara heard the threat there. Hopefully Gilbert did, too, because she'd never known Kenan to give idle threats.

"Let go of me," Walter said, his face a shade of red that bespoke punishment and death.

"Don't strike her," Kenan said.

"She's a traitor. I can slice her open if I want."

"Nay, good sir." The wavering voice came from behind Sara. Reid cleared his throat. "She's no traitor to ye." Sara's already clenched stomach quivered with panic for the thin man who was mostly arms and legs without muscle.

Walter yanked his fist back from Kenan. Reid walked forward holding a wooden box. He didn't look at her but kept his gaze pinned to her father.

"Aren't ye supposed to be at Dunvegan?" Walter asked, waving away Gilbert who seemed ready to take on the unarmed, fragile-looking man.

Sara began to shield Reid but stopped.

Supposed to be at Dunvegan? Her father knew Reid? And knew he should be at Dunvegan?

Reid cleared his throat. "I came with Lady Seraphina because she asked me to carry this. She brought ye this to assure yer victory."

Sara's inhale stopped as Reid lifted the lid, swinging it back on little iron hinges. He tilted it toward Walter.

"Oh, Reid," she whispered, her shoulders curling with the pain of regret in her chest. What had he done?

"What is this?" Walter asked, but a calmness in his voice said he had a guess.

"'Tis the great Fairy Flag, milord," Reid said. "Yer daughter stole it for ye. So ye see, Lady Seraphina is no traitor to Clan Macdonald."

CHAPTER THIRTY-ONE

"Absence lessens half-hearted passions, and increases great ones, as the wind puts out candles and yet stirs up the fire."

François VI *Duc De La Rochefoucauld, 1613-1680*

"If ye didn't throw the ladder down to her, and I didn't, who did?" Simon asked John as they sat at the tables that still hadn't been taken down outside Dunvegan's wall in the village.

Rory stood brushing Airgid's dappled coat longer than needed as he listened. He'd been training with his warriors and meeting with the leaders of each group within his clan: archers, cavalry, the blacksmith, and farrier. A rainstorm had blown in from sea, but they'd persisted until every resident had a weapon for self-defense if Walter Macdonald led a siege.

Three more ferries had already been constructed in the last two days to carry vulnerable villagers behind Dunvegan's mighty curtain wall when the time came. The business allowed him to stay numb inside, which was better than the pain that nearly crippled him when he watched Sara ride away.

"Margaret," John answered, but Simon was already shaking his head.

"She and Theo went to check on the lass, and she was already liberated," Simon said. "And before ye can say it, wee Eleri didn't do it, or she would have waited for her to reach the top before running off."

"Reid Hodges then." John crossed his one whole arm over his chest. "The man has a soft spot for Sara, even rode off with her the morning she snuck away." Reid had told Rory that he'd go with Sara, but he wasn't any real protection. He could barely hold a weapon.

"Think she went back to Dunscaith?" Simon asked, making Rory's hand pause in mid-swipe along Airgid's flank. He'd given her enough coin to see her safely off the isle. *Merciful God, don't let her return to that devil.*

"That bastard of a father will kill her if she did," John said. "Hope she didn't."

"Chief MacLeod." A woman's voice cut into Rory's eavesdropping, and he straightened to find Henrietta Blounce standing there, her usual gaggle of apprentice midwives behind her. She'd been one of Sara's biggest critics.

"Aye," he said, nodding to her and the other lasses.

"Ye should know that Winnie Mar has left Dunvegan," Henrietta said. She crossed her arms. "She said she has an interest in learning midwifery," her brows rose high on her forehead, "but she hasn't shown up for any of my lessons, and now she seems to have taken herself off somewhere."

Rory dropped his brush into the bucket of water. "When did she leave?"

Henrietta looked up and then to her hand, her fingers ticking off days before meeting his gaze with her direct stare. "Saw her last the early morning of Monday, the day Sir Jamie was brutally sent to God." She passed the sign of the cross before her as if warding off the murderous evil. The ladies behind her did the same in comical symmetry.

Simon and John had risen and were listening closely. "Never liked that woman," John said.

"Wicked tongue," Simon added. "Always wanted everyone out of the castle as if she was the lady there."

"And she could yell like a true banshee," John said, sticking his finger in his ear to wiggle it.

Henrietta studied them without agreeing or disagreeing. She turned her frown back to Rory. "Thought ye should know who is living at Dunvegan and who has decided to desert us before the war begins."

"Like a rat jumping ship," Simon said.

"Stinking rat," John said, shaking his head.

Rory rubbed his chin. "There may be no war. We're just preparing."

Henrietta turned away but left a parting comment. "We shall have war when we were promised peace with the wedding." She shook her head, and the other ladies mimicked her.

"Old goat," John mumbled.

Simon spat on the ground and scuffed the spot with his boot. "Acts like Rory here brought this war on himself."

"There's no pleasing some people," John added as they shuffled off toward the ferry.

And yet, Rory had acted to please his clan above what he felt was right. Under forceful advice, he'd sent Sara away. Ten years ago, he'd tried to appease his people after Madeline's trickery by swearing to never trust a woman again. He'd spent his whole life trying to please his father, but the man never softened toward him.

Rory's chest was tight as he led Airgid back to his barn situated to the side of Dunvegan. After feeding his loyal, hardworking mount an apple, Rory walked back out into the midday grayness. Since Sara had left, it seemed the sun had given up on trying to burn through the clouds. The heaviness made it hard for him to draw a full inhale.

When he'd stood on the roof in the pre-dawn light, watching Sara leave, a part of him left with her. Maybe she'd taken his scarred soul that she'd said Madeline had cut to pieces. Sara had stitched it back together, and then he'd let her take it with her.

Rory walked down the path that wound through the cottages making up Dunvegan Village. Buckets of water sat along the perimeter of each house, ready to be thrown on thatched roofs if the Macdonalds rode through with torches, trying to burn them down. Jok had suggested taking the offensive and marching on Dunscaith, but Rory was trying to prevent war, not start it.

Rory realized his feet were taking him toward the one-room cottage that Winnie Mar had occupied when she wasn't playing lady of the castle. He stopped before her cottage, studying it. He remembered her taking pride in it last year, but now it had tall weeds around the base as if she'd abandoned it months ago.

He threw open the door. It was empty like Henrietta had said. A single bed was made up, and the basic furnishings were sitting as they should: table, two chairs, washing pitcher, and a chest for clothes, which was empty. Walking behind the cottage, Rory found a fire pit with charred wood. He kicked at the crisscrossed pieces, watching them fall apart. He was about to turn away when something white caught his gaze. He crouched, pushing at the remaining coals with a stick.

"Daingead," he said as he unearthed a charred mushroom. It looked like a wrinkled Destroying Angel mushroom. Winnie could have taken one from Jamie's room to study and decided to get rid of it. Or…she was the source of the deadly mushrooms to begin with.

Rory straightened. The wind tugged at his hair as he breathed in the fresh scent of the sea and listened to the murmur of voices lower in the village. But it didn't clear his head nor loosen the tight knot in his gut. Walking, he found himself at Airgid's stall again, leading him out and throwing the saddle back onto his sturdy back. The horse looked at him with large brown eyes. His ears flicked as if sensing Rory's turbulent mood.

"Where are ye off to?" Jok asked as Rory led Airgid back out.

"Ye think she went to her aunt's, to Morag's?" Rory asked his friend.

Jok's grin faded to seriousness. "At first, but then she might have sailed over to the mainland."

"She took the bag of coins?"

Jok nodded. "Had me tie it to her satchel."

"I'll be back by nightfall," Rory said and mounted Airgid to break into a slow run while his mind churned much faster than the horse's feet.

Rory slowed and stopped before the burned chapel. Wind blew the damp, acrid smell of destruction.

He looked to the south. His warrior instincts told him that Walter Macdonald would come riding soon. That war was inevitable.

He stared at the ruin, the roof destroyed and the colorful windows shattered. A shell of blackened stone blocks was all that was left. Their bones would be there, too, if Sara hadn't knocked under the floor of the burning church.

"Bloody hell," he said, his fist pushing against his forehead. Sara had saved him, saved all of them trapped in the church. Even when she'd been raised by a man who hated them. No matter what orders her father wrote to her, she wouldn't have killed Jamie, not unless he attacked her. She would've just let them all burn. He pressed Airgid into a run.

An hour later, Morag's cottage came into view. Black crows circled above it, landing on the thatched roof and fence. There were no horses tied there.

Rory dismounted, ignoring the crows, and looped the reins over the post near a bucket that held clean rainwater for Airgid.

Rap. Rap. Rap. "Morag Gunn," he called through the door.

"Rory MacLeod," she called back through the door. He waited, but she didn't open it.

"Open the door. Is Sara here?"

A bar scraped off the door on the inside, and it swung open. "'Tis about damn time you came after her, you dull-headed arse," Morag said.

He glanced over the white-haired woman's head, but the front room looked vacant. "Sara?" he called.

"Seraphina isn't here," Morag said, disdain evident in her voice. "You sent her away, and she won't stay where she's not wanted." Her words stabbed at him, more so because they were true.

"Where has she gone?"

Her face was hard, her lips thin, and her eyes narrowed. She wore her white hair in a long, neat braid that lay over one straight shoulder.

"To stop this bloody war."

"What?" His muscles tensed. "How?"

"By riding to her father's and stealing back that damn flag."

"Did she steal the flag for him?" he asked.

Morag jabbed his chest with a fingernail cut to a point. "Why would she ride into Hell to get it back if she'd sent it there? Of course not." Her frown called him all sorts of foul names, and her nail may have drawn blood.

"I gave her coins to leave to the mainland," he said, absently rubbing the jabbed spot on his chest.

Morag pointed at the table where a familiar pouch sat. "She doesn't want your money, MacLeod."

He strode past her, scooping up the bag. It was heavy. "Daingead."

"My niece is proud." Morag crossed her arms. "Those coins don't take the place of you standing by her, believing her."

He felt his blood rush, heating his face. "My people think she killed Jamie and stole the Fairy Flag."

Morag crossed her arms. "Sara said you compared her to Madeline, that you broke some foolhardy vow and can't forgive yourself enough to see reason."

At the girl's name, Rory's chest hurt harder. "'Tis not foolhardy to swear not to let another girl die because of me. I wanted Sara to leave to protect her. I will not have her blood spilled on my account. Not again."

Morag stared at him, her eyes narrowing. She tilted her head as if she was hearing something. "You think Madeline's blood is on your hands? That 'tis your fault she died?"

He looked away from her searching gaze. "Because of me, she got close, and my father had to punish her before everyone to stop it from happening again."

Silence. And then Morag said, "You don't know, do you?"

He looked back at her. "Know what?"

CHAPTER THIRTY-TWO

"She's mad, but she's magic.
There's no lie in her fire."

Charles Bukowski, 1920-1994, German-American poet

Morag met his gaze without blinking, the wrinkles deep in her forehead. "Alasdair didn't slash that poor girl's throat because of you, because you gave away secrets or told her where to find the flag. She would have died even if you'd never become involved with her."

Rory clenched his fists, trying not to slip back into the horror of that day when he was barely a man. "Father held her before everyone and said I was the reason she was dying."

Morag shook her head. "Well, he couldn't tell everyone the truth, now could he?"

"What truth?" Rory asked, his breathing shallow.

"That Madeline had found out the secret of he and Elspet, my sister." She flipped her hand. "Yes, Madeline was a spy for the Macdonald Clan, and she probably fell in love with the handsome young second son of Chief MacLeod. But what sealed her fate was when she sent word to Walter Macdonald that his wife was having relations with his enemy and had born him twin girls, Eliza and Eleri."

Rory watched her, his brows furrowed. "But she stole the flag."

Morag shrugged. "It never left Dunvegan, did it?"

"She seduced Jamie to get it."

Morag tilted her head again. "Who told you that? Jamie? Alasdair?" She shook her head. "No. Madeline was killed because Alasdair went insane with fear and fury that Elspet and one of his daughters, trapped at Dunscaith, would be killed by Walter. And he took that fear out on Madeline's throat, blaming you because he couldn't reveal his secrets." Morag flapped her hand again. "And then that fool brother of yours made you swear that vow, which you did, I suppose, because you were in shock over watching that poor girl bleed to death in front of you."

She shook her head and huffed. "Walter ended up torturing my sister and locking Eliza up. Alasdair, having deprived himself of the woman responsible, took out his continued worry and anger on you, Rory." She stepped up to him, poking him with her words. "But you did not endanger your clan by loving a Macdonald. Your. Father. Did."

He didn't say anything as his churning mind made sense of what the crone had revealed. All these years he'd felt he was to blame, as if he was the one who'd made the slash across Madeline's throat. And he'd been punished over and over for it until any confidence he'd had as a lad was shredded, and the shame had followed him into manhood.

The woman sat down at her table as if she'd suddenly grown weary. "I thought you'd learned something during your stay in England, Rory MacLeod."

"I learned that life is unfair and cruel." He ran his hands over his head, pressing against the ache throbbing there.

Morag folded her hands before her on the table.

"You learned to look beyond the prejudices you were raised under," she said. "You looked at each of those men unfairly held with you, Kenan Macdonald, Cyrus MacKinnon, and Asher MacNicol, and realized they were not the enemy you'd been told they were. They are warriors and sons and brothers, Scotsmen like you. And yet now"—she swooped an arm out—"you fall back on the easy distrust of a Macdonald."

"There was evidence," he said but then thought of the mushroom he'd found in Winnie's fire.

"Was it evidence or misleading deception?" she countered with a grin. "Like Jamie telling you Madeline seduced him to get the flag."

She stared hard at him, her eyes narrowing. "Trust what you feel is the truth. Read Sara's heart and her actions you've seen yourself. Go against the prejudices you've been raised to believe. We're asked to put our faith in God even though we have little proof. 'Tis time you put your faith in someone your heart tells you is true."

. . .

Reid had the Fairy Flag all along. Reid Hodges? Why? How?

Walter touched the flag in the box with reverence while Reid held up the wooden case. Her father looked at Reid. "Ye've done well, man."

"Lady Seraphina brought it," Reid said. "I merely carried it for her."

Sara stared at the man she realized she didn't know at all. "I…" She didn't know what to say. Kenan was staring at her with such a hard look that she gave him a small shake of her head.

Walter laughed, a deep belly laugh, and grabbed Sara into his arms, hugging her. Her head tipped back with the squeezing force of it. He smelled of sweat and smoke. "That's my lass!" He held her shoulders and shook her, grinning. "Made the second son fall in love with ye, killed his brother, and stole the Fairy Flag right out from under him."

"She didn't kill Jamie MacLeod. I did."

The familiar voice made Sara's gaze snap past her father's weathered face. She stepped back from him, her breath halting.

"He didn't eat enough of the mushrooms to make him die quickly, so I had to smother him, too," Winnie Mar said and smiled. "But everyone at Dunvegan thinks Sara was behind it all." She snorted through her pert nose. "As if you'd have the courage to do such things."

"Winnie Mar?" Sara said, her hands fisted at her sides. "You killed your lover?"

Winnie's smile turned into a feral grimace as she glanced beside her at Gilbert. "I never loved Jamie MacLeod. I killed the chief of our enemy. I did my duty to infiltrate Dunvegan and wreak havoc." She slid her arm through Gilbert's. "I will always be loyal to the Macdonald Clan."

Winnie nodded to Reid. "Me and my brother that is. My last name is Hodges, not Mar."

Sara turned back to Reid, eyes wide. He still held the wooden box as Walter closed the lid. "I will take it inside, milord," Reid said, "to yer library."

"Reid?" Sara said, but he wouldn't meet her eyes as he strode past and into the keep.

Kenan took her arm. "I'll take ye inside," he said.

Walter smiled broadly. "I'd thought to put ye in the dungeon or stocks, but Seraphina, the Flame of Dunscaith, is loyal." He laughed. "And we will be victorious over those bloody MacLeods now that we have the flag. Once and for all." He swung his arms up into the air as if he were drunk on glory. Whether or not the Fairy Flag truly held the power to bring victory, it had bolstered him and would do the same for the Macdonald warriors waiting to march north.

"When do they march on Dunvegan?" Sara asked Kenan as they walked through the great hall that had been her home and then her Hell over the last years since their mother had died.

"He says in a few days' time, but now that he has the flag…it could be on the morrow. He wants to test the catapult first." They climbed the steps to the next level where the family bedchambers were and walked down to the room she had shared with Eliza.

"Is there any way to sabotage it?" she asked. "To give us more time."

"Time for what?" Kenan asked. "With that flag, he will go to war. There's no stopping him now."

Sara tugged his arm, glancing down the empty hall. "Kenan…I didn't know about Reid carrying the flag here. I came here to steal the flag back."

He stared at her, his frown unchanging. "Ye'd be locked in the dungeon if ye'd ridden in here with nothing to offer. Winnie had already arrived to say she'd killed Jamie." He looked away and rubbed his jaw. "Which I'm glad to hear ye did not do. Killing changes a person."

"How long have Reid and Winnie been spies at Dunvegan?"

"Reid about three years, Winnie a bit over a year." He looked annoyed. "I, of course, was kept in the dark about such things."

"I didn't recognize them."

"Ye wouldn't. They lived with the Mackinnons for years. When Father sent word for them to return, he kept them hidden in case any MacLeod spies were here at Dunscaith."

"How do you know this?"

"Winnie threw it in my face when she arrived like a triumphant queen." Kenan shook his head. "Father sees me as a traitor. I'd probably be locked in the dungeon if he thought the Macdonald army would follow him." He allowed a confident grin. "But they follow me. I'm the one who trained them, who works with them every day. And I'll be the next chief despite Father wanting to put Gilbert in charge."

"You're the better chief," she said. "'Tis a wonder Winnie has latched onto Gilbert and not you."

"Oh, she's tried, but I wouldn't do that to Gilbert, no matter what an arse he is." He made a pinched face. "And she's rather cloying, and"—his brows rose with a tinge of wry humor—"she's just killed her lover."

"You're wise," she said, patting his arm. Even with the Hell storm whirling around her, Kenan could always tease a smile out of her.

He opened the door, and she inhaled the familiar scent of her room. Beeswax and flowers. The beds sat on opposite walls with a woven rug in between before a swept hearth. Just as it had always been. It made her miss Eliza. "I hope Eliza is safer at Dunvegan than here." Sara walked inside. "When I left, she was."

Her middle felt hollow again now that the anxiety

of arriving had burned away. "If you march on Dunvegan," Sara said, looking at Kenan, "get Eliza and Eleri to Aunt Morag's."

"I will," he said. "The crafty woman will get them away to safety somehow while her crows attack any foes."

"Margaret and Theodore Harris are also helpful and loyal to the twins." Sara rubbed her hands down her face. *Sweet Mother Mary, must it come to war?*

Kenan stopped before her, taking her hands away to hold in his. "And Rory? What has happened? Aunt Morag thought ye two…"

He trailed off as tears welled unbidden in her eyes. "I thought…I thought we might be…" She shook her head. "But he sent me away."

"Why?"

"He thinks I killed Jamie and stole the flag."

"We need to tell him about Winnie and Reid," Kenan said, his jaw set in a hard line.

"He didn't even say goodbye to me the morning I left. Only sent some coins to help me flee." There could be no love there.

"I'll make him see the truth."

A flutter of hope rose in her stomach, but sorrow weighed it down like a butterfly caught in a net. She shook her head. "I told him I hadn't done those things, but he doesn't believe me. Without trust, there's nothing but ashes between us."

She let Kenan pull her into a gentle hug, like when they were children and Gilbert had done something cruel. "I'm so sorry, Sara."

"I wish…I wish I could fly away somewhere and start anew." She looked up at him, squeezing her eyes to rid them of tears. "Like a phoenix."

Kenan's face softened, letting up on his hold. "Ye've been reading the myths?"

"I don't have the books."

Kenan stepped over to the hearth to start a fire to ward off the chill from the coming night. "I have several in my chamber. The myth of Icarus flying too close to the sun."

"The one where his wings, held together by wax, melt?" she asked, watching him strike flint, sparking a bit of wool between his fingers.

He blew gently on the ignited bundle before adding it to the straw kindling and dry peat he'd stacked on the grate to allow more air to feed it. "Aye. When I was imprisoned in England, I would dream of flying away. I drew plans for making lightweight wings out of thin hides when I returned to Dunscaith."

Her mouth dropped open. "You've made wings?"

A grin broke across his serious lips. "Aye, and they are sewn together, not glued with wax. I used Leonardo da Vinci's plans, but modified them to glide, not flap. Men aren't strong enough to flap."

"Have you tried them? Do they work?"

"They're finished, but I've yet to try them." Kenan pointed a finger upward. "I have them hidden on the roof, so Father and Gilbert don't find them. They'd laugh and destroy them."

"Or figure out how to make them into a weapon."

His smile fell into a hard look of dislike. Their family could not be more divided. Gilbert and Father against Kenan, Eliza, and Sara. And a home divided was weak, just like a country, just like a clan.

Sara felt heat burn up her neck like a wildfire out

of control. Rory knew that. And she was dividing his clan, those who felt she was innocent and those who believed she was the enemy in their midst, poisoning their chief and stealing their flag. Even without proof, their beliefs condemned her. And Rory was now the chief and responsible for keeping his clan strong and united as the threat of war increased.

She closed her eyes for a moment. Even if he believed her, it wasn't enough.

"I'll come for ye for supper," Kenan said, standing out of his crouch. He walked over to her and wiped a tear off her cheek with his thumb. "I will have words with Rory." Despite the tender touch, his words ground out like stone caught in a mill.

"Don't."

"I won't kill him." Kenan's face was tight. "But anyone who hurts my sister will hurt." He kissed her forehead and left.

Sara sat in a chair before the fire. "House divided," she said. "A clan divided is weak." How about a heart? If a heart was divided, would it die? Hers was shattered into splinters. She leaned forward, holding her face in her hands, her eyes shut.

Rap. Rap.

The brief knocks were soft. Sara lifted her head.

Rap. Rap. Rap.

Sara rose and walked to the door, opening it a crack. "Reid?"

He nodded and glanced from side to side. "Can I come in please, milady?"

She opened her door wider, and he walked in. Pinched under his arm was the wooden box. "I've come to give ye back the Fairy Flag."

CHAPTER THIRTY-THREE

"There is no fire like passion, there is no shark like hatred, there is no snare like folly, there is no torrent like greed."

Gautama Buddha, 564BC

Sara ushered Reid inside and slid the bar across the door. "I don't understand any of this, Reid. I didn't know you took it. I don't even know who you are."

His brow was furrowed, his eyes sad. "I apologize that I didn't tell ye back at Dunvegan that I was loyal to yer clan, milady. I was sent there three years ago to get close to Lord Alasdair. When he died this past winter, I remained in the household sending information to yer father about what I heard. My sister had come by then, masquerading as a common woman who meant to set up home in the village. Even though I'd infiltrated the castle, yer father thought she could gain more information from Jamie's bed."

His words came fast, and he shook his head. "I didn't know she was going to kill him and in such a terrible way." The box in his hands seemed to weigh too much for him, and he set it on a table near the fire. Reid looked like a man about to buckle under the stress of his mission.

"Sit." She pulled up a chair for him across from her own.

From his leather pouch, he pulled a scarf that was

the same pale gold color as the silk flag. "Ye can switch this out for the flag."

He pushed the scarf into her hands, and she stared in confusion at it for a long moment before raising her gaze to Reid. "But you carried the Fairy Flag all the way here," Sara said. "Why are you giving it back to me?"

Reid dropped his face in his hands, unknowingly mimicking her own small collapse before he knocked. "I saw the box under Lady Eleri's bed when I came to retrieve ye one day. 'Twas always part of my purpose at Dunvegan, ordered by yer father, milady. Find the Fairy Flag and bring it to Dunscaith." He looked up at her. "That was all before I met ye at Dunvegan." He stood as if nervous energy pushed him from his seat and paced before the fire. "When I saw the box sitting there, I came back when Lady Eleri left with ye, and I buried it in the woods."

Three steps forward, swivel, and three steps back. "When everyone started to blame ye and then Jamie was poisoned, I didn't know what to do." He looked at her. "I was supposed to give it to Chief Macdonald, but I didn't want ye to suffer for it. When ye were sent away, I took it with us to fulfill my mission. I wrestled with telling ye the whole way here."

"But you told my father I took it." She tried to keep her words unintrusive as he talked. It was the most he'd ever said to her.

"He was going to hit ye," Reid said, shaking his head. "I didn't know how to stop him. When Kenan did, I grabbed the box, knowing that if Chief Macdonald thought ye brought him the flag, he'd celebrate ye instead of hurting ye. I...I couldn't stand to see ye come to harm, milady."

It was true that she'd be in Dunscaith's dungeon right now instead of her old room if she hadn't shown up with the Fairy Flag. Still seated, Sara looked up. "Thank you, Reid. You are clever and brave."

He exhaled. "And a bloody fool."

Her brows pinched together. "A fool?"

He looked into the fire. "I've lived with the MacLeods for three years. Master Rory was always fair. Lady Eleri and Mistress Margaret were kind. I don't want them to be hurt in this war. I don't want to be the one responsible for it. 'Tis bad enough that my sister is a murderer. And yer father, milady…"

He shook his head again. "Trying to burn them in God's house. Such unholy actions are heavy sins I cannot be part of." He passed the sign of the cross before him, the weight of his conscience making his shoulders roll forward. "I'm not brave enough to suffer God's wrath."

"So you're giving me the flag?"

He looked up at her. "Aye, milady." He inhaled fully. "I'm giving ye the flag to either fly over the Macdonald army or to return it to the MacLeod Clan." He shook his head. "I don't know what's right anymore."

And Reid expected her to know what was right? She was to decide the fate of two huge clans after she'd been abandoned by both.

Sara released a long breath. "Does anyone know you're giving it to me? Winnie?"

He shook his head. "Nay. I would never tell her." He frowned with deep disappointment. "Winnie wasn't always so calculating. When we were young, she aspired to become the lady of a castle. Now she will do anything to obtain her goal. When Jamie said he didn't want her in Dunvegan anymore, she…reacted poorly."

Poorly? She'd tortured and killed the man.

"Then she returned to Dunscaith to pick up her relationship with yer brother, Gilbert. She's told me she plans to be lady of Dunscaith or Dunvegan if the Macdonalds take it away from the MacLeods." He stared into the fire. "All of it means bloodshed."

"And Scotland will slowly bleed to death," Sara said.

His face turned to her. "We should be guarding our borders and coastlines against foreign enemies, not fighting against one another."

Sara's gaze drifted to the box. It belonged to the MacLeods, and she didn't think Rory would use it against a Scottish clan. He wanted to make Scotland strong.

"It belongs with the MacLeods, with Rory." Even if Rory had sent her away.

Reid's face fell in his hands. "I shouldn't have taken it, but once I told Winnie there was no putting it back."

"Reid, *you* should return the flag to Dunvegan," she said and swallowed hard. "Tell them…" She felt tears in her eyes but blinked them back. "Tell them I took it, and you returned it. Then you can live in safety there. If the flag disappears, and you are here, my father might decide you're a traitor."

She might be blamed, but Kenan would help get her to mainland Scotland. She'd look for her mother's family, the Gunns.

He shook his head. "I'm done with lying, and I

won't do something to hurt ye, milady."

She stroked the false flag still in her hands as he talked, letting the relief wash over her. Despite everything, she didn't want Rory to think she'd lied to him.

"I'll return to Dunvegan," Reid said, "and let them know I've seen Chief Macdonald readying for war. I plan to ride away at first light. And I won't mention the flag to Lord Rory." He looked at her. "Maybe ye should destroy it."

The flag was a piece of history whether it was magic or not. Destroying it was like destroying a piece of Scotland. Sara couldn't imagine doing that.

She followed him to the door. "Thank you, Master Reid, for all your service and protection."

"I only wish I was more worthy, milady." He slid out into the dark corridor.

Sara turned, leaning back against the door, and stared at the box. It was square and ancient, the wood stained and dry. The thought of throwing it in the fire made prickles slide under her skin. *No.* She would hide it so her father couldn't use it. But where? 'Twas a wonder she hadn't noticed its pointed corners in Reid's satchels. She'd been too heartbroken to notice much of anything.

Moving the false flag aside, she opened the lid and stared down at the yellowish silk of the real Fairy Flag. The flag opened as she pulled it out, exposing its design of crosses stitched with gold thread and red rowan berries scattered across it, the colors having faded over the centuries. Lifting her top petticoat, Sara caught the edge of the flag in her waistband, tucking it gingerly around her like a short inner skirt. The rest of it slid down like another petticoat, and she lowered the outer skirt over it. "Safe and with me."

She folded the false flag to put it inside the box. Looking into the bottom, she saw a small piece of paper and drew it out. It had sat under the real flag.

This flag was given to Clan MacLeod by a princess from the fairy realm. Clan MacLeod is the rightful keeper of this flag, and we will destroy anyone who takes it.

Two signatures sat below in the stilted lettering of a child learning to write.

Jamie MacLeod and Rory MacLeod

Sara ran her finger over Rory's name. Had he and his brother hidden this note inside the box when they were boys? A warning to future enemies and thieves?

Whether there was power in the rectangular piece of silk or not, it did belong to Clan MacLeod, and she would see it returned. She would prove to Rory that she hadn't taken it.

She set the false flag in the box and closed the lid. She'd have to return it to the library before anyone noticed it was missing. Sara stood before the flames dancing in the hearth. The note was crisp between her fingers, and she almost threw it in. But she tucked it into her bodice.

It was a small piece of Rory. She pressed her palm against it. *Rory.* His unique amber eyes, so piercing, staring into her own as they teased each other over the chessboard and then later as they came together. Their mouths and hands exploring every inch of each other, taking and giving. Trusting. It had been as false as the yellow scarf now in the box.

• • •

"We will break into three armies," Rory said to Jok and Brodrick. "Left and right flanks, and I will be part of the forward push. Keep your armies back," he said, looking at both men in their eyes until they nodded.

"Then I will feign retreat to bring the Macdonalds into our trap. Once they follow us onto the upper moor above Dunscaith," he said, pointing to a map he'd drawn out from scouting the Sleat peninsula in years past, "the left and right flanks will charge in."

"They'll be surrounded," Jok said, nodding.

"What if they're flying the Fairy Flag overhead?" Brodrick asked.

"Shoot it with a flaming arrow," Rory said. "We will have a vat of burning pitch for each of the three armies. Light one of the arrows with whisky-soaked wool balled up on the tip and shoot the damn flag."

"'Tis a bloody shame," Brodrick said, but he nodded, knowing it couldn't save them if the Macdonalds were flying it.

"And what if we see Lady Sara?" Jok asked.

Without hesitation, Rory said, "Keep her alive and get her out of there."

Brodrick's face opened in surprise. "Ye mean to bring her back? After she stole the flag and killed Jamie?"

Rory turned his hard stare on the man. "Evidence points to her innocence," Rory said. "She's to be brought safely here."

"What evidence?" Brodrick asked.

Rory took two steps forward so he stood nose to

nose with the man who'd judged Sara guilty from the start. Rory didn't bother to hide the threat in his gaze and stance. "Evidence that I, yer chief, has seen and weighed. If ye cannot uphold my orders, ye may leave Dunvegan today or remain behind in the pit to think about yer loyalties, Brodrick MacLeod."

Brodrick's face reddened, and he gave a nod. "I march with Clan MacLeod."

"Then ye follow *my* orders and keep yer thoughts to yerself." Tamped fury swirled like a whirlwind of fire up inside Rory. If the man wanted to be knocked on his arse and thrown in the pit, Rory would oblige him. "I will have no traitors in my ranks."

Brodrick stood straight. "I am no traitor to Clan MacLeod." He balanced on the edge of insolence but held himself just from it.

Jok's hand landed on Rory's shoulder. "Brodrick knows how to follow orders. Don't ye, Brodrick?"

"Aye."

Rory inhaled, grappling with control, but he finally took a step back, and Jok dropped his hand. Rory turned on his heel. "We ride!"

"To Dunscaith!" the men yelled, their call rising up like a wave across the one thousand strong, half on horses and half on foot. "To victory!"

Rory mounted Airgid while Jok and Brodrick mounted their own horses and rode out to lead their armies. Jok led the cavalry and Brodrick led the archers. Rory led those men fighting on foot with swords and shields.

The march would be brisk but slow enough not to wear out his men and their mounts. They'd need their energy to fight the Macdonalds, especially if they flew the Fairy Flag. Not that Rory really believed in fairy magic. But he knew the influence it would have over the men on both sides, because *they* believed in the Fairy Flag's power. So, he wanted it taken out of the battle as soon as possible.

An hour later, as they marched past Morag's cottage, she came outside to watch. Rory saw more than one man pass the sign of the cross before himself at the sight of the white-haired woman with her black crows. The birds flapped overhead and on the posts near her, jostling for a closer position to the woman who held up bits of oatcake for them to eat.

Her expression was neutral, watching as if she were a chronicler who would then go inside to write about the MacLeods riding off to war against the Macdonalds. Would future Skye inhabitants think he was foolish to march against a clan flying the Fairy Flag? Rory glowered as he watched ahead of him over the rolling countryside.

Would they speculate that the true reason Rory marched, using every weapon he had and all his men, was to find and bring Sara back to Dunvegan?

To bring her back to him?

. . .

"I've heard you've obtained the pagan flag," Father Lockerby said to Walter Macdonald.

Sara watched her father shovel more pigeon pie into his maw, munching away at it with the same single-mindedness with which he ordered people about. He didn't answer the priest but patted the wooden box that sat beside him on the table in Dunscaith's great hall. The box's presence, with the false flag inside, had made it hard for Sara to breathe.

The priest's eyes narrowed. "Do you plan to use it?"

Sara forced herself to eat some of the hens' eggs that had been baked and served with fresh yeast rolls. She'd snuck the false flag in the box back to the library during the night Reid had given it to her. Her father had been so busy with preparations that he'd blessedly left it there until that morning.

Gilbert sat farther down the table. "We'll unfurl it when we reach Dunvegan, and it'll make our warriors multiply in number and strength." He sat his tankard down with a *clunk*.

Kenan watched it all with a silent frown. Would he go against their father? Kenan hadn't encouraged the feud before, but since he'd returned from the English prison, he'd openly argued against it. He'd pressed the need for peace until he was faced with choosing to go along with their father's plan or killing him. Sara didn't think he'd decided yet.

The disgruntled priest kissed the crucifix he wore on twine around his neck. "'Tis pagan magic. It should be burned, not flown about as if calling Lucifer to aid ye."

Walter frowned at the priest. "God has brought it to me, and I will use what He has provided."

"God did not bring it to ye," Lockerby snapped, "she did." He pointed a long finger toward Sara as if she were indeed Lucifer. "Using it is a sin of great magnitude."

Walter stood slowly, dropping his eating knife so it clanged on the pewter plate. He walked over to the priest, but the man didn't cower. They were of equal height, but the priest had a way of looking like he stared down with condemnation as if he were God on his heavenly throne. Her father's voice started at an even volume and increased. "For generations, the MacLeods have been our foes, and the only reason we have not taken Dunvegan and MacLeod territory is because of that damn flag."

The priest tried to get in words. "That is not—"

"And now we have it, and we will win the land my ancestors died for!" Growing fury and self-righteous indignation flared red in Walter's face, but Father Lockerby didn't seem to care.

"They should be dying for God, not for land!" Father Lockerby yelled back. "I did not condemn ye for burning St. Mary's Chapel, a house of God, but using pagan magic…" He shook his head. "Flying it above yer army…'Tis blasphemy!"

Walter threw his arm out to the side. "Be gone, priest! We have no need of yer services." He turned away. "The MacLeods, on the other hand, will need yer last rites."

"We will need him for the wedding vows," Winnie said as she entered the room. Having missed most of the shouting, her mouth curled up in a playful smile, and she walked over to touch Gilbert's arm as if to proclaim that he was hers.

Father Lockerby marched toward the double doors leading to the bailey. "I'll remain, taking confessions for those souls who wish to recant their sinful or pagan ways."

Walter raised his tankard, toasting the cleric. "Good day, ye grumpy old bull." He smiled.

Apparently, the joy filling him at the thought of conquering his lifelong enemy made him more forgiving. That forgiveness wouldn't save her if he discovered that she'd switched out the real Fairy Flag.

Walter walked back to the table, sitting near the box, as if he couldn't be parted from it. His fingers toyed with the latch, and Sara's breath caught as he raised the lid, looking down into the darkness of the box.

"What shall I do, Father?" Sara asked, trying to keep the panic from her voice as she tried to distract him. "I would be of help. My friend, Beatrice, and I can prepare Dunscaith for a siege just in case?"

His face turned to her, and he let the lid fall shut. "My daughter," he said, studying her. "Ye've done well bringing me this weapon. If the MacLeods bring war here, this," he thumped the box with his hand, "will stop them in their tracks. No need to increase supplies or move the villagers inside the walls."

"Father," Kenan said, unable to sit quietly by, "preparation doesn't lessen the power of the flag." Sara knew Kenan didn't put much stock in the magic of the flag, either, but saying that outright would turn their father into an even more stubborn arse. "'Twould be best that Sara and our attendants store and prepare food for the villagers and alert them in case they must retreat inside the safety of our walls."

Walter pointed at him, his face red. "Ye concern yerself with my armies, not women's work."

"I'll start preparing," Sara said.

"I don't want anyone sleeping in my hall because ye've scared them," Walter said.

She nodded. "I'll remind them to listen for our

warning bell."

Gilbert stood. "'Tis best to let the womenfolk work on something else or they'll get underfoot."

Underfoot? Gilbert would get her foot kicked under his plaid if he kept talking that way. Sara let her breath out slowly, and Kenan tipped his head to her, his brow rising in a look of surprised admiration for her control.

Rapid footsteps bounded down the stairs in the corner tower, and one of Kenan's warriors, Ian, emerged. "Riders are breaking through the forest."

Kenan rose, his hand on his sheathed sword. "English?"

"Nay," Ian said. "They're Scots. I think MacLeods." Sara's heart leaped with a rapid thumping.

Walter pushed his chair back, making it tumble. "They've come for the flag. Saves us a trip to Dunvegan." He grinned widely and grabbed the box, striding toward the door. "'Tis time to defeat these bastards." Gilbert jogged after him.

"Be safe, my love," Winnie called.

"Kenan, wait," Sara said, running to him. She rose on her toes, her fingers curling into his tunic.

"I need to direct our men, Sara," he said, his eyes following his father and brother.

She yanked, and he lowered his ear. The words burst from her numb lips. "I replaced the Fairy Flag in that box with a silk scarf."

For the space of two heartbeats, Kenan stared at her. He exhaled, scrubbing a hand over his mouth before he stared directly at her.

"Get out of here, Sara. He *will* kill ye."

CHAPTER THIRTY-FOUR

"Deliberate violence is more to be quenched than a fire."

Heraclitus, Philosopher, 500 BC

Sara followed her brother as he ran from the great hall. His voice rose as he burst outside into the bailey, issuing orders to organize the Macdonald troops.

A woman ran past him into the entryway, catching Sara's arm to pull her back into the great hall. Beatrice had her natural wide-eyed, frightened-fawn expression. "MacLeods are coming to conquer us," she said. "What do we do?"

Winnie picked up a pear that had been left on the table and bit into it, speaking while chewing. "We remain calm and act like ladies."

Sara looked into Beatrice's eyes. "Go through the village. Any woman and child who fears can come inside the castle."

"That's not what the chief said," Winnie said. "We'll be overrun."

"Start by putting them in my bedchamber," Sara said.

"We have the Fairy Flag," Winnie said. "All will be well."

Relief slid over Beatrice's face, making Sara's heart hurt. Because they didn't have the Fairy Flag, she did, tied under her petticoat. A flutter of remorse beat like bat wings inside her. She could run outside and pull the flag out of her petticoats, delivering it to her father. Although she despised her father and what he was doing, she loved her people, people like Beatrice who believed in the flag's power.

Sara held tightly to Beatrice's arms. "Go now. Bring those who are frightened."

Beatrice ran out, determination, and the thought of the Fairy Flag, giving her courage. Sara hurried to the double doors leading into the bailey.

"'Tis a lie!" Her father's voice thundered over the din of horses being saddled and swords being strapped to every man with two arms. Sara's insides twisted as she watched with horror. Walter lifted the scarf out of the wooden box. He let the box drop, and it splintered, as he held the yellow silk up with two hands. "A foking trick."

He will kill ye. Her brother's words pierced her chest as surely as if Walter Macdonald had drawn his sword and stabbed her with it. Sara leaped back inside the doorframe, barely able to breathe, her heart thumping wildly. In that instant, seeing her father's reaction to being betrayed, she believed he pushed her mother from Dunscaith's roof.

Kenan grabbed it from him. "Fly it anyway. People don't know what it looks like, MacLeod or Macdonald." There were soldiers nearby who could hear. He looked at them. "For all we know, this is the Fairy Flag. It hasn't been seen for two decades. 'Tis yellow silk and sits in the box."

Father Lockerby strode up to the scarf, touching it. "If this isn't the pagan flag, where is it?"

"I looked at it the night Reid Hodges brought it,"

Walter said. "'Tis been replaced since then by a traitor." He looked around, and Sara pulled back farther into the alcove inside the door. "Seraphina Macdonald!" His voice rattled through Sara like an earthquake.

"We must find it," Gilbert called.

"Nay!" the priest yelled back. "Trust in God, not some pagan cloth."

Sara peeked back out in time to see Kenan catch Walter's arm. "There's no time to hunt for it. 'Tis inside Dunscaith, keeping the castle safe. Fly this flag or none at all."

Father Lockerby's eyes were wide. "'Tis inside the castle somewhere." The priest turned, striding back inside, walking right past Sara into the great hall.

Kenan's friend, Angus, rode his horse into the bailey. "The Lion of Skye leads them in a charge across the moor. Some on horse, most on foot. Looks to be about three hundred men."

"Say the flag is in the box, and give it back to them," Gilbert said, shoving the scarf back inside the box, but the fall had left it lopsided, the corner chipped off.

"To make them leave?" Walter growled. "I don't want them to leave. I want them conquered, whether here or at Dunvegan." He looked straight at Gilbert. "Kill them all, and Dunvegan is yours."

He'd give Dunvegan to Gilbert? Sara looked back into the hall where Winnie stood finishing the pear. Sara's eyes narrowed. If the woman couldn't get Dunvegan through Jamie, she'd get it through Gilbert.

The priest dashed up to Winnie. "Do ye know where the real Fairy Flag is?"

She pointed toward the doors. "They took it out there."

"Daft woman. That's a fake." He turned, running toward the stairs. "It must be inside the castle. It must be destroyed!"

Sara's hands flattened on her skirts, knowing it was safely tucked between the layers. She stepped back as two men carried a caldron between them into the hall. It held black pitch.

"What is that for?" Winnie asked, worry tightening her previously annoyed features.

"The chief ordered it inside in case it must be carried above to pour over MacLeods."

"*If* they get inside the bailey," the other man said. "Which they won't." He grinned at the ladies. "Because we have the Fairy Flag." They jogged back out.

Apparently, not everyone had heard her father's explosion in the bailey. But how long would it take to spread, muting her clan's confidence?

Sara hurried back to the double doors, peering out. She heard Winnie laugh behind her. "You're like a chicken running back and forth without its head."

Sara's father and brothers had ridden out of the gates, and Macdonald armies were organizing, many on horses and the rest on foot. Walter yelled for the massive catapult to be brought forward. She saw no flag or scarf flying up high.

Standing on tiptoe, she could make out the oncoming MacLeods, straight down the center of the moor toward them. She squinted, and her breath caught. Even if he was too far away for Sara to see his expression, she could see Rory's broad frame, riding his gray charger with total confidence at the head of his army.

He was coming for the Fairy Flag. If she'd been able to get it back to him, would it have stopped this battle? She could run out to Rory, handing him the flag. Her fingers slid around her waistline where the edge of the flag was caught. If she flew it over her head, would that be the third flying of the Fairy Flag, using up all its magic? If there was magic.

Which clan would claim she was flying it for them? Her father would despite his suspicion that she'd replaced the flag with the scarf. But if she ran toward Rory, would he think she flew the flag for him, for MacLeods?

Sara ran her hands over her forehead, letting them rest on the top of her head as she tried to decide what to do. Her breaths were coming too fast, making her chin feel numb and sparks start to glitter in her sight. Dropping her hands, she leaned against the door, forcing even breaths between her parted lips. It took her a moment to realize the gates to the bailey were closing.

"No!" she yelled. "There are villagers coming."

"Orders from the chief," one of the warriors barring the gate yelled at her.

Her father wasn't only protecting Dunscaith, he was trapping the Fairy Flag inside since he'd seen it when Reid first brought it.

"Bloody priest! Are you mad?" Winnie's shrill voice made Sara spin around toward her.

"Fire?" Sara said, running back into the great hall where flames had caught onto three of the tapestries hanging on the walls. The dry threads became a banquet of many colors for the fire as it gorged over the neatly stitched images.

"Father Lockerby?" Sara yelled. "What are you doing?"

The priest's face was contorted in a manic smile, his eyes wide. "In the name of God and His everlasting son!" He held his torch to another tapestry. "We will destroy the pagan idol."

Sara ran up to him, grabbing his arm, but he shoved her back and brandished his torch before him. "Don't try to stop me or ye will die with the Fairy Flag."

"We will all die, you mad arse," Winnie yelled, running out of the great hall toward the double doors.

"Please, Father Lockerby," Sara yelled over the sound of crackling flames. "The bailey doors are locked. We'll be trapped in all the smoke."

Mania, wild and vicious, encompassed his features. "I should have burned with the chapel when I helped Walter Macdonald in his sinful plans, so I will be purified by the flames here, destroying the pagan flag."

"You knew about the plan to burn the MacLeods in the chapel?"

He spun, baring his teeth. "Walter Macdonald promised he'd burn the Fairy Flag himself if I helped him."

Her father lied to everyone. He'd lie to God when he finally died.

Sara threw her arm over her mouth and nose as the acrid smoke billowed, and the fire crackled over the dry tapestries. There was no stopping the priest when he noticed the caldron of pitch. With a cackle that sent chills racing through her, she watched him touch his torch to the flammable pitch. It caught easily. He threw his torch on the table where the remnants of their dinner sat.

"No!" she yelled as he tipped the already wobbly caldron over, the burning pitch pouring out slowly to cover the rugs on the wooden floor, like a flow of lava burning a path through a helpless town.

Coughing, she ran back to the front doors, which were closing. Winnie stood on the outside of the narrowing crack. "He can't be stopped," Sara yelled as she ran up to the woman, realizing Winnie wasn't opening the doors to let her out.

"Your father agrees, Seraphina," Winnie called through. "You should have burned in the chapel." Winnie's face was hard and serious as she slammed the doors together right in Sara's face.

Sara worked the latch frantically, pushing her shoulder against the crack between the two heavy oak doors. But the sound of logs or boards scraping against the doors on the outside made Sara scream with fury. "Let me out!"

The smoke billowed, choking her. It was like St. Mary's Chapel all over again except now she was trapped inside and there was no tunnel underneath to crawl out.

Hurrying back to the great hall, Sara stopped to stare at Father Lockerby as he stood on the table, having kicked the food off into the growing patch of fire under him. His arms were raised. "Blessed be the Lord, cleanse me of my wickedness with these flames!"

He was determined to die, but she was determined to live.

Coughing, she ran toward the steps. *Groan! Crack!*

Turning back to the room, she saw the heavy caldron drop out of sight as the floor under it gave way. No, she couldn't go down below, not with the flaming floor falling upon her head. She grabbed her skirts in her hands and raced up the turning stairs. Higher and higher. She coughed, covering her mouth. She must get to fresh air.

Thighs starting to ache from use didn't stop Sara from climbing. She reached the third floor and pushed through a door to the roof. Cold wind flew around her, yanking her hair, and she sucked in large inhales. She slammed the door shut behind her, trying to contain the smoke for the time being, and ran across Dunscaith's vacant roof, all the guards having run out to battle.

The low stone wall met her hips as her hands grasped the cold, rough stone. Rory's army had stopped in a line across the moor above the village, and Macdonald forces stood before them. Her father yelled, but she couldn't hear what he said. Rory pointed toward the castle where smoke billowed out now from all the windows. She saw her brother, Kenan, break away from the army, racing back toward the castle.

"You can't do anything to save it," she said. *To save me.*

The fire would eat up through the floors, one at a time while filling every crevice with deadly smoke. Eventually, it would feed on the wood under her feet. Although the walls of the castle were made of stone, the floors and the roof were wood.

Like fire eating upward through wooden floors, destroying a building from the inside out, fiery guilt did the same within a person. *I should have fought to stay, to prove my innocence, to tell him…* Tears burned in her already stinging eyes.

Sara stood upon a stone seat built into the wall so that she was higher. Was this where her mother stood before her father pushed her? The wind snatched at her skirts and hair, whipping it around her face. Her breath caught as she looked toward the field. "Rory," she said, her lips suddenly numb. He'd seen her.

With a yell, taken up by many MacLeods, another two armies flooded out of the woods on either side, increasing the MacLeod army like the legend of the flag said would happen. But Rory didn't wait for his men to join him.

Sara held her breath as she watched him dodge between Macdonald men and horses. He only used his shield to block strikes so he could race past warriors, riding Airgid straight toward Dunscaith Castle.

She glanced back at the closed door where smoke snaked out of the cracks around it. Her gaze scanned the roof, but there were no ropes or chains to aid her. "'Tis too late."

CHAPTER THIRTY-FIVE

"I have always felt it is my destiny to build a machine
that would allow man to fly."

Leonardo da Vinci, 1452-1519

Rory used his knees to guide Airgid through the me-
lee of Macdonald warriors. *Sara.* He must get to Sara.
She was trapped in Dunscaith, and the castle was on
fire. The smoke came to him on the wind, bringing
memories of being trapped in the chapel. *Daingead!*
She must have gone to the roof because the entrance
was consumed.

Rory saw Kenan yelling up to a guard who raised
the toothy portcullis. As soon as he could, Kenan
ducked under it to race through the bailey. Gilbert
ran after him. Winnie Mar escaped the smoke-filled
bailey on Gilbert's arm. She'd gone to Dunscaith?

Rory ducked low over Airgid's neck as he clopped
under the still-rising portcullis. He swung down from
his mount as Kenan turned to him. The doors of the
castle were braced. "Bloody foking hell!" Rory yelled.
"Someone trapped her inside!" He and Kenan
worked quickly to kick the braced wood away. Rory
yanked the door open, and a huge cloud of smoke
billowed out like poisonous gray exhales from a giant
while flames licked out like lethal tentacles.

"'Tis impossible," Kenan called to him, and they
stood staring at the fiery maw.

Rory's hands fisted at his sides. "I'll drape myself and run—"

"Ye'll be burned before ye can reach the steps," Kenan said. "Even if ye made it through, ye wouldn't be able to bring Sara down that way."

"I won't leave her to burn!" The words roared out of Rory as if he yelled back at the monstrous flames. He couldn't let her die. His chest squeezed as he gazed up the four stories. Sara stood at the top, balanced on a step with smoke rising up from behind her. "I'll climb up."

He ran to the castle wall, trying to find finger holds. But he was only able to climb a few feet before the smooth stone gave him no aid. His blood raced as if to supply him with berserker strength even though he could not scale the bloody wall.

In times of siege, the smoothness would deter the enemy from climbing, but right now, he cursed the masons who'd sanded away any finger or footholds.

Rory shook off Kenan's arm as he tried to snatch him down and threw himself at the unclimbable wall once more. "I must reach her," Rory yelled. "Sara! I'm coming for ye!"

"You can't climb it." Sara's words were barely heard over the sounds of war and the crackle of feasting fire.

He could see lines on her dirty cheeks. The evidence of tears shook him to the core. "I won't let ye burn, Sara," he yelled up. "Ye're the phoenix, remember?"

She spread her arms as if to show she didn't have wings. "I wish I had Phoenix's wings." Then her arm covered her mouth as coughing wracked her body.

The note of desperation caught at Rory's throat, and he coughed, too, as the smoke billowed forth, filling the bailey.

"Wings!" Kenan yelled. "My wings are up there." He coughed, too. "Tucked in a corner by the west turret. Get them, Sara!"

"Wings?" Rory asked, looking at the man. Had the smoke and thought of losing his sister struck him mad?

Kenan grabbed his upper arms, shaking them, a hopeful grin on his gray-streaked face. "After we returned...I studied da Vinci's plans." Kenan pulled Rory into the center of the bailey.

Sara had disappeared along the roof. *Crash!*

"Sara!" Rory called as the massive crash from somewhere inside continued to rumble with the sounds of splintering wood and whooshing fire. "Sara! Where are ye?"

"Here!" Her voice came a moment before she reappeared on the edge of the wall, her arms full of folded tan hides.

Rory almost sank to his knees in relief, his heart hammering. She hadn't fallen through the roof to be consumed by the flames below. Not yet anyway. "Stand only on stone, not wood," he called.

"What do I do with this?" Her eyes sought out her brother. The wind was blowing from the sea inland, making the smoke blow past her out toward the fighting on the moor.

"Open them up," Kenan said, spreading his arms wide. "I changed da Vinci's design by attaching the front points. There's a bar there for ye to hold on to."

Rory watched her clumsy movements as she tried to extend the massive pieces of tanned parchment.

"Be careful not to puncture them or they won't hold ye aloft," Kenan yelled.

"Sweet Holy Mother Mary!" she yelled. "I don't want to be aloft."

"Ye do," Kenan yelled, "at least for a bit. Hold the whole thing behind ye and tie the rope around yer waist."

They watched her fumble with the rope. She wore a red gown, and her hair blew in the smoke-filled wind, rising and falling on the currents of heat and air.

Kenan's hands were raised up as if he were helping her fit them on her back. "Slide your arms in the leather straps there and hold onto the bar." He cursed and Rory looked at him.

"What?"

"I haven't tested them. The materials are heavy for her and 'tis made for someone my size."

Rory grabbed his shoulder. "Ye have to get her down."

"I know, but she's terrified of heights, especially since Mother fell," Kenan said. He looked back up at Sara, speaking loud and calm. "Ye're going to have to get yer feet through the leather strap behind ye, so they don't drag ye straight down."

"Fok," Rory said, scratching his hands through his hair so hard he might have drawn blood.

Sara glanced behind her at the length of the contraption.

"Somehow, get your legs out behind ye," Rory yelled. "Slide the loop closer to the point at the front." She disappeared for a moment, and Rory held his breath until her head reappeared.

Kenan was almost jumping up and down with his

need to fit the wings to his sister. "Slide your arms in the leather straps," Kenan said. "Then ye are going to stand up on that ledge, point the nose out, not down, out over the moor—"

"Nay, she'll land in the fighting," Rory said.

Kenan looked back up. "Try to fly over them toward the forest."

"Fly?" Her eyes were wide, and her voice held fear. It twisted Rory's stomach.

"Sara," he called, and her face turned to him, their gazes connecting. "Ye can do this. Yer brother is brilliant, and this is yer way out of that inferno. Like Phoenix, ye'll spread yer wings and aim for the forest. I will ride out and catch ye."

"You'll catch me?" she asked, panic making her words sound like curses.

"Just stay aloft."

"Or land if ye're close to the ground before ye hit the trees," Kenan yelled. "Keep the point up. The wind will carry ye the way ye point but keep yer legs behind ye."

Sara's lips moved as if she were reciting all the instructions Kenan was throwing at her. Either that or she was praying.

"Aye, God, keep her aloft," Rory added to the prayer. He turned to mount Airgid and stopped as a deep voice cut across the bailey.

"Ye foking bastard, burning down my castle!" Walter Macdonald rode his horse under the portcullis straight at Rory as if to run him down.

Rory lunged to the side, hitting the ground in a roll that brought him to his feet. He had no time for this.

Walter glanced above. "What the hell is she doing?"

"She's going to fly out of there," Kenan said, pulling his sword.

"And I'm going to catch her," Rory said, leaping to his feet.

Walter laughed. 'Twas chilling despite the heat. "She stole the Fairy Flag from ye. Brought the damn thing here to me and then stole it back. She's a traitor to us both."

She stole the Fairy Flag. The words funneled through Rory's head.

Walter tipped his face to his daughter. "Ye will burn, Seraphina, ye traitor!"

Traitor to us both. Blood rushed in Rory's ears, and he had to shake his head to clear it. Sara stood with Kenan's wings strapped to her, her beautiful face smudged with smoke, her eyes wide with fear. She didn't refute Walter's condemning words.

She just stared down into Rory's eyes.

Faith.

Air moved in and out of him, and his blood slowed with his heart. *Faith.* Rory realized that he had faith in the beautiful woman above him. No matter what truths or lies Walter yelled, Rory knew Sara had a golden, caring heart. Whatever she did, she did it for good reasons, and he would never turn his back on her again.

The Macdonald chief turned his mount from the castle. "And now ye will die, too," he said.

The decision to kill Walter Macdonald was decided the moment he condemned his daughter to burn.

CHAPTER THIRTY-SIX

"A heart filled with love is like a phoenix that no
cage can imprison."

*Jalal ad-Din Muhammad Rumi, 1207-1273,
Persian poet & philosopher*

Sara felt the heat against her back as the fire broke
through the door and the roof. Staring down, she
pulled in a mouthful of smoke as she gasped. Her father's cruel words had filtered up to her, and his
saying them to Rory turned her stomach to stone.

"Climb onto the ledge," Kenan called out to her,
going toward his own horse and mounting. "I'll catch
ye if Rory…" He didn't finish his sentence because
Rory roared, running straight at her father's horse
that barreled down on him.

At the last second, Rory dodged to the side in a
vertical leap, his sword slashing out as an extension of
his arm. If her arms weren't strapped to Kenan's bi-
zarre contraption, Sara's hands would have flown to
her mouth. Rory's sword shot out with his momen-
tum, sliding through Walter Macdonald's weakest
point, his throat.

The horse kept riding as her father's head slid
from his shoulders and his body slumped, falling to
the side and off the saddle, foot caught in the stirrup.
The horse dragged his beheaded body out through
the open gate, trailing fresh blood from the open

stump of his neck. People screamed at the sight as the horse continued toward the battle on the moor.

Relief, not horror, threaded through Sara, and she closed her eyes. *Forgive him, Lord.* Her heart wasn't in her prayer, but the man was her father.

Rory hadn't slowed in his run toward Airgid. He turned back to Sara once he'd mounted. "Fly, Sara! Fly!"

"Wait until he gets beyond the village," Kenan called up to her, seemingly unaffected by their father's head sitting several yards away. Kenan held his arms out to her. "Unless the roof is caving in or ye can't stand the smoke."

She stood up on the seat before the short wall. The wings were heavy across her back, and she looked over her shoulder at what she could see. Wind and currents of heat buffeted her, catching the wings and trying to pull her off her feet. She dropped her arms down, thankful Kenan had built the center bar to collapse so the sides of the glider could slant down to stop the breeze from taking her before she was ready.

The feeling gave her hope because the contraption felt too heavy to stay aloft.

"Only step up when ye're ready to jump," her brother yelled. "And make sure that bar in the front is open and rigid."

Her heart beat with near panic as she stared down the drop. What had her mother thought as she looked down? Had she had time to contemplate anything while defending herself? "Sweet Mother Mary."

"Sara, ye can do this," Kenan called. "I know ye can."

"I can do this." *I'm not afraid of heights,* she

thought. "No, I'm merely afraid of smacking into the ground," she said, feeling like she might vomit. Would that make her lighter?

She tried to take a deep breath, but the smoke made her cough. She caught sight of Rory breaking through the edge of the village, pushing Airgid toward the field. Many of the warriors had stopped fighting and surrounded her father's horse. Men pulled his body from the stirrup. Rory's army surrounded them, waiting to see if they'd still fight.

"Is he out there?" Kenan yelled.

"Almost."

Boom! Crash!

Sara yelped, trying to see behind her. Fire. Smoke. The flames roared up from a hole near the doorway that led below, which was now engulfed.

"Fly, Sara!" Kenan yelled. "Now!"

• • •

"Get out of my way!" Rory's voice tore through the rumbling of men and horses.

"Look!" someone yelled, and Rory saw Jok pointing behind him. "On the castle roof!"

Rory turned Airgid in a loop behind the last group of his men. "Sara," he said on an exhale.

He could see her far off, standing on the edge of the castle roof. Fire licked up into the sky behind her with billowing smoke puffing like a huge chimney. She wore red so she was easy to spot. He watched her rise onto the wall. "God protect her," he said.

"She's a Phoenix," Brodrick yelled, pointing with his bloodied sword.

"Rising from the fire," came from another warrior.

"Seraphina, the Flame of Dunscaith," one of the Macdonalds called.

She teetered forward and jumped.

A collective rumble of awestruck curses rose over the two staring armies, their feud momentarily forgotten as they watched. Rory sat on Airgid, holding his breath, his muscles taut and ready.

Wind caught under Kenan's contraption, and she rose in the air.

"Bloody hell, she's flying!"

"She's turned into a bird!"

But Sara was still a flesh-and-blood woman desperate to save herself from burning with Dunscaith. "Feet up, Sara," Rory murmured.

The nose of the false wings pointed slightly upward, but she was still lowering too fast. Rory saw Kenan riding out the gates and through the village, relying on his horse not to hit buildings as he stared up at his sister, his arms raised as if to catch her. But Sara quickly outpaced him, and then the wind swept under her. Sara pitched upward, her red dress flapping out behind her, and her hair streaming with it.

"From the flames!"

"The phoenix rises."

The men of both armies were in awe, watching Sara fly closer but still too high. Rory pressed into Airgid's side, and they took off. "Make way," he roared, and men leaped to the sides as he tore a path through them to intercept Sara.

"Level out," he yelled up to her.

"Bloody foking hell," she yelled, her voice a mixture of absolute fear and desperate determination.

"Point the nose a bit back down," he called, turning Airgid to follow her. The horse, used to quick changes of direction during battle, pivoted to chase the beautiful bird who wore red silk instead of feathers. Rory guided Airgid with his knees, leaning one way or the other as he stared up at Sara.

She'd managed to catch one foot in the loop at the back of the machine, and her other foot wrapped around the first. Maybe she needed to drop her feet.

"Make way," he called as he chased her, and what once was a frenzy of fighting was now clusters of men staring up into the sky. Some held their arms up as if wanting to catch her, too.

"Turn before ye reach the woods," he called up.

"Turn?"

"Tip the nose one way."

She let out a small scream as the machine tipped, turning her away from the woods.

"Drop one foot down, Sara!"

"Kenan said not to!"

"We need to get ye down!"

She'd lowered to the level of the tops of the tree canopy, from which she'd turned away. Rory rose in his stirrups as Airgid chased after her.

"Down a bit more, Sara!"

Kenan pulled his mount alongside Airgid, and they surged forward together. "We need to grab her," Kenan said.

Sara's arms were extended outward now as she pushed the bar she was holding forward and her body backward, and it seemed to slow her in the air. Rory was able to catch up to her. "Keep circling and slowing," he yelled.

"Dearest Lord, get me down," he heard her pray. She turned again in a wide arc, and Rory raced to put himself into her path.

As she was closing in, he rose up again in the stirrups while Airgid ran. Rory lifted his arms. "Drop yer legs!"

Without questioning him again, Sara dropped her legs. Rory grabbed them and was immediately yanked off his horse into the air. "Bloody ballocks!" he yelled as he flew, the two of them dangling over the men who ducked to avoid his boots.

Sara screamed. "I can't hold on with your weight."

"Hold on. Lower the nose!" he yelled.

His weight pulled her backward, but she still held the bar, and the rope around her waist kept her from falling straight down. They were closing in on the ground. "Slow up! Slow! Slow!" But neither of them knew how to slow the winged machine. Rory's boots brushed the grass, and he resisted the human desire to cling to the earth and jump down. Not without Sara.

As they flew close to the ground before the forest, the wind, as if tired of tossing its toy, abandoned them, and the machine slowed even more. His feet touched down, but he fell forward. Refusing to let go of Sara's legs, he let the wings drag him until finally their bellies scraped across the grass. They stopped.

Without the wind whipping past his ears, his voice was loud. "Sara?"

Her breaths came fast and hard. "I'm alive."

He let go of her legs and found his knees under him. Without waiting to stand, he crawled to her where she lay under the wide sprawl of the wings.

Around them, horses thundered as men rode to the fallen phoenix.

"Sara!" Kenan's voice rose above the others.

"I'm well," she called out. "I think."

Rory crawled up alongside her spread body, lying in the grass and wildflowers, her forehead resting on her arm. "Are ye hurt anywhere?"

She turned her face to his. "I don't believe so."

He smiled broadly and caught her to him, but she was stiff in his arms. His smile faltered. "My prayers are answered that ye are safe," he said.

She stared into his eyes. "You didn't let go. This time." Accusation edged her words.

"Lift the wings carefully," Kenan called, and the stretched parchment rose slowly while Sara's gaze left Rory's, moving to her arms. She pulled them out of the straps.

Rory's fingers dropped to her waist. "I need to untie her middle." Once the knot gave way, Kenan and several men, from both sides, lifted the wings off her. Sara pushed into a sitting position.

Despite the hundreds of men standing around them, no one said anything. She looked around and then took Rory's proffered hand, letting him help her rise. Her hair was tousled and tangled, and black soot smeared across her gown and the smoothness of her face. But she was still radiant, her back straight and her cheeks full of rosy color.

Slowly at first, a cheer rose, building in strength.

"The phoenix has risen from the flames!" a Macdonald warrior shouted.

"To the phoenix!" the others called, and the entire field of two thousand warriors, Macdonald and

MacLeod together, beat their swords against their shields in applause.

Before it died down, Rory grabbed Kenan's shoulder. "We need to end this," Rory said.

Kenan nodded. The two men stood side by side. When the noise lowered like the wind fading from a storm, Kenan spoke first. "My father has died a warrior's death, and I now stand in his place." A cheer rose sharp and powerful from Kenan's men, making Rory wonder how loyal they had been to Walter Macdonald. "Dunscaith burns."

"Started by Father Lockerby to burn the Fairy Flag inside," Sara said.

The men cursed, their faces filled with anger. Kenan continued. "We must work to put it out and then rebuild."

Kenan looked at Rory and then back out at his men. "Rory MacLeod and I were imprisoned together in England, as ye know. Both of our old, warring chiefs have died, and a new generation is beginning."

Rory's gaze fell on Brodrick as he began to speak. "A new generation that fights the tyranny of the English and not fellow Scotsmen." His gaze slid along his men who had loosely gathered to the left while Macdonalds stood opposite on the right. "A united Scotland is strong. A divided Scotland will fall to its foreign enemies."

Kenan turned, grabbing Sara's hand to bring her to stand between Rory and him. "My sister, Seraphina, has proven that we can survive the flames and destruction of our past, rising up from the ashes both on MacLeod land and Macdonald. And from those ashes, we rebuild and train together to defend our country."

Rory watched the men look across at their enemy. Anger and revenge still marred their faces, but they did not spit or curse or refuse. They were battle weary and had seen their comrades injured as well as the Macdonald chief riding without a head.

"Today," Rory said, "we separate and honor our dead and heal our wounded."

"And then we rebuild," Kenan said.

There wasn't a cheer. It was more like an affirmative grunt that rose and fell like a shallow wave. There was work to do to fix decades of anger and resentment, encouraged by two old chiefs who gloried in fighting the battles between neighbors instead of the bigger war against invaders of Scotland.

Jok's voice rose. "Let's start by putting out that raging inferno." He pointed toward Dunscaith where flames shot out the top.

"Where is the Fairy Flag?" a Macdonald warrior asked.

Rory exhaled and pointed to the castle. Everyone turned to stare at it.

"See to the injured and dead," Rory called. "And then we will put out the fire. MacLeods will leave at first light." Around them, the men moved off. The battle had lasted less than half an hour before Walter's headless body had halted the action.

Kenan stood next to Rory. "Did ye have that speech already planned?" Rory asked. "Because it was…good." His hand slapped down on Kenan's shoulder. "Rebuilding from the ashes."

"Created on the spot."

"If ye don't like being a chief, ye could be a bard,"

Rory said, his tone light although he felt the weight of unsaid words between Sara and him.

Kenan turned and strode off toward Walter's body on the ground near his horse.

Sara stood beside Rory, her eyes on her ancestral castle. "'Tis a miracle ye came away from that alive," he said, his words low.

She didn't look away from the fire. "I was certain I would die this day," she said, the wind catching her words so he almost didn't hear them.

The thought of her lifeless eyes, her lovely lips that would never smile again… It tore through him like a cannonball. Rory moved to stand before her, and her gaze rose to his. "I would have ye return with me to Dunvegan."

Her lips pinched tighter before she spoke. "Why?"

He caught the back of his head with one hand. "Eliza is there. And Gus misses ye."

She crossed her arms, her brows arching higher. "Did Gus tell you that?"

A gust of breath escaped Rory. "I'm a foking arse, Sara."

Jok ran up to them. "No MacLeods dead but eleven injured. Injuries aren't serious."

Daingead! He'd never get a quiet moment here to talk with Sara.

Jok's face shifted between them. "Brodrick and I will lead the men to form a wet fire block around the inside of the wall."

"Good," Rory said, and Jok ran off.

Rory stepped closer to her, and she took a step back. "Come back with me to Dunvegan," he said again. "So we can…talk."

Sara met his gaze evenly. "About you being a foking arse?"

"Aye."

"About you abandoning me, throwing me out of Dunvegan."

Excuses popped into Rory's head. He'd sent money with her to go somewhere safe. He had to think about leading his clan, keeping them safe. He needed to make certain no one tried to harm Sara with her staying at Dunvegan.

But he said none of it, because none of it made up for the fact that he had abandoned her, and he knew how that felt.

"Sara," he said while meeting her gaze. "See the truth in my eyes. When I thought ye would die up there, die in the fire, it made the foking flag mean nothing. I am exceedingly sorry."

She looked back for a long time, her face unreadable. "I'll discuss visiting the twins with Kenan." Sara turned and walked down the hill toward the village. With each step she took away from him, another knot formed in Rory's gut.

CHAPTER THIRTY-SEVEN

*"I thought my fire was out and stirred the ashes…
I burnt my fingers."*

*Antonio Machado, 1875-1939, Spanish poet &
playwright*

Sara looked down from her mount at her brother
while she tried to ignore the large warrior mounting
his dappled gray charger, Airgid. Rory wore a cloak
with tawny fur that made him look even more lion-
like. "If things are unsettled at Dunvegan, I'll send
word to you from Morag's," Sara said to Kenan.

"I'll be here trying to dig out Dunscaith and start
rebuilding," Kenan said.

"The twins and I will help."

Kenan looked over his shoulder at Rory, and
Sara's gaze followed. A white bandage had been
wrapped around Rory's left bicep and a cut on his
forehead had been stitched. How could wounds make
a man even more attractive? *Lord help me.*

*See the truth in my eyes. The foking flag means
nothing.* His words ribboned through her mind as she
fought to hold onto her anger and distrust for fear of
being hurt again. *I am exceedingly sorry.*

Her brother tugged on her stirrup, making sure it
was the right length. "I hear tales of ye being a phoenix or some Celtic goddess," he said.

"As long as they don't think I'm an angel." She

looked down toward the village. "What of Gilbert?"

"I'll try to track him down after I bury Father."

"Do you think he'll marry Winnie Mar?"

Kenan shrugged. "Wedding a lying murderer is not wise, but Gilbert's never thought much past his immediate comforts." He looked out amongst the villagers who had started to haul away rubble from the castle. "And I will keep watch for Reid Hodges."

"As will I in case he returns to Dunvegan," Sara said. "He harbors guilt and is appalled by what his sister did."

Kenan nodded, handing her Lily's reins. "Keep safe, sister."

The journey back to Dunvegan would take two days, but the army under Brodrick decided to ride ahead with the injured. Sara was thankful that miraculously no one was killed.

Looking down, Sara smoothed her petticoat, hiding the slip of yellow silk. She'd changed her smock and sooty gown into a sturdy green woolen petticoat and bodice that Beatrice had found for her, but she'd tucked the flag back around her in between the layers. On her person was the only place she felt it was safe, especially because no one knew it still existed.

She rode along with the armies around her, but only Jok seemed to stay close. Rory stayed in front of the warriors. Sara's stomach still twisted with unresolved questions about the future.

Rory said that he wanted her to return, and he'd apologized. But he'd distrusted her and let others sway him to make her leave. Anger made her hands tighten around her reins, and Lily tossed her head.

"Pardon, sweet," Sara said and patted Lily's neck,

loosening her hold.

Jok pushed his horse up to walk even with Sara and handed her a bladder of spring water. She took a long drink of the cool water they'd gathered at Dunscaith's fast-flowing spring. Stoppering it, Sara handed it back to him.

They rode for another hour before Jok spoke. "We learned from Kenan that Winnie Mar killed Jamie, and her brother, Reid, stole the flag."

Sara kept her face forward and her tongue still.

"I'm sorry I didn't trust ye, milady."

Another apology. She should feel pleased, vindicated, but none of that mattered if Rory couldn't trust her.

"'Twas the pressure of his men that pushed him to send ye away," he continued. Jok lowered his voice. "Ye know about Madeline?"

Sara nodded but kept her eyes forward. Just the woman's name made her spine straighten. "Not every Macdonald woman is another Madeline." She was proud to have kept the emotion out of her tone.

"Aye," Jok conceded. They rode in silence for another mile when Jok spoke again. "Seeing Madeline killed and then hearing it was because of him in front of the whole clan...Well, it changed Rory. But..." Jok paused until she looked across at him. "Lady Sara, ye're helping to change him back."

They rode for another minute in silence, and then Sara said, "You continue to guard his back."

"Always will," Jok said, still looking forward. "Ever since he punched Brodrick for saying I was touched by Lucifer because my hair color and freckles were unnatural."

Sara felt her face warm. What would Brodrick think of the fiery marks on her back? "Brodrick said that?" she asked.

"Aye." Jok turned a grin on her. "We were eight at the time."

Her lips twitched thinking of young Rory, lean and angry, punching Jamie's best friend for his cruel teasing. A lightness opened up the smallest amount, and Sara breathed deeper as she stared forward.

· · ·

Jok held his battle shield ready as he watched the crows swooping and flapping while Sara sat with Morag outside the cottage. Sara hadn't seen Rory since the night before when he stalked amongst his men, giving orders. The rest of the MacLeod warriors rode by. Some of them nodded to Sara, some of them kept their gazes straight ahead. A few smiled at her.

"Rory stopped here?" Sara asked when her aunt told her about his visit. "For what reason?"

Morag shrugged. "He comes here periodically, because he knows I'm wise." She looked into Sara's eyes. "And he knows I don't lie."

"I don't lie, either." Sara's cheeks warmed as she remembered that she sat with the Fairy Flag wrapped around her. "So glad he has faith in someone. It certainly isn't me."

"Ballocks," Morag said. "You should talk with him."

"I try to, but then he's"—she flapped her arms—"gone." Three crows on the roof line lifted one wing each as if imitating Sara. "I've talked with Kenan and

Jok and now you about Rory, but he rode on ahead."

"He has business back at Dunvegan. His people were expecting war with the Macdonalds, a siege. It needs to be undone, and the people calmed."

"Of course," Sara said, feeling selfish. She rose from the stump that she'd used as a chair. Morag remained sitting, and a crow swooped down to take Sara's spot.

Sara kissed Morag's cheek. It was smooth, timeless, despite her white and silver hair. "I will let you know what happens. Eliza and I might be back soon if things go poorly." She glanced at the forest that hid the path toward Dunvegan and the sea.

"You never know how rabble will react," Morag said. "If you're not threatened with stoning and decide to stay at Dunvegan, bring Eliza and Eleri to visit. I want to work on the girl's back some more."

Jok helped Sara mount Lily and they continued at the back of the MacLeod army toward Dunvegan.

"The crows…" Jok said, glancing back. "They live with yer aunt?"

"As far as I know, they remain outdoors, but they seem exceedingly loyal to her."

"And protective," he said, rubbing at his neck as if one might have pecked him.

They rode without talking the rest of the way. Sara listened to the *clip-clop* crunch of the horses' hooves on the packed dirt and pebbles. The clouds played across the sky, hiding and revealing the sun that was sinking in the west, and the breeze tugged the shorter curls around her face. They passed the rise that hid the beach where she'd first seen Rory, and she longed to walk upon it again, letting the sound of the waves lull away her agitation.

They clopped past the burned chapel. It looked like a charred maw open to the sky with its broken windows and gaping black hole that had been the roof. In the twilight, the soot-blackened walls cast far-reaching shadows that seemed like monsters' pointed claws. A shiver made Sara wrap her cloak tighter around her shoulders.

Perhaps a new priest would motivate the village to rebuild. Father Lockerby, even if he'd lived, wouldn't have.

As they climbed the rise that led into Dunvegan Village, smoke tinged the breeze, and Sara's heart bolted. "Do you smell that?" Sara asked Jok, her hand against her chest.

Jok frowned. "Smoke."

CHAPTER THIRTY-EIGHT

"Nor shall this peace sleep with her; but as when
The bird of wonder dies, the maiden phoenix,
Her ashes new-create another heir
As great in admiration as herself."

William Shakespeare

Sara could tell Jok wanted to race ahead, but he kept pace with her. Sara was torn between surging forward and turning back to escape to the beach or Morag's cottage. But that would be cowardly, and Sara had learned from jumping off a four-story castle tied to Kenan's machine that she was no coward. No matter what happened in the future, she knew that for certain.

Lily's ears twitched, picking up on the smell and Sara's unease. Jok and she increased the horses' gaits, riding to the top of the crest. Sara pulled back on the reins, stopping Lily, and stared down along the path that led into the center of Dunvegan Village all the way to the castle. People lined the road. They held torches, and a flame was passing from person to person, lighting them on both sides of the road.

"What is this?" Sara asked.

"They don't have pitchforks and hatchets," Jok said, and he started forward. Was he mad? Sara kept Lily reined in.

He stopped, turning his gaze back to her. "Lady

Seraphina, 'tis safe."

I'm no coward. Sara pressed Lily to follow Jok down the middle of the road. When she glanced to the sides, the faces looking up at her were friendly. Some faces were curious, some wide-eyed, but there were no snarls or curses. No one spat. Even the elderly midwife, Henrietta, nodded to her without her normal sneer.

Sara looked forward, her gaze landing on Rory. He stood upon the table before the castle, holding a torch. He wore a crisp white tunic and clean plaid and looked handsome and full of authority. Sara's stomach tightened, catching her breath as she studied his serious face.

Eleri and Eliza stood with Margaret to one side, and they waved, Eliza rising onto her toes in excitement. As Sara rode closer, Gus tried to run to her, but the girls held his lead.

Simon and John stood together, each holding a lit torch. Simon waved. "Wave for me," John said.

"I can't," Simon said. "I only have one hand free for my own wave."

"Welcome, Lady Sara," John called.

Sara's heart thumped hard, but she managed a small smile and nod for the two elderly men. It was the first time she'd seen them outside Dunvegan's protective wall.

Jok dismounted when they reached the table and led his horse off to the side while Sara continued to sit on Lily waiting for some indication as to what further she should do. The people who had lined the road gathered behind her, the torches giving the square a flickering glow in the twilight. More and more people came, villagers and the warriors who'd fought at Dunscaith. She could see the mass of bodies on the hillsides surrounding the town, their torches bright.

Did they expect an apology from her? For what? Being a Macdonald? The thought made her hands grip the reins tightly.

"Lady Seraphina Macdonald," Rory said, his words ringing in the stillness like a deep call, as if his words were for everyone. "I, Rory MacLeod, chief of Clan MacLeod of Dunvegan, welcome ye." He looked directly at her. "And…I was wrong."

Sara's breath caught as the moment stretched out before her. Rory was not only admitting his mistake to her but to his entire clan, many of whom had seen him swear to never trust a woman after Madeline was killed.

Rory continued. "My brother, Jamie MacLeod, was poisoned and smothered by Winnie Mar, who then stole the Fairy Flag and escaped to Dunscaith."

The truth was Reid had taken it, but then he'd given it back to Sara. It was complicated, and the damn flag was currently wrapped around her hips, so she didn't correct him.

"Father Lockerby destroyed Dunscaith Castle with fire, burning the Fairy Flag."

Sara couldn't let this go on, even if Rory had composed a speech. She wouldn't start what she hoped would be a new peace between their clans with a lie. Would they think she was keeping the flag for herself? That whoever she decided to support would get the legendary weapon?

"To escape Dunscaith, Lady Seraphina rose from the flames to fly on wings out over the field, making the fighting pause," Rory continued.

Had she done that? Had she stopped the battle? She'd merely been trying to escape burning to death.

"The Flame of Dunscaith is a phoenix," someone called from the crowd and a cheer grew, making her face heat.

"She saved our men and brought peace!" another called out. The cheer rose higher.

Oh Mother Mary. Sara looked at the faces behind and around her. She turned back to Rory and held up a hand, shaking her head. His brows pinched. Without waiting for the crowd to quiet, Sara threw her leg over Lily and jumped to the ground. She strode to the table, lifted her skirts, and climbed up next to Rory.

The nearness of him and the drama unfolding with her at the center made her tremble, but she didn't reach out for his support.

"Sara?" he said.

She looked up into his eyes. They were dark in the shadows, intense. "Rory, do you have faith in me?"

"Aye," he said without hesitation, and her heart leaped in time with it. "I…" he continued, "I forgot how to have faith in people." His hand came up to her cheek, sliding a thumb across it. "But that was wrong in so many ways. Ye helped me find my faith again." Rory's thumb slid gently across her cheek.

"I have faith in you, too," she said and realized she did. As he'd broken from the tree line and saw her on Dunscaith's roof, she'd known he would try to save her.

Sara turned toward the crowd. "I am humbled by you all." Her voice rose, and the villagers and warriors stood still as if desperate to catch each of her words.

"But I'm just a woman, a woman who wants peace between our clans, between all the clans of Scotland. Peace and cooperation make our country strong."

Another wave of cheering crested. "Seraphina the phoenix!" was shouted and repeated.

Sara's fingers went to the back of her waist, and she tugged the strings holding her petticoat in place.

Rory's mouth brushed her ear. "What are ye doing?"

"I found this at Dunscaith." And before she could worry more about what everyone would think, she dropped her outer petticoat, revealing the short yellow silk skirt tucked into the waist of her red under petticoat.

The people before her grew quiet, and the muteness spread quickly all the way to the back.

Sara's hands shook as she carefully pulled the silk edge from her waistband, smoothing it with reverence before folding it against herself. She turned, handing it to Rory. "It belongs with the MacLeods."

His expression was blank. "Ye had it with ye when ye flew over all of us?"

She nodded. "Lockerby was going to burn it with the castle." She lowered her voice. "Perhaps I should have left it."

"The Fairy Flag was tied around her as she flew over the battle at Dunscaith," a voice in the crowd called out. It was Brodrick. "Seraphina Macdonald unfurled the flag. 'Tis why neither clan suffered any deaths."

"And peace was struck," Henrietta said.

People were silent for the space of a heartbeat, and then they erupted in even louder cheers, the roar growing as the news spread back across the multitude.

"She saved both clans!"

"And the Fairy Flag!"

The roar of approval raised gooseflesh along Sara's arms. People hugged each other and raised their fists up in the air in celebration.

"I knew she'd save us!" John called.

Rory looked down to meet her gaze, a grin growing on his lips. His mouth moved near her ear so she could hear him above the celebration. "Ye honor us."

She gazed into his amber eyes. "I only wanted to give it back." Her brow pinched. "Is the flag used up? Because I unfurled it the third time?"

He brushed some curls back from her upturned face. "I never had confidence in its magic." He leaned back to her ear, and heat bloomed in her at the feel of his warm breath. "I have confidence in ye, Sara. I knew it when yer father said ye'd brought the flag to him."

She frowned into his smile. "I don't understand."

"He said ye'd brought the Fairy Flag to him and I didn't believe him because ye'd said ye hadn't taken it. My faith in ye was too strong. I realized then that I love ye."

Her breath caught, and she stared into his eyes. "You love me?" Her heart thumped wildly.

He nodded, and a smile broke along her lips. She threw her arms around his neck. "I love you, too."

Rory's arms hugged around her, pulling her closer as their lips met in a kiss that enveloped them both. The cheers continued, but the love and faith they'd found in each other wrapped around them, blocking out everything except their love.

EPILOGUE

Wind tugged at the wreath tied in Sara's hair as Rory MacLeod kissed her. Kenan Macdonald watched the final part of his sister's wedding there on the white sand beach with a mixture of happiness and envy.

After Sara's return to Dunvegan, Rory had asked her to marry him. They'd chosen to say their vows outdoors where they'd met, near water where no fire could threaten them.

Rory's dog, Gus, trotted along the shore, sniffing at the water as it rushed in and out, tumbling pieces of crystallized seaweed. Eliza and Eleri, inseparable since they'd been introduced, laughed and threw barley seeds at the couple for luck. Beatrice had come from Dunscaith to witness the union, and Aunt Morag had left her crows for the day to attend the ceremony.

Cyrus Mackinnon had ridden down to spend a few days in enemy territory, as his father called MacLeod land. He wanted to see Kenan's flying machine, so Kenan had hauled his repaired wings to the top of the hill bordering the sea, Cnoc Mor a Ghrobain, and would demonstrate later. It had survived the flames and Sara's crash landing with minor injury.

A crowd of onlookers cheered when Rory and Sara turned to smile, their clasped hands raised high. The joy on his sister's face warmed Kenan. She would be happy, and so would his twin half sisters. He on the other hand had a castle to rebuild, a resentful brother to guard against, a clan to support, and a life to put back together. Kenan's time at Carlisle Castle in England had done more than steal a year and a half of his life. It had stolen his belief in humanity. Ash MacNicol was right. People were inherently selfish and untrustworthy.

He rubbed the scar on his palm. Their brotherhood was the only thing Kenan trusted.

"Holy Lord!" Rory's red-haired friend, Jok, called, pointing toward the top of Cnoc Mor a Ghrobain.

"What the hell?" Kenan's friend, Tomas, asked, and a gasping murmur rose above the sound of the waves.

"Is it a bird?" Eleri asked.

"Your wings!" Sara called at the same time.

Kenan's gaze snapped to the sky where a large flying triangle surged and dropped with the buffeting wind. "Bloody hell!" he yelled, running into the surf before stopping to watch. "Those are my wings!" Had the wind wiggled them loose from the rocks he'd placed on them? Nay! There was a person clinging to them, hanging underneath. "Someone's stealing my wings!"

The entire wedding party stood along the shore, watching as a small person held onto the bar.

"'Tis a child," Rory called, covering his squinted eyes against the sun.

"Too big," Morag said. "'Tis a woman."

The woman turned the machine toward the land, the wind whipping it sideways. "Daingead," Kenan swore, his hands resting atop his head.

"I can't see her," the old man, Simon, called.

"Watch the wings," John said. "She's not doing

anything but holding on."

The wind carried the faintest words across the glittering sea to Kenan. "Bloody foking hell!"

"Doesn't seem to know how to fly that thing," Simon said.

As more curse words carried to them, Morag chuckled beside Kenan. She'd waded out in the surf with him, the bottom third of her dress soaked and moving with the water. "She's having a hell of a time," his aunt said.

Kenan dropped his hands. "She's going to ruin them."

"She's going to crash," Cyrus called.

"You best go save her," Morag said, sounding almost jolly.

Kenan yanked off his boots and white tunic, throwing them toward the shore. He trudged out through the surf, his feet kicking up the sand, shells, and crystallized seaweed underneath. Once the water was to his waist, he unbuckled his belt, yanked off his plaid, and lifted them up, throwing them back to shore.

The lass screamed, and he pivoted back around in time to see his flying machine hit the water. "Bloody hell." Kenan dove under, swimming with all his might.

Continue the Brotherhood of Solway Moss series with Kenan Macdonald in Book #2.

When a brash woman from a feuding clan crashes Kenan's creation based on Leonardo da Vinci's plans for a flying machine, he captures her, demanding that she help him rebuild it. He doesn't expect her to capture him back. But she has reasons for her risky sabotage and even riskier abduction. She needs to convince the Macdonald chief to save her clan.

• • •

To stay up to date on Heather's writing projects, sales, conference schedule and more, please subscribe to her once-a-month newsletter at:
https://www.heathermccollum.com/about/newsletter/

ACKNOWLEDGMENTS

Thank you, lovers of historical romance, for joining me in this new series! The families are growing and strengthening the Isle of Skye with each book.

Thank you to my wonderful agent, Kevan Lyon, who deals with all the 21st-century publishing details while I'm romping around 16th-century Scotland. And to my heroic editor, Alethea Spiridon, who always has a word of encouragement when I can't wrangle my characters into behaving. Thank you, too, to all the editors, publicists, artists, and manuscript formatters and coordinators at Entangled Publishing. We make a great team!

Also…

At the end of each of my books, I ask that you, my awesome readers, please remind yourselves of the whispered symptoms of ovarian cancer. I am now an eleven-year survivor, one of the lucky ones. Please don't rely on luck. If you experience any of these symptoms consistently for three weeks or more, go see your GYN.

- Bloating
- Eating less and feeling full faster
- Abdominal pain
- Trouble with your bladder

Other symptoms may include indigestion, back pain, pain with intercourse, constipation, fatigue, and menstrual irregularities.

*Don't miss the exciting new books
Entangled has to offer.*

Follow us!

f @EntangledPublishing

⭘ @Entangled_Publishing

♪ @EntangledPub